Bloody hell,
what was wrong with him?

*P*hilip was normally not prone to lascivious thoughts, especially when he was working. Of course, he had never worked in such proximity to a woman before. A woman whose skirts rustled with her every movement, inspiring thoughts of the curvaceous form beneath. A woman who smelled just like she'd stepped out of the confectioner's.

A woman who was not his fiancée.

Meredith frowned, and worried her lower lip beneath her teeth, drawing his attention to her mouth. And what a lovely mouth it was. He couldn't decide if it were more likely that those full, moist, delectable lips has been fashioned by an angel or by the devil himself. Miss Chilton-Grizedale portrayed the epitome of a proper lady, but there was nothing proper about that rosy, lush mouth or the heated thoughts it inspired.

He closed his eyes and was overtaken by a vivid image of himself pulling her into his arms. He could almost feel her curves pressed against him. Lowering his head, he touched his lips to hers. Warm. Soft. She tasted delicious . . . like a rich, luscious dessert. He deepened the kiss, slipping his tongue into the heat of her mouth and . . .

"Is something amiss, Lord Greybourne?"

Jacquie D'Alessandro

Who Will Take This Man?

AVON BOOKS

An Imprint of HarperCollinsPublishers

This is a work of fiction. Names, characters, places, and incidents are products of the author's imagination or are used fictitiously and are not to be construed as real. Any resemblance to actual events, locales, organizations, or persons, living or dead, is entirely coincidental.

AVON BOOKS
An Imprint of HarperCollinsPublishers
10 East 53rd Street
New York, New York 10022-5299

First Avon Books paperback printing: October 2003

Avon Trademark Reg. U.S. Pat. Off. and in Other Countries, Marca Registrada, Hecho en U.S.A.
HarperCollins® is a registered trademark of HarperCollins Publishers Inc.

Printed in the U.S.A.

10 9 8 7 6 5 4 3 2 1

This book is dedicated with my love and gratitude to Jenni Grizzle. Jenni, when the chips were down, you brought salsa and turned the blues into a party. And to Wendy Etherington for bringing chocolate and champagne to the party. Thanks for being such terrific buds. I'm not sure what I did to deserve such loyal friends, but I'm sure glad I did it!

And, as always, to my wonderful, supportive husband, Joe, a man who didn't have to ask twice Will You Take Me?, and my incredible, makes-me-so-proud son, Christopher, aka I'll Take You Too, Junior.

Acknowledgments

I would like to take this opportunity to thank the following people for their invaluable help and support:

My editors, Carrie Feron and Erika Tsang, for their kindness, cheerleading, and wonderful ideas; my agents, Damaris Rowland and Steve Axelrod, for their faith and wisdom; my husband, Joe, for all the hours he spent helping me with my research; my mom and dad, Kay and Jim Johnson, for a lifetime of love and support; my sister, Kathy Guse, whom I am very proud of; my in-laws, Lea and Art D'Alessandro, for the priceless gift of their son; my sister-in-law, Brenda D'Alessandro, for being lots of fun and the world's best shopper; Melissa Beaty, Belinda Allen, and Ann Wonycott for the great booksignings; Kathy Baker, DeeAnn Kline, and George Scott, booksellers extraordinaire, for their kindness and support; Michelle, Steve, and Lindsey Grossman for all the laughs and fun and for being such great peeps; and a cyber hug to Connie Brockway, Marsha Canham, Virginia Henley, Jill Gregory, Sandy Hingston, Julia London, Kathleen Givens, Sherri Browning, and Julie Ortolon. You Looney Loopies are the best!

Thanks to Debbie Beazley, Angie Bowman, Linda Chambers, Dana Grindstaff, Alison Kane, Paula Mullin, Jennifer Murray, Jeannie Pierannunzi, Sharon Ramsey, Lauren Ronco, and Lori Snow, not just for the fun of tennis, but for providing so much inspiration for future stories.

A very special thank-you to the members of Georgia Romance Writers.

And finally, thank you to all the wonderful readers who have taken the time to write or e-mail me. I love hearing from you!

Prologue

Dear Philip,

Due to your continued refusal to see to your own arrangements, I am writing to inform you that your damn wedding has been planned. Precisely whom you will be marrying has not yet been determined, but rest assured, the nuptials will take place in London on September first, and unlike the last damn wedding I arranged for you three years ago, I expect you to show up this time. Indeed, I demand it. While you've been traipsing about Egyptian sand dunes in search of rusty relics, my health has fallen into a decline. According to Doctor Gibbens I have less than a year left, and I'll see you married and assuming your proper place in Society, perhaps even with an heir on the way, before I cock up my toes.

As you no longer have the luxury of time to engage in a lengthy courtship, I have hired a matchmaker to find you a suitable wife. Unfortunately, given the scandal that ensued when you failed to appear for your last damn wedding, Miss Chilton-Grizedale faces a daunting challenge. However, she is a formidable negotiator and has promised to find a chit who will make you an admirable viscountess. With Miss Chilton-Grizedale overseeing the wedding arrangements down to the last detail, all you need to do is show up. Make damn certain you do.

With regards,
Your father

One

Meredith Chilton-Grizedale pursed her lips and stroked her chin as she slowly circled Lady Sarah Markham, who stood upon the dressmaker's platform. Meredith's gaze critiqued the slender form garbed in the elegant, pale blue wedding gown, noting every detail, from the demure square neckline to the elaborate ruffled flounce. A satisfied smile threatened to curl her lips upward, but she staunchly subdued it. One could not afford to be too effusive when dealing with Madame Renée, Oxford Street's most exclusive milliner. For every compliment Madame received, she clearly felt compelled to increase her already exorbitant prices.

"You look lovely, Lady Sarah," Meredith said. "Lord Greybourne will be besotted the moment he sees you." A tiny flutter of something that felt suspiciously like envy rippled through Meredith, surprising and irritating her. She slapped the feeling aside like a bothersome insect and gazed at the beautiful young woman standing before her. Pride instantly supplanted her errant twinge of envy.

Oh, she had indeed arranged a brilliant match on Lord Greybourne's behalf. Lady Sarah was a diamond of the first water. Sweet, innocent, amenable, possessed of a gentle temperament, lively conversation, a singing voice that could rival the angels, and a formidable talent for the pianoforte. The negotiations, which Meredith had handled between Lady Sarah's father, the Duke of Hedington, and Lord Greybourne's father, the Earl of Ravensly, had proven quite delicate and tricky, even for a matchmaker of her considerable experience. What with the scandal that had ensued three years ago when Lord Greybourne had not returned to England from roaming the wilds of foreign locales to honor the marriage agreement his father had entered into on his behalf, coupled with the fact that he'd incomprehensibly walked away from the comforts of Society to live in *uncivilized* conditions where heathen traits abounded in order to study artifacts, only Lord Greybourne's title and family connections kept him from being hopelessly unmarriageable. Indeed, it had taken an enormous amount of time, flattery, and diplomacy on Meredith's part to convince the duke that Lord Greybourne was the perfect match for Lady Sarah—a task made all the more difficult considering the hordes of eligible titled, and unmarked-by-scandal, young men buzzing around her.

But convince Lord Hedington she did. A sigh of immense satisfaction eased past Meredith's lips, and she was hard-pressed not to twist about and physically pat herself on the back. Thanks to her—if she might say so herself—*inspired* efforts, the most anticipated wedding of the Season would take place in two days at St. Paul's Cathedral. A wedding so grand, a marriage so brilliant, so talked-about, that Meredith's reputation as the foremost matchmaker in England was assured.

Ever since the betrothal announcement two months past, anxious mamas were courting her attention, inviting her to tea and their musicales and soirees, asking her to whom their darling daughters would most be suited. And which eligible bachelors were serious about choosing a bride this Season.

As she had so many times over the past few months, Meredith again found herself wondering why a man born into the upper echelons of Society, the heir to an earldom, a man who would never have to spend his life doing anything save seek pleasure, would spend a decade living in rustic conditions, digging up artifacts belonging to *dead* people. Everything practical in Meredith revolted at the very thought. Clearly Lord Greybourne harbored some very unusual beliefs and tendencies, and, she feared, his manners would most certainly need some dusting off. Even his father had hinted that his son might require a bit of "polishing."

Even so, she did not doubt that she could shine him up enough to make a grand showing at the wedding. After all, her reputation, her livelihood depended upon the success of this wedding. She could only hope that after the ceremony he would prove to be an affable and kind husband. Because, based on the enormous gilt-framed painting of him hanging in his father's drawing room, Lord Greybourne had not been blessed with a bounty of physical attractions.

An image of that painting flashed through her mind. Poor Lord Greybourne. Where his father, the earl, was quite handsome, Lord Greybourne was . . . not. His painting depicted a pale, pudgy-faced, unsmiling countenance decorated with thick spectacles magnifying unremarkable brown eyes. Definitely not the most attractive of fellows. Of course, the painting *had* been commissioned fourteen years earlier, when he was but a youth of fifteen. Meredith hoped his years abroad had improved him somewhat, although it did not really matter. In addition to being a Paragon, Lady Sarah did not, like many young women her age, harbor unrealistic romantic notions regarding marriage. *Thank goodness. Because the dear girl is taking on more the frog than the prince, I'm afraid.*

Yes, Lady Sarah knew it was her duty to marry, and marry well, according to her father's dictates. Meredith blessed the fact that Lady Sarah was not difficult like a growing number of modern young ladies who professed to want their marriages to be love matches. Meredith fought the urge to snicker at such nonsense. Love matches indeed. Love had nothing to do with a successful marriage.

Meredith looked up at Lady Sarah, who, based on her expression, was not as happy as she should be. "Now, don't frown, Lady Sarah," Meredith scolded gently. "You'll wrinkle your forehead. Is something amiss? The dress—"

"The dress is fine," Lady Sarah said. Her huge pansy-blue eyes, reflecting unmistakable distress, met Meredith's in the mirror. "I was just thinking about what you said . . . about Lord Greybourne being besotted the moment he sees me. Do you truly think he will be?"

"My darling girl, you cannot doubt it for a moment! I shall need to be standing by with the hartshorn to revive him when he falls prostrate at your feet."

Lady Sarah's eyes widened. "Oh, dear. Whatever shall I do with a husband who *swoons*?"

Meredith barely refrained from looking toward the ceiling. Lady Sarah possessed many admirable qualities. Unfortunately, a sense of humor was not among them. "I was speaking figuratively, not literally, my dear. Of course Lord Greybourne is not prone to swooning." *I hope.* "Why, with all his traveling about and exploring, he is of course the most hale and hearty of men." *I can only hope and pray.*

When Lady Sarah still appeared concerned, Meredith grasped her hands—her icy cold hands, she noted. "There is nothing to worry about, dear heart. Feeling a bit anxious in the days before your wedding is completely natural and quite expected. Just remember this: You are going to be the most beautiful bride, your groom shall prove to be the most gallant and exciting of men, and your wedding shall be Society's most talked-about event for years to come." *And will ensure my reputation and future.*

Instantly her imagination took flight, and in her mind's eye she saw herself in the future, ensconced in a modest cottage in Bath, or perhaps Cardiff, taking the waters, enjoying the sea air, basking in the admiration and respect of everyone she met . . . her squalid past so deeply buried that it could never again be resurrected. This match represented the culmination of her hard-fought battle to make a place—a *respectable* place—in the world for herself, but it was only the beginning. Her services as a matchmaker would be the most sought-after, her opinions the most respected, her financial future set, all the while providing a service that she felt *compelled* to provide. Every woman deserved the protection and care of a kind, decent husband. How different her life would have been if Mama had found such a man . . .

"Father received word that Lord Greybourne's ship was scheduled to dock this morning," Lady Sarah said, pulling Meredith from her reverie. "He sent 'round an invitation for Lord Greybourne and his father to dine with us this evening." A becoming blush suffused Lady Sarah's satiny-smooth cheeks. "I am most anxious to meet the man who will be my husband."

Meredith smiled at her. "And I am certain he cannot wait to meet you." Of course, with the wedding only two days away, that did not afford Meredith much time to reacquaint Lord Greybourne with any rules of Society he may have forgotten during his travels, but she was comforted by the fact that he *had* spent his first twenty years among the *ton*. True, he was a bit of a diamond in the rough, but at least he wasn't a lump of coal in a cave. She hoped.

But even if he were, she'd make him into a presentable groom. After the ceremony, well, then he would be Lady Sarah's problem, er, project.

A loud commotion sounded from outside. "What do you suppose that is?" Lady Sarah asked, craning her neck to peek beyond the forest-green curtain separating the dressing area from the front of Madame Renée's shop.

"I'll see," Meredith said. Walking into the front of the shop, she peered out the front picture window. A row of stopped carriages lined the street, and a crowd of pedestrians milled about, blocking her view. Rising onto her toes, she noted a lopsided bread cart at the front of the traffic snarl—clearly the source of the problem. She was about to turn away when she noticed a giant of a man standing near the overturned cart raise his ham-sized fist, which clutched a whip. Good lord, he meant to strike that man holding that puppy! Meredith's hand flew to her lips, but before she could even emit a gasp, another man, whose back was turned toward her, executed a lightning-fast maneuver with his walking stick and fist, whereupon the giant went down like a tenpin. The savior then tossed what appeared to be a coin up to the man still standing upon the lopsided cart, then calmly tucked his silver-tipped walking stick under his arm and strode away, disappearing into the crowd.

Hoping to catch another glimpse of the brave man, Meredith craned her neck, but he was lost in the crowd. An odd flutter shivered through her, settling in her stomach. Heavens. What an extraordinary, brave man. And he moved like . . . like a swift, sleek, predatory animal. Graceful. Strong. Heroic. His knowledge of fighting marked him as a ruffian—completely unrespectable, but still . . . what did such a man look like? He'd used his walking stick like a weapon. Perhaps it was a weapon, as the silver tip bore some sort of unusual design unfamiliar to her. Another flutter quivered down her spine, and looking down, she realized her palms were pressed to her chest.

Shaking her hands as if to rid them of dirt, she frowned in annoyance at her fanciful thoughts. Botheration. It mattered not what he looked like. What mattered was Lady Sarah and the wedding. Weaving her way among the rows of bolts of colorful silks, satins, wools, and muslins, she pushed back the curtain leading to the dressing area. And discovered Lady Sarah on her hands and knees on the floor, struggling to rise.

Meredith rushed forward. "Lady Sarah! What happened?" She extended her hands to help the young woman gain her feet.

Lady Sarah's beautiful face puckered into a rueful grimace. "I wanted to see what all the fuss outside was about, but when I attempted to step down from the dressmaker's platform, I tripped on my hem and fell."

"Are you hurt?"

"I don't believe so." Lady Sarah gingerly shook both arms and legs, then her features relaxed. "Nothing's damaged. Except my pride, of course."

Before the relief at that statement could take hold of Meredith, Lady Sarah pressed one hand to her brow, and clutched at Meredith's sleeve with the other. "Oh, dear. I fear I suddenly have the most dreadful headache."

"Did you strike your head when you fell?"

"No . . . at least I do not recall doing so." She closed her eyes. "Oh, my. I believe I need to lie down."

Meredith immediately led Lady Sarah toward the chintz-covered chaise in the far corner of the room, helping the young woman recline against the pillows.

"*Mon Dieu,*" came Madame Renée's voice from the doorway. "What has happened?"

"Lady Sarah is feeling unwell," Meredith reported, trying to keep her voice calm. She touched her hand to Lady Sarah's brow, relieved when she discerned no signs of fever. "She's suffering from the headache."

"Ah, do not be concerned, Mademoiselle Meredith," Madame said. "I see this always with zee nervous brides.

I shall brew her my special tisane and she will feel *très magnifique* this quickly." She snapped her fingers.

Meredith looked down at Lady Sarah's waxy complexion, and prayed Madame's assessment was correct. But at least the wedding was still two days away. Surely that would be more than sufficient time for Lady Sarah to recover.

Surely it would.

Two

Pacing the confines of the small private office off an alcove near the vestry at St. Paul's, Philip Whitmore, Viscount Greybourne, prayed for all he was worth that his bride would not show up.

His stomach cramping with tension, he pulled his gold pocket watch from his waistcoat and consulted the time. Mere minutes remained before the ceremony was scheduled to begin. Would Lady Sarah come? *God help me if she does.*

Damn it all, what an utterly impossible situation this was. Had he made Lady Sarah understand? He'd only had that one opportunity to speak privately with her, when he'd dined at her father's townhouse the evening before last. Due to her suffering a fall earlier in the day and subsequently finding herself the victim of a vicious headache, she had not joined the party for dinner. He squeezed his eyes shut. *First the fall and then the headache.* Bloody hell, he'd feared it would come to this.

After dinner, however, Lady Sarah had made an appearance. Following several minutes of small talk, he'd suggested she show him the gallery, and she'd obliged. And he'd taken the opportunity to tell her . . . warn her. She'd listened to his tale with what appeared to be merely polite interest, and at the end of his recitation had murmured, "How . . . interesting. I shall think upon it," then had excused herself, claiming the headache. When he'd called upon her yesterday he'd been informed by the butler that she still suffered the headache and was not receiving visitors. He'd tried to speak to her father, but the duke was not at home. Philip had left a note for his grace, but had not received a reply, indicating he'd obviously arrived home too late to respond. And Philip had spent the remainder of his time at the warehouse, searching through the numerous crates for the one item that could bring salvation. He'd been unsuccessful, which meant that one way or another, this day was about to take a very unpleasant turn.

Surely someone would send word to him soon, or Lady Sarah would herself arrive. Or not arrive. He raked his hands through his hair and tugged on his confining cravat. Either way, he was damned. Honor demanded that he marry Lady Sarah. But honor also demanded that he not. Her image rose in his mind's eye. Such a lovely young woman. The thought of taking her for his wife should have pleased him enormously. Instead the very idea cramped his insides with dread.

A knock sounded, and he quickly strode to the door and opened it. His father entered the room, and Philip closed the door behind him with a soft click. Turning, he met his father's gaze and waited for him to speak. The signs of Father's illness were starkly visible in the ribbon of sunlight streaming through the window. Deep lines bracketed his mouth, and his complexion was sallow and pale. He was considerably thinner than when Philip had left England, his face bordering on gaunt, the shadow of circles staining dark gray beneath his eyes.

But those eyes remained unchanged. Piercing blue and rapier-sharp, they could cut with a single frigid glance—as Philip knew all too well. Gray strands marked his temples, but his ebony hair remained thick. He looked like an older, tired, paler version of the hearty man from a decade earlier. A man with whom Philip had shared little other than cold silence and tension after Philip's mother's death—a situation made all the more painful as he and Father had enjoyed a warmer relationship prior to Mother's death. A man who had made a deal with Philip, one that had afforded him the opportunity to pursue his dreams, albeit only until "someday," asking only one thing in return.

Father had not reacted well when he learned it was the one thing Philip could not give him.

His father walked slowly toward him, his eyes taking in every aspect of Philip's appearance. He halted when only two feet separated them. A wealth of memories hit Philip like a blow, rushing images through his mind, ending, as thoughts of Father always did, with the reverberation of his quiet, condemning words: *A man is only as good as his word, Philip. If you'd kept yours, your mother wouldn't have—*

"The ceremony is about to begin," Father said, his expression unreadable.

"I know."

"Unfortunately, your bride has not yet arrived."

Thank God. "I see."

"You told her." The words were a statement, not a question.

"I did."

"We'd agreed that you would not."

"No. You *requested* that I not tell her. I never agreed that I wouldn't." Philip's hands clenched at his sides. "I *had* to tell her. She had the right to know."

"Did you tell Lord Hedington as well?"

Philip shook his head. "Lady Sarah requested that I not, at least not until she'd thought upon the matter."

"Well, with each passing minute without her here, it becomes clearer what her thoughts on the matter were."

Philip could only hope his father was correct.

* * *

Meredith stood in the shadows cast by the columns in the marble-tiled vestibule of St. Paul's, trying her very best to look dignified and contain her excitement, praying she did not resemble a child with her face pressed against the window at the confectioner's shop. A procession of elegant carriages wended their way toward the magnificent west entrance of the cathedral, dispensing Society's finest for the wedding of Lady Sarah Markham and Viscount Greybourne. A hum of excited whispers echoed from the throng of guests entering the church, their voices swallowed by the swell of organ music as they passed Meredith. She caught snatches of their words as they glided by.

". . . heard Greybourne was nearly killed during an altercation with some tribe of . . ."

". . . supposedly wants to start his own museum with some American colleague. . . ."

"His importing business venture is rumored to be wildly successful. . . ."

"Amazing that he managed to snare Lady Sarah, what with his odd interests and that scandalous debacle three years ago. . . ."

On and on they came, all of Society's finest, walking through the magnificent columned entrance to proceed down the nave, passing under the architectural splendor of the dome, until over five hundred guests filled St. Paul's pews. All except the one guest Meredith most particularly wanted to see.

Where was the bride?

Dear God, she hoped Lady Sarah was not still suffering from that tumble at the dressmaker's. No, surely not. If so, her father would have sent word. Meredith had been most anxious to speak to Lady Sarah yesterday, to find out how her meeting with Lord Greybourne had gone the evening before. But when she'd called upon her in the early afternoon, Lord Hedington had informed her that Lady Sarah was unable to receive visitors due to the lingering headache. Meredith's alarm clearly showed, for Lord Hedington had quickly assured her that Lady Sarah had taken a restorative tisane and, after some much-needed sleep, would be perfectly fit for the wedding. He reported that Lady Sarah and Lord Greybourne had spent over an hour together touring the gallery the evening before, and had gotten along "smashingly well," news that calmed a tiny fraction of Meredith's jitters. In addition, he said that in spite of his disheveled clothing and abominable cravat—which would surely be solved after employing a proper valet—Lord Greybourne seemed a decent sort of fellow.

Thank goodness. Not that she'd had the opportunity to meet the groom herself and put her own fears to rest. Oh, she'd tried, without success, to meet with Lord Greybourne to assess what, if any, last-minute emergency etiquette lessons he might require, but the man had remained as elusive as fog. He'd responded to her trio of calls upon him with a trio of terse notes stating that he was "busy."

Busy? What on earth could be keeping him so busy he couldn't take a quarter hour out of his schedule to see her? Busy seeing to his own pleasures, no doubt. Rudeness, that's all it was.

The cathedral's clock struck the hour. The ceremony was now scheduled to begin.

And still no sign of the bride.

A cold chill of unease slithered down her spine, a sensation not the least relieved by Lord Hedington striding into the vestibule, his brows bunched into a severe frown. Meredith emerged from the shadows.

"Your grace, are you certain Lady Sarah was feeling well?"

"She claimed she felt fine, but I'm worried, I admit. The chit is never late. Prides herself on her promptness, unlike most females." He shook his head. "I should never have agreed to come to the church without her, but she was so insistent—" His words broke off, and he heaved a sigh of clear relief. "Here comes the Hedington carriage now. Thank goodness."

Meredith looked out the door and relief rushed through her at the sight of the elegant black coach, drawn by four matching grays. The coachman halted the carriage in the cathedral's curved drive, and a liveried footman hopped down and trotted up the steps.

"Your grace," the young man said, "I have a message for Lord Greybourne." He held out a wax-sealed envelope. "Lady Sarah instructed me to deliver it just before the ceremony was to begin."

"Lady Sarah instructed *you?*" The duke looked over the footman's shoulder toward the coach. "Where *is* Lady Sarah?"

The footman's eyes rounded. "Is she not here? She departed for St. Paul's only moments after you left, your grace."

"But if you have the carriage, what did she travel in?" the duke asked, his voice tight.

"Baron Weycroft called, your grace," the footman reported, "Lady Sarah, along with her abigail, departed with him in his coach."

The duke's expression turned to one of confusion. "Weycroft, you say? I've not seen him, either. Well, at least she is not alone, although it's deuced odd that they've not arrived. Ye gods, I hope they haven't broken a wheel or some such."

"We did not pass them on the road here, your grace," the footman said, his countenance as confused and concerned as the duke's.

"The note," Meredith said, nodding toward the vellum, and pushing down her rising sense of dread. "Let us deliver it to Lord Greybourne at once. Surely it will offer the answers we seek."

* * *

A knock sounded at the door and Philip and his father exchanged a glance. Unease slithered through Philip. Had Lady Sarah arrived? "Come in," he said.

The door opened and Lord Hedington stalked into the room, every line of his body bristling with obvious tension and concern. With his bushy brows, jowly cheeks, oversized ears, and the folds of skin drooping under his protruding eyes, Lord Hedington bore a striking, and remarkably unfortunate, resemblance to a hound. An unfamiliar woman, fashionably garbed in a dark blue gown, remained standing in the open doorway. Her gaze panned the room, as if looking for someone else, then their gazes met. Philip fancied that confusion, and then surprise, flared in her eyes.

"May I assist you, Miss . . . ?"

Color washed over her cheeks, and she performed a quick curtsy. "I am Miss Meredith Chilton-Grizedale, my lord. I am—"

"She's the matchmaker who arranged for you to marry my daughter," Lord Hedington said in a tight voice from behind Philip.

Philip stared at her, certain he failed to hide his surprise. Upon hearing his father talk about the formidable Miss Chilton-Grizedale, he'd formed a mental picture of a stern, gray-haired, grandmotherly sort that in no way resembled this young woman standing before him. Pushing his glasses higher on his nose, he noted that she appeared as surprised as he. He was staring, but couldn't seem to drag his gaze away from her. And for the life of him, he couldn't understand why. Obviously due to his surprise, for she certainly was not a woman one would ever call beautiful. Her features were too irregular. Too unconventional.

Recalling himself, he offered her a formal bow. "A pleasure to meet you, miss." After she entered the room,

Philip closed the door behind her, then turned toward Lord Hedington. "Has Lady Sarah arrived?"

The duke raised his quizzing glass, thus now resembling a hound with one magnified eye, and peered at Philip. "No," said Lord Hedington, "and she certainly should have, as she departed for St. Paul's over an hour ago." He thrust out his hand. "But she sent this note to you. It just arrived. I demand you open it at once and tell me what the devil is going on."

Philip took the envelope and stared at it for several long seconds. He briefly squeezed his eyes shut, prayed his relief did not show, then forced his gaze upward from the vellum. Three pairs of eyes stared at him with varying degrees of distress. His father appeared more than a bit suspicious. Lady Sarah's father appeared worried. And Miss Meredith Chilton-Grizedale appeared deeply troubled.

Philip broke the seal. The slight crackling of the vellum as he unfolded it echoed in the silent room. Drawing a deep breath, he lowered his gaze to the paper.

Lord Greybourne,

As you requested, I have thought upon the matter we discussed during our meeting. Indeed, I have thought about nothing else. Given the evidence you presented regarding your friend's wife, along with your expertise and strong belief in the power of the curse, and the fact that I have suffered from a fall and the headache, I cannot deny my fear that if we were to marry, the third event would come to pass. Therefore, this letter is to inform you that I will not marry you, and for my own safety, I have taken steps to ensure I shall not be forced to do so. I apologize for the inconvenience my not coming to the church will cause you, but as you pointed out during our meeting, this is the best way. Please advise

*my father that I am well and safe, and that a letter
from me explaining everything awaits him at home.*

Lady Sarah Markham

Philip had barely finished scanning the few lines when
Lord Hedington tapped his quizzing glass upon the vellum and demanded, "For God's sake, what does she
write? Is she all right?"

Philip raised his gaze and met the duke's eyes. "Yes,
your grace."

"Then why the devil is she not here? Where is she?"

Calm descended over Philip, and he drew his first easy
breath in what seemed like months. She'd jilted him. Thank
God. "I do not know exactly where she is, but she does
not wish for you to worry about her safety. Still, I believe
the main point is that she is not here. Nor is she coming."

"Not coming?" the duke thundered. "Balderdash. Of
course she's coming. She's getting married. Here. To you.
Today." He yanked his watch fob from his waistcoat
pocket and snapped it opened. "Five minutes ago."

"I'm afraid not." Philip handed the single sheet of vellum to the duke, who snatched the paper from his fingers.
Seconds after scanning the words, the duke's fierce scowl
darkened further.

"What the devil is this 'curse' she refers to?" he asked,
passing the paper to Philip's father. Philip noted that a
wide-eyed Miss Chilton-Grizedale, whose complexion
had taken on a faintly greenish hue, had sidled closer to
his father to peer at the letter.

Before Philip could reply, his father looked up from the
note and their eyes met. The icy anger and disappointment in his father's gaze hit Philip hard. Harder than it
should have. Certainly harder than he wanted to admit.
Damn it, he was no longer a green lad who sought his father's approval.

Father, instead of directing his ire where he clearly wanted to, turned the full force of his frigidly calm fury upon Lord Hedington. "This is an outrage. What sort of addlepated, beef-witted chit is your daughter, Hedington? How dare she write that she will not marry my son. And *you*." He swung his attention toward Miss Chilton-Grizedale, pointing at her in an accusatory fashion. "I engaged you to find my son a suitable wife, not some daft flibbertigibbet who babbles about curses and would cry off on her wedding day."

Anger flashed in Miss Chilton-Grizedale's eyes, and she opened her mouth to speak, but Lord Hedington's outraged voice cut off whatever she was about to say.

"Addlepated? Beef-witted?" the duke fumed. "Daft? How dare you refer to my daughter in such terms, especially when it is clear from this note"—he snatched it from Philip's father's hand and waved it about like flag—"that something *your* nincompoop son said to her set her on this disastrous course." He swung his attention to Miss Chilton-Grizedale. "And how dare *you* have arranged a union for my daughter with such an unsuitable man. You assured me that the scandal three years ago was merely a misunderstanding, that Greybourne was respectable in every way. Yet he's clearly frightened my Sarah with this idiotic chatter, *and* his cravat is an utter disgrace. One should *never* trust a man sporting untidy neckware."

Crimson rushed into Miss Chilton-Grizedale's pale, greenish cheeks, and she lifted her chin. "Before you *gentlemen* say anything *else* you might regret, or toss about any further accusations or aspersions upon my character, I believe we should hear what Lord Greybourne has to say about the matter."

Hmmm. Quite the imperious piece, although he couldn't help but applaud the woman's level-headed nerve. He'd be hard-pressed to name many *men* who would show such spirit and common sense in the face of two such angry fathers.

Clearing his throat, then adjusting his spectacles, Philip drew a deep breath in preparation of telling the very undone Lord Hedington and the greenish-skinned Miss Chilton-Grizedale the same story he'd related to his father two days ago upon his return to England.

"Something happened while I was in Egypt, something which prevents me from marrying Lady Sarah. Or anyone else."

After several seconds of deafening silence, understanding, edged with steel, dawned in Lord Hedington's eyes. "I see. You fancy yourself in love with some woman you met abroad. That is unfortunate, because your duty demands—"

"This has nothing to do with another woman, your grace. The problem is that I am . . . cursed."

No one spoke for several long seconds. Finally Lord Hedington cleared his throat and, after casting a surreptitious glance at Miss Chilton-Grizedale, said in a low voice, "It is, I believe, quite common for men to occasionally suffer from such an . . . affliction. My daughter's abundant beauty will surely rekindle your . . . urges."

A choking sound erupted from Miss Chilton-Grizedale, and Philip's father paled. Philip actually felt a blush creeping up his neck. Bloody hell, he could not *possibly* be having this conversation. He dragged his hands down his face. "Your grace, I am *not* impotent."

There was no mistaking the duke's, or Philip's father's, relief. Before anyone could speak, Philip continued, "I am speaking of a *curse,* one written on a broken stone tablet I discovered just before sailing from Alexandria."

Philip's mind drifted back to Alexandria, to the day, months earlier, when he'd found the stone. Squinting against the bright sun, breathing in the hot, dry air that felt and smelled like no other . . . air redolent with the scent of history and ancient civilizations. Air that he would miss with an ache he couldn't describe when he departed the following day for the country of his birth. To honor an agreement he'd made a decade earlier. An agreement he could postpone no longer, now that his father was dying.

He'd been nearly ready to quit for the day—his last day—but his reluctance to put away his tools—for the last time—to wipe the dust and dirt and sand from his hands—for the last time—propelled him to continue. And minutes later . . .

"The day before I was to depart Alexandria for my voyage back to England, I made a discovery—an alabaster box. Inside the box was an intriguing stone with writing upon it in an ancient language. As ancient languages are of special interest to me, I was especially excited about the find. I took the box and retired to my cabin on board the *Dream Keeper* in preparation for our departure at dawn. When I deciphered the stone, I realized it was a curse."

Lord Hedington's countenance resembled a thundercloud. "What sort of person places any credence in such nonsense—"

"It is not nonsense, your grace. Such things were very common in ancient times, and indeed still exist today in many cultures." Philip drew a deep breath, then continued. "Based on the translation and my estimation of the age of the stone, which is called the Stone of Tears, I judged that the curse was most likely cast during the first or second century B.C. I've deduced that it was composed by a man who, just prior to his marriage, discovered that his betrothed had betrayed him with another. The curse was cast upon the man's betrothed, and it called for three events to occur—two during the days just prior to the wedding, and the third two days after the wedding. Before the wedding, the curse decreed, the bride-to-be would suffer a non-life-threatening fall, then a severe headache. I believe these were meant to symbolize her 'fall' from grace and the 'pain' the man's bride-to-be inflicted upon him. Then, two days after the wedding, the bride would . . . die."

Silence followed his words. Then the duke lifted his quizzing glass and peered at Philip. "So you believe, based on some scribblings on an old piece of rock, that if you were to marry my daughter, she would die two days after the wedding. Does that sum it up?"

"Yes, actually, that sums it up perfectly. The curse specified that the bride of anyone who read the stone would suffer the curse—or his wife, if he were already married. And *I* have read the stone. At first I held out some hope that perhaps the curse had been broken over the centuries, but unfortunately recent events dash that hope. You will recall that two days ago, Lady Sarah suffered a non-life-threatening fall, and then a severe headache. Just as the curse portends."

"Coincidence—"

"It is *not,* your grace. It is proof which cannot be ignored, especially when coupled with the missive I received several hours after my return to England."

"Meaning precisely what?"

"During the first week of our voyage home, I pored over the stone, looking for any small clue I might have missed. When not in my cabin, I kept the stone hidden so as not to risk anyone else finding and translating it. However, several days into our journey, while studying the stone, I heard a loud booming noise. Concerned, I ran from my cabin." He dragged his hands down his face. "I thought I'd hidden the stone, but apparently in my haste I failed to do so. When I returned, I discovered one of my colleagues, Edward Binsmore, in my cabin. He'd come to check on me due to the noise. When he entered my cabin, he saw the stone on my desk and, being as knowledgeable with the ancient languages as I am, he translated it. We both instantly realized the ramifications of him doing so, as Edward had a wife awaiting his arrival in England."

Philip looked at his audience and struggled to keep his voice steady. "We prayed the entire journey, and the moment we docked in London, Edward departed for his home just outside the city. Several hours later, a message arrived from him." His throat tight, he withdrew Edward's note from his waistcoat and handed it to the duke. "Mary was dead. She'd passed away without warning. The date of her death was exactly two days after Edward had translated the Stone of Tears."

While the duke scanned the missive, Philip went on, "As you see from the note, Edward reports that during the two days prior to her death, Mary had suffered a fall in the garden, followed by the onset of a severe headache. The letter convinced me, and him as well, that the curse remains unbroken." He plunged his fingers through his hair. "I quite understand that it is difficult to believe in such things. That which cannot be seen or touched, things that indeed stretch the bounds of credulity, are hard to accept. Or are dismissed as coincidence. However, based on my years of study and research, *I* no longer believe in coincidence. And my belief in the power of this curse is supported—most tragically—by Edward, who is considered an expert on such matters. And will also be supported by my American colleague, Andrew Stanton, who sits amongst the wedding guests."

The duke's face turned crimson. "I don't believe in this tomfoolery you are spouting."

"That is certainly your choice, but that does not make these curses any less real. My friend Edward Binsmore's wife is dead as a result of this one."

The duke waved his hand in a dismissive gesture, but a flicker of uncertainty flashed in his eyes. "Sarah informed me about her fall at the dressmaker's shop. Clearly the chit must have struck her head during the incident if she even listened to this cock-and-bull tale. I cannot believe you passed along such a nonsensical tale."

Philip looked steadily at Lord Hedington, hoping the man would see the depth of his sincerity. "I could not be responsible for your daughter's death. And I very much believe that if we had married she would have died. You may not believe in the curse," he said quietly, "but given the facts I presented, can you honestly tell me that you would be willing to risk your daughter's *life* on the possibility that I am wrong?"

Lord Hedington pressed his lips tightly together, then finally shook his head.

"Given the circumstances," Philip continued, "I told Lady Sarah I quite understood if she chose to cry off. Indeed, I strongly encouraged her to do so."

Lord Hedington's face paled a bit. "And if she hadn't?"

Philip's gaze did not waver. "I would not have married her. Not today. I cannot consider doing so until I determine if there is a way to break the curse."

"Then why the bloody hell did you come here today?" the duke demanded.

"I did not know of Lady Sarah's decision. I tried to see her yesterday, but she remained indisposed. If she'd chosen to come to the church today, I wanted to talk to her, explain again why we could not marry, at least at this time. Encourage her to consider a postponement. I couldn't just abandon my bride at the altar."

"As you did three years ago," Philip's father said in a frigid voice. Philip turned toward his father and they exchanged a long look. He and Father had already engaged in this argument the day Philip arrived back in London, but the icy expression in the earl's eyes clearly indicated they were about to have it again, regardless of the fact that they had an audience.

"I am gravely disappointed in you, Philip," his father said quietly. "When I agreed to finance your antiquarian studies and expeditions abroad, clearly it was a very grave error on my part not to have stipulated a date by which you were to return and marry, but it foolishly had not occurred to me that you would still be trotting about the globe on the eve of your thirtieth birthday. I honored my part of the bargain. It is to your great dishonor that you refuse to do the same."

"It is not dishonorable to save a woman's *life,* Father."

He made a dismissive sound. "Your reasons are based on superstition, coincidence, and nonsense, and quite frankly sound like nothing more than a pitiful excuse to renege on your duty. Sadly, I cannot say that I am unduly surprised by this turn of events. You brought embarrassment and scandal to the family when you did not return to honor the marriage I arranged for you three years ago."

"An arrangement you made without my prior knowledge or consent." He yanked on the damn cravat that strangled him like a noose. "The reason I returned to England now was to honor our agreement and marry."

"Because I'm dying."

"Because I always intended to do so. Someday. Your health made me realize that someday is now."

"Yet the first thing you tell me is that you will not honor our agreement. Because of some silly stone."

Frustration clenched Philip's hands. From the corner of his eye he noted that Lord Hedington and Miss Chilton-Grizedale were listening to this exchange with wide-eyed, rapt attention. Well, the hell with them. They certainly weren't the first people to disapprove of him. "My honor and integrity mean everything to me. If I were *not* honorable, I would have remained silent. Married Lady Sarah, and after her untimely demise two days later, I would have simply gone on with my life in the way I wished, returning to Egypt or Greece or Rome, having honored my agreement to marry."

His words hung in the air between them, the ticking of the mantel clock the only sound breaking the prolonged silence.

Finally Miss Chilton-Grizedale cleared her throat. "You mentioned trying to determine if there is a way to break the curse, my lord. Do you think there is a way to do so?"

He turned toward her. The greenish hue had left her skin. She studied him through serious, aqua-blue eyes, and he mentally approved her calm outward demeanor. Imperious though she was, she was obviously not the frail sort of female who flew into the boughs at the slightest provocation, and her thought processes were clear and concise. He could see why his father considered her a good strategist.

"I do not know if there is a way to break the curse," Phillip admitted. "There often is. Unfortunately the Stone of Tears itself is broken, so if there is a remedy to the curse, it is missing. I am, however, hopeful that the other portion might be amongst the artifacts and items that either sailed on my ship or on the second ship which departed several days before mine. I've learned that that ship, the *Sea Raven,* has not yet docked—most likely due to weather or repair delays—but I am expecting it any day now. And even before it arrives, there are dozens of packed crates to unseal and examine."

"Wouldn't you remember finding such a piece of rock?" she asked.

Philip shook his head in frustration. "I do not recall seeing any such stone. However, that does not mean that it is not amongst the artifacts. I did not see every item that was packed away. It is quite possible that it was sent back to

England on a previous shipment and is already awaiting me in the British Museum. Rest assured I will devote myself to the search. But in the meantime, we must deal with the situation at hand."

"Which is the bride's absence at your wedding," Miss Chilton-Grizedale murmured.

"And your refusal to marry," Philip's father added in a tight voice.

He turned to his father and met glacial blue eyes. "Yes. At least I refuse until such time as I discover a way to break the curse, assuming there is a way. If I am able to find a way to break the curse, I shall not hesitate to marry Lady Sarah."

"And if there isn't a remedy? Or you cannot discover it?"

"Then I cannot marry. Anyone. Ever."

Father's lips narrowed into a tight line. "You gave me your word."

"But that was before—"

"Before nothing. Promises were made. Agreements struck. I shudder to think of the social and financial consequences should you not marry Lady Sarah."

"The financial consequences will be substantial, I assure you," Lord Hedington broke in, his tone ominous.

"Good God, if this ridiculous curse story gets out," his father fumed, "the scandal will ruin us all. People will believe you are insane."

"Is that what you think? That I've gone mad?" Father's reaction was exactly what he'd expected, yet it was impossible to suppress the hurt and frustration from his voice.

Color suffused his father's pale cheeks. "I would almost prefer that to believing you've made up this asinine excuse to sidestep your duty and promise. Again."

"You once told me that a man is only as good as his

word." A long look passed between them, fraught with memories of a dark day standing over Mother's casket. "It is advice I took to heart. I give you my word that avoiding my duty is not what I am doing."

His father squeezed his eyes shut for several seconds, then met Philip's gaze. "If I were to pretend to believe all this rubbish, I'd say that clearly *you* believe very strongly in this curse. However, that belief is misguided, and, for all our sakes, you must put aside these . . . notions and attempt to correct this debacle you've created. You've spent too many years away from civilization, immersed in ancient customs that simply do not apply in today's modern world."

"There is no mistaking the words scripted on the stone."

"They are *words,* Philip. Nothing more. From what you've told me, they are the ramblings of a jilted, jealous man. They have no power—unless you insist upon giving power to them. Do not do so."

"I'm afraid I cannot oblige you, Father, other than to assure you that I shall devote myself to the search for the missing piece of stone."

Lord Hedington harrumphed. "As I'm not certain at this moment what to believe or make of this curse story, I have to agree with Ravensly that no word of it is to leave this room." His scowl encompassed the entire group. "Agreed?"

Everyone nodded and murmured their assent.

"And I want to find my daughter."

"Both excellent plans, your grace," Philip agreed. "However, I believe the more pressing matter at the moment is the hundreds of guests waiting in the church." He dragged his hands down his face, his gaze alternating between Father, Lord Hedington, and Miss Chilton-Grizedale. "Since we've agreed for now not to mention the curse, we shall have to agree upon another excuse, for I'm afraid we can no longer delay a formal announcement that today's wedding will not be taking place."

Grim-faced, Lord Hedington and Father headed toward the door. Just as Philip fell into step behind them, a low moan, followed by a thud, sounded behind him. He looked over his shoulder and froze.

Miss Chilton-Grizedale lay sprawled in a heap on the floor.

Meredith came awake slowly. Someone was massaging her hand in the most delightful manner. She forced her heavy eyelids open and suddenly found herself staring up into Lord Greybourne's bespectacled brown eyes. The instant their gazes met, his expression filled with relief. She blinked. He did not look at all like a frog. He looked scholarly, but in a disheveled sort of way. Eminently masculine and strong. And he smelled delightful. Like sandalwood and freshly laundered linen. Yes, he looked most decidedly un-frog-like. And suddenly puzzled.

"No, of course there are no frogs here, Miss Chilton-Grizedale."

Heavens, had she spoken out loud? Surely not. A buzzing commenced in her ears, and she stared into his face. He seemed like a decent man. . . . *announce that today's wedding will not be taking place . . . not taking place.*

And he'd just ruined her life. Dear God.

"Glad you've finally come around," he said. "Had thought you were made of sterner stuff, but clearly I was mistaken."

A frown pulled down her brows. "Come around? What do you mean?"

"You swooned."

"I did no such thing. I am not prone to the vapors."

Good heavens, what was wrong with her tongue? It felt thick and foreign in her mouth.

He smiled. A crooked half smile that creased a dimple in his cheek. "Well, for one not prone to the vapors, you sunk like a papyrus brick tossed in the Nile. Do you feel well enough to sit up?"

Sit up? She cast her gaze about and realized with no small amount of chagrin that she was lying on her back on a sofa. And that Lord Greybourne sat perched upon the edge of the sofa, his hip pressed against hers, her one hand clasped between his wide palms, which continued to gently caress her skin. Heat radiated up her arm, spreading warmth through her entire body—warmth that had nothing to do with the consternation suffusing her. He was entirely too close, and she was entirely too . . . prone.

Good heavens, she *had* swooned! The reason for her vapors came rushing back in a wave. Lady Sarah . . . no bride . . . no wedding . . . cursed groom—who was indeed rough around the edges, in ways she'd never imagined.

Snatching her hand from his, she lifted her head, but the movement served no purpose other than to accentuate the odd floating sensation behind her eyes. A low moan passed her lips.

"Take some deep breaths," Lord Greybourne said, and demonstrated by drawing in a mighty breath that puffed out his chest, then slowly exhaling. His warm breath tickled the curls surrounding her face.

"Do you think I don't know how to breathe?" She hadn't meant to sound quite so testy, but this disastrous debacle coupled with his closeness to her person had clearly tossed her off kilter.

"I'm not certain. I *do* know that you won't require a demonstration on how to swoon. You already know how to do that."

Good heavens, he was nothing short of insufferable. Here they were, faced with utter travesty and social ruin, and he was making jokes! Closing her eyes, she took a half dozen deep breaths. Feeling considerably better, she again attempted to sit up, but discovered she couldn't move. "You're sitting on my gown, Lord Greybourne."

He shifted, then, grasping her shoulders, lifted her in a no-nonsense fashion into a sitting position, all but plopping her onto her bottom. Embarrassment, combined with a healthy dose of irritation—directed at herself or him, she wasn't certain—pricked her. "This may come as a shock, my lord, but I am not a sack of potatoes to be hauled about." The jarring movement knocked a long curl loose from her carefully arranged coiffure, and the lock flopped over her eye.

Pushing aside her hair with impatient fingers, she realized she no longer wore her bonnet.

"I removed it," he said, before she could question him. "I thought perhaps the ribbon tied beneath your chin might restrict your breathing." A half smile touched his lips and he tugged at his cravat. "God knows this thing constricts my airflow. You might also want to fix your gown." He waved his hand vaguely in the direction of her neck.

Dipping her chin, she realized with chagrin that her fichu was loose and pulled askew, exposing an expanse of skin that, while not indecent, was certainly far more of her bosom than normally saw the light of day.

She sizzled him with an outraged glare, but his lips curved upward in a patently unrepentant grin. "Didn't want a choking female on my hands."

Any gratitude she may have harbored for his assistance evaporated. "I merely felt *light-headed,* my lord—"

"Happy to hear you admit it."

"—and as such, it was hardly necessary for you to make so free with my attire."

"Ah. Then I suppose I shouldn't have straightened your garters."

Her eyes goggled, and the ill-mannered lout had the audacity to *wink* at her.

"I am teasing you, Miss Chilton-Grizedale. I merely wanted to bring some color back into your pale cheeks. I would not dream of touching your garters without your express permission. Probably."

Heat raced up her neck. This man was beyond insufferable—he was incorrigible. Uncouth. "I can assure you, you shall never receive such permission. And a gentleman would never say such a scandalous thing."

Again that dimple in his cheek flashed. "I'm certain you are correct."

Before she could fashion a reply, he rose. Crossing to a ceramic pitcher resting on the desk, he poured water into a crystal tumbler. He moved with lithe grace, and the knowledge that he'd untied and removed her bonnet, loosened her fichu, that his fingers had surely brushed over her throat, touched her hair, rushed heat through her—a fiery warmth that felt like something decidedly more than mere embarrassment.

Returning to her, he handed her the glass. "Drink this."

She somehow resisted the urge to toss the contents into his face. The tepid liquid eased her dry throat, and she assimilated the fact that she'd swooned—for the first time in her life. He clearly thought her some weak-willed twit. In her eight and twenty years she'd suffered worse things, recovered from worse, without succumbing to such missish nonsense. But dear God, this situation was a disaster.

Lady Sarah had abandoned Lord Greybourne at the altar—certainly a circumstance rife with scandal. But one made all the worse, from Meredith's point of view, because the wedding in question—the most talked-about, anticipated wedding in years—was one Meredith had arranged. And as much as she might wish it otherwise, every member of Society would remember *that* snippet of information. Remember it, and revile her because of it. Blame her for arranging such an unacceptable match, just as Lord Ravensly and Lord Hedington had done.

All her grand plans for her future evaporated like a trail of steam escaping a teakettle. Her reputation, her respectability for which she'd fought so hard, worked so tirelessly to establish, teetered on the edge of extinction. And all because of him.

Her gaze wandered around the room, and for the first time she realized that she and Lord Greybourne were alone. Just another facet of this debacle that could result in disaster. "Where are your father and Lord Hedington?"

"They went to announce to the congregation that Lady Sarah had taken ill and therefore the wedding could not take place today." He exhaled a long breath. "Isn't it odd how two statements that are both true can still somehow be a lie?"

"Not a lie," Meredith said, hastily adjusting her fichu and straightening her dark blue skirts. "I prefer to call it an omission of certain pertinent facts."

He cocked his head and studied her. "A definition that sounds very much like that for 'lie.'"

"Not at all," Meredith said briskly. "A lie is making false statements. 'Tis not a lie to simply not tell everything you know."

"Actually, I believe that is called a 'lie of omission.'"

"It appears you possess an overactive conscience, Lord Greybourne." At least she could be grateful that he *had* a conscience—dusty relic though it most likely was.

"More a case of liking my facts and definitions to be neatly aligned."

"Must be your scientific nature."

"Yes." The low hum of muffled voices drifted into the

room. Lord Greybourne rose and walked to the window. His lips flattened. "People are leaving the church. Clearly the announcement has been made." For several seconds he appeared lost in a brown study, then suddenly his eyes focused directly on her. "It has just occurred to me that this episode no doubt bodes poorly for you and your matchmaking enterprise."

Meredith stared at him, grimly noting that his position by the window bathed him with a golden halo of light— quite a feat for a man she regarded as the devil himself.

"Bodes poorly?" She nearly laughed at his understatement. "Ruination of gargantuan proportions more aptly describes the future of my matchmaking enterprise." She did not bother to voice the obvious—that this entire mess was his fault—him and his wretched curse. Surely there must be a way to fix this? She chewed on her bottom lip for several seconds, and a possible solution sprang to mind.

"I'm certain we can agree that the cancellation of today's ceremony is problematic, not just for me, but for everyone involved," she said. "If, however, you and Lady Sarah were to marry at a future date, preferably soon, that would dispel any scandal, and everyone would see that I did indeed make a wonderful match."

He nodded slowly, stroking his chin. "I agree with your theory. However, you are forgetting about the curse."

She debated whether to baldly state her opinion regarding the curse.

Clearly her skepticism showed, because he said, "Just because we cannot see or touch something does not make it any less real, does not mean it does not exist." He stepped closer to her, and she had to force herself to stand her ground and not retreat. His expression was so earnest, his eyes behind his lenses glowing with intensity. "Religions the world over worship a variety of gods that cannot be seen. I cannot see nor touch the air in this room, yet the fact that I can breathe tells me it is here."

At his words she drew in an involuntary breath, instantly noting that the air she could not see or touch smelled like Lord Greybourne. Fresh, clean, and masculine. And rife with potentially ruinous scandal.

"Surely you will be able to find a cure, or remedy, or whatever one finds to rid oneself of such things. You seem a bright sort of fellow."

His lips twitched. "Why, thank you. I—"

"Although your manners and appearance are in desperate need of refurbishment. We shall work to correct the damage years away from proper Society have wrought upon you before your wedding to Lady Sarah is rescheduled."

He cocked a brow. "And what, precisely, is wrong with my appearance?"

She mimicked his haughty expression and ticked items off on her fingers. "Hair too long and unkempt. Cravat disastrous. Waistcoat partially unbuttoned. Shirtfront wrinkled, cuffs too long. Jacket buttons unpolished, breeches too snug, boots scuffed. Do you not have a valet?"

He muttered something that sounded suspiciously like *bloody domineering piece.* "I'm afraid I haven't had the time to employ a valet as yet. I've been rather preoccupied with trying to find the missing piece of stone—which I am determined to do."

"Yes, you certainly must find it. We shall need to reschedule the wedding as soon as possible. Tell me, what did you think of Lady Sarah?"

He shrugged. "She was acceptable."

"Acceptable?" She barely managed to choke out the word. Good lord, on top of everything else, the man was daft. "She is a diamond of the first water. She will make the perfect viscountess and hostess. Not only that, in financial terms, and in terms of your estates, the match is highly advantageous."

"You say that as if I care a jot about such things, Miss Chilton-Grizedale."

She stared at him. "Do you not?"

He looked as if he were debating how to answer, then he said, "Actually, no. I do not. Society and all its trappings hold no appeal for me. They never have. Parties, soirees, the Season, none of it interests me. My holdings are already substantial enough. I do not require more land."

She barely suppressed a snort of disbelief. A man not interested in increasing his holdings? Not lured by the appeal of Society's trappings? Either he thought her a gullible fool or the years he'd spent gathering artifacts under the desert sun had greatly depleted his mental acuity.

He adjusted his glasses, and Meredith noticed his hands. Large, well-formed, long-fingered hands, browned by the sun. Hands that had massaged hers only moments ago. They looked strong and capable and manly in a way that stirred her in an odd, unfamiliar manner.

"Honor dictates I marry—and I need to do so before Father succumbs," he said, his voice dragging her gaze back to his. "So you see, as far as I'm concerned, whomever you chose, diamond or not, would not much matter. I'm not necessarily particular about the bride, so long as she is not overly off-putting—in which case, Lady Sarah is acceptable."

Being a practical person herself, Meredith couldn't find fault with his logic. Still, it irked that he appeared less than bowled over by her coup of snaring the much-sought-after Lady Sarah for him.

"What if you are unable to undo this curse of yours, Lord Greybourne?"

"Failure is simply not an option I will consider, Miss Chilton-Grizedale."

Since she wished to postpone thinking about the dreadful ramifications should he fail, she asked, "How long do you estimate it will take you to search through your crates?"

He frowned and considered. "With help, perhaps a fortnight."

The wheels in her head whirred. "That should give us ample time to come up with a contingency plan."

"And what sort of plan do you suggest, Miss Chilton-Grizedale? Believe me, I am open to suggestions. But I fail to see any, as the facts are quite irrefutable: If I do not break the curse, I cannot marry. And I *must* marry. However, with this curse hanging about my neck, I would risk the life of any woman I married—something I am not willing to do. And I cannot imagine any woman being willing to do so."

Unfortunately, Meredith was hard-pressed to immediately name anyone who would want to marry even the heir to an earldom, only to risk expiring two days later. "But surely—"

"Tell me, Miss Chilton-Grizedale, would *you* be willing to take such a risk?" He stepped closer to her, and suddenly the room seemed to shrink significantly. "Would *you* want to risk losing your life by becoming my bride?"

Meredith fought the urge to back up, to fan herself to relieve the heat creeping up her neck. Instead she lifted her chin and faced him squarely. "Naturally I would not wish to die two days after my wedding, if I were to believe in such things as curses. Which, in spite of your compelling arguments, I am still inclined to regard as a series of unfortunate coincidences. However, the point is moot, my lord, as I have no desire to ever marry."

Surprise flickered behind his spectacles. "That places you in a category of females that I believe you might be in all by yourself."

"I have never objected to solitude." She tilted her head and studied him for several seconds, then asked, "Do you normally place people into 'categories'?"

"I'm afraid so. Almost instantaneously. People, objects, most everything. Always have. A trait quite common among scientists."

"Actually, I tend to do the same thing, yet I am not a scientist."

"Interesting. Tell me, Miss Chilton-Grizedale, what category have you placed *me* in?"

Without even thinking, she blurted out, "The 'not what I expected' category."

The instant the words passed her lips, mortification suffused her. Heavens, she hoped he wouldn't ask what she meant, for she couldn't very well tell him that she'd been expecting an older version of the pudgy, toady youth in the painting, and he was so very much . . . *not* that.

He regarded her with an intensity that filled her with the urge to fidget. "That is very interesting, Miss Chilton-Grizedale, for that is the precise category I placed *you* in."

Feeling uncharacteristically unnerved by his regard, Meredith stepped away from him and adopted her most brisk tone. "Now that we are all categorized, let us get back to our present dilemma." Her brain raced, trying to cast the situation in the best light. "Today is the first of the month. I believe the best plan is to reschedule the wedding for, let us say, the twenty-second. That should give you more than enough time to search your crates." *And give me ample time to polish you into more marriageable material so no one will doubt what a brilliant match I've made.* "We'll plan something small and private this time, in your father's drawing room, perhaps." In her mind's eye she envisioned the placement of the flowers, and the complimentary, effusive announcement in *The Times* the following day, praising her skills, reestablishing her reputation. "We've only to convince Lady Sarah that this is the best course. Do you think you can uncurse yourself by then?"

"That is certainly my intention."

A tiny flicker of hope coughed to life in Meredith's breast. Yes, perhaps this *could* possibly be salvaged. Of course, the situation was a debacle. However, it was not a *complete and total* debacle. She clung to that thought like a lifeline, lest she crumble into a heap. Damn it all, this was so unfair! She'd worked so hard. Had sacrificed so much to finally earn the respect she'd so desperately wanted. She couldn't lose it . . . not again. Yet the thought of having to go through it all again . . . the lying and cheating and stealing. She briefly squeezed her eyes shut. No. It couldn't come to that. He'd cure his curse and all would be well. It *had* to be.

A knock sounded at the door, and Lord Greybourne called, "Come in."

Lord Hedington marched into the room, looking as if he were a volcano on the verge of erupting.

"You advised the guests?" Lord Greybourne asked.

"Yes. I told them Sarah had fallen ill, but gossip about one or the other of you crying off is already rampant. No doubt this damnable story will make the front page of *The Times*."

Meredith cleared her throat. "Lord Greybourne and I were just discussing how best to salvage this situation, your grace. He is hopeful of finding the missing piece of the stone, and thereby being able to reverse the curse. Based on that, I shall reschedule the wedding to take place on the twenty-second. I'll send the announcement to *The Times* immediately to squelch any gossip."

Lord Hedington's gaze bounced between them, then his head jerked in a nod. "Very well. But I expect to be assured that no harm will come to my daughter. If I am not confident of her safety, there will be no wedding, scandal be damned. And now I plan to return home and retrieve this note Sarah claims to have left me." Turning on his heel, he quit the room.

Meredith looked at Lord Greybourne. "I offer you my assistance, my lord, in searching for the stone."

"Thank you. I don't suppose by any chance you are a farmer, Miss Chilton-Grizedale?"

Good Lord, the man *was* daft. "A farmer? Certainly not. Why do you ask?"

"Because I fear this will very much be like looking for a needle amongst the haystacks."

Narrowed eyes assessed the collection of Egyptian artifacts resting on red velvet behind the glass display case in the British Museum. How fitting that the artifacts should lie upon such a color—the shade of blood. Blood that had already been shed. And blood that would soon be shed.

Your blood, Greybourne. You shall suffer for the pain you've caused. Soon.

Very soon.

Three

Meredith walked slowly up the walkway leading to her modest house on Hadlow Street. While the area was far from the most fashionable in London, it was still respectable, and she loved her house with the fierce pride of someone who had worked hard for something she wanted. And more than anything Meredith had wanted a home. A *real* home. A *respectable* home.

Oh, she well knew she'd never be a member of Society, but her association with the *ton,* even though it was on the fringes, afforded her a measure of the respectability she'd craved her entire life.

Yet now her footsteps slowed to a snail's pace. She dreaded opening the front door and having to tell the three people she loved most in the world that she'd failed. That the life, the facade she'd so carefully constructed stood in danger of collapsing like a house of cards. Was it possible that Albert, Charlotte, and Hope already knew? Gossip traveled so quickly—

The oak door swung open to reveal Albert Goddard's expectant smile. Charlotte Carlyle stood behind him, her normally solemn gray eyes wide with anticipation. Charlotte's daughter Hope peeked around her mother's dark green skirt, and the instant she saw Meredith, the child raced toward her.

"Aunt Merrie!" Hope hugged her chubby little four-year-old arms around Meredith's legs, and Meredith leaned down to press a kiss to the child's shiny golden curls. "I *missted* you, Aunt Merrie," Hope proclaimed, looking up, her gray eyes exact replicas of Charlotte's, shining with pleasure.

"And I missed you as well, poppet." The area surrounding Meredith's heart went hollow. More than her future had been compromised today. With her current situation, what would become of Hope and Charlotte? Of Albert?

Arranging her features into what she hoped would pass for unconcern, she looked toward the doorway. The instant her gaze met Albert's she knew she'd failed in her attempt for nonchalance. His smile froze, then slowly faded, his entire expression turning to one of narrow-eyed wariness.

Damnation, he knew her too well, and after eleven years, she supposed that was to be expected. Still, his eyes were far too knowing for a mere twenty-year-old. But of course, Albert had seen and survived more than most twenty-year-olds. Her gaze shifted to Charlotte, her cook's apron still tied around her trim waist, her eyes reflecting the same cautious wariness as Albert's. Charlotte knew her as well as Albert, although Charlotte had only joined Meredith's "family" five years ago, shortly before giving birth to Hope. As there was no hiding the truth from either of them, she decided not to prolong the misery.

With Hope's small hand nestled in hers, Meredith walked up the cobbled pathway. When she stepped into the small parquet-floored foyer, she untied her bonnet and handed it to Albert.

"We need to talk," she said without preamble to Albert and Charlotte.

Still holding Hope's hand, Meredith led the way down the corridor to the drawing room. Hope immediately dashed to her child-sized chair and table in the corner and began drawing in her sketch pad. Meredith clasped her hands in front of her and faced her two dearest friends.

"I'm afraid I have some rather disturbing news." She described the morning's events at the church, concluding with, "As much as I'd like to be optimistic, I'm afraid I must be practical. This debacle, though no fault of my own, is going to have disastrous repercussions on my reputation as a matchmaker. Indeed, it is only a matter of time, perhaps hours, before requests to cancel my services start arriving. While I remain hopeful that Lord Greybourne will find the missing piece of the stone and end the curse, I'd be foolish not to make plans in the event that he is unsuccessful. Even if this proves to be merely a postponement, rather than a permanent canceling of the nuptials, with all the gossip already flying about, it could take months to repair the damage. If he fails . . ." She pressed her fingers to her temples in an attempt to keep the few remaining remnants of her rapidly disappearing sanity from escaping. "Good Lord, in that case, I am well and truly ruined. My livelihood is destroyed. . . ." And she well knew how limited the choices were for women to earn a living. *I won't go back. . . . I'll never go back.*

Albert narrowed his eyes. "If ye ask me, this curse is mighty suspicious-like. Maybe this Greybourne bloke is makin' it all up so he don't have to get married."

Meredith slowly shook her head. "I don't think so."

"Yer just too trustin', that's all," Albert said.

"I'm not saying *I* believe in this curse. In truth, I'm not quite sure exactly *how* I feel about it. As incredible as it seems, I somehow find I cannot discount it. And there is no doubt in my mind that Lord Greybourne believes in it absolutely."

"Well, that just proves that the bloke's half daft." Albert pointed his index finger at her. "I think ye should stay away from him, Miss Merrie. I don't trust him one bit. And in the meanwhile, don't ye worry none about funds. I'll take on some nighttime labor, maybe down at the docks. Or we can resettle somewhere else, somewhere

where the gossip ain't been heard. Maybe somewhere near the sea like we always talked about. We'll get by, just like always."

"Of course we will," said Charlotte. "I can take on some sewing—"

"I don't want for us to just *get by*." Meredith's chest tightened, and she clenched her hands to tamp down the panic threatening to overwhelm her. "We've worked too hard, too long. I cannot, will not, allow this situation to destroy my good name, respectability, and reputation. The chance for a secure future for all of us. For Hope. And the only way to ensure that it does not ruin anything is to make certain that Lord Greybourne marries Lady Sarah."

"Well then, we'll just make certain that that's wot happens," Albert decreed, as if it were the simplest thing in the world. "Why, we'll just offer to help Lord Greybourne find his missin' rock, and before ye can say 'Brummel's a dandy' we'll have this problem fixed and the bloke married off."

A tired smile tugged at Meredith's lips. Dear Albert. Somehow, when she hadn't been looking, he'd grown into a tower of strength. Certainly a far cry from the sick, broken child she'd found discarded in the gutter, left for dead. Here she was supposed to be taking care of him, but now it appeared he was taking care of her, bearing her troubles upon his broad shoulders.

He rose and limped across the carpet to her, then wrapped a strong arm around her shoulders. "We've faced worse than this, Miss Merrie, and come through all right. Why, if it's necessary, I'll dress meself up like a bride and marry the bloke meself." He squeezed her shoulders and shot her a wink, and because she knew he was trying to cheer her up, Meredith forced a smile.

Slanting a sideways glance toward Charlotte, Meredith asked, "I believe Albert would make quite a lovely bride, don't you, Charlotte?" She reached out and playfully pinched Albert's cheeks. "After all, he's so very handsome."

Meredith felt Albert tense at her teasing question, and Charlotte's face blazed crimson. But then her dear friend merely shrugged and said, "Lovely or not, I suspect that at *some* point Lord Greybourne would notice there was something amiss with his bride. How long do you think it would escape his notice when his wife's *beard* began to grow?"

Albert stroked his clean-shaven jaw. "Hmmm. Yes, that could present a problem." His expression sobered and he clasped Meredith's hands. "I'll not have ye worryin' 'bout something ye cannot change, Miss Merrie. We'll try to find this stone, and if we do, well then, the bloke and Lady Sarah will marry and all will be fine. And if we don't find the stone—"

"I'll be ruined."

Albert's expression turned fierce. "Never. Nothin' could ever dim ye in my eyes."

"Nor mine," Charlotte added softly. "Nor Hope's." She rose and hugged Meredith. "Albert is right. This will all work out fine. And if it doesn't, we'll leave London. Go somewhere new. Start again."

Meredith forced a smile and hugged her friends, but her heart felt heavy. Dear God, how many times could she go somewhere new and start again? She was so *tired* of doing that.

Unfortunately, she suspected it was exactly what she was going to have to do. But maybe, just maybe, everything would be all right.

Sitting at the breakfast table the next morning, Meredith opened *The Times*. The bold newsprint headline stared back at her: *Is Cursed Viscount the Most Unmarriageable Man in England?*

Any hope that her announcement of the wedding being rescheduled for the twenty-second would avert gossip disintegrated. Her heart plummeted to her feet, dragging her cramped stomach along for the tumultuous journey as she quickly scanned the words, her dread increasing with each paragraph. Three entire pages, not to mention the entire left column of the front page, were devoted to the story.

Her gaze scanned over the words, each one burning into her mind, incinerating any foolish hopes she might have harbored that perhaps her reputation could somehow remain partially intact. Every detail, from the curse, to Lord Greybourne's bargain with his father, to speculation regarding Lady Sarah's mysterious "illness," was printed for all to read.

Heavens, with the accuracy of his story, one had to wonder if the reporter had been secreted behind the curtains while Lord Greybourne had told his tale of the curse. The entire incident was detailed, from his finding the stone, to the death of his friend's wife, to his vow to somehow break the curse. Meredith read the final lines of the article with dread.

Is this curse real, or just a ploy concocted to dissolve a betrothal that Greybourne or Lady Sarah—or perhaps both of them—realized they did not want after they'd met? Was Lady Sarah merely ill, as her father stated—or did she cry off rather than risk dying two days after her marriage? Many women would give a great deal to marry the heir to an earldom—but would they be willing to die for it? I rather think not. The wedding has been rescheduled for the twenty-second, but will it actually take place? One cannot help but suspect this rescheduling is naught but a ploy for Grey-

bourne and Miss Chilton-Grizedale to save
face. And all this begs the questions—if the
curse is real, how will Lord Greybourne honor
his vow to marry? Indeed, should the curse
prove real, one must wonder, who will take
this man? Should Lord Greybourne discover a
way to break this curse, will he and Lady
Sarah still marry? If not, perhaps he can
again engage Miss Chilton-Grizedale's matchmaking services to aid him in his quest for a
bride. Certainly no one else will be hiring her
after this debacle.

Meredith's gaze riveted on that last line, each word re-
verberating like a death knell. She squeezed her eyes shut
and wrapped her arms around her middle in a fruitless effort to contain the pain seizing her. Damn it all, this could
not be happening to her.

Hot tears pressed behind her eyes, and she gritted her
teeth to stem the moisture. Tears were futile signs of
weakness, and she was not weak. Not any longer. Mama's
voice tickled her memory. *Stop running, Meredith. You
cannot escape your past.*

*Yes, I can, Mama. I did escape. I did not give up as you
did. I fought hard for what I have—*

Had. What she'd *had*. Because now it was gone.

The bottom dropped out of her stomach, and she
pressed her fingertips against her temples in a vain attempt to temper the rhythmic pounding in her head. No. It
wasn't gone. Not yet. And by damn, she wouldn't give it
up without a fight.

"Are you all right, Miss Merrie?"

At the deep-voiced question, Meredith's eyes popped
open. Albert stood in the threshold, a look of concern
pinching his dark brows. She instantly noted the vellum-
laden salver he held.

Forcing a wan smile, she said, "I'm fine, Albert. Just a bit tired."

Albert didn't smile in response. Indeed, his dark eyes flashed, and he planted his free hand on his hip and glared at her. "Now, that's a bald-faced lie if ever I heard one, and I've heard plenty," he said with his characteristic brutal bluntness. "'Tis like a ghostie yer lookin', all pale and scared-like." His frown furrowed deeper and he jerked his head toward the newspaper. "I read it. I'd like to get that reporter bloke alone for five minutes. Probably he were eavesdroppin'."

"Perhaps, but how he learned of the curse doesn't really matter at this point." Her gaze rested on the salver. "I guess we both know what those are. No sense pretending they're invitations to tea."

"Yer most likely correct. I can't get anything done wot for answerin' the door." At that moment the brass knocker sounded.

"Leave those with me," Meredith said.

Albert set the salver on the table, then limped across the floor toward the corridor, his left boot scraping against the wood. The fact that his limp was so pronounced this morning indicated that he'd either not slept well last night or that the weather was damp. Perhaps a combination of both.

At the threshold he turned and gazed at Meredith with an intense expression. "Don't you worry none, Miss Merrie. Albert won't let no one ever hurt you." He quit the room, and Meredith heard the fading, soft scrape of his boot along the runner in the corridor.

Her gaze fell to the note-laden salver. Although she knew without reading them what they contained, one by one she broke the wax seals and read the contents. Each note was very much like the last. Just a few hastily scribbled lines, worded in such a way that she could almost feel the heat of censure rising from vellum to scorch her skin. *I shall no longer require your services. I wish to terminate our association.*

The exact wording didn't matter. Each letter represented the same thing: another shovelful of dirt upon the grave in which her reputation and respectability now lay.

Something had do be done. And quickly.

But what?

Philip stared at the newspaper in disgust. "How the bloody hell did this reporter find out about the curse?"

Andrew Stanton, his American friend and antiquarian colleague, looked up from his breakfast in surprise. "You told me everyone had agreed at St. Paul's not to talk about it."

"We did. But somehow this damned reporter found out. Like bloody rabid dogs after a bone." He tossed *The Times* aside, and blew out a frustrated breath. "I warned you London would be like this."

"Actually, you told me that England was stodgy and dull and boring, and I'm afraid I must disagree. Only hours after our arrival we engaged in a very satisfactory street brawl, resulting in you getting yourself a pet."

Philip shot him a dark look. "Yes, a puppy is exactly what I wanted."

"You don't fool me. I've seen you doting on the beast. I'll wager that the moment he's feeling in top form you'll be frolicking in the park with him." Before Philip could icily point out that he did not *frolick,* Andrew blithely continued, "And then there was the heated argument with your father, topped off by the debacle at St. Paul's yesterday. No, I most certainly have not been bored. Indeed, I cannot wait to see what happens next."

"Have you always been such a bloody pest?" Philip asked with a scowl.

"Not until I met you." He grinned. "You taught me well."

"Well, the next time you're about to be chopped to pieces by machete-wielding hooligans, remind me not to intervene."

Andrew shuddered at the memory. "Yes, you and your walking stick quite saved the day. How was I to know that woman was the machete-wielding hooligan's sister?"

After accepting more coffee from a footman, Philip said, "I received a note from Edward this morning."

Andrew's amusement instantly faded. "How is he?"

"He claims he is well, but I'm certain he is not. He visited Mary's grave. . . ." A powerful wave of guilt engulfed Philip. Poor Mary Binsmore. And poor Edward. His friend had been devoted to his wife of two decades. He made a mental note to consult with his solicitor about setting up a trust for Edward. Of course a financial gesture was woefully inadequate, but he had to do something. *If it weren't for me, Mary Binsmore would still be alive—*

Cutting off the disturbing thought, he continued, "He wishes to aid in the search through the crates for the missing piece of stone. I wrote back that I'd welcome his help. God knows we need the assistance, and keeping busy will help him to focus on something other than his loss. I suggested he join you at the British Museum in going through the crates delivered there, while I continue my search at the warehouse."

"An excellent plan." Andrew drained his china cup, then rose, his height and muscular build dwarfing the hovering footman. "I'm off to the museum. I'll report to you immediately should we find something."

"I'll do the same."

No sooner had his friend departed than Bakari entered the breakfast room, his dark brown face set in its usual inscrutable mask, his hands precisely folded against his midsection. Dressed in his customary loose silk shirt, drawstring trousers, soft leather ankle boots, and turban,

Bakari had caused quite a stir among the rest of the formal, liveried staff. Philip eyed his manservant warily. It was always impossible to tell if Bakari was about to impart good news or bad news.

"Your father."

Ah. Bad news. Suppressing a resigned sigh, Philip said, "Show him in."

Seconds later the earl entered, his gait surprisingly brisk given his complexion bore an unhealthy pale hue. The guilt and regret that lurked within Philip rose sharply from the recesses of his heart, where it dwelled like a hulking beast. Although he was not anxious to engage in another argument with Father, he was glad to see him up and about. Mother had experienced much the same her last months—one good day interspersed with an ever-increasing number of bad days—until there were no more days at all.

Settling himself in the chair across from Philip, Father's chilly gaze raked over Philip's lack of cravat, loose-fitting shirt, and rolled-back sleeves before flicking over the discarded newspaper. After accepting coffee from a footman, Father said, "Damned thorough story. Almost as if the man were in the room with us. I find his intimate knowledge of something we'd agreed should be kept quiet quite . . . curious."

"Are you implying that I provided *The Times* with this information?"

"Did you?"

As he had so many times before, Philip deflected the hurt his father's doubt arrowed at him. "No, I did not. No doubt someone overheard us. We were not exactly whispering." Philip dragged his hands down his face. "Besides, I cannot see that it really makes much difference how the story was found out. Indeed, perhaps it is better that it is known. It might cut down on the speculation."

A humorless laugh escaped his father. "You've been away from Society far too long. No, this is just the sort of story that whets the appetite and causes speculation and innuendo to run rampant. I'm just grateful that Catherine isn't in London, being subjected to this mess."

Philip's heart squeezed at the mention of his sister. She was the one thing he'd missed during his years abroad, and he couldn't wait to see her. Her son had contracted a sudden stomach ailment, regrettably postponing her travel plans. "Well, she's soon to be subjected, I'm afraid," Philip said. "I received a note from her this morning. Spencer has recovered and Catherine expects to arrive in London this afternoon."

"I see. Well, we shall have to prepare her," his father said. "The gossipmongers will pounce upon this situation like a pack of hounds on a trapped fox. Indeed, the gossip is already spreading, even amongst the servants."

"How do you know?"

"Evans keeps me informed. I'm convinced there isn't a butler in all of England who knows more than he. Would you care to hear the latest?"

Philip suspected he didn't want to know, but somehow he heard himself answering, "Of course."

"According to Evans, who, I might add, relayed the following with an enormous amount of hemming and hawing and throat-clearing, is that Lady Sarah cried off for two reasons: One, she did not want to die from your curse, and two, even without the curse she still would have jilted you, as she had no wish to become the bride of a man who is unable to . . . perform his husbandly duties."

Philip winced. "Ah. I see. Since it is impossible to conceive that any woman wouldn't wish to marry the heir to an earldom unless for very compelling reasons, tongues are wagging with the notion that the compelling reason is I will not be able to consummate my marriage."

"I'm afraid so. Not the sort of conjecture a man likes to have to defend himself against." He stirred a bit of sugar into his coffee. "Have you any news of Lady Sarah?"

"Not yet, but I've sent 'round a note advising her of my intention to call upon her later today." He patted his mouth with his napkin, then set the square of linen on the polished cherrywood table next to his plate. "And toward that end, I shall depart for the warehouse to continue with the unpacking of the crates." Rising, Philip strode toward the door.

"What in God's name are you wearing?" came his father's outraged voice.

Philip halted and looked down at his loose-fitting, drawstring-waisted trousers. "Comfortable clothing. I'm going to be working in a warehouse, Father, not attending a ball." With that, he exited the breakfast room. As he approached the foyer, the brass knocker sounded, and Bakari opened the door. Philip caught the sound of a familiar, throaty female voice. *Her* voice. The dictatorial matchmaker. He noted with some annoyance that his footsteps quickened.

"Will see if Lord Greybourne is available," Bakari said, holding a calling card between his fingers.

"I'm available, Bakari." He stepped around the butler and met Miss Chilton-Grizedale's startled expression. His gaze swept over her, the details of her ensemble clicking in his mind. Peacock-blue muslin gown with matching spencer. Bonnet that framed her piquant face in a way that reminded him of a stamen surrounded by soft petals. A frown pulled down his brows. No, that didn't sound quite right. But damn it all, she did somehow remind him of flowers. Perhaps it was her fragrance? He inhaled and instantly discarded the notion. No, she did not smell like flowers. She smelled like—he leaned a bit closer to her and inhaled again—like freshly baked cake.

No, it was her coloring, he suddenly realized, that brought flowers to mind. Her skin looked as soft as roses, her cheekbones blushed with peach, and her lips were colored with a delicate pinkish red, all colors he recalled from his mother's formal country gardens at Ravensly Manor.

Bakari harrumphed. "Might want to invite lady in," came his dry whisper behind him, "not gawk at her in the doorway."

Annoyed at himself, Philip instantly stepped back. Damn. Clearly some brushing up on his manners *was* called for. "Please come in, Miss Chilton-Grizedale."

She inclined her head in a regal fashion and entered the foyer. "Thank you, Lord Greybourne. I apologize for calling so early, but I believe it is essential that we get a timely start. I am ready to depart whenever you are." Her gaze flicked over his attire, and her eyes widened.

"Depart? But you've just arrived." Looking pert and fresh and smelling good enough to nibble upon.

Bloody hell, where had *that* thought come from? Clearly it entered his head because he harbored a weakness for freshly baked cake. Yes, that's all it was.

"I've come to accompany you. To help you look through the crates to locate the other half of the stone." Her clear, aqua gaze met his questioningly. "Where exactly are we going?"

"The crates are stored in a warehouse near the docks. I cannot ask you to accompany me to such an area, or to help me with such a task, Miss Chilton-Grizedale. It is tedious, dirty, exhausting work."

She lifted her chin and somehow managed to appear to look down the slope of her pert nose at him—amazing, considering he stood a good six inches taller than she. "First, there is no need to *ask* me, my lord, as I have *offered* my assistance. Second, I am quite accustomed to

work and do not tire easily. And as for the docks, you need
not worry about protecting me, as I am armed. Third—"

"*Armed?*"

"Of course." She held her reticule aloft. "Filled with
stones. One cosh to the head will fell any brigand. A very
practical device I learned long ago to carry with me at all
times."

He stared at the innocent-looking beaded bag dangling
from her wrist by a velvet drawstring. She'd learned this
trick long ago? What sort of upbringing had the very
proper Miss Chilton-Grizedale had that would warrant
arming herself? "Are you normally in the habit of, er, delivering coshes to the head?"

"Hardly ever." He raised his gaze and met eyes flickering with mischief. "Unless, of course, a gentleman makes
the error of trying to dissuade me from doing something I
wish to do."

"I see. And in that case you—"

"Cosh first, then ask questions later, I'm afraid." She
twirled the little bag around in a circle, then continued in
a brisk tone, "And third, the time spent together will provide the dual purpose for me to reacquaint you with some
of the rules of Society you have clearly forgotten. As for
this expedition proving distressing to my clothing, I harbor no fear of my garments becoming dirty, as—brace
yourself—they can be laundered. And last, I shall not find
any task tedious that might result in the ending of this
curse. Have you seen *The Times?*"

"I'm afraid so, although how they gained the information about the curse, I do not know."

"Creepers, no doubt." At his questioning look, she clarified, "Newspaper informers. They earn their living ferreting out information—most often information that the
persons involved would prefer not to have offered up for
public consumption."

"And how do they gather this information?"

"They steal or intercept correspondence, eavesdrop, bribe servants, any number of devious ways. No doubt one of them overheard us talking in St. Paul's yesterday."

Philip shook his head. "Incredible. The lengths that people will go . . . just incredible."

"Not at all. It's quite common. Actually, I find you thinking such a practice to be incredible quite amazing. Forgive my bluntness, my lord, but you seem to hold a rather naive view of the world, for one who is so well traveled."

"Naive?" An incredulous laugh escaped him. "I have no illusions about people and their motives, Miss Chilton-Grizedale, and I did not have to leave England to form those opinions. If anything, my travels abroad renewed my faith in my fellow man. In one way, however, I suppose you are correct, although I would call myself 'unpracticed' as opposed to naive. While I have been exposed to dishonesty in many forms, my time and thoughts have, for many years, been focused on objects and people from the past. I fear I cannot claim any expertise in the area of modern human behavior. In fact, what I know of it leaves me largely unimpressed."

She regarded him through serious eyes. "Yet I believe that human behavior is most likely very much the same today as it was hundreds, even thousands, of years ago."

Her statement surprised him. And piqued his curiosity and interest. But before he could respond, Bakari interjected, "Invite lady to stay for breakfast? Or tea?"

Another wave of annoyance washed over Philip. What on earth was the matter with him? He might have developed a few rough edges during his time away from polite Society, but he did hold a *few* social graces. Unfortunately, something about Miss Chilton-Grizedale clearly did not bode well for him recalling *any* of his manners.

"Forgive me," he said. "May I interest you in something to eat? Or tea, perhaps?"

"No, thank you." Her gaze swept over his attire. "How long before you are ready to depart?"

Depart? Oh, yes. The crates. The stone. The curse. His life with Lady Sarah. "I need a few moments to collect my journals."

"And to change into some proper attire."

He folded his arms across his chest. "I must say, I am growing weary of these repeated comments on my clothing. Nor do I particularly care to be on the receiving end of such a peremptory order."

She raised her brows. "Peremptory order? I prefer to call it a strong suggestion."

"Yes, I'm certain you do. And there is nothing wrong with what I am wearing."

"Perhaps if you were tromping about in the desert, or along the Nile. You just admitted that you lack knowledge of modern human behavior. I, however, am something of an expert on the subject. Pray believe me when I tell you that your present attire is unacceptable for going out-of-doors." She pursed her lips into a prim line. "It is also unacceptable for receiving guests. All in all, it is simply unacceptable."

Philip turned to Bakari. "Do I look unacceptable?"

Bakari merely harrumphed and strode from the foyer in an altogether unhelpful manner. Philip swiveled his attention back to Miss Chilton-Grizedale. "If you think I'm going to truss myself up like a goose in form-fitting, fussy, dandified clothes just to look 'acceptable' to strangers I care nothing about, you're sadly mistaken."

"The members of Society, whether you are personally acquainted with them or not, are your peers, Lord Greybourne, not strangers. Such august company lends one respectability. How can you take that so lightly?"

"And how can you take it so seriously?"

Her chin lifted a notch. "Perhaps because, as a woman who must depend upon herself for her livelihood, my respectability is of the utmost importance to me—and is something I take very seriously. Lady Sarah is not a stranger. Nor is your sister, whom I've heard so much about. Are you saying that you care nothing for them?"

"*Catherine* would not be so shallow as to condemn me because I'm not clad in the latest fashion."

Bright red stained her cheeks at his arch observation. "But like it or not, your behavior will reflect upon both your fiancée and your sister, not to mention your father. If you won't think of your own reputation, think of theirs." Her brows lifted. "Or is a world adventurer such as yourself too selfish to do so?"

Annoyance flooded him at her words. Damn irritating woman. Even more so because he couldn't deny she had a valid point. Now that he was back in the confining restraints of "civilization" his actions *would* reflect on others. For ten years he hadn't had to think about anyone except himself. His departure from England had marked the first time in his life he'd been able to say and do anything he damn well felt like saying or doing, without the censure of Society's—or Father's—glare beating down upon him. It was a freedom he'd reveled in, and one he did not relish curtailing in any way. But he'd rather suffer a cobra bite than do anything to hurt Catherine.

"I'll change my clothing," he said, unable to keep the snarl from his voice.

She shot him a satisfied—no, a *smug*—smile that all but screamed, *Of course you will,* upping his irritation several notches. Muttering under his breath about autocratic females, he retired to his bedchamber, returning several minutes later, his concessions consisting of changing into a "proper" pair of breeches and yanking on a jacket over his loose-fitting shirt, purposely leaving his jacket unbuttoned.

When she raised her brows and appeared about to comment, he said, "I am going to a *warehouse*. To *work*. Not to have my portrait painted. This is the best you'll get from me. It's this or I wear nothing at all."

She appeared startled, then narrowed her eyes. "You wouldn't dare."

He moved closer to her, surprising him when she stood her ground, but he was cheered by her sharp intake of breath. "Did you know that temperatures in Egypt, in Syria, can reach levels where you actually can see the heat radiating off the ground? I am quite accustomed to wearing a minimum of clothing. Or none at all. So daring me would not be wise, Miss Chilton-Grizedale."

A blush suffused her cheeks, and her lips compressed into a flat line of disapproval. "If you think to shock me with such words, Lord Greybourne, you are doomed to failure. If you wish to shame yourself, your fiancée, and your family, I cannot stop you. I can only hope you will act in a decorous manner."

He heaved out a dramatic sigh. "I suppose that means I shall not get to disrobe in the foyer. Pity." Extending his elbow, he said, "Shall we?"

He looked into her eyes, noting their extraordinary clear Aegean-blue color. They sparkled with determination and stubbornness, along with something else, not so easily defined. Unless he was mistaken, which he rarely was in such assessments, a hint of secrets simmered in Miss Chilton-Grizedale's eyes as well, piquing his curiosity and interest.

That, along with her penchant for loading her reticule with stones, was casting her in the light of an intriguing puzzle.

And he harbored an incredible weakness for puzzles.

Four

 Meredith sat upon the luxurious gray velvet squabs of Lord Greybourne's coach, and studied her traveling companion. At first she'd done so covertly, from the corner of her eye as she'd feigned looking out the window at the shops and people lining Oxford Street. However, his attention was so wrapped up in studying the contents of the worn leather journal setting upon his lap, she soon abandoned the ruse and simply looked at him with frank curiosity.

The man sitting across from her was the complete antithesis of the boy in the painting hanging in the drawing room at his father's London townhouse. His skin was not pale, but a warm, golden brown that bespoke of time spent in the sun. Golden streaks highlighted his thick, wavy dark brown hair that was once again haphazardly coiffed, as if his fingers had tunneled through the strands. Indeed, even as the thought crossed her mind, he lifted one hand and raked it through his hair.

Her gaze wandered slowly downward. Nothing about the adult Lord Greybourne could be described as soft or pudgy. He looked lean and hard and thoroughly masculine. His midnight-blue cutaway jacket, in spite of its numerous wrinkles, hugged his broad shoulders, and the fawn breeches he'd changed into emphasized his muscular legs in a way that, if she were the sort of woman to do so, might induce her to heave a purely feminine sigh.

Fortunately, she was not at all the sort of woman to heave feminine sighs.

In further contrast to his youthful self, although his clothing was finely made of quality cloth, Lord Greybourne projected an undone appearance, no doubt the result of his askew cravat and those thick strands of hair falling over his forehead, in a fashion which, if she were the sort of woman to be tempted, might tempt her to reach out and brush those silky strands back into place.

Fortunately, she was not at all the sort of woman to be tempted.

He looked up and their eyes met, his surrounded by round, wire-framed spectacles. In the painting, Lord Greybourne's eyes had appeared to be a dull, flat brown. The artist had utterly failed to capture the intelligence and compelling intensity in those eyes. And there could be no denying that Lord Greybourne's countenance was no longer that of a youth. All the softness had been replaced by lean angles, a firm, square jaw, and high cheekbones. His nose was the same—bold and blade-straight. And his mouth . . .

Her gaze riveted on his lips. His mouth was lovely in a way that she had not noticed in the painting. It was full. And firm—yet somehow appeared fascinatingly soft at the same time. Just the sort of mouth that, if she were a different sort of woman, might entice her to want to taste.

Fortunately, she was not at all the sort of woman to be enticed.

"Are you all right, Miss Chilton-Grizedale? You look a bit flushed."

Damnation! She snapped her gaze up to his and arranged her features into her most prim expression. "I'm fine, thank you. It is merely warm in the carriage." She resisted the urge to lift her hand to fan herself. Just as well, as, with her luck, she'd lift her hand and swing her stone-laden reticule around and cosh herself on the head with it. Instead she nodded toward the journal resting on his lap.

"What are you reading?" she asked, refraining from pointing out his lack of manners in ignoring her. Clearly she would need to pick her battles with this man, and her inner voice cautioned that having him ignore her might be in her best interests.

"I'm searching through a volume of my notes from my travels. I'm hopeful that I may have made a notation or sketch at some point that might provide a clue."

"Have you had any success?"

"No. My notes fill over one hundred volumes, and although I examined them during my return voyage to England to no avail, I was hoping that perhaps I might find something I'd missed." He closed the book, then tied a length of worn leather around it.

"What do your notes contain?"

"Sketches of artifacts and hieroglyphs, descriptions, folklore and stories told to me, personal observations. Things of that nature."

"You learned enough to fill more than one hundred volumes?" An incredulous laugh escaped her. "Heavens, I find it a chore to compose a single-page letter."

"In truth, I experienced more than I could ever have time to record in writing." An expression that seemed to combine longing and passion entered his eyes. "Egypt, Turkey, Greece, Italy, Morocco . . . they are impossible to adequately describe, yet they're so vivid in my memory, if I close my eyes, I feel as if I am still there."

"You loved those places."

"Yes."

"You did not want to leave."

He studied her before replying. "You are correct. England is the place of my birth, yet it no longer feels like . . . home." One corner of his mouth quirked upward.

"I wouldn't expect you to understand what I mean. Indeed, I barely do myself."

" 'Tis true that I do not know what places such as Egypt and Greece look like, but I know about the importance, the *necessity,* of being in a place that feels like home. And how out of sorts one can feel when they are not there."

He nodded slowly, his gaze never leaving hers. "Yes, that is exactly how I feel. Out of sorts."

Something in his tone, in the way he was looking at her, with all that focused attention, stalled her breath. And rendered *her* most definitely out of sorts. In a way that irritated and confused her. What on earth was it about this man that robbed her of her usual aplomb?

In an effort to break the spell between them, she averted her gaze and said, "A friend of mine offered to help us sort through the artifacts, should we require his services." Actually, both Albert and Charlotte had wanted to accompany her today, but Meredith had convinced them to wait a day. She wanted to first ascertain what sort of conditions they would be working under, and she was glad she'd insisted. The fact that they would be near the docks . . . Charlotte *hated* the docks.

"*His* services? Is your friend an antiquarian?"

"No. Actually, Albert is my butler, and one of my dearest friends."

If he was surprised by her referring to her butler as a dear friend, he did not show it. Instead, he nodded. "Excellent. My American colleague and friend, Andrew Stanton, is at the British Museum today, looking over artifacts there. Another friend and antiquarian, Edward Binsmore, has also offered his help."

The name sounded familiar, and after a second's thought, recognition hit her. "The gentleman whose wife passed away?"

"Yes. I think he is looking for a way to keep busy."

"It's probably best for him," Meredith said softly.

"Grief is sometimes harder to bear when nothing but hour upon hour of loneliness yawns in front of you."

"You sound as if you speak from experience."

Meredith's gaze flew to his. He was watching her, his eyes soft with understanding, as if he, too, had known such sadness. She swallowed to ease the sudden lump clogging her throat. "I think most adults have experienced grief in one of its many forms." He looked as if he were about to question her, and as she had no desire to answer any questions, she forestalled him by asking, "Can you show me the stone the curse is written upon and tell me exactly what it says? It seems that would better enable me to know what I am looking for."

He frowned. "I have hidden the Stone of Tears so as not to risk anyone else finding it and translating it. However, I have written down the English translation in my journal." Opening the worn leather book, he passed it to her. "I cannot see any harm in letting you read it, as you will never take a bride."

Meredith set the journal on her lap, then looked down at the neat, precise handwriting on the yellowed page and read.

As my betrothed betrayed me with another,
So shall the same fate befall your lover.
To the ends of the earth
From this day forth,
Ye are the cursed,
Condemned to hell's worst.
For true love's very breath
Is destined for death.
Grace will fall, a stumble she'll take,
Then suffer the pain of hell's headache.
If ye have the gift of wedded bliss,
She will die before you kiss.
Or two days after the vows are said,

Your bride, so cursed, shall be found dead.
Once your intended has been lo
Nothing can save her from
There is but one key
To set the cursed f
Follow the b
As she
And

An involuntary shiver snaked down Meredith's spine, and she fought the urge to snap the book closed and not gaze upon the eerie words any longer.

Lord Greybourne leaned forward and ran his finger over the last lines. "That is where the stone is broken, leaving only these fragments of words and sentences."

The sight of his large, tanned hand hovering just above her lap snaked another shiver—of an entirely different nature—through Meredith. Swallowing to moisten her suddenly dry throat, she asked, "How large is the stone?"

He turned over his hand, resting it palm up on the journal. "About the size of my hand, and approximately two inches thick. I judge the missing piece is about this size, or a bit smaller." He curled his hand into a fist.

Her gaze riveted on his fisted hand, the weight of which pressed upon her thighs through the book. She swore she could feel the warmth of that masculine hand right through the journal, an unsettling, disturbing sensation that seemed to heat her from the inside out. An overwhelming urge to shift in her seat hit her, and she had to force herself to remain still. He seemed oblivious to how improper his casual familiarity was. And she most assuredly would have told him—if she'd been able to find her voice.

Thankfully, the coach slowed, and Lord Greybourne leaned back, his hand slipping from the journal. He looked out the window, allowing Meredith to expel a breath she hadn't even realized she held.

"The warehouse is just ahead," he reported.

Excellent. She couldn't wait to exit the confines of this carriage, which seemed to grow more restraining with each passing moment.

A few minutes later, feeling much recovered from the short walk from the carriage, Meredith stepped into the vast, dimly lit warehouse. Row upon row of wooden crates stood stacked. Dozens of crates. Hundreds of crates. Very *large* crates.

"Good heavens. How many of these belong to you?"

"Everything in approximately the back third of the building."

She turned and stared at him. "Surely you jest."

"I'm afraid not."

"Did you leave anything at all behind in the countries you visited?"

He laughed, the deep, unrestrained sound echoing in the vast chamber. "Not all of my crates are filled with artifacts. Many of them contain fabrics, rugs, spices, and furniture I purchased for a business venture my father and I are involved with."

"I see." She stared at the seemingly endless rows of crates. "Where do we begin?"

"Follow me." He headed down one narrow aisle, his boot heels thudding against the rough wooden floor. She followed him as he turned again and again, until she felt like a rat in a maze. Finally they arrived at an office.

Extracting a key from his waistcoat pocket, he unlocked the door and indicated she should enter. She crossed the threshold and found herself in a cramped room, the limited space dominated by an oversized beechwood desk. Crossing to the desk, Lord Greybourne opened the top drawer and withdrew two thick ledgers.

"The plan is to open a crate, remove its contents, check them against these ledgers, then repack the crate. The ledgers contain itemized lists of the contents of each crate, all of which are numbered."

"If that is the case, then why must we unpack each crate? Why can we not simply look at the itemized list to see if something such as 'half a curse stone' is noted?"

"Several reasons. First, I've already examined these ledgers, and nothing faintly resembling 'half a curse stone' is listed. Second, it is highly possible that it is listed, but inaccurately described. Therefore a visual examination of the contents is necessary. Third, as I was not the only person cataloging the items and packing the crates, I cannot swear that unintentional errors were not made. And last, it is possible that I did not find a 'half a curse stone' listed because it may very well be part of another item listed. For instance, when I found my piece of the stone, it was in an alabaster box, therefore—"

"The listing may only read 'alabaster box' without listing the actual contents of the box."

"Exactly." He crossed to the corner of the office where blankets were piled, and hefted up an armful. "I'll set these on the floor to protect the artifacts and open a crate. I suggest we do one crate together to familiarize you with the procedure, then we can each work on a separate crate. Does that meet with your approval?"

The sooner they started, the quicker they'd find the stone. Then the wedding could take place, her life could be restored to normal, and she would forget all about Lord Greybourne. "Let us begin."

Two hours later, Philip looked up from cataloging a particularly fine clay vase he recalled finding in Turkey. His gaze settled upon Miss Chilton-Grizedale, and his breathing hitched.

Due to the hot, stuffy air in the warehouse, she'd discarded her cream lace fichu, just as he'd discarded his jacket. She was bent over the crate, reaching inside to withdraw another artifact. The material of her gown molded itself to the feminine curve of her buttocks. The very *lovely* feminine curve of her buttocks.

Ever since she'd settled herself across from him in his carriage—a conveyance which had seemed quite roomy until that moment—he'd been disturbingly *aware* of her. No doubt because of her scent . . . that delicious fragrance of freshly baked cake that whetted the appetite. Bloody hell, women weren't supposed to smell like that. Like something sinfully edible that made a man want to take a bite.

A golden shaft of morning sunlight gleamed through the window, capturing her in its glow. There was something very *vibrant* about this woman. Underneath her calm, decorous exterior, he sensed suppressed energy. Vitality. Passion.

And then there was her coloring. Shiny midnight curls contrasting with a porcelain complexion, properly pale except for twin brushes of peach staining her cheeks. All set off by those striking blue-green eyes whose color reminded him of the turquoise Aegean, not to mention her full, deep rose lips . . .

Everything about her seemed so very *vivid*. Colorful. Outstanding. Like a single spot of bright color painted upon an otherwise white canvas. She reminded him of a sunset in the desert—the rich, vibrant hues of the evening sun painting the sky a stunning contrast to the golden beige of the endless sand.

She shifted, and an image—a most unwanted and vivid image—of him stealing up behind her, touching his lips to the vulnerable skin on her nape, pressing his body against her feminine form, flashed through his mind, leaving a trail of heat in its wake.

He shook his head to dispel the sensual image, shook it

so vigorously his spectacles slid down his nose. Bloody hell, what was wrong with him? He was normally not prone to such lascivious thoughts, especially when he was working. Of course, he had never worked in such proximity to a woman before. A woman whose skirts rustled with her every movement, inspiring thoughts of the curvaceous form beneath. A woman who smelled like she'd just stepped out of the damn confectioner's.

A woman who was not his fiancée.

That thought brought him up short and blinked the remnants of the disturbingly provocative image from his mind. He grimly set his jaw. Yes, she was not his fiancée. Excellent. Now he was back on the correct path. He found this woman imperious and annoying. Her goal was to turn him into some simpering, dandified, ruffle-cuffed fop. Yes, yes, that was much better. She was the *enemy.*

Yet, when he attempted to pull his gaze from the enemy's enticing curves, he failed completely. He watched as she carefully lifted a wooden bowl from the crate and gently set it on the blanket spread on the floor. Turning, she made a notation in the ledger, affording him the opportunity to admire her profile.

Her nose tilted slightly upward, and her chin was set at an angle that could only be described as stubborn. She frowned, and worried her lower lip between her teeth, drawing his attention to her mouth. And bloody hell, what a lovely mouth it was. How could he not have noticed it before now? He couldn't decide if it was more likely that those full, moist, delectable lips had been fashioned by an angel or by the devil himself. Miss Chilton-Grizedale portrayed the epitome of a proper lady, but there was nothing proper about that rosy, lush mouth, or the heated thoughts it inspired.

He closed his eyes and was overtaken by a vivid image of himself pulling her into his arms. He could almost feel her curves pressed against him. Lowering his head, he touched his lips to hers. Warm. Soft. She tasted delicious . . . like a rich, luscious dessert. He deepened the kiss, slipping his tongue into the heat of her mouth and—

"Is something amiss, Lord Greybourne?"

Philip's eyes popped open. She was staring at him with quizzical concern. Heat crept up his neck, and he had to fight the urge to jerk at his already loosened cravat. He swallowed twice to locate his voice. "Amiss? No. Why do you ask?"

"You groaned. Did you hurt yourself?"

"No." Aching was certainly not the same as hurting. As unobtrusively as possible, he shifted, moving his arm so the ledger he held shielded that which ached. Damn. This was a devil of an inconvenient time for his months of celibacy to catch up with him.

Ah! Yes, surely these uncharacteristic lustful urges she inspired were due to the fact that it had been months— *many* months—since he'd last had a woman. He grabbed on to that explanation like a mongrel with a bone. Of course, that was all this was. His body was simply reacting to her in response to his long abstinence. Why, he'd feel the same if confined in close quarters with *any* woman. The fact that this . . . *termagant* had inspired lustful thoughts just proved that theory.

He felt considerably cheered until his inner voice chimed in. *You spent over an hour alone with Lady Sarah—your fiancée—in the privacy of the dimly lit gallery, and not once did your thoughts stray to* that.

"Did you discover something?" she asked.

Yes. That you're having the most unsettling, unwanted, uncharacteristic effect upon me. And I don't like it one bit. "No." He forced a smile he hoped didn't appear as tight as it felt. "Just a bit of a cramp from all the crouching." Nodding toward the pile of artifacts carefully lined up on the blanket, he asked, "Anything interesting in your crate?"

"All of it is interesting. Fascinating, in fact. But nothing even remotely resembling what we're looking for." She waved her hand in an arc encompassing the artifacts spread around her. "This is truly amazing. Incredible that you found all these things. Amazing that they were once held by people who lived centuries ago. You must have been filled with wonder every time you discovered something else."

"Yes. Filled with wonder. That describes it exactly."

"Did you actually dig these things from the ground?"

"Some of them, yes. Some were purchased with my own personal funds, others by funds allocated by the museum. And still others were bartered for English goods."

"Fascinating," she murmured. Reaching down again, she picked up a small bowl. "Who would barter away something this beautiful?"

"Someone who was starving. Someone who may have stolen it. Someone desperate." Some perverse devil in him prodded him forward, almost as if daring his mind and body not to react to her, as if he required proof that the past few minutes were nothing more than an aberration. He stopped when only several feet separated them. "Desperate situations often force people to act in ways they might not otherwise."

Something flashed in her eyes, something dark and pain-filled. In a blink that haunted look disappeared, and if it hadn't been so stark and vivid, he would have thought he'd imagined it.

"I'm certain you're right," she said softly. She looked at the bowl cradled in her hand and ran a fingertip over the glossy inside. "I've never seen anything like this. It looks like flattened pearls. What is it called?"

"Mother of pearl. I estimate this piece hails from approximately the sixteenth century, and most likely belonged to a noblewoman."

"How do you know that?"

"Mother of pearl comes from the inside of mollusk

shells and is associated with the moon and water, thus making it very feminine in nature. While not as valuable as pearls, mother of pearl was still costly and would have only belonged to someone of wealth."

Her finger continued to slowly move over the smooth inside of the bowl, a hypnotic motion that riveted his attention in a way that dispelled his hope that his body would not react further to her. "There's something so lovely, so magical about pearls," she said in a soft, trance-like voice. "I recall as a child seeing a painting of a woman with long ropes of lustrous pearls wound through her dark hair. I thought she surely must be the most beautiful woman ever born. She was smiling in the portrait, and I knew the reason she was so happy was because she wore those pearls." A wistful-looking smile touched her lips. "I told myself that someday I would wear pearls like that in my hair."

He instantly imagined her with ropes of the creamy gems wound through her midnight curls. "And have you?"

She looked up and their eyes met. He could almost see the curtain fall over the glimpse into the past she'd taken as the memories were chased from her eyes. "No. Nor do I expect to. It was merely a childish yearning."

"My mother was very fond of pearls," Philip said. "They were once thought to be the tears of the gods. They are symbols of innocence; therefore, they are talismans for the innocent and are said to keep children safe."

"Wouldn't it be lovely, then, if every child could have one? To feel safe."

"Indeed it would." Something in her voice piqued his already overly inquisitive nature, and he wondered if she was speaking of any child in particular.

"Did you know," he said, in an attempt to restart the conversation rather than simply gawk at her, "that the Greeks and Romans believed pearls were born in oysters when a drop of dew or rain penetrated between the shell?"

The instant the question crossed his lips, he wished he could snatch it back. Surely her eyes would glaze over with boredom at such a topic. He may not have been among Society in a great while, but he recalled—all too well—that stories of historical lore were not popular to discuss with ladies.

But her eyes instantly lit with unmistakable interest. "Really?"

"Yes, although the ancient Chinese adhered to an even more unusual theory. They believed that pearls were conceived in the brains of dragons. They were very rare gems, and therefore guarded between the dragon's teeth. The only way for the pearl to be taken was to slay the dragon."

"I'm certain the dragon had something to say about that."

Looking at her, her eyes bright with amusement, he couldn't suppress the grin pulling at his lips. She certainly didn't seem such the autocratic termagant now, what with those streaks of dust in her hair. Indeed, he could not recall the last time he'd felt such an easy camaraderie with a woman, at least a proper Englishwoman. In his youth he'd always felt awkward and clumsy in their presence, as if he'd tied a knot in his tongue. Even as a young man, before he'd left England, he'd always lacked the smooth sophistication and charming finesse so many of his contemporaries displayed. Thankfully he'd outgrown his awkwardness and shyness as he'd matured during his years abroad, and been exposed to other cultures.

His gaze roamed her face, slightly flushed, no doubt from the overly warm air in the warehouse. A bit of dirt marked her cheek, and without thinking, he reached out to wipe it off.

The instant his fingers touched her smooth cheek he realized his error. Her skin was like velvet cream. So incredibly soft. And pale. His hand looked dark and rough next to her complexion, as if it didn't belong there. Which it most emphatically did not.

Feeling like a complete ass, especially given the way she'd gone perfectly still, except for her eyes, which widened to the size of saucers, he lowered his hand and stepped back. "There was a smudge of dirt on your face."

She blinked several times, as if coming out of a trance, and hectic color stained her cheeks, enchanting him far more than it should have. Bloody hell, this . . . whatever it was . . . attraction, awareness, whatever name he assigned to it, was no aberration. And whatever had sparked this attraction, he consigned it to the devil.

A shaky-sounding laugh escaped her, and she, too, retreated several steps. "Quite all right. Heaven knows I don't want to be going about with a dirty face."

He desperately searched his mind for something, anything, to say, but damn it, the only thing he could focus on was horrendously inappropriate, even for him. He could hardly ask, *May I touch you again?* Gone was the ease he'd felt only moments before. In a heartbeat this woman brought back all the awkwardness he'd thought he'd conquered. Just another reason to dislike her. And he did dislike her. Didn't he?

The fact that his fingertips still tingled where they'd brushed against her skin did not bode well for the disliking-her theory.

Just as it occurred to him that the growing silence was becoming oppressive, the sound of a door slamming startled him from his Miss Chilton-Grizedale-induced stupor. A deep voice called out, "Are you here, Greybourne?"

Philip drew in a shaky, relieved breath at the interruption, but then frowned. "That sounds like Lord Hedington." Raising his voice, he said, "Yes, I'm here. Near the back."

"Perhaps he brings word of Lady Sarah." There was no missing her hopeful tone.

"Yes. Lady Sarah." *Your fiancée. The mother of your future children. The woman who should be occupying your thoughts.*

Meredith pressed her lips together and, leaning down, brushed at a bit of dust clinging to her gown in an effort to collect herself. She hoped Lord Hedington was here with news regarding Lady Sarah, but regardless of his reason, she thanked the stars above for his precipitous arrival.

Lord Greybourne had the oddest, most unwelcome effect on her. The mere innocent brush of his fingers across her cheek had heated her as if he'd set fire to her gown. Surely it was merely the result of being alone with him for such a prolonged period. Yes, that explained why, even while her attention was focused on cataloging the artifacts, she'd been intensely aware of him. Of his every movement. The sound of him removing items from the crate. The occasional heaving of a sigh.

She should have been discussing etiquette with him, but between her fascination with the artifacts and her preoccupation with him, all thoughts of manners had fled from her head.

Their eyes had met four times. And four times it had felt as if every particle of air had been sucked from the room. Four times he'd smile in his lopsided way, the way that creased that dimple in his cheek, then asked if she was all right. And four times she'd answered that she was fine.

But she'd lied four times. She was not fine. This man kindled feelings in her, longings, that confused and frightened her. And she did not like to be confused or frightened.

She could not overlook his obvious faults regarding his manners and outspoken nature, yet when it came to discussing his work, he was proving himself—and she was finding him—intelligent, entertaining, and disturbingly attractive.

And that was very bad.

"There you are," said the duke as he rounded the corner, a fierce scowl puckering his features. "I—" He halted at the sight of her, then, lifting his quizzing glass, he glared at her. "You!" he said.

"Miss Chilton-Grizedale is helping in the search for the missing piece of the stone tablet, your grace," Philip said. "Have you any news?"

The duke's jaw worked back and forth as he alternated his glare between them. "Yes, I have news." He stepped closer to Meredith and pointed an accusing finger at her. "This is entirely your fault."

Before Meredith could say a word, Lord Greybourne stepped between her and the irate duke. "Perhaps you'd like to explain yourself," Lord Greybourne said in a soft voice that did little to belie the steel underneath. Since she could not see around him, she moved to the side, to stand next to him.

Lord Hedington, his houndlike face flushed deep red, looked like a canine teapot on the verge of spewing a stream of steam. "I blame you as well, Greybourne." Reaching into the pocket of his brocade waistcoat, he extracted a folded piece of ivory vellum. "This note arrived an hour ago from my daughter ... the new Baroness Weycroft. In order to ensure that she would not be forced to marry *you,* she married Lord Weycroft by special license yesterday."

The duke's words echoed in the silent warehouse. Meredith's heart seemed to stall, but she knew her pulse was beating, for she could feel it thumping, no, pounding, in her ears. From the corner of her eye, she saw Lord Greybourne go perfectly still.

"Apparently the idea came to her after your conversation in the gallery," the duke fumed. "Seems the chit has carried a tendre for Weycroft for years, but knowing it was her duty to marry in accordance to my wishes, she agreed to the match with you." His gaze swung to Meredith, nearly freezing her with the arctic blast. "A match *you* arranged. A match you assured me would be beneficial to my family and to my daughter."

He focused his attention on Philip once again. "According to her letter, when she finally met you, she found herself not at all drawn to you, a fact which made her realize exactly how strongly she felt for Weycroft. Your talk of curses and falling and headaches frightened her, convincing her that if she married you, she would indeed die. But of course, she also knew I would not agree to dissolve the betrothal.

"The morning after meeting with you, she wrote to Weycroft, explaining everything. Apparently Weycroft carried a tendre for Sarah as well. Unwilling to allow her to come to harm by marrying you, he procured a special license. He came for her yesterday, under the guise of escorting her to her wedding at St. Paul's. They were married and are now on their way to the continent for an extended wedding trip."

The irate duke swiveled his attention back to Meredith, and leveled her with a look filled with utter disgust. "The scandal attached to this will cast a black mark upon my family, and I hold you personally responsible, Miss Chilton-Grizedale. I shall make it my personal crusade to ensure that you never again foist your matchmaking 'skills' upon anyone." He turned to Lord Greybourne. "As for you, the only bright spot in this entire disaster is that my daughter did not marry an imbecile such as yourself, whereupon she would have given birth to a future generation of imbeciles. Although, rumor has it that you wouldn't have been able to give her a child anyway."

Meredith could not suppress her gasp at the duke's unmistakable implication. She risked a glance at Lord Greybourne. His lips were pressed together and a muscle ticked in his jaw.

Lord Greybourne took one step forward, every line of his body taut with obvious tension. "You may say what you wish to me, but you will recall there is a lady present. You are about to cross a line that, I assure you, you'll regret crossing." His voice was barely above a whisper, but there was no mistaking the menace emanating from him.

"Are you threatening me?" the duke asked, the bravado in his voice lessened by his hasty backward step.

"I am warning you that my patience with you is about to end. Now, unless there is something else in Lady Sarah's note that you wish to tell me, I believe there is nothing more to say." He nodded to the left. "The exit is that way."

Favoring them both with one last scathing look through his quizzing glass, the duke turned on his heel and stalked away. The sound of his boots against the wooden floor faded, then a door slammed closed and the warehouse was silent.

Meredith forced herself to take long, deep, calming breaths. A half sob, half laugh rose in her throat, and she pressed her hands to her lips to contain it. Dear God, she hadn't thought this situation could get any worse, but now with Lady Sarah married, this situation was indeed very much worse. It was, in fact, a complete debacle.

Lord Greybourne stepped in front of her. Behind his spectacles, his brown eyes simmered with anger, although there was no mistaking his concern. Reaching out, he gently grasped her shoulders. "I'm sorry you were subjected to such inexcusable rudeness and crude innuendo. Are you all right?"

Meredith simply stared at him for several seconds. Clearly he believed she was distraught due to the duke's remark regarding Lord Greybourne's . . . manliness. Little did Lord Greybourne know that thanks to her past, very little shocked Meredith. Nor could she fathom that anyone could so much as look at Lord Greybourne and have a doubt regarding his masculinity.

Lowering her hands from her mouth, she swallowed to find her voice. "I'm fine."

"Well, I'm not. I'd have to place myself firmly in the category of 'vastly annoyed.'" His gaze roamed over her face and his hands tightened on her shoulders. "You're not going to faint again, are you?"

"Certainly not." She stepped back, and his hands lowered to his sides. The warm imprint from his palms seeped through her gown, shooting tingles down her arms. "You may place me firmly in the category of 'females who do not succumb to vapors.'"

He cocked a brow. "I happen to know that is not precisely true."

"The episode at St. Paul's was an aberration, I assure you."

While he did not appear entirely convinced, he said, "Glad to hear it."

"You came to my defense in a very gentlemanly way. Thank you."

"I'm certain you don't mean to sound so surprised."

Indeed, she was surprised—stunned, actually—although she had not meant to sound as if she were. But she'd have to reflect upon that later. Right now there were other, bigger issues to contemplate.

Unable to stand still, Meredith paced in front of him. "Unfortunately, with the duke's news, we must now recategorize our situation from 'bad' to 'utterly disastrous.' Your bride is well and truly lost, ruining our plan for you to marry on the twenty-second, and my reputation as a matchmaker is in tatters. And with your father's ill health, time is short. There must be a way to somehow turn this situation around. But how?"

"I'm open to suggestions. Even if we are successful in finding the missing piece of stone, my marrying is out of the question without a bride." A humorless sound escaped him. "Between this curse hanging over my head, the unflattering story in the newspaper, and the gossip Lord Hedington alluded to circulating about my ability to . . . perform, it seems that the answer to the question posed in today's issue of *The Times* is yes—the cursed viscount *is* the most unmarriageable man in England."

Unmarriageable. The word echoed through Meredith's mind. Damnation, there must be a way—

She swung around to face him. "Unmarriageable," she repeated, her drawn-out pronunciation of the word in direct contrast to her runaway thoughts. "Yes, one might very well christen you the Most Unmarriageable Man in England."

He inclined his head in a mock bow. "A title of dubious honor. And one I'm surprised you sound so . . . enthusiastic about. Perhaps you'd care to share your thoughts?"

"Actually I was thinking you exhibited a moment of brilliance, my lord."

He walked toward her, his gaze never wavering from hers, not stopping until only two feet separated them. Awareness skittered down her spine, and she forced herself to stand her ground when everything inside her urged her to retreat.

"A *moment* of brilliance? In sharp contrast to all my other moments, I suppose. A lovely compliment, although your stunned tone when uttering it took off a bit of the shine. And brilliant though I may be—albeit only for a moment—I'm afraid I'm in the dark as to what I said to inspire you so."

"I think we can agree that Lady Sarah marrying Lord

Weycroft places us both in an awkward situation." At his nod, she continued, "Well then, if you are the Most Un-marriageable Man in England, and it seems quite clear you are, the matchmaker who could marry you off would score an incredible coup. If I were successful in such an undertaking, you would gain a wife, and my reputation would be reinstated."

"My moment of brilliance clearly remains upon me, as I'm following your thought process, and what you've de-scribed is a good plan. However, I cannot marry unless I am able to break the curse."

"Which a brilliant man such as yourself will certainly be able to do."

"*If* we are able to locate the missing piece of the Stone of Tears. Assuming we are successful, whom did you have in mind that I would marry?"

Meredith's brow puckered, and she once again com-menced pacing. "Hmmm. Yes, that is problematic. Yet surely in all of London there must be one unsuperstitious woman willing to be courted by a cursed, gossip-ridden viscount of questionable masculinity who will most likely fill their homes with ancient relics."

"I beg you to cease before all these complimentary words swell my head."

She ignored his dust-dry tone and continued pacing. "Of course, in order to ensure the reinstatement of my reputation, I must match you with just the perfect woman. Not just any woman will do."

"Well, thank goodness for that."

"But who?" She paced, puzzling it over in her mind, then she halted and snapped her fingers. "Of course! The perfect woman for the Most Unmarriageable Man in En-gland is the Most Unmarriageable Woman in England!"

"Ah. Yes, she sounds delightful."

Again she ignored him. "I can see the Society pages now—England's Most Unmarriageable Man Weds England's Most Unmarriageable Woman—and praise to Meredith Chilton-Grizedale, the acclaimed Matchmaker of Mayfair, for bringing them together." She pursed her lips and tapped her index finger against her chin. "But who is this Most Unmarriageable Woman?"

He cleared his throat. "Actually, I believe I know."

Meredith halted, and turned toward him eagerly. "Excellent. Who?"

"You, Miss Chilton-Grizedale. By the time Society reads tomorrow's edition of *The Times, you* will be the Most Unmarriageable Woman in England."

Five

 Philip watched all the color leach from Miss Chilton-Grizedale's cheeks as his words hung in the air like a heavy fog. Where seconds ago her eyes had danced with excitement, they now resembled shards of aquamarine ice. Her lips curved in what he suspected she meant as a smile, but which came out more like a grimace, inexplicably tweaking his pride.

"How amusing you are, my lord. I can hardly be considered unmarriageable, as, since I've no desire to ever marry, I was never considered marriageable." Her tone was light, but sounded forced. And what was that look that had flashed in her eyes? Fear? Sadness? His curiosity about her doubled. Why would she not want to marry? Bah, probably no man would have the dictatorial piece. But the instant the thought entered his mind, he rejected it. Surely there was some man, somewhere, who wouldn't find her autocratic ways *completely* off-putting. And as he was coming to learn, she wasn't autocratic *all* the time.

Had she given her heart to someone who did not return her feelings? Or did she, even now, love a man who either would not or could not marry her?

The thought filled him with an unpleasant sensation that felt suspiciously like jealousy. "I thought most women wanted nothing more than to marry."

"I am not most women, Lord Greybourne."

No, she was not most women, a fact that increasingly intrigued him far more than it should.

Lifting her chin, she said in a brisk tone, "Besides, a woman such as myself would never do for a man like you."

"A woman such as yourself? Meaning what, exactly?"

Color crept into her pale cheeks. "I meant a woman not of the peerage. You are a viscount, the heir to an earldom. You must marry a woman from your social class."

He stared at her intently, wishing he could read her thoughts, for although her explanation made perfect sense, he strongly suspected that she had let something slip, had revealed something she had not meant to. *A woman such as myself . . .*

"Yes, I suppose you are correct. But until I am free of this curse, not to mention this unfortunate bit of gossip, I cannot imagine any woman being eager to marry me."

"You can dispel the gossip very easily, my lord. Simply take a mistress, and be certain to be seen with her. At the opera, the theater."

It was, of course, an excellent suggestion. Taking a mistress, combined with a bit of well-timed lack of discretion—not difficult, given his already tarnished reputation—would put to bed any doubts regarding his ability to perform. However, the fact that she so calmly suggested it, in that dispassionate voice, coupled with the fact that he had absolutely no desire to take a mistress, annoyed him. Why didn't the idea appeal to him? He'd been celibate for months. Perhaps there *was* something wrong with him.

But one look at Miss Chilton-Grizedale heated his blood in a way that he recognized all too well. No, there was nothing wrong with him—aside from this inexplicable desire for the wrong woman.

"I shall consider your suggestion regarding a mistress," he said coolly. "But that still leaves us with the problem of the curse and locating this 'unmarriageable' woman you suggested."

She pursed her lips and frowned. "Upon consideration, I think focusing on an 'unmarriageable' woman might not be in our best interest. We could achieve the same goals of marrying you off and restoring my reputation by pursuing a highly marriageable woman. Therefore, I think it wiser to concentrate on a proper young woman, one very much like Lady Sarah."

"Rather like beauty and the beast," he murmured.

She stiffened. "I shall do my utmost to find you a wife who is beautiful, my lord."

He stared at her for several seconds, then said carefully, "I meant that *I* am the beast, Miss Chilton-Grizedale." His heart leapt in a way it most certainly should not have at the notion that she did not consider him a beast. That perhaps she found him attractive, as he increasingly found her.

Crimson stained her cheeks. "Y-yes, of course. But naturally I shall concentrate my endeavors on women I think you'll find attractive. In fact . . ." Her voice trailed off, and, nodding to herself, she began pacing. He tracked her progress, his gaze alternating between her furrowed brow and pursed lips. Each time she moved past him, he caught an elusive whiff of her scrumptious scent, a fragrance that all but set him to salivating. And those pursed lips . . . He drew in a long, careful breath. Those lips looked puckered as if to offer him a kiss, an offer he knew he would never refuse.

Suddenly she halted and faced him, her eyes bright, her frown vanished. "I believe I have a plan, my lord."

"Pray, do not keep me in suspense, Miss Chilton-Grizedale."

"In spite of the fact that this curse renders you—at least temporarily—unmarriageable, I think it will also provoke a great deal of interest and curiosity about you. We must make that work to our advantage. With all these rumors flying about, we shall toss a few of our own choosing into the mix. We'll make it known that it is merely a matter of time before the curse is broken, and in the meanwhile, through the hosting of an exclusive soiree—perhaps a dinner party—I shall find you a wife. Cursed as you may be, with the imminent promise of no longer being cursed, marriage-minded mamas will be unwilling to allow the heir to an earldom slip through their fingers."

"And if I cannot—"

Reaching out, she touched her fingers to his lips, effectively cutting off his words, and his very breath. Shaking her head, she whispered, "Don't say it. You will. You must. For your integrity and to keep your promise to your father before his health further fails, and for the sake of my livelihood and reputation."

He wanted to tell her that it was a very real possibility that he would never find the missing piece of stone, never be able to solve the curse, would never be able to marry. But to do so would have required him to move, something completely beyond him at the moment. And movement might have dislodged her fingers from his lips, something he was most reluctant to do. The touch of her fingers against his lips simultaneously paralyzed him and sizzled a bolt of heat through him.

He wasn't certain what reaction must have shown on his face, because her eyes widened and her lips formed an O of surprise. She snatched her hand away as if he'd bitten her, then retreated two hasty steps.

"I beg your pardon, my lord."

His lips tingled from her touch, and it required a great deal of will not to run his tongue over his bottom lip to taste the spot she'd just touched. He moved his hand in a dismissive gesture—only to discover that his hand was not quite steady.

"No harm done," he said lightly. " 'Tis better not to vocalize some things." *Like the fact that I find you fascinating. Intriguing. That I like the way you speak your mind and present your ideas in a clear, concise, nonconvoluted way. That you affect me in a way that I find very unsettling. And that I would like to know much more about you.*

No, it was definitely better that he not vocalize such things.

Clearing his throat, he said, "I believe your plan is sound. As I know next to nothing about planning soirees, I think it might be wise to enlist my sister Catherine's help. She is scheduled to arrive in London this afternoon."

"An excellent suggestion, my lord. An invitation from Lady Bickley would most certainly be looked upon with more favor than one coming from me. Do you think she would be willing to act as hostess?"

"I'm certain she would be happy to do anything at all to help. I'll send a note, inviting her to dinner this evening to discuss the details . . . if you are free to join us?"

"Yes, thank you. The sooner we put our plan into action, the better."

Pulling his watch fob from his pocket, he checked the time. "Since it already grows late, and as I must send off the invitation to Catherine, then speak with my father to tell him the latest developments, I suggest we finish our respective crates, then depart."

She nodded her agreement, then returned to her work area. Philip forced himself to do the same. But, unable to stop himself, he turned his back to her, then rubbed his index finger over his lips where she'd touched him.

She was coming to his home. This evening. The very thought made his heart pound in a way that it most certainly should not. But there was no ignoring the fact that it did. The question was, what did he plan to do about it?

Albert closed the door to Miss Merrie's house with more force than he'd intended. Muttering darkly under his breath, he limped across the foyer and dropped the missive that had just been delivered onto the salver resting on the mahogany table—along with the dozen other messages already there.

"Was that another one?" came Charlotte's soft-spoken voice behind him.

He froze, and his heart skipped several beats. Damn it all, he had to stop reacting this way every time they were in the same room. But how to stop? He'd been a mere lad of fifteen when Miss Merrie had invited a beaten and pregnant Charlotte to join their "family," rescuing her as she'd rescued him years earlier. But he was no longer a lad, and there was nothing brotherlike about his feelings for Charlotte.

Drawing a deep breath, he turned slowly, trying to make the movement appear smooth. Unfortunately, in his attempt to appear less awkward, he nearly tripped on his own feet. He lurched forward, and Charlotte grasped his shoulders to steady him, just as he grabbed her upper arms to keep from pitching face first onto the floor.

His balance regained, everything in him stilled. The warmth of her hands seared imprints on his shoulders that sizzled down to his feet. Her arms felt slender beneath his palms. If he pulled her closer, the top of her head would nestle perfectly under his chin.

She looked up at him, her gray eyes filled with concern. Just concern. Not a flicker of any of the emotions churning through him. Not the slightest indication that she felt anything more for him than she ever had—respect, fondness, and friendship.

Damn it all to hell and back, he wished that was all he still felt for her. But somehow, his feelings of respect, fondness, and friendship had flared into something more. Something that rendered him clumsy and tongue-tied in her presence. Something that made him achingly aware of her every minute of the day, that made his heart beat faster at the sound of her voice, that tensed his every muscle when they stood in the same room. That made him spend sleepless, restless nights, aching in his lonely bed. For her.

The thought of her guessing, of realizing how he felt, clenched his stomach into a tight knot. She wouldn't laugh—she was too kind for that—but the thought of seeing pity in her eyes, of feeling sorry for him for his hopeless feelings . . . he couldn't bear it.

"Are you all right?" she asked.

Gritting his teeth, he slowly released her arms. "Fine," he said, more brusquely than he'd meant to. He took an awkward step back from her, careful to keep his weight balanced on his good leg, then jerked his jacket back into place.

Her gaze shifted to the pile of letters. "I guess we know what those are. More cancellations."

Not yet trusting his voice, he merely nodded.

"Poor Meredith," Charlotte said. "She's worked so hard, she doesn't deserve to be cast away like this." Her eyes narrowed, and her lips pressed into a thin line. "But that's how people are. They use you, then toss you aside like so much trash. You and I know that better than most, don't we, Albert?"

"Yes. But not all folks are that way, Charlotte." He savored the sound of her name on his tongue. "Miss Merrie ain't like that—you and I know that better'n most."

Her fierce expression relaxed a bit. "If only everyone were like her."

"Impossible to wish that all folks were good," he said gently.

She looked at the floor, twisting her hands together. "Yes. But sometimes I can't help but wish for impossible things."

Her quiet voice grabbed him by the heart, and unable to stop himself, he gently touched his fingers under her chin to raise her face. He held his breath, waiting for her to recoil, but to his surprise she stood her ground. Her skin felt like . . . he didn't know. Like the softest thing he'd ever felt. Her gaze met his, and his heart thumped so hard he knew she had to hear it. "Wot do ye wish for, Charlotte?"

For a long moment she said nothing, and he simply stood, absorbing the feel of her warm skin beneath his fingertips, the sight of her eyes, so fathomless and full of shadows from past hurts and pains. The desire to make all her dreams come true, to destroy anyone or anything that would ever dare hurt her, throbbed through him. His gaze roamed her face, touching on the faint scar bisecting her left brow, and the slight bump on the bridge of her nose. An image of her, beaten and bruised, flashed through his mind.

Never again. He'd never allow anyone to ever hurt her again. To be near her and never be able to touch her, love her, would be nothing short of torture for him, but it was the way it had to be. She deserved so much more than the likes of him.

And even if, impossibly, his ruined leg and physical limitations didn't matter, her words, those fervent words he'd heard her speak to Miss Merrie when she first came to them, haunted him, making him know that there was no future for them. *I'll never let another man touch me again* she'd said through her cracked, swollen lips. *Never again. I'd kill myself, or him, first.*

It had taken a long time for her to come to trust him, but trust him she did—at least as far as she trusted anyone. He'd do nothing to risk that. Ever. If this was all he could have of her, so be it. But God forgive him, he wanted so much more.

"What do I wish for?" she repeated softly. "All my wishes are for Hope. I want her to have a good life. A safe life. Happiness. I don't want her to ever have to do . . . the things I've done."

Her voice went totally flat, as did her eyes, and Albert's heart squeezed. "Hope is goin' to have a grand life, Charlotte. You, me, Miss Merrie, we're all goin' to see to it."

The hint of a smile touched her lips, warming her eyes. "Thank you, Albert. You are a dear boy. And a wonderful friend."

He tried hard not to let his idiotic disappointment show. Damn it, he wasn't a boy. He was man. Soon to turn one and twenty. He wanted to remind her, but what was the point? Forcing a smile, he said, "Ye're welcome. 'Tis an honor to be yer friend."

The clip clop of an approaching carriage caught his attention. Walking to the narrow window beside the front door, he moved the curtain aside.

"A fancy carriage," he reported. "Stoppin' in front. Must be another note delivery from another of them fancy ladies wantin' to—"

His words sliced off as a footman opened the carriage door and Miss Merrie emerged, followed by a tall gentleman wearing spectacles.

Albert's eyes narrowed as he watched the gentleman escort Miss Merrie up the walkway. Because the walkway was narrow, they proceeded single file, with the gentleman falling in behind Miss Merrie. The man's gaze wandered down Miss Merrie's back, taking note of her backside in a way that set Albert's teeth on edge. Without waiting for them to climb the steps, he flung open the door.

"Everythin' all right here, Miss Merrie?" he asked, scowling at the man.

"Everything is fine, thank you, Albert." After climbing the steps, Miss Merrie performed a quick introduction.

To Albert's surprise, the Greybourne bloke extended his hand. "Good to meet you, Goddard."

Albert wasn't certain he returned the sentiment, but, scowl firmly in place, he shook the gentleman's hand

"Thank you for seeing me home, Lord Greybourne.

Are you certain I cannot offer you some refreshment before you leave?"

"No, thank you. However, I look forward to seeing you later this evening. Shall I send my carriage? Say at eight?"

"That will be fine." She inclined her head in a regal fashion. "Good afternoon."

Lord Greybourne bowed, then returned to his carriage. Albert stood on the porch and glared at him until the carriage was no longer in sight. Entering the foyer, Miss Merrie was handing Charlotte her shawl.

"So that bloke's Lord Greybourne," Albert said.

Meredith turned toward Albert's stern voice, a tone she was not accustomed to hearing from him. His severe frown paused her fingers in the act of untying her bonnet. "That was Lord Greybourne, yes."

"And ye're seein' him this evenin'?"

"Yes. I'm joining him and his sister and one of his antiquarian colleagues for dinner at Lord Greybourne's townhouse."

Albert's brows collapsed even farther. "I'd watch myself with that one if I were you, Miss Merrie. He's got designs on ye."

Heat scorched Meredith's cheeks, and she prayed neither Albert nor Charlotte would notice. "Good heavens, Albert, what a thing to say! Of course he does not. I'm trying to find him a bride."

"Ye already found him one. But based on the way he was oglin' ye, it appears he's forgotten all about her."

She barely kept herself from pressing her hand against her chest where her heart thudded. Was Albert correct? Had Lord Greybourne ogled her? Something that felt suspiciously like a smile tugged at her mouth, and she clamped her lips together. Good heavens, she should be outraged! Being ogled was highly uncouth. Certainly she should not feel . . . flattered. Nor be experiencing this rush of warm pleasure. No, of course she was outraged.

"What do you mean, 'ogling'?"

"I saw the way he looked at ye. Like ye were a treat in the confectioner's shop, and he were cravin' a bit of sweet."

Another unwanted, inappropriate, inexplicable wave of pleasure washed through her. Botheration, this was what happened when one did not get one's proper rest. She'd make it a point to retire early this evening and sleep late tomorrow.

Adopting her most prim expression, she said, "He was doing nothing of the kind. His expressions are easy to misinterpret due to his thick spectacles." When Albert appeared about to argue the point further, she quickly added, "I have some news."

She quickly told Albert and Charlotte about the search for the missing stone, Lady Sarah's marriage, and her plan to find Lord Greybourne another wife. "We shall discuss plans to meet that goal at dinner this evening." Out of the corner of her eye she spied the pile of letters resting on the table. Putting on her bravest face, she smiled at both Albert and Charlotte. "I'm certain everything is going to be just fine."

But she could see in their worried expressions that she'd failed to convince them.

Yet how could she hope to do so when she herself was far from convinced?

Six

Philip paced in front of the fireplace in the library, and stared once again at the mantel clock.

"You seem nervous," Andrew remarked in an amused drawl.

"Not nervous. Filled with anticipation. I haven't seen Catherine in ten years." He watched Andrew tug his midnight-blue jacket into place. "Speaking of nervous, that's the dozenth time you've straightened your attire."

"Wouldn't want your sister to think you've befriended a disreputable ne'er-do-well."

"Ah. In that case you'd best leave before she arrives." Ceasing his restless pacing, he stared into the flames dancing in the fireplace, childhood memories washing over him. "She always looked like an angel, but good God, she was a mischievous devil. Always sending the butler off on some false errand so we could slide down the curving banister at Ravensly Manor, or convincing me to join her on late night raids of the kitchens to filch biscuits."

Yes, one year his junior, Catherine had been everything he was not as a child—fun-loving and playful. She taught him how to laugh and smile, how to take time for fun, coaxing him from his shyness, and accepted him exactly as he was—awkward, clumsy, diffident, serious, bespectacled, and pudgy.

"You've spoken of her so often over the years, I feel as

if I know her," Andrew said. "You were fortunate to have each other."

"She was my best friend," he said simply. "When I left England, leaving her was the most difficult part. But she'd been recently married, and was expecting a child, and I'd been assured of her happiness." His jaw clenched. "But as you know, her letters indicate that her cordial relationship with her husband changed drastically when she presented him with a less-than-physically-perfect heir."

"Yes. It's hardly the boy's fault he was born with a clubfoot. The man should be happy he was blessed with a child."

At Andrew's sharp tone, Philip turned to his friend and offered a grim smile at his dark scowl. "I appreciate the outrage on Catherine's behalf. Believe me, it cannot possibly match mine. I greatly look forward to engaging in a little private discussion with my swine of a brother-in-law."

"Happy to participate in that 'chat' should you require any assistance."

A knock sounded at the door. At his call to enter, Bakari opened the door. "Lady Bickley," he intoned, then stepped aside.

Catherine stepped over the threshold, and a lump clogged Philip's throat at the sight of her. Clad in a pale green muslin day gown, her shiny chestnut curls framing her lovely face, she looked very much like the image he carried in his mind and heart, only more so. More beautiful, more slim, more elegant. An air of regal serenity surrounded her—not unusual for a proper English lady. Yet it had always been the flashes of deviltry so often present in her golden brown eyes that were so unexpected. And endearing.

He walked slowly toward her, across the expanse of the Persian rug to where she remained framed in the doorway, like a stunning portrait. Before he'd taken half a dozen steps, however, her lips twitched in that infectious, engag-

ing way of hers, and she ran toward him. He caught her up
in his arms, swung her around in an exuberant manner,
and was instantly inundated with her delicate floral scent,
exactly the same as he recalled. No matter what sort of
mischief Catherine had engaged in, she'd always smelled
as if she'd just stepped out of the garden. After one final
twirl, he set her down, then they held each other at arm's
length while giving each other a thorough look-over.

"You look exactly the same," he declared, "only more
lovely, if that is possible."

She laughed, a delightful sound that filled him with nos-
talgia. "Well, I'm afraid *you* look completely different."

"For the better, I hope."

"For the *much* better."

"Is that to insinuate my appearance was lacking before
I went abroad?"

"Not at all. Ten years ago, you were a darling boy. Now
you're a—"

"Darling man?"

"Exactly." She squeezed his shoulders. "And so
strong," she teased in the exaggerated way he so vividly
recalled. "Clearly, living in rustic conditions agrees with
you." Her smile faded, and her eyes turned misty. A myriad of emotions flashed in her eyes, so quickly he couldn't
decipher them. Resting her palm against his cheek, she
said, "It is so wonderful to have you home, Philip. I've
missed you very much."

Her voice hitched, and looking into her eyes, he realized that there were subtle changes. This was not the care-
free girl he'd left behind. Shadows flickered in her eyes,
shadows a casual observer wouldn't notice, but he knew
her very well. Clearly Father's illness and her unhappy
marriage had taken their toll on her vivacious spirit. He
looked forward to speaking to her privately, to hear about
her son and husband, things she wouldn't confide to him
in front of Andrew.

"And I've missed you, Imp." She smiled at his use of her childhood sobriquet. Grabbing her hand, he kissed her fingers in his most gallant gesture, then offered her his arm. "Come, you must meet Andrew."

They turned and made their way across the room to the fireplace where Andrew stood. Leaning his head toward Catherine, Philip whispered, making certain he spoke loud enough for his friend to hear, "Do not believe a word he says. He is an outrageous flirt and an accomplished mischief maker."

Drawing to a halt near the hearth, Philip said, "May I present my friend and colleague, Mr. Andrew Stanton. Andrew, my sister, Catherine Ashfield, Lady Bickley."

Catherine smiled and offered her hand. "A pleasure to meet you, Mr. Stanton, although I feel I already know you through Philip's letters."

Andrew said nothing for several seconds, then seemed to gather himself, and reaching out, he took her hand and formally bowed over it. "It is an honor, Lady Bickley. As Philip was kind enough to share snippets of your letters with me and often regaled me with stories of your childhood, I, too, feel as if we are already acquainted. The miniature of you he carried did not do you justice."

"Thank you." Catherine shot Philip an arch look. "Childhood stories? Oh, dear. You must not believe everything my brother tells you, Mr. Stanton."

"I assure you he painted you in the most flattering light." One corner of Andrew's mouth lifted. "Usually."

"Come, let us sit," Philip said. "Miss Chilton-Grizedale isn't expected to arrive for another hour, which gives us some time to catch up."

"Yes," Catherine agreed. "I want to hear about . . . everything."

Once they were seated, Philip asked, "As neither Spencer nor Bickley joined us this evening, I take it that you traveled to London alone?"

A pained expression flashed in Catherine's eyes, so quickly that if Philip didn't know her well, he would not have recognized it as such. "Yes. Bertrand is immersed in his duties at Bickley Manor. I left Spencer in Little Longstone, under the care of Mrs. Carlton, his governess. Traveling is difficult for him, and he does not particularly care for London." Then her face lit up with a look of deep, motherly love. "However, he is most anxious to meet his wildly adventurous uncle and made me promise to extract your promise to visit us in Little Longstone the *instant* you return from your wedding trip." She reached out and clasped his hand. "I visited with Father earlier and he told me everything. I'm so sorry about your canceled wedding, Philip. But do not worry. The idea you wrote me of hosting a party is excellent. With the soiree Miss Chilton-Grizedale and I will arrange, we'll find you a lovely bride in no time."

Philip leaned nonchalantly against the marble mantel in the drawing room, ankles crossed, half smile in place, swirling a snifter of after-dinner brandy. Outwardly, he knew he appeared relaxed and composed. Inwardly, a mass of tense confusion writhed through him like snakes in a pit. As he had all during dinner—wildly unsuccessfully— he now again tried his damnedest to keep up with the conversation buzzing between Miss Chilton-Grizedale and Catherine, but his mind was not cooperating. No, he was far too preoccupied. With *her*—the annoying matchmaker, whom he was finding more annoying with each passing minute. More and more annoying because it was no longer her autocratic nature he was finding irksome— although there was no denying that still rubbed him the wrong way. No, it was this damnable attraction and awareness he was experiencing that was now the source of his mounting irritation.

The excellent meal had done little to hold his attention,

in spite of the fact that the Mediterranean influences in the courses indicated that Bakari had obviously gone to great pains to see to it that his very English cook, Mrs. Smythe, had prepared the food according to his tastes. Judging by the number of harrumphs Bakari had muttered, and Mrs. Smythe's formidable demeanor, Philip judged this had been no easy task.

The delicately poached turbot had been lost upon him as he'd attempted to divert his gaze away from Miss Chilton-Grizedale—and failed utterly. She sat on his left, giving him an unimpeded view of her profile. Her dark hair was arranged in a Grecian-style knot, with a bronze ribbon that matched her gown woven through the shiny strands. His gaze touched upon her smooth skin, the curve of her cheek, the sweep of her lashes. With every sip from her wine goblet, his attention was drawn to her lovely mouth.

Every time she'd leaned forward to say something to Catherine, he'd desperately tried not to notice how the movement pulled the coppery-bronze silk of her gown just a bit tighter across the generous swell of her breasts. Every word she uttered to Catherine regarding this party they were planning with the precision of a military invasion provided him with another opportunity to enjoy her voice.

In fact, she was speaking to Catherine now, both women perched upon the brocade settee. A delicate blush colored Miss Chilton-Grizedale's cheeks, and her eyes were alight with interest. She moved her hands in animated gestures as she spoke, punctuating her words. Her voice was rich and warm, with just a slightly husky timbre that made it sound as if she'd just awoken. From bed. His bed.

An image instantly formed in his mind, of them, together, naked, limbs entwined, her whispering his name in that husky voice . . . *Philip . . . please, Philip . . .*

"Philip . . . please. What do you think?"

Catherine's voice snapped him back from his runaway thoughts like a cobra bite. He looked around and noted three pairs of eyes regarding him with varying degrees of quizzical expressions. Andrew, who sat on an overstuffed wing chair across from the ladies, bore an expression that appeared more amused than questioning. Heat crept up Philip's neck. He adjusted his spectacles, then, convention be damned, he loosened his confining cravat.

"Afraid I was in a bit of a brown study. What were you saying?"

Catherine's lips quirked upward. Alternating her gaze between Andrew and Miss Chilton-Grizedale, she reported in a teasing voice, "My brother has changed very little in the past decade, I see. His mind, always filled with thoughts of his studies, often wandered off during our conversations. I recall one time relating a fascinating story to him of a musicale I'd attended. After the fifth 'That's nice, Catherine' he'd uttered, I said, 'And then I jumped into the Thames and swam across to Vauxhall.' He simply nodded. However, when I said, 'The pyramids at Giza were built by Sir Christopher Wren,' that comment quickly rewarded me with his attention—something you might both wish to remember the next time Philip's mind wanders."

"Thank you for the advice, Lady Bickley," said Andrew. He turned to Philip. "Is that what you were contemplating just now, Philip? The beauty of the . . . pyramids?"

Philip shot Andrew a quelling look. Normally he enjoyed his friend's irreverent sense of humor—but not now. Not when he felt so unsettled and undone. "No. I was merely . . . preoccupied." Careful to avoid looking at Miss Chilton-Grizedale, he focused his attention on Catherine. "What do I think about what?"

"Holding the gathering here at your townhouse the evening after next, with me acting as hostess. Miss Chilton-Grizedale and I thought a dinner with dancing afterward would best suit our purposes."

"Can you arrange something that quickly?"

"With the proper help and staff, a coronation could be arranged that quickly." Sadness shadowed Catherine's eyes. "And with father's illness, time is of the essence."

"To assist me in my search for a wife for you, it would help to know what sort of qualities you admire in a woman," Miss Chilton-Grizedale said in that brisk, no-nonsense tone of hers.

Something that sounded suspiciously like a guffaw arose from Andrew. Philip shot his friend a frown, and when Catherine and Miss Chilton-Grizedale looked his way, Andrew started coughing. Waving his hand, Andrew reached for his brandy and gasped, "I'm fine. Really." After taking a sip, Andrew grinned at Philip. "Yes, Philip. What sort of qualities do you admire in a woman?"

All eyes turned his way, and when Philip remained silent, Miss Chilton-Grizedale said, "I'm not saying I shall be able to meet all your criteria, Lord Greybourne, especially as time is short. However, it might prove helpful to know if there are any characteristics that you find particularly attractive or overly off-putting. In fact, if you wouldn't object to loaning me the use of your desk and a piece of vellum, I'd like to jot down some notes."

This was not a conversation he particularly wished to have, especially given the devilish gleam he recognized all too well in Andrew's eyes. But since he couldn't think of a way to refuse her request without reinforcing her belief that his manners were sorely lacking, he led the way to his desk. Extracting a piece of thick ivory vellum from the top drawer, he held out the maroon leather chair for her.

"Thank you," she murmured, sitting down with fluid grace. Her bronze skirts brushed his breeches, and her delicious scent wafted into his head. Scones. Tonight she smelled like warm, freshly baked, buttered scones. Damn it all, he had a particular weakness for warm, freshly baked, buttered scones. He stepped quickly back from her.

"Philip harbors a fondness for willowy blondes," Andrew said, rising to stand near the fireplace, "especially since he met so few during his travels. And if her features are those of a classic beauty, so much the better." He made a *tsk*ing noise. "Too bad Lady Sarah ran off. Physically, she was exactly the sort he likes."

"Classically beautiful blondes," Miss Chilton-Grizedale repeated in a serious tone, making a note. "Excellent. What else, my lord?"

A scowl bunched Philip's brows. Damn it all, as recently as two days ago he would have agreed with Andrew. But now . . .

"My brother enjoys music," Catherine added, "therefore someone with a talent for the pianoforte, or a pleasant singing voice, would be preferable." She turned toward him. "Don't you agree, Philip?"

"Er, yes. Musical talent is nice."

"Someone who has at least a passing interest in antiquarian studies would no doubt be helpful," Catherine added. "For conversational purposes."

"Indeed," agreed Andrew, who was clearly enjoying this conversation far too much. "Being of a scientific and intellectual bent, Philip prefers ladies who are conversant in subjects other than fashion and the weather. However, she should most certainly be a practical woman who won't expect romantic drivel. Philip isn't the sort to make the grand romantic gesture."

"Oh, I agree," Catherine said, before Philip could reply. "Romance is simply not in Philip's nature." She smiled and wagged her finger at him. "Don't look so stricken, Philip, dear. Most men are notoriously unromantic."

"I am not stricken, nor am I unroman—"

Miss Chilton-Grizedale's *tsk*ing cut off his words. She shot him a look of clear disapproval. "How vexing this is. Based on these comments, I'd made a *perfect* match for you, Lord Greybourne."

"I did not intentionally curse myself, Miss Chilton-Grizedale."

"But that does not make you any less cursed, now, does it, my lord?"

"How kind of you to point that out. Have you always had this compelling need to state the obvious?"

"I prefer to call it a reiteration of the pertinent facts—"

"Yes, I'm certain you do."

"—and no, I only need to do so when certain people lose sight of the situation."

"Ah. Certain people who are not showing a *moment* of brilliance, perhaps?"

She smiled sweetly. "I would not have presumed to imply as much—"

"Ha!"

"—but now that you mention it, yes." Before he could reply, she turned to Catherine and asked, "Where were we? Oh, yes. The bride-to-be's traits. What else?"

Catherine's bemused gaze bounced between him and Miss Chilton-Grizedale, then she said, "She should, of course, be accomplished in handling the servants and know how to run the household."

Miss Chilton-Grizedale, he noted, jotted down copious notes, her bottom lip caught between her teeth with concentration.

Catherine stroked her chin. "What else? Oh, yes. A love of dusty relics is an absolute must."

"I fear no such woman exists," Andrew chimed in. "A woman who does not abhor them would be enough to ask for."

"All right," Catherine agreed. "Philip, what else do you like?"

"I'm surprised you've bothered to ask. I like—"

"Animals," Andrew said. "She must love large animals. He already has a puppy that, based on the size of its paws, promises to grow to the size of a pony."

Catherine turned toward him. "A puppy? Did you bring him home from Egypt?"

"No. I found him on the way home from the docks. Abandoned."

"Where is he now?"

"Resting in Bakari's quarters. The beast had an injury which Bakari bandaged. He's keeping him as still as possible for a few days to give its leg a chance to heal."

Catherine gave him a fond smile. "You always did have a soft spot for abandoned creatures."

"I've always felt a special kinship toward them," Philip said quietly.

Miss Chilton-Grizedale's hand moved swiftly across the vellum for several more seconds, then she looked up. "Anything else?"

"She should be an accomplished dancer," Catherine said, which brought a guffaw from Andrew.

"Oh, most assuredly," Andrew agreed, "so she can teach Philip how to dance."

A confused frown puckered Catherine's brow. "As I recall, Philip is a passable dancer."

"Such effusive praise will surely swell my head," Philip murmured.

Andrew laughed. "My dear Lady Bickley, the last time I saw him engaging in a dance, the din he raised sounded like a stomping herd of elephants."

"Camels," said Philip. "It was *camels,* not elephants. Several camels broke free of their tethers during a soiree in Alexandria and caused quite a commotion." He glared at Andrew. "So all that stomping wasn't me at all."

Catherine coughed to cover an obvious laugh. "My relief knows no bounds. To continue, your future wife should possess at least a passing knowledge of French. And don't you think she should know how to embroider, Philip? Even as a child you liked having your initials decorate your handkerchiefs."

"Oh, absolutely," Philip said. "Please be certain to add that to your list, Miss Chilton-Grizedale. 'Must know how to embroider.' I couldn't possibly consider marrying a woman who was not handy with a needle and thread."

Clearly his dry tone was not lost upon Miss Chilton-Grizedale. She looked up and their eyes met. One corner of her mouth twitched, and clear amusement glittered in her eyes. "I've not only added 'expert embroiderer' to the list, my lord, but I've placed a star next to it as well to denote its category as one of the utmost importance."

She smiled at him, a simple gesture that sped up his heart to a ridiculous rate. A reluctant answering grin pulled at his lips, evaporating a measure of his irritation. Andrew issued a loud ahem, recalling Philip's attention, and he realized he'd been grinning at Miss Chilton-Grizedale like an idiotic green schoolboy experiencing his first crush. She blinked twice, as if she, too, had forgotten the presence of others.

"Was there anything else you'd like added to the list, my lord?" she asked. "Perhaps something you find particularly abhorrent?"

"Philip detests liars," Andrew said. "And didn't we run into our share of them with those corrupt artifact dealers. Liars and thieves, nearly every one of them. Thankfully Philip possesses an excellent eye for spotting a forgery."

Philip nodded slowly. "I cannot deny that I hate being lied to."

Miss Chilton-Grizedale made a notation on the vellum. "So noted," she said in a voice that sounded somewhat strained, "although I believe it is safe to say that no one enjoys being told falsehoods." She turned her attention to Catherine. "Since that appears to finish this list, would you like to begin making up the guest list now, Lady Bickley?"

"Of course. That way I can send out the invitations early tomorrow."

While Catherine and Miss Chilton-Grizedale sat at the desk near the windows, their heads close together as they plotted out the guest list, Philip and Andrew settled themselves on the opposite side of the room, near the marble fireplace, and began a game of chess. As Philip concentrated on resettling his ruffled feathers, they played in silence for some time, before Andrew said, "Edward came to the museum today."

Guilt pricked Philip, and he raked his hand through his hair. "Damn, I've been so preoccupied with my own problems this evening, I completely forgot to ask about Edward. How were his spirits?" He didn't add that he'd sent around a note to his solicitor late this afternoon instructing him to open an account in Edward's name.

"Subdued. He's planning to come again tomorrow."

"Good. Focusing on something other than Mary will no doubt help him."

"I agree. Obviously he's mourning his wife, but it's difficult to tell exactly what he's thinking. He's not an easy man to read." Feeling the weight of Andrew's stare, Philip looked up from the chessboard and found his friend's gaze resting pointedly on him. "Not like some people."

Philip raised his brows. "Meaning?"

Andrew leaned forward and lowered his voice. "Meaning that you are easier to read than a book, my friend."

Philip stiffened. "I don't know what you're talking about."

"The hell you don't. I mean *her.*" He jerked his head toward the other side of the room. "That little exchange of words between you was quite telling. Not to mention the fact that you've been looking at her as if she's an oasis and you're dying of thirst."

Bloody hell. Had he truly been that obvious? And when the devil had Andrew turned into such an enthusiastic observer of human behavior?

Andrew's gaze flicked over to the two women in the corner, then he regarded Philip with an inscrutable expression. "Easy to see what the attraction is."

To his annoyance, everything inside Philip tensed. Forcing a light tone, he said, "She is pretty, yes."

"Actually, I don't believe 'pretty' describes her at all. She is distinctive. Unusual. Striking. But not pretty."

"Indeed? I hadn't particularly noticed."

"I see. Then I suppose you didn't notice any of her other attributes, either."

"Such as?"

"Such as the darker blue ring that surrounds her aqua irises, making her eyes appear like bottomless pools. Or the way her pale skin turns a delicate peach when she's animated about something, or how incredibly shiny all that dark hair is. How long do you suppose her hair is? I suspect it at least reaches her waist." He heaved a long sigh. "There's nothing like a curvaceous woman with long, long hair. But I suppose you didn't notice the fact that she is quite the curvy piece, either."

Philip dropped all pretense of studying the chessboard. Unwanted, unwelcome jealousy pumped through him, along with a healthy dose of anger. "We've returned to civilization, Andrew. That is hardly a proper way to describe a lady."

The look Andrew shot him was one of pure innocence. "So there *is* some decorum buried in there. I meant no disrespect, of course. I was merely obliging your request to list her attributes—ones that I believe any man with eyes would instantly note, by the way. Except you, it seems. Interesting. Especially as you are normally most observant."

Oh, he'd observed. Observed everything about her, including her striking eyes, her complexion, her lovely hair, and the hints of her feminine form beneath her bronze-hued gown. It just irked that Andrew had also noted them.

"Too bad she isn't one of those willowy blondes you prefer," Andrew mused, "Although I imagine it wouldn't matter. From everything you've told me, I gather you're expected to marry some 'Lady' something-or-other as opposed to a regular 'Miss.' "

"Yes, that is what is expected," Philip said. The words felt like desert sand upon his tongue.

"Yet there have been many occasions when I've known you to do the exact opposite of what was expected, Philip."

Philip studied his friend for several seconds before replying. "That was in Egypt. Turkey. Greece. This is England. I returned here to do what is expected of me."

"To marry someone you barely know. You're abandoning the life you love abroad, your explorations, giving up your freedom."

This was a familiar argument between himself and Andrew. "I'm honoring an agreement that *granted me* my freedom for the past ten years. And between the British Museum and the private museum you and I plan to co-found, I shall have more than enough to keep me busy."

"I suppose. But you've given up a great deal. It certainly seems that you should have the woman you want. I myself would never marry for less than love."

Philip couldn't contain his bark of surprised laughter. "I find it difficult to envision you in the role of lovesick suitor, Andrew. I've seen you in the company of numerous women over the years, yet none seemed to have captured your heart."

"Perhaps because my heart was already otherwise engaged."

Philip stared, nonplussed. Although it was sometimes difficult to determine if Andrew was speaking in jest, those quietly spoken words held no trace of amusement. He'd known Andrew for five years, had lived in close quarters with him all that time, shared life-and-death experiences with him, yet this was the first mention of this unrequited love.

"*Is* your heart otherwise engaged?"

A fleeting expression of what looked like pain flashed in Andrew's eyes. Then a rueful, sheepish grin pulled up one corner of his mouth. "Caught."

Unable to hide his surprise, Philip asked, "Is she American?"

"No. I met her years ago. During my travels."

"And you fell in love with her?"

"Yes. My fate was sealed the moment I laid eyes upon her."

"Well, then why didn't you marry her?"

"Unfortunately the lady was already married."

"I see." Silence settled over them while Philip digested this new information about his friend. "Do you love her still?" he finally asked.

Once again their eyes met, and Philip was struck by the bleak expression in Andrew's dark eyes. "I will always love her."

"Did she . . . love you in return?"

"No." The word came out as a harsh whisper. "She was true to her husband, to her marriage vows. She did not know of my feelings. She did nothing to encourage them. I simply lost my heart to her."

Philip tried to suppress his pity and amazement. He'd never seen Andrew so serious, so undone. So sad. Reaching out, he squeezed Andrew's shoulder in a gesture of sympathy. "I'm sorry, Andrew. I had no idea."

"I know. And I'm not certain why I told you, except . . ." He shook his head, then pressed his lips together, as if having a difficult time forming the words, uncharacteristic of the normally unreserved Andrew. "I know you're a man of integrity, Philip. A man of your word. A man who must choose a wife. I suppose I'm just hoping that you will choose . . . carefully. And follow your heart. I was not able to do so, and it is a pain I would not wish upon anyone, most especially my closest friend. Perhaps your betrothed marrying another was fate. A sign that you were meant for another."

Before Philip could fashion a reply, Andrew's expression changed, replacing his air of melancholy with his normal lopsided grin. He inclined his head toward the chessboard and moved his queen. "Checkmate."

Philip shook Andrew's hand, then turned toward Catherine and Miss Chilton-Grizedale who had arisen and were crossing the room. "Have you finished with the guest list?"

"Yes. The invitations will be sent out tomorrow. And we can hope that by the evening after next, you will have found someone who appeals to you. Miss Chilton-Grizedale and I have made up a list of candidates that is certain to please you."

A knot settled in his stomach. "Excellent. Now we can only hope that I am able to break the curse. For if not, it doesn't matter how perfect a woman you find for me, I will not be able to marry her."

Silence fell over the group like a shroud of fog. Finally Miss Chilton-Grizedale said, in her practical, brisk way, "I believe our best course is to remain hopeful. Nothing breeds bad luck more than a pessimistic outlook." Her gaze wandered to the mantel clock. "Good heavens, I had no idea it was so late. I really must be going."

"I must go as well," Catherine said.

They all walked to the foyer, where Bakari called for both Philip's and Catherine's carriages.

After tying her bonnet beneath her chin, Catherine hugged Philip. "Thank you for a delightful evening. I've missed sharing meals with you."

"Thank you for your help. If there is anything I can do—"

"You can continue searching for the missing piece of stone so that the wedding can take place." Turning toward Andrew, she inclined her head. "A pleasure, Mr. Stanton."

Andrew bowed over her gloved hand. "The pleasure was mine, Lady Bickley."

Philip walked Catherine down the walkway to the waiting carriage. After seeing her safely inside, he returned to the foyer, where Miss Chilton-Grizedale and Andrew were sharing a laugh over something. An uncomfortable wave of jealousy washed through him. He forced a smile, then reached for his walking stick.

Andrew noted his walking stick and asked, "Going somewhere, Philip?"

"I am seeing Miss Chilton-Grizedale home."

Her cheeks flooded with color. "That is not at all necessary, my lord. I would not wish to indispose you."

"I insist. Whereas my sister lives just down the road and has two footmen in addition to her coachman to protect her, you live quite a distance from here, and there are all manner of criminals who lurk about at night." He raised his brows. "You've harped on my lack of decorum, yet when I make a gentlemanly gesture, you argue."

She appeared to bristle. "Harp? I prefer to call it reminding."

"I'm certain you do."

"There's no point in arguing with him, Miss Chilton-Grizedale," Andrew broke in. "Philip can be quite stubborn. Indeed, I suggest that you add 'capable of putting up with pigheadedness' on your list of qualities in his future wife."

She laughed. *Humph.* He didn't think Andrew's comment was particularly humorous. Then an enchanting smile lit Miss Chilton-Grizedale's face—a smile directed at Andrew—a fact which further tensed Philip's muscles.

"I'll add it as soon as I return home." She held out her hand to Andrew. "Good evening, Mr. Stanton."

Andrew raised her hand and bestowed a kiss upon Miss Chilton-Grizedale's gloved fingers—a kiss that, even to Philip's dim memory of all things decorous, lasted considerably longer than was strictly proper. "A delight, Miss Chilton-Grizedale. I've not been fortunate enough to spend the evening in such lovely company for a long time. I hope we meet again soon." Turning toward Philip, he said, "I'll see you in the morning." With that he climbed the stairs, heading toward his bedchamber.

Philip escorted Miss Chilton-Grizedale to his waiting carriage, then settled himself on the velvet squabs directly across from her.

The instant the door clicked shut, Meredith questioned the wisdom of allowing Lord Greybourne to escort her home. Only hours earlier, this coach had seemed spacious. Now it felt as if the interior did not contain enough air to breathe. She had only to reach out her hand to touch him. Looking down, she noted that the bronze skirt of her gown brushed his breeches. It was difficult to see his features in the dim interior, but she felt the weight of his regard. The intimacy of this dark, close space sped up her heart in a way she found most disturbing. She closed her eyes, hoping to erase the image of him sitting just across from her, but there was no escaping the knowledge he was there. His masculine scent invaded her senses, that lovely aroma of freshly laundered clothing and sandalwood, mixed with a musky fragrance she couldn't identify. He smelled like no other man, and she knew that even blind she could pick him out of a crowd of thousands.

"I thank you for your assistance this evening," he said, his deep voice rising out of the dark shadows.

Opening her eyes, she forced a smile, hoping that the dim interior would keep him from noting just how forced it was. "You're welcome; however, your sister deserves much of the credit. With my reputation in disfavor, the successful outcome of this dinner party would be dubious indeed. However, I am hopeful that we shall find you another bride as well suited to you as Lady Sarah was."

"Not to put too fine a point on it, Miss Chilton-Grizedale, but it is obvious that Lady Sarah and I were not well suited at all—at least *she* did not find *me* at all suitable. Or attractive in any way."

"Lady Sarah was clearly daft." Dear God, she had not meant to speak that thought out loud. Forcing her hands to remain folded on her lap as opposed to clamping them over her runaway lips, she stammered, "S-socially, you were suited in every way."

"Ah, yes. I suppose we were. But when one's heart is otherwise engaged, as Lady Sarah's clearly was with Lord Weycroft, that muddies the waters."

Relieved that he did not pursue her comment, Meredith raised her chin. "Actually, it does not muddy the waters at all, my lord. Lady Sarah's affection for the baron would have faded with time once you and she were wed. It is simply a matter of mind over heart. The heart is willful and capricious. It does not know what is best, and, if listened to, will more often than not lead one toward an unwise path. The mind, however, is methodical and precise. Practical and sensible. When the heart and mind are at odds, one should always listen to the mind."

"Such a pragmatic, unromantic statement from a woman whose occupation it is to arrange marriages."

"The successful arrangement of marriages has nothing to do with romance, my lord, as I'd think a man in your position would know. My understanding of that concept is what has enabled me to be successful in my matchmaking endeavors. The advantageous combining of estates, political aspirations, families, and titles is what is important. Couples can develop a fondness for each other over time."

"And if they don't?"

"Then they should strive for civility, with each pursuing their own interests."

"My interests lie in studying antiquities. In learning about people and civilizations from other corners of the world. I plan to be very involved with displays at the British Museum, and it is my intention to found a museum of my own. For me to pursue those interests alone sounds very . . . isolated. Lonely. As was much of my work abroad. I would much prefer a partner with whom I could share all things."

His deep voice wrapped around her like a cloak, seducing her with its warmth. She moistened her dry lips, and noted that his gaze flickered briefly down to her mouth. "Are you saying that you wish for me to make a love match for you? Because you must remember that due to your father's illness, our time is limited."

"According to Andrew, it does not take long to fall in love."

She raised her brows. "He is an expert in such matters?"

"I don't know that I would call him that, but he *is* in love with someone."

They passed under a gas lamp, and Meredith saw he regarded her with a speculative expression. "You look disappointed at that news, Miss Chilton-Grizedale."

"I am, Lord Greybourne."

"May I inquire why?"

She raised her chin a notch. "I'd hoped to offer Mr. Stanton my services to find him a bride."

For the space of half a dozen heartbeats, the only sound was the squeak of the carriage making its way slowly down the street. Then, to her surprise, he threw back his head and laughed. Whatever she'd expected his reaction to be, it certainly hadn't been amusement.

Annoyance flooded her, an emotion that actually pleased her. *Good. Certainly I cannot find an annoying man attractive.*

"I fail to see what is so amusing, my lord. Although it may not seem so to you, I assure you that prior to the debacle caused by *your* curse, my services as a matchmaker were highly sought after. Last year alone I arranged seven successful unions. The most notable of those, Miss Lydia Weymouth and Sir Percy Carmenster, was what convinced your father to seek out my services on your behalf."

His laughter tapered off, and shaking his head, he said, "Forgive me. I was not laughing at you, dear lady. Indeed, I was laughing at myself. Laughing because your words made me happy."

Meredith frowned. Happy? What had she said that could have possibly made him *happy*? She cast her mind back, but before she could reach an answer, he said, "With Andrew's affections already spoken for, I'd say that means that you'll simply have to devote all your attention to me."

Unfortunately, Meredith did not think that devoting all her attention to Lord Greybourne would prove difficult.

And that scared her to death.

When Philip arrived back home, he was greeted by an empty foyer. "Hello?" he said, removing his hat.

A harrumph sounded behind him, startling him. Turning swiftly, he found himself facing Bakari. Damn, the man moved like a cat—silent and stealthy. It was a talent that had stood them in good stead during numerous adventures over the years—such as the time Bakari had furtively rescued Philip from that band of artifact thieves—but one that was quite disconcerting in the foyer.

Philip noted the man seemed a bit out of breath. "Is all well?"

Bakari grunted. "Dog."

"Ah. I see." Philip hid a smile. Apparently, under Bakari's tutelage, the puppy, whom he'd yet to name, was recovering. Excellent.

The sound of footfalls upon the stairs drew Philip's attention. Andrew, who still wore the same garments he'd worn to dinner, and whose face bore a slight sheen of perspiration as if he'd been exerting himself, joined them in the foyer.

Philip raised his brows. "I thought you'd retired—or are breeches, boots, and cutaway jackets a sleeping-wear fashion trend I've missed?"

"Not at all," Andrew said. "I decided to wait until you arrived home, to see how your carriage ride with Miss Chilton-Grizedale went." Tilting his head left, then right, he made a great show of studying Philip's face. Then he shook his head. "Just as I suspected."

"What?"

"Your time alone with her did not go as you wanted."

"Meaning?"

"You did not kiss her."

Bakari harrumphed.

Annoyance slithered down Philip's spine. "First of all, how could you possibly know that, and secondly, why would you think I would do such a thing? Allow me to remind you that we are now in *England*—staid, proper, and all that. One simply does not go about kissing ladies. There are rules. Propriety."

Andrew's face was the picture of skepticism. "Since when are you such a stickler for rules and propriety? Need I remind you what happened the last time you strictly adhered to the rules?"

Bakari drew in a sharp breath and, waving his hands about, muttered some incantation. Then he shook his head. "Bad. Very bad."

Philip raked his hands through his hair. "No, you need not remind me, and yes, it was bad."

"*Very* bad," Bakari insisted.

"I damn near drowned because you insisted we cross the river as the ancients had—in a damn tippy canoe," Andrew said with a dark scowl, clearly ignoring the 'you need not remind me' part.

"Bloody hell, you should have told me you could not swim! *Before* we left the shore. Did I not pull you safely to land—in spite of your flailing arms and legs, which if I may remind *you*, inflicted numerous bruising blows to my body, several of them to very tender areas?"

"Got in a few good ones," Andrew agreed. "But it was no less than you deserved. The entire incident shaved a decade from my life."

"And would have been avoided if you'd told me the truth."

"Saying he can't swim is not the sort of thing a man goes around bragging about," Andrew insisted. "And it wouldn't have come up if you hadn't insisted on following the 'cross the river in the canoe' rules." His eyes narrowed. "And don't be thinking you've changed the subject. I know you didn't kiss her because, as I said earlier, I can read you very well, my friend, and that frustration I see simmering below the surface is not that which you would bear had you kissed her. And second, I thought you would do such a thing because it is so clearly obvious you want to."

Bakari harrumphed *and* cleared his throat.

Philip clenched his jaw. Damn, but it was irritating when Andrew was right. Bloody hell, he'd wanted to kiss her. Desperately. Why hadn't he? It was just a simple kiss, after all. But the instant that thought entered his mind, he realized the answer—he hadn't kissed her because some instinct told him that there wouldn't have been anything even remotely resembling simple in kissing her. "And I suppose you would have kissed her."

If Andrew heard the tightness in his tone, he ignored it. "Yes. If I were that attracted to a woman and was presented with the opportunity, I would kiss her."

"And the fact that I am to—I hope—soon be married to someone else?"

Andrew shrugged. "You're not married yet, old man. And that's not why you didn't kiss her, and we both know it."

Philip narrowed his eyes. "I'm certain there's a ship departing for America within the hour," he said—a comment about which Andrew looked completely unconcerned.

"Should kiss girl you want," Bakari said softly. "Girl might want you, too." Then, after a low bow, Bakari left the foyer heading toward his chambers, his soft leather slippers silent on the marble floor.

Girl might want you, too. Bloody hell. Bakari normally only spoke on average a dozen words a month. Which meant he'd already surpassed his usual quota with that speech. Excellent. Philip was not anxious to hear anything else.

He looked toward Andrew, whose face bore a suspiciously innocent expression. "Don't say a word," Philip warned.

"I wasn't going to. Bakari said it all. In amazingly few words. A rather scary talent, don't you agree?"

"One that you might wish to emulate—uttering fewer words, that is."

"As you wish. I'm off to bed." He started toward the stairs. At the landing, he turned around and issued Philip a mock salute. "Sweet dreams, my friend."

Sweet dreams, indeed. With his muscles tense and his thoughts racing, sleep was nowhere in his immediate future. Deciding a brandy might relax him, Philip walked down the corridor toward his study. Entering the room, he headed immediately for the decanters and poured himself a fingerful of the potent liquor. As he raised the snifter to his lips, his gaze fell upon his desk. His hand froze halfway to his mouth, and he stared.

One of his journals lay open on his desk, with several more volumes stacked in a haphazard pile near the inkwell. He didn't recall leaving the books in such a manner; indeed, he wouldn't, as he was very careful with them. Setting his drink down next to the decanters, he strode toward the mahogany desk.

The journal was opened to a page upon which he'd sketched a detailed picture of the hieroglyphics and drawings on a tomb in Alexandria. His gaze skipped over the page, noting it appeared undamaged, then settled on the stack of journals.

A frown tugged his brows downward. Had one of the servants been looking through his belongings? It must be so, as neither Andrew nor Bakari would do so without asking his permission, nor would either not carefully replace the journals upon the shelf.

But why would one of the servants do such a thing? No doubt curiosity about him and his travels. Understandable, but he needed to discover the offender first thing tomorrow morning and address the issue. Not only did he not like the thought of someone looking through his things, but these journals were irreplaceable. He certainly didn't want some curiosity-seeker inadvertently damaging or misplacing them.

Heaving out a long, irritated breath, he closed the open journal, then picked it up. He was about to turn to slide it back into its proper spot on the shelf when he spied a piece of foolscap on the desk, underneath where the journal had rested. Cramped, unfamiliar writing was scribbled across the surface. Puzzled, he picked up the note and squinted in the dim light to scan the few words.

You will suffer.

Philip frowned and ran his finger over the print. The ink smeared slightly.

This had been written recently. *Very* recently. But by whom? Someone in his house? Or had an outsider gained entry? Striding quickly to the French windows, he tested them, noting they were all securely locked. Had an intruder gained entry some other way? It seemed very odd that clearly neither Andrew, Bakari, nor any of the other servants heard or saw someone entering the townhouse. He recalled that Bakari had not been in the foyer when he arrived home—he'd been tending to the dog. And the front door had not been locked. Philip dragged his hands down his face. How long had Bakari left the foyer unattended? Bloody hell, someone could have walked right in the front door! Unless that someone had already been in the house. . . .

He looked at the note again. *You will suffer*.

Who the devil had written it—and why?

A shaky hand lifted the generous pour of brandy to trembling lips. *A narrow escape. Far too narrow for comfort. I must take more care in the future.* A quick gulp of the potent liquor provided a much-needed warmth. After several more swallows, the glass was set down, and a noticeably steadier hand lifted a dagger. The polished, keenly sharpened blade reflected the candlelight.

Your untimely arrival home interrupted me, Greybourne, forcing me to abandon my search. But I'll find what I'm looking for. And when I do, your life is over.

Seven

THE LONDON TIMES

The marriage between Lady Sarah Markham and Lord Greybourne will *not* take place on the twenty-second of this month as previously announced, in light of Lady Sarah's abrupt marriage to Baron Weycroft yesterday. Why would she do such an unexpected thing? Yes, there is this supposed curse to consider, but it is difficult to put much credence in such a story. Is this curse something that Lord Greybourne fabricated to avoid the altar? He wouldn't be the first man to do his utmost to remain a bachelor, yet why he would conspire to not wed this Season's Most Sought-After young lady certainly leads to some interesting questions. And what about Lady Sarah herself? Surely this curse could not be her only reason to reject Greybourne. After all, why would she choose to marry a mere baron when she could have married the heir to an earldom? Perhaps there is something to the popular belief that his years abroad affected more than Greybourne's mental capabilities. One certainly must wonder what on earth Miss Chilton-Grizedale was thinking when she attempted to make this disastrous match.

Meredith closed her eyes and rested her face in her hands. She'd known the gossip would be relentless once word of Lady Sarah's—or rather Baroness Weycroft's—marriage got out, but this was even worse than she'd anticipated. Yet it wasn't so much the story regarding Lady Sarah's marriage or her own matchmaking failure that distressed her so—after all, those things were inarguably true. No, it was the sly innuendos regarding the reason behind Lady Sarah's defection that riled her. Good heavens, any fool could see there was nothing mentally or physically wrong with Lord Greybourne. Such cruel rumors were no doubt very embarrassing for him. Sympathy for him, along with a healthy dose of outrage on his behalf, flooded her.

"Guess ye've seen *The Times,*" came Albert's voice from the doorway.

Meredith raised her head and stared at him through gritty eyes. "I'm afraid so."

"I hate to see ye so upset, Miss Merrie. Yer eyes look like bruises."

Bruises? Not the most flattering assessment, but Albert was correct. In spite of her intention to enjoy a good night's sleep, she'd spent a restless, fitful night. But not because of the gossip. No, her thoughts had been filled with Lord Greybourne and the increasingly disturbing way he made her feel—warm and heated, trembly and excited all at the same time. Being in his company was an aspect her mind dreaded and her heart anticipated. And as always, with her practical nature, her mind won. However, the battle had proven particularly bloody this time. She'd always managed to beat back her feminine longings and urges whenever they raised their heads, but since meeting Lord Greybourne, her longings and urges were not so easily dismissed.

Rising, she straightened her shoulders. "While this all looks bad on the surface, I'm confident that we can turn all the gossip to our advantage. Human nature being what it is, there won't be a woman in London who won't be at least curious to know if the rumors regarding Lord Greybourne are true. These same women will attend the soiree Lady Bickley is hosting at Lord Greybourne's home, and *poof*!" She snapped her fingers. "We'll have a bride for Lord Greybourne in no time." Surely those words should have filled her with satisfaction rather than a sensation that felt unpleasantly like a cramp.

"I hope ye're right, Miss Merrie."

"Of course I'm right. And now I have a favor to ask of you, Albert. I know you'd normally take Charlotte and Hope to the park this morning, but would you postpone your visit until this afternoon and accompany me to the warehouse instead?"

"To help look for the missin' piece of stone?"

"Yes."

Albert looked at her in that penetrating way he had—as if he could read her mind. She tried her best to keep her features impassive, but knew it was a futile effort with Albert.

"Of course. But ye don't just want me there to look for that bit of rock. . . ." His eyes widened, then narrowed to slits. "Did that Greybourne bloke say somethin' untoward to ye? Has he shown himself to be the ill-mannered lout ye believe he is? I *told* ye not to trust him."

How to tell Albert that it wasn't Lord Greybourne but *herself* she did not trust? "Lord Greybourne's behavior has been exemplary." *Occasionally.* "However, it is not proper for me to be alone with him in the warehouse. There is enough gossip circulating already. I've no desire to add to it."

Albert's angry expression relaxed. "So I'd be like a chaperone of sorts."

"Exactly. And helping to locate the missing stone at the same time. We can spend the morning there, then return here. I'll ask Charlotte to prepare a basket of cheese and biscuits, and the four of us can all go to the park together this afternoon."

Albert nodded. "I'll tell Charlotte about the change in plans, then see to the gig." With that, he quit the room, the scrape of his boot sounding against the parquet floor.

Meredith drew in a relieved breath. Now she did not have to face the prospect of hours alone in Lord Greybourne's company. Her heart tried to voice a protest, but her mind firmly quashed it. It was better this way. And this was the way it had to be. Anything else was impossible.

Philip folded *The Times* and tossed it down on the breakfast table with an exclamation of disgust.

"How dreadful is it?" came Andrew's voice from the doorway.

Philip shrugged. "Not that bad, I suppose, as long as I do not object to the inferences that I am"—he ticked off points on his fingers—"a liar, daft, and unable to . . . perform."

Andrew winced. "Particularly nasty, that last one."

"Yes."

Andrew's ebony eyes took on a wicked gleam. "Perhaps this inability to perform is the real reason you have not kissed the object of your affections."

"Do you know who's a bigger bloody pain in the arse than you?" Philip asked pleasantly.

"Who?"

"Nobody."

Chuckling, Andrew walked to the sideboard and helped himself to a hefty portion of eggs and thinly sliced ham, then seated himself across from Philip.

Keeping his tone light, Philip said, "Thought you might like to accompany me to the warehouse today."

Andrew looked up from his eggs in surprise. "Instead of me going to the museum and continuing my search through the crates there? Why?"

"Well, you said Edward was planning to go the museum today, and I could use your assistance at the warehouse."

"Won't Miss Chilton-Grizedale be there?"

"I'm not certain. We did not discuss her plans for to-day."

"But you think she may go to the warehouse?"

"Possibly. However, she cannot help me open those heavy crates, and she lacks your expertise in antiquities."

Andrew nodded thoughtfully, slowly chewing a mouth-ful of egg. He swallowed, then touched his napkin to the corner of his lips. "I see. You don't want to risk being alone with her."

Bloody hell. When the devil had he become so trans-parent? He felt like a damn piece of glass. Knowing there was no point in prevaricating, he jerked his head in a nod. "That's about the size of it, yes."

Andrew looked back down at his breakfast plate, but not before Philip caught his slight grin, along with a noise that sounded suspiciously like a jackass's bray. "Happy to come with you," Andrew said. "I have a feeling this is go-ing to prove a most interesting morning."

Philip, with Andrew's help, had just removed the wooden tops from two crates when the squeak of hinges an-nounced that someone had arrived. To his annoyance, Philip's heart galloped off like a horse out of the gate when Miss Chilton-Grizedale called out, "Lord Grey-bourne, are you here?"

"Yes, I'm here." Bloody hell, was that rusty, croaky sound his voice? He cleared his throat, then tried again. "In the same place as yesterday."

To his surprise he heard the low murmur of voices, as if she were conversing with someone. The tap of ladylike footfalls sounded upon the wooden floor, accompanied by another set of heavier footsteps. A man's, he decided. A man with a limp.

Seconds later Miss Chilton-Grizedale, followed by Albert Goddard, appeared from around a stack of boxes. Goddard, Philip noted, stood behind Miss Chilton-Grizedale like a scowling sentinel guarding the crown jewels.

Today she wore a plain brown gown, clearly in deference to the dusty task at hand. Her bright blue gaze met his, and for one insane second it felt as if he'd been punched in the heart. She, however, clearly experienced no such battering, as she merely inclined her head in his direction. "Lord Greybourne." Her gaze shifted to where Andrew stood, several yards away, and to Philip's annoyance, her face lit up like a bloody gas lamp.

"Mr. Stanton, how nice to see you again."

"Likewise, Miss Chilton-Grizedale."

She shifted to the side to make room for Goddard, who stepped forward with a decided limp. "May I present my friend Mr. Albert Goddard, who, as I mentioned yesterday, offered to help us search for the stone. Albert, this is Lord Greybourne's colleague, Mr. Stanton. You met Lord Greybourne yesterday."

"Good to see you again, Goddard," Philip said, offering the young man a smile. He extended his hand, and to his surprise Goddard looked at him with a narrow-eyed glare. Just when Philip thought Goddard meant to ignore him, he reached out and gave Philip's hand a perfunctory shake. "Lord Greybourne," he said, or rather snarled.

Goddard's greeting to Andrew, Philip noted, was much friendlier. Clearly Andrew was to be on the receiving end of all the friendly greetings.

"I thought perhaps Albert and I could work on the

same crate so I might show him our system, Lord Grey-bourne," Miss Chilton-Grizedale said, "if that meets with your approval."

"Of course." An excellent plan. It would keep her well away from him. Indeed, with both Goddard *and* Andrew here, the work would move at a rapid pace, and there would be no reason to come into close contact with Miss Chilton-Grizedale at all. He should be very pleased. So why the devil wasn't he?

They moved into their respective work areas, but Philip quickly realized that rather than concentrating solely on the contents of his crate, most of his attention was focused on the low murmur of conversation, interspersed with her occasional sultry laugh, taking place between Miss Chilton-Grizedale and Goddard. In fact, so intent was he upon eavesdropping on them, he failed to note that Andrew stood directly next to him—until he turned his head and practically found himself nose to nose with his friend.

"Egad, Andrew," he said, taking several hasty steps backward. "What are you doing, sneaking up on me like that?"

"Sneaking? I was standing beside you for better than a minute, attempting—to no avail, I might add—to gain your attention. In another brown study, were you?"

"Yes." Another bloody Miss Chilton-Grizedale–induced brown study.

Andrew stepped closer and nodded toward the couple, whose heads were bent close together. "What do you make of the *friend*?" Andrew whispered.

Pretending to examine the bronze oil lamp he held, Philip whispered back, "He's her butler."

"Her friend *and* her butler," Andrew said in a musing tone. "He also loves her."

"I beg your pardon?"

"He loves her. Can you not see it?"

Philip turned his attention back to Goddard and Miss Chilton-Grizedale, and swallowed the denial that hovered on his tongue. For as much as he wanted to refute Andrew's statement, he could not. It was there for the world to see, in the way Goddard looked at her, smiled at her, laughed with her, was so solicitous of her. He wore his feelings on his sleeve like a badge of honor that proclaimed, *I love this woman, and will do my utmost to protect and defend her.*

"I can see it," Philip said quietly. "And she obviously cares deeply for him as well." The words made his heart ache with a hurt he couldn't name.

Andrew shot him a meaningful look. "Yes, yet I sense that she brought him here today for the same reason you dragged me here."

Philip stilled. Could Andrew be right? Had she brought along Goddard to ensure they would not be alone together? If so, had she done so merely for propriety's sake—or did she, like him, feel this unsettling . . . whatever it was, between them? Could she possibly be as attracted to him as he was to her?

It was with a huge sigh of relief that Philip entered his townhouse early that afternoon. Andrew had continued on to the museum, but Philip felt the strong need for a little time alone. They'd searched through a half dozen more crates and had been unsuccessful.

He'd endured all he could of avoiding looking at Miss Chilton-Grizedale, keeping himself away from her, forcing himself not to breathe too deeply when in her vicinity so as not to smell the delightful scent of fresh-baked goods—muffins this morning—that seemed to surround her like a halo of deliciousness. And damn it all, he'd grown weary of Goddard's sharp-eyed stares as well. If the man's eyeballs had been equipped with daggers, Philip would have bled to death on the warehouse floor.

Yet even after enjoying a savory meal of poached fish and creamy peas, he remained restless, unable to relax. When Bakari entered the dining room, Philip asked, "How is the dog feeling today?"

"Better." He harrumphed. "Restless."

I know exactly how he feels. "Do you suppose he's up for a walk in the park?"

Bakari studied him for several seconds through solemn dark eyes, then inclined his head. "Walk in park do you both much good."

Twenty minutes later found Philip entering Hyde Park, or rather being pulled into the park by an energetic ball of floppy-eared, golden-haired fur who was clearly so ecstatic at being outdoors, he did not know where to look or what to smell first. At first the pup had balked at the leather lead, but once they exited the townhouse, the lead was clearly forgotten, except as a way to pull Philip along.

"I don't believe you've quite gotten the hang of this," Philip said, tucking his walking stick under his arm and breaking into a jog to keep up. "*I'm* the master. You're supposed to follow *my* commands. *I'm* supposed to lead *you* about."

The dog paid absolutely no heed, dashing from one tree to the next, his tongue lolling in canine joy. A bandage still surrounded his hind leg, but obviously he'd suffered no permanent damage, for he was a whirling dervish of activity. And after being cooped up for the past several days in Bakari's chamber, Philip didn't have the heart to try to curb his enthusiasm today. The dog—whom he absolutely did need to name—caught sight of a colorful butterfly, and the chase was on. With a chuckle, Philip broke into a run. "Let's go show that butterfly who's faster," he said. The dog needed no second invitation.

"A perfect day for the park," Meredith said to Charlotte as they walked along the shady path in Hyde Park. Hope, clutching her favorite doll, skipped several yards ahead.

"Perfect," Charlotte agreed.

Yes, it was a lovely afternoon, the sun's warmth tempered by a cool breeze that brought the scent of flowers and the rustling of oak leaves. Exactly the sort of afternoon to forget one's worries for a little while by strolling through the park. So surely she would soon forget her worries.

Like the fact that in spite of Albert's and Mr. Stanton's presence in the warehouse, she'd remained painfully aware of Lord Greybourne. Surely she must have suffered some form of ear strain—if there were such a thing— from trying to catch bits of his conversations with Mr. Stanton. The deep timbre of his voice elicited a reaction in her she could not understand. How could the mere *sound* of him ripple pleasure down her spine?

"I'm sorry Albert did not feel up to joining us," she said, desperate to direct her attention elsewhere. "I'm afraid all that standing he did at the warehouse tired his leg. It must be particularly paining him, to refuse a visit to the park. I feel terrible about it, as I'd asked him to accompany me to the warehouse."

"He was happy to go, Meredith."

A fond smile curved Meredith's lips. "He is such a dear boy." She chuckled and turned toward Charlotte. "I must remember to begin saying he is a dear *man*."

Charlotte jerked her head in a nod. "Yes, he is."

"It is nearly impossible to fathom that in only a few short months he will turn one and twenty. We must plan a special celebration for him."

"Speaking of special celebrations, how are the plans for tomorrow evening's party progressing? Did Lady Bickley say in the note she sent you this morning?"

Surprise filled Meredith at the almost desperate note in Charlotte's voice, not to mention her uncharacteristic query regarding Meredith's correspondence. Clearly she wished to change the subject—but why? And why did she have to choose a topic that would only remind Meredith of the man she was trying desperately to forget?

"Lady Bickley wrote that the invitations were delivered this morning, and she'd already received two affirmative replies. I am confident that I shall soon find a suitable bride for Lord Greybourne and have him happily married off."

An image rose in her mind's eye, of him garbed in wedding attire, his eyes filled with warmth and desire as he lowered his head to kiss his bride. Jealousy hit her like a backhanded slap, and she heartily wished she could blindfold her cursed mind's eye.

She squeezed her eyes tightly shut to the count of five to erase the image, but when she opened her eyes, her attention was caught by the sight of a tall man running toward them, being pulled by a golden-haired puppy.

She halted as if she'd walked into a wall. Damnation! How could she possibly hope to forget the man when she saw him everywhere she went!

Lord Greybourne's gaze settled on her, and his steps faltered. The puppy, however strained forward, and Lord Greybourne allowed himself to be led, albeit at a much slower pace, as if he were not anxious to come closer. There was, however, no way to avoid each other, therefore Meredith stiffened her spine, and affixed a smile upon her lips.

When they drew within speaking distance, she said, "Good afternoon, Lord Greybourne." She'd intended to keep walking, to allow this meeting to result in nothing more than an exchange of greetings, but she'd forgotten about Hope—Hope, who adored dogs. Hope, who promptly squealed with delight at the energetic puppy. The child crouched down and was instantly bombarded with frantic puppy kisses all over her face.

"Thank heavens you happened along," Lord Grey-bourne said, pausing beside her, "else that dog would have run me all the way to Scotland. I quite believe he thinks he's a quarterhorse and I'm a plow to be dragged behind."

His hair stood up at odd angles, no doubt from a combination of the breeze and his impatient fingers. His dark blue jacket was not only wrinkled, but bore numerous strands of golden puppy fur, as did his breeches. And no doubt his cravat would have been askew, if he'd been wearing one. Instead his bare throat rose from his rumpled shirt. He looked undone and thoroughly masculine in a way that had everything feminine in her melting.

Melting? Good heavens, she wasn't melting! She was appalled at his attire. Of course she was.

Drawing herself up, she asked in her primmest voice, "Did your cravat fly off during a sudden freakish breeze, Lord Greybourne?"

"No." The fiend shot her an unrepentant wink and smile. "Didn't wear one."

Lest she give in to temptation and actually return that infectious smile, she dragged her gaze away and looked down at the giggling Hope and the prancing, yipping, ecstatic puppy. She noticed the bandage on the dog's hind leg, and something tickled her memory, and she looked at the dog more closely. He looked familiar. Her gaze shifted to Lord Greybourne's walking stick. The silver head bore an unusual design. . . .

The pieces suddenly clicked together in her mind. Her heart thumped in slow, hard beats as recognition hit her. Raising her gaze, she found him looking at her with a compelling expression that gave her the sudden urge to fan herself.

"You rescued this dog," she said. "On Oxford Street." She clearly remembered her reaction to the scene—the odd flutter that had shivered through her, settling in her stomach. Vividly recalled thinking what a brave, extraordinary man. And that he moved like a swift, sleek, predatory animal. Graceful. Strong. Heroic. Wondering what he looked like.

Well, she need wonder no longer. That brave, extraordinary, heroic man stood not three feet away from her. Another flutter eased through her. *Oh, my.*

To her amazement, a dull red flush that was clearly embarrassment crept up his neck. Pushing his spectacles higher on his nose, he asked, "You were there?"

"I was inside the seamstress's shop with Lady Sarah. I heard a commotion and looked out the window. I saw someone dispatch that giant of a man, but as I didn't see the rescuer's face, I didn't realize that someone was you." She pointed toward his walking stick. "I thought the design was familiar, but didn't place it until I saw you with the bandaged puppy."

"I did nothing more than anyone else would have done under the circumstances."

Meredith did not argue the point, but she did not believe for an instant that almost anyone else would have behaved in a similarly brave fashion. No, she knew too much of human nature to credit that anyone—let alone a peer—would risk himself against that angry giant of a man to save a street mongrel. Indeed, a crowd had stood by and watched without raising a finger. Except Lord Greybourne. Their eyes met, and something warm spread through her, like honey on a summer day. Her breath caught in her throat, and it was all she could do to refrain from heaving out a gushing, feminine sigh.

"Miss Chilton-Grizedale, it seems that this time it is *you* who is remiss with your manners. May I be so bold as to request an introduction to your friends?" His smiling gaze bounced between Charlotte and Hope.

Consternation burned Meredith's cheeks, and she pulled

herself together. "Of course. Lord Greybourne, may I present my dear friend Mrs. Charlotte Carlyle."

Charlotte performed a quick, rather awkward curtsy. "Lord Greybourne."

"A pleasure, Mrs. Carlyle."

"And the little imp who appears to be your puppy's new best friend is Mrs. Carlyle's daughter, Hope."

Lord Greybourne hunkered down to his haunches next to where Hope had seated herself on the grass. The puppy, clearly tired from his exertions, was curled up in the child's lap, alongside Hope's doll. The dog's eyes drooped closed in canine bliss as Hope gently petted his golden fur.

"Hello, Hope," he said with a smile. "It seems my dog likes you very much."

"Oh, and I like him very much." She smiled an angel's smile at Lord Greybourne. "He's very kissy. He kissed me *and* Princess Darymple," she confided, nodding toward her doll.

"Yes, well, he's quite fond of lovely young ladies *and* Princesses. He told me so."

Charlotte reached down and touched Hope's halo of bright yellow curls. "This gentleman is Lord Greybourne, Hope."

"Hello. Are you a friend of my mum's or Aunt Merrie's friend?" she asked.

"I'm your Aunt Merrie's friend."

Hope nodded solemnly. "Is she going to marry you?"

Philip stilled, and stared at the child, taken aback. "I beg your pardon?"

"It's what Aunt Merrie does. She *marries* people."

"Ah. I see. Well, in that case . . . yes, she is going to marry me." He looked up at Miss Chilton-Grizedale's flaming face, and with his gaze steady on hers, he added softly, "I hope."

Feeling the weight of the child's stare, he forced his attention back to her. Her gray eyes rounded to saucers. "Are you the cursed gentleman?"

"I'm afraid so."

Reaching out, she patted his arm in what he assumed was meant as a comforting gesture. "There's no need to worry. Aunt Merrie will help you. And if she can't, Uncle Albert said he would wear a bridal gown and marry you himself."

Philip wasn't certain whether he should be horrified or amused. Amusement won, and he chuckled. "I hope it won't come to that."

"I hope not. Because I want Uncle Albert to marry—"

Hope's words were halted when her mother touched her fingers to the child's shiny hair. Damn. He very much wanted Hope to finish her sentence. Had she been about to say "Aunt Merrie"?

Crouching down next to her daughter, Mrs. Carlyle said softly, "Hope, do you remember what Mama said about listening to other people's conversation?"

Hope hung her head. "Yes, Mama. Not s'posed to."

"And if you do hear something . . . ?"

"Not s'posed to repeat it."

Mrs. Carlyle pressed a kiss to Hope's tiny nose. "Good girl." The woman stood, and Philip followed suit. Finding himself standing quite close to Mrs. Carlyle, Philip took his first good look at her. It was difficult to judge her age, for while she'd appeared youthful at a distance, he now noted the lines etched on her forehead. A faint scar bisected her left brow, then disappeared into her hairline near her temple. There was no missing the shadows of past sufferings lingering in her gray eyes. She was pretty, but in such an understated way, one would need to look twice to see it. Her speech pattern struck him as rather odd—she spoke well, but he heard an unmistakable trace of Cockney under her well-modulated voice.

"What is your dog's name?" Hope asked.

"He doesn't have one yet," Philip admitted. "Actually, today is his first day out since being hurt. Do you have a suggestion for a name?" His glance included Miss Chilton-Grizedale and Mrs. Carlyle.

Miss Chilton-Grizedale looked down at the sleeping puppy sprawled, belly up, on Hope's lap. "He really must learn to relax," she murmured, her lips twitching.

Captivated by her mischievous grin, he chuckled. "Judging by the paces he put me through arriving here, he was due for a rest. I fear, however, that sleeping is not his natural state."

"Therefore naming him 'Sleepy' wouldn't do at all," Miss Chilton-Grizedale said.

"I'm afraid not."

"Something pretty," said Hope. "Like Princess."

"A good suggestion," Philip said, "but perhaps better suited for a girl puppy."

"Then Prince," Hope said, nodding her head.

Philip thought for several seconds, then nodded. "Prince. I like it. It's regal, and royal, and masculine." He smiled down at the child, who beamed at him in return. "Prince it is. Thank you, Miss Carlyle, for your assistance."

"You're welcome. I'm very smart. I'm almost *five*, you know."

"A very important age," Philip said with a great deal of solemnity.

"Aunt Merrie is baking a cake for my birthday. She bakes yummy things. Every morning."

He instantly recalled Miss Chilton-Grizedale's scrumptious scent. *She smells like yummy things.* "You're having a party, then?" he asked.

She nodded, her blond curls bouncing. "At our house."

"And do you live near your Aunt Merrie?"

"Oh, yes. My bedchamber is just two doors away from hers."

"Mrs. Carlyle and Hope live with me," Miss Chilton-Grizedale broke in.

"And Uncle Albert, and Princess Darymple, too," Hope added.

Philip digested this bit of news, his curiosity piqued about the Chilton-Grizedale household. Hope called her "Aunt Merrie." What was Mrs. Carlyle's relation to Miss Chilton-Grizedale? He could not see any family resemblance, but that did not mean they weren't related. He and Catherine looked decidedly dissimilar. And what of "Uncle" Albert? Since his last name was Goddard, he obviously was not Mrs. Carlyle's husband. Very curious. And just another bit of mystery surrounding her he unfortunately found fascinating—as if he needed anything else to further kindle his growing interest in her.

He turned toward Miss Chilton-Grizedale, not at all noticing how enticing she looked with the sunlight dancing over her. "Your niece is delightful." His gaze bounced between Miss Chilton-Grizedale and Mrs. Carlyle. "Are you sisters?"

"Not in a blood-relation sense," Miss Chilton-Grizedale said. "Mrs. Carlyle is a dear friend of long standing. She has lived with me since her husband passed away, just several weeks before Hope's birth."

It wasn't what she said, but the way she said it, that caught his interest. As if she were reciting a memorized verse. Her expression gave nothing away—in complete contrast to Mrs. Carlyle, whose cheeks bore twin flags of bright color, whose hands were clenched together at her waist, and whose eyes were averted, her lips pressed together in a thin line. Because she recalled a painful time in her life? Perhaps. But her distress looked more like embarrassment than sadness.

"My condolences on the loss of your husband, Mrs. Carlyle."

"Th-thank you," she said, not looking at him.

Inclining his head toward Miss Chilton-Grizedale, he said, "My apologies for interrupting your stroll, but I must thank you for bringing Prince to a halt. It appears, however, that I shall need to carry the little fellow home."

Bending down, he gently scooped Prince off Hope's lap, cradling the sleeping beast in his arms like a babe. "A pleasure to meet you, Mrs. Carlyle, and you as well, Miss Carlyle. Thank you for helping me name Prince."

The child scrambled to her feet and smiled up at him. "Welcome. Can I see Prince again soon?"

"As I imagine I'll be spending a great deal of time in the park with Prince, I'm certain we'll see each other again." He smiled at Hope, then turned his attention to Miss Chilton-Grizedale. Their eyes met, and a tingle shot through him. Damn it all, he liked the look of her. More every time he saw her. Which was bad. Which meant that he should endeavor to see less of her. Certainly not more of her. He needed to leave. Now.

Instead, his voice developed a mind of its own, and working together with his mouth—which had also developed a mind of its own—he found himself asking, "Would you like to join me on a visit to Vauxhall this evening, Miss Chilton-Grizedale?"

She appeared to be quite torn, and hoping to nudge her toward acceptance, he coaxed, "Mr. Stanton and my sister Catherine are accompanying me. Joining us would afford you a perfect opportunity to further harangue me on my lack of decorum."

"Harangue? I prefer to call it gently reminding."

"I'm certain you do. You could also discuss your matchmaking services with Mr. Stanton. . . ."

Clearly she had not considered this, for her eyes lit up

with enthusiasm. "Why, yes, I could. A marvelous suggestion. In that case, I'd love to join you."

A breath he hadn't realized he held blew past his lips, and he smiled, pushing aside the bothersome fact that she had not shown much animation about the outing until he'd reminded her of Andrew's bachelor state.

"Excellent. We'll come 'round for you at nine?"

"That will be fine."

Yes, indeed, that will be very fine. He very nearly jumped up and clicked his heels together. "I'd best be off, ladies." He made the trio a formal bow, then started walking backward. "Must get Prince home."

"Watch behind you," Miss Chilton-Grizedale warned.

He halted abruptly and swiftly turned around. Good God, he'd almost backed into a thorn bush. Drawing a deep, calming breath, he stepped to the side. He heard Hope giggle behind him, and, hoping his face was not overly red, he turned to face them, offering a jaunty salute to show he was unharmed.

Unfortunately, his sudden stop awakened Prince, who, after issuing a huge yawn, squirmed to be let down. Philip gently settled the puppy on the grass, bracing himself for the upcoming mad dash down the path.

Prince, however, buried his nose in a mound of grass.

"Come along now," Philip said tugging gently on the lead.

Prince dug his paws in and continued to smell the grass.

Bloody hell, the dog had nearly yanked his arm from the socket earlier, but now, when time was of the essence, he couldn't get the beast to move. At this rate, they wouldn't reach home until Michaelmas.

"I'll see that you get a nice, big beef bone to chew on the minute we arrive home," Philip bribed, trying to urge Prince along, but Prince was having none of it.

"How about a biscuit?" Nothing. Not even a tail wag. "Ham? Cozy pillow to sleep on? Your own rug by the fire?" Philip dragged a hand down his face. "Five pounds. I'll give you five pounds if you run like you did earlier. All right, ten pounds. My kingdom. My entire bloody kingdom if you come along now."

Clearly Prince was not a beast open to bribery.

Looking up, Philip noted that Miss Chilton-Grizedale, Mrs. Carlyle, and Hope had nearly reached a curve in the path. Thank goodness. Seconds later, they turned, disappearing from his sight. He instantly scooped up Prince in his arms, and broke into a run. Prince, clearly enjoying this game, licked Philip's chin and yipped.

"All right, I'll still give you the beef bone. But you're not getting the ten pounds. And you should be bloody grateful. If not for me, you'd be named Princess."

Prince, golden ears flapping back in the breeze, yipped again, and Philip increased his pace. There was no time to lose. He needed to call upon Catherine, then go to the museum to speak to Andrew—to inform both of them that they were going to Vauxhall this evening.

Eight

  Meredith walked along Vauxhall's graveled South Walk, and attempted to accomplish the impossible: ignore the man walking beside her.

Botheration, how could she hope to turn a blind eye when she was so acutely aware of him? When hints of his clean, masculine scent teased her senses? Lady Bickley and Mr. Stanton strolled several yards ahead, and she focused her attention on their backs with the zeal a pirate would bestow upon a booty of gold coins, but to no avail. Lord Greybourne remained no more than a foot away, and every nerve in her body tingled with that knowledge.

At least being outdoors proved a welcome improvement over sitting opposite him in the confines of the carriage. Seated upon the plush gray velvet squabs in the elegant black lacquer coach, he'd been close enough to reach out and touch. Close enough to catch teasing whiffs of his tantalizing scent that filled her with the urge to lean forward and simply bury her face against his neck and breathe. Close enough so that their knees bumped every time the carriage hit a rut in the road. And each time her heart had tripped over itself, shooting unwanted, heated sensations through her.

And that posed a tremendous problem.

Not only for the discomfort those unwanted sensations brought her, but his nearness had rendered her uncharacteristically mute. Thank goodness Lady Bickley had kept up a lively conversation, chatting in an animated fashion about tomorrow night's party. And thank goodness as well for the coach's dim interior, which hid the fiery color she knew colored her cheeks.

Unfortunately, she now faced the even more daunting prospect of strolling beside Lord Greybourne in Vauxhall's enticing atmosphere, which by its very nature lent itself to romance. The fragrant gardens, the dimly lit paths surrounded by stately elms, their foliage festooned with twinkling lamps, the narrow lanes that led to even more dimly lit places where all manner of scandalous behavior occurred . . .

The mere thought pulsed heat through her, and she was once again rendered mute. Good lord, the man was going to think her a complete nodcock. She should be discussing decorum with him, but the task was impossible when her thoughts were focused on very *un*decorous matters. Why did *he* not say something? Toss her some sort of conversational gambit, as she was clearly incapable of thinking of one on her own.

Their shoulders bumped, and she drew in a sharp breath at the contact. She turned toward him, and discovered him gazing at her with such intensity, her stride faltered. Reaching out, he grasped her upper arm to steady her, then brought them to a halt.

"Are you all right, Miss Chilton-Grizedale?"

Meredith stared at his handsome, compelling face, and the bottom dropped out of her stomach. *No, I am not all right at all, and it is entirely your fault. You have me feeling things I do not want to feel. Wanting things I can never have. Desiring you in a way that will lead to nothing but heartbreak.*

The warmth of his hand seeped through her gown, heating her skin in a way that begged for her to step closer, press herself against him. Terrified that she would do just that, her mind instructed her feet to step back, away from him—a command her feet blithely ignored.

Swallowing to moisten her dust dry throat, she said, "I . . . I'm fine."

"This gravel can be quite treacherous. Did you twist your ankle?"

"No, I merely stumbled. No damage done."

"Good." He released her arm with a lack of haste she foolishly fancied might be reluctance. "Would you like to continue walking? Andrew and my sister are quite far ahead of us."

Meredith turned and noted that indeed the other couple had already disappeared from view. She moved forward, and he fell into step next to her. Other couples strolled along, but without the security of Mr. Stanton's and Lady Bickley's presence, Meredith was very much aware of being alone with Lord Greybourne. She quickened her pace.

"Are we engaged in a race, Miss Chilton-Grizedale?" he asked in a voice laced with amusement.

"No, I just thought perhaps we should catch up with Mr. Stanton and Lady Bickley. We would not want to lose them."

"Never fear. If I know Catherine, she is on her way to secure a prominent supper box. By the time we arrive, Andrew will have already ordered wine, thus relieving me of the burden of choosing a vintage." He chuckled. "Thank goodness the Gardens are renowned for their excellent wines, as Andrew is most definitely not a connoisseur. Brandy is much more his preference."

A bit more relaxed now that the mood seemed lightened, Meredith pointed ahead to the three triumphal arches spanning the walk. "At this distance, it almost appears as if the authentic Ruins of Palmyra reside in Vauxhall."

Philip focused his attention on the arches, vastly relieved to have something to concentrate on other than his companion. After a brief perusal he said, "They are a reasonable facsimile, but cannot compare to the actual ruins."

"I did not realize your travels spanned to the Syrian desert, my lord."

Impressed by her knowledge of the ruins' location, he said, "Syria was but one of many places I visited over the course of the past decade."

"The ruins were magnificent, I imagine."

An image instantly crystallized in his mind, so vivid he felt as if he once again stood in the ancient city. "Among the vast array of ruins I studied, Palmyra stands out, mostly because of its sheer dramatic scope. The contrast of color is remarkable, and quite impossible to describe, I'm afraid. During the day the ruins are bleached white by the relentless sun, against an infinite sky so dazzlingly blue it hurts the eyes to look at it. At sunset, shadows fall over the ruins as the sky lightens from that vivid blue to yellow, then deepens to orange, then to an almost blood red. And then the sky would grow darker, darker, until the city simply vanished into the desert night, gone until the sun rose again."

He turned his head to look at her. She was gazing at him, a dreamy look in her eyes, as if she, too, could see Palmyra as clearly as he. "It sounds extraordinary," she whispered. "Incredible. Beautiful."

"Yes. All those things. And more." His gaze roamed over her face, touching upon each unique feature, settling last on her lovely mouth. He wanted to touch her. Kiss her. With an intensity that he could no longer ignore.

Pulling his gaze from her, he quickly took note of their surroundings. "Come," he said, placing his hand gently under her elbow to steer her toward a path leading away from the pavilions and colonnade. "It is such a lovely evening, let us walk and talk a bit longer before joining Andrew and Catherine in the supper box. There are several things I'm wondering about, and perhaps you'd satisfy my curiosity."

He glanced down at her. She blinked rapidly, and the faraway expression vanished from her eyes. "Certainly, my lord. At least I'll try. What are you curious about?"

"*You,* Miss Chilton-Grizedale. How is it that you came to be a matchmaker?"

She hesitated for a second, then said, "In the usual manner. At a young age I possessed an innate sense regarding which gentleman and lady among my family's acquaintances would suit one another, and I enjoyed dropping hints regarding my choices. Amazingly enough, quite a number of my suggestions came to pass. As I grew older, I read the Society pages, and mentally paired off members of the peerage. I would read the banns and often think, heavens, no—he shouldn't marry *her*! Lady so and so would be a much wiser match. Soon the village mamas began seeking my advice for their daughters. I eventually moved to London, and little by little my reputation grew."

Just as it had struck him in the park this afternoon, it was not her words that didn't ring true, but the manner in which she said them. As if she were reciting a speech she'd memorized. He had the distinct impression that if he asked her the same question two months from now, he'd receive the same answer—word for word. And unlike many women he'd met, he sensed a reluctance in her to talk about herself.

She slid him a sideways glance. "Your father hiring me on your behalf to find you a suitable bride was my most prestigious commission to date."

"Yet even if you do succeed in finding a woman willing to marry me, I can only do so if I am able to break the curse."

"I refuse to take a pessimistic view regarding breaking the curse. And I cannot imagine any woman not wanting to marry you."

He slowed his pace and looked at her. "Indeed? Why is that?"

His question clearly flustered her. "Well, because you are"—she waved her hand around, as if trying to conjure the words she sought from the air—"titled. Wealthy."

Disappointment and something that felt suspiciously like hurt filled him. Was that all she saw? "And those are the sole criteria you use when arranging suitable matches?"

"Certainly not." She flashed a grin. "It helps enormously that you have all your hair and teeth."

"And if I didn't have all my hair and teeth?"

"I still cannot imagine any woman not wanting to marry you."

"Why?"

"Are you casting about for compliments, my lord?" Her voice held an unmistakable trace of amusement.

Damn it, he was. Shamefully. He knew he was far from handsome. Knew his years traveling about had tarnished the shine of his manners. Knew his interests would bore any female to tears. Still, he longed to hear her dispute what he knew. She was clearly striving to keep the conversation light, while he conspired to maneuver her into a dark corner. He should be ashamed of himself. Appalled. And he'd strive to dredge up all those proper feelings— after he'd kissed her.

"Do you have any compliments to give, Miss Chilton-Grizedale?"

She heaved out a dramatic sigh. "I suppose I could think of one. If pressed."

"Let me guess. My ears do not stick out nor droop like a hound's."

She laughed. "Precisely. And there are no warts upon your nose."

"Careful. Such praise will go straight to my head."

"Then I'd best not point out that there's no paunch about your middle. Or that your eyes are—" Her words snapped off as if she'd chopped them with an axe.

"My eyes are what, Miss Chilton-Grizedale?"

She hesitated for several heartbeats, then whispered, "Kind. Your eyes are kind."

Lovely, simple words. Surely they shouldn't have pumped such heat through him.

Meredith risked a glance at him. He was looking at her with an intensity that turned her throat to dust. Averting her gaze, she swallowed, then said, "It is your turn now, my lord."

"To give you compliments? Very well. I think you are—"

"No!" The word burst from her lips, followed by a nervous laugh. "No," she repeated more softly. "I meant it is your turn to tell me how you fell into your present profession as an antiquarian." Yes, that's what she'd meant, but a part of her couldn't help but wonder what he'd been about to say.

"Ah, well, it is interesting that you would phrase it that way, as I literally did 'fall' into my love for antiquities. When I was but a lad of five, I accidentally fell into a well at Ravensly Manor, the family's country estate in Kent."

"Oh, dear. Were you hurt?"

"Only my pride. Luckily the well was shallow, as I was quite clumsy as a child. I recall one governess who referred to me as 'The Accident Ship Looking for a Port to Dock.' She only muttered that under her breath, of course, but I was clumsy—not deaf."

There was no mistaking the tinge of hurt in his voice, and she instantly recalled the painting hanging over the mantel in his father's drawing room. A pudgy, bespectacled boy on the brink of manhood. He'd no doubt been a pudgy, bespectacled child as well, one whom the governess thought it was acceptable to call names. Sympathy, along with a healthy dose of outrage on his behalf, swept through her.

"I hope your father showed that governess the door—without benefit of a reference."

"Is that what you'd have done?"

"Without hesitation. I cannot abide people who say or do hurtful things to those they are supposed to look after, to those who depend upon them. Those who are smaller or weaker than they. It is the worst sort of betrayal." Her hands fisted as the words flowed, unstoppable, low, and fervent. Embarrassed by her intensity, and praying he did not read too much into it, she quickly said, "So you were at the bottom of the well . . ."

"Yes, where I discovered gobs of oozing mud. It quite cushioned my fall, but it also ate my shoes. When I lifted my foot, there came this horrible sucking sound. Then my foot, encased only in my stocking, emerged. I plunged my hands into the mud, and discovered it was only about a foot deep. Underneath the mud was a hard substance I realized was stone. I felt around for my shoe, and while doing so, I found something small and round. I pulled it free and managed to wipe off enough of the mud to see it was a coin. Feeling around, I located three more. That evening, I showed the coins to my father. They were made of gold, and appeared to be very old. The next morning we traveled to London, to the British Museum.

"The curator was beside himself over the find, explaining that he believed the coins hailed back from when the Romans invaded Britain in 43 A.D. He said that a Roman soldier may have hidden the coins in the well, but was killed in the fighting before he could return for them. Such a scenario fired my imagination, and from that moment on, I've been fascinated by the study of the past and the remains of ancient civilizations. Over the next several years I dug countless holes on the estate's property, and while most families took the waters in Bath, my father brought me to the Salisbury Plain to see Stonehenge and to Northumberland to explore Hadrian's Wall. So, like you, I knew my calling from a very young age."

She hesitated, then said carefully, "I realize this is none of my affair, Lord Greybourne, but it sounds as if you were close to your father when you were a boy. Yet there is no mistaking the tension between you now."

Several seconds of silence met her observation, and she wondered if she'd offended him. Finally he said, "Our relationship changed when my mother passed away."

"I see," she murmured, even though she didn't. "I'm sorry."

"As am I."

"I hope you are able to set aside your differences before it's . . . too late."

"That is my hope as well. However, I'm not certain it's possible. Some wounds never heal."

"Yes, I know. But I would urge you to do whatever necessary to mend your relationship with your father. You don't realize how fortunate you are to *have* a father."

"Your father is dead?"

The question hit Meredith like a backhanded slap, making her realize that she'd allowed this conversation to veer down a road she did not wish to tread upon. "Yes, he's dead." At least she supposed he was. It was what she told herself. Determined to change the subject, she asked, "Whatever happened to the coins you found in the well?"

"We donated three of them to the museum. I kept one for myself."

"Do you still have it?"

"I do. Would you like to see it?"

"Very much."

He paused, lightly grasping her arm to turn her to face him. To her surprise he proceeded to loosen his cravat. "Wh-what are you doing?"

"Showing you the coin." With his cravat unknotted, he parted the edges of his snowy shirt, exposing the column of his throat. Reaching inside the V, he withdrew a chain hanging around his neck from which dangled a small circular object. However, he didn't pull the chain over his head. Instead he stepped closer, then held out the disk.

She went perfectly still. They stood in a deeply shadowed curve of the narrow pathway, lit only by the faint glow of moonlight sifting through the trees. The noise, music, crowds, and illuminated lamps of the grove were far in the distance, cloaking them in intimacy. A fragrant breeze brushed her gown against his boots. No more than two feet separated them. Two feet that could be erased in one step. One step that would bring her flush against him. She heard him breathing. Could he hear her heart pounding?

Her gaze riveted on the coin he held out to her. Unable to stop herself, she raised her hand, noting that it shook slightly. He settled the coin against her palm. His fingers brushed hers as he did so, sizzling heat up her arm.

Warm. The gold was warm from where it had rested against his skin only seconds before. Her fingers involuntarily closed over the coin, absorbing the heat, pressing it into her palm. Slowly opening her fingers, she stared at the round disk. "I cannot see it very well, I'm afraid."

He stepped closer. Now only inches separated them. "Is that better?"

"Er, yes." But she lied. It was so much worse. Now she could clearly distinguish his scent. Feel the warmth emanating from his body. See his bare throat work as he swallowed. Her mind screamed at her to back away, but her feet refused to move. Still holding the coin, she looked up at him. The dim light did not prevent her from noting his serious, intent expression as he stared. At her lips.

He cupped her face between his broad palms and gently feathered his thumbs across her cheeks. "So soft," he whispered. "So incredibly soft." He lowered his head, slowly, as if to give her the opportunity to pull away, to end this madness. Instead, she closed her eyes and waited . . .

Philip brushed his mouth lightly over hers, fighting against the rising urge to simply yank her into his arms and devour her. Instead he gently drew her closer, until her body was flush against his, trapping her hand, which still held the coin, against his chest. He ran the tip of his tongue along her plump bottom lip, and her lips parted, inviting him into the warm heaven of her mouth.

Delicious. She tasted exactly as she smelled—sweet, seductive, and delicious. Like something from the confectioner's shop. Desire pumped through his veins like a drug, ensnaring his senses. A long, feminine moan sounded from her, and he touched his fingers to her throat to absorb the vibration, while his other hand skimmed down to the small of her back, urging her closer, tighter against him.

She released the coin, splaying her fingers against his chest. She had to feel his heart slapping against his ribs. Had to feel his arousal pressing against her. His tongue explored the silky secrets of her lovely mouth, and the exquisite friction of her tongue rubbing against his nearly brought him to his knees.

More. Had to touch more of her. Without breaking their kiss, he pulled on the satin ribbons securing her bonnet beneath her chin, then pushed the bonnet back, exposing her hair. He sifted his fingers through the thick, silky strands, scattering pins that pinged gently as they hit the graveled ground. Soft. Fragrant. More.

Gently fisting his hands in her hair, he tilted her head back, giving him access to her jaw and the vulnerable curve of her neck. He noted with satisfaction that her pulse jumped wildly against his lips, and he touched his tongue to the frantic beat. With a sigh, she rose up on her toes, sifting the fingers of one hand through the hair at his nape, while the hand that pressed his chest moved upward until the tips of her fingers touched the exposed skin at the base of his throat where he'd parted his shirt.

The feel of her fingers on his skin, touching his hair, undid him. He reclaimed her lips with a need he could not stem, which was fired further by her heated response. The feel of her pressed against him, the taste of her in his mouth pummeled him with fists of hot want and need, stealing his subtlety, vanquishing his finesse. His hands, normally so steady, patient, and calm that they could spend hours piecing together minute fragments of broken pottery, roamed unsteady, impatient, and restless up and down her back.

She shifted against him, her softness rubbing against his erection, and a shudder racked him. He had to stop. Now. While there still remained a remote chance that he could. With an effort that cost him, he raised his head and looked down at her.

Her eyes were closed, and rapid, shallow breaths puffed from between her parted lips. Her dark hair lay in tangled disarray about her shoulders. Longing battered him, but he clenched his jaw and forced himself not to give in to the overwhelming need to kiss her again. Her eyelids fluttered open, and their gazes locked.

Damn. While he welcomed the intimacy and privacy afforded by the darkness, he also cursed it, as it hid the nuances of her expression from him. He wanted to see her eyes. Her skin. Were her pupils dilated? Did a flush of arousal stain her cheeks?

She remained pressed against him, forcibly reminding him of his aching erection. God knows he wanted her—with a ferocity completely unfamiliar to him. Was it simply the fact that it had been so long since he'd had a woman? Or was it this particular woman that had him so painfully aroused?

He squeezed his eyes shut and tried to imagine someone else wrapped in his arms, his fingers tangled in her hair, and failed. Utterly. He saw only her. This was not a case of any-woman-would-satisfy-him. Only this particular woman would do.

The silence grew heavy with the need to say something, but what? No doubt a true gentleman would apologize and heartily beg her pardon, but the fact that he'd deliberately lured her into the dark recesses of Vauxhall with the express intention of kissing her proved his gentlemanly tendencies were tarnished. *Tarnished?* His inner voice scoffed. *More like rusted beyond repair.* And how could he apologize for something he was not sorry for?

Still, the words echoing through his brain, *I want you, I want you,* were probably best left unsaid. So he brushed back a tangled curl from her forehead and whispered the one word that hovered on the tip of his tongue.

"Meredith."

The sound of her name, whispered in that aroused-rough voice, yanked Meredith from the sensual fog surrounding her. She blinked rapidly as reality returned with a thump. Every nerve tingled with awareness, hummed with pleasure. The feminine flesh between her legs felt heavy and moist, and ached with a low throb, made all the more acute by the hardness pressing against her belly. His obvious arousal quashed those rumors that he could not . . . perform—not that she'd believed them for an instant anyway. And the way he kissed . . .

God help her, he'd kissed her senseless. How many hours had she lain awake, wondering what it would feel like to be kissed in such a way, trying to bludgeon back her curiosity and desires? She knew all too well where such thoughts led, and it was a path she'd vowed never to follow. Yet she'd allowed Lord Greybourne to lead her into the intimate and private darkness, knowing in her heart that he would kiss her. And desperately wanting him to.

But she had not counted on him making her feel like . . . this. So alive. So aching. So wanting. And so bereft when he stopped. She'd wanted to know the feel and taste of his kiss. And now she knew. And she wanted more. And that was utterly impossible.

She wished she could claim outrage, brand him a cad, but her honor wouldn't permit such a patent falsehood, nor allow her to place any blame for what had happened between them on his shoulders. She could have stopped him. Should have stopped him. But she'd chosen not to. And now, as she always had, she would simply have to live with the consequences of her actions. But in this case her actions could well threaten the respectability for which she'd fought so long and hard. What on earth was she thinking to risk it all for a clandestine kiss?

With as much dignity as she could muster, she disentangled her fingers from his thick, silky hair, pulled her other hand away from the warmth of his chest, then stepped back, out of the circle of his arms.

Deftly twisting her disarrayed hair into a passable chignon, she pulled her bonnet back into place, securely tying the bow beneath her chin. "We must go back," she said, feeling much more in control now that her hair was tidy. Now that he was no longer touching her.

"I don't think that's possible."

"Lady Bickley and Mr. Stanton must be concerned by our prolonged absence."

"That is not what I meant." Reaching out, he ran a single fingertip over her cheek, stilling her with a whisper of a touch. "But I think you knew that. I think you know, as I do, that we cannot erase what just happened between us. That from now on, everything will fall into one of two categories—before we kissed, and after we kissed."

Those words, spoken in that low, fervent voice, threatened to weaken her still-wobbly knees. Stepping back, out of his reach, she raised her chin and adopted her most brisk tone. "Nonsense. We can and will forget it."

"I will not forget it, Meredith. Not if I live to be one hundred."

Dear God, neither would she. But one of them had to be sensible. "Please understand that I accept my share of the blame for this." She attempted a lighthearted laugh, and was quite impressed with the results. "Clearly the romantic atmosphere adversely affected both our judgments. We must not make such a to-do over a meaningless kiss."

"You truly believe that? That it was nothing more than the atmosphere? That nothing significant passed between us?" He stepped closer to her, and although he did not touch her, his nearness made her heart skip several beats. "You honestly believe it will not happen again?"

"Yes." The word sounded forced even to her own ears. "Once can be discounted as simply poor judgment. Twice would—"

"Place it in a different category altogether."

"Yes."

"A category labeled 'a mistake of gargantuan proportions.'"

"I'm glad you agree." Relieved that they'd reached an understanding, she plunged on before he could change his mind or further discuss their kiss—a topic she longed to forget. "We really must rejoin the others."

He inclined his head, and they proceeded back toward the supper boxes in silence. Meredith kept her distance from him, careful not to brush her arm against his. No good could come of this impossible attraction to him. They belonged in different worlds. He was destined to marry a woman of his own class—once he broke the curse. And if he failed to break the curse, he couldn't marry. Either way, she could only ever be a temporary diversion for him, a plaything to be tossed aside when the games were finished, and she would never allow herself to be that to any man. An image of her mother's face rose in her mind, and she squeezed her eyes shut. No. She would never make the same mistakes Mama had made. Never do what Mama had done.

Charlotte cracked opened her bedchamber door and peeked into the corridor. The light flickering beneath Albert's door indicated he'd finally lit his candles and retired for the evening. Assured that she would be alone, she hurried to the kitchen to make herself a much-needed pot of hot, soothing tea. She pushed open the kitchen door and halted as if she'd walked into a brick wall. Albert leaned against the wooden work counter, a biscuit in one hand, a steaming cup in the other hand. Her appearance in the doorway froze his hand halfway to his lips. He appeared as startled and disconcerted as she.

Charlotte's heart slapped against her ribs as she took in his appearance. His light brown hair was badly disheveled, as if he'd overindulged in his habit of raking his long fingers through the thick strands. The glow from the low burning flame in the grate cast his lean features into stark shadows, accentuating the shading along his jawline from the nighttime stubble of his beard. Her gaze traveled downward, and her heart threatened to cease slapping altogether.

He wore the dark blue flannel robe she'd given him for his last birthday, almost a year ago. At the time, she hadn't thought twice about purchasing such a personal item for him—he was Albert, after all. Part of her family. But after he'd opened her gift, he'd hugged her, pressing a warm kiss to her forehead. Simple gestures of gratitude, nothing more. Yet it was as if she'd taken a blow to the head. He'd never done such a thing before. Indeed, it sometimes seemed that Albert went out of his way *not* to touch her— as if he sensed her aversion to a man's hands on her—and she'd appreciated his sensitivity.

That hug and tender kiss to her forehead were the first time in her life a man had ever touched her with kindness and gentle care. With friendship. Without expecting or wanting more from her. It was a revelation, and one that had set her on this destructive course of impossible, unacceptable feelings for Albert.

Her gaze traveled downward, and her mouth went dry. The robe gaped open at the chest, revealing a V of hair-dusted skin. Skin she instantly wanted to touch her lips to. The robe ended just below his knees, revealing his calves, one noticeably more muscular than the other due to his injured leg. His feet were bare. Desire, strong and unwanted, gushed through her, and she bit her bottom lip to contain the moan of longing that threatened to spring free. If she'd been capable of it, she would have laughed at herself and the sheer irony of this situation.

When she'd arrived on Meredith's doorstep five years ago, badly beaten and pregnant with a child, the identity of whose father she could only guess at, she'd sworn she'd never want another man to touch her again for as long as she lived. And she'd kept that vow. Until she'd given Albert that damnable robe.

God help her, she had to make these feelings go away, but how? He was a loving, caring, decent young man who deserved a beautiful, innocent, adoring young woman. Not a jaded, homely, used-up former whore five years his senior. He knew what she'd been, how she'd lived her life before Meredith took her in. He'd always been kind enough to never throw her past in her face, but that only made her love him more.

"I thought you'd gone to bed," they said simultaneously.

Charlotte forced a weak smile, trying her utmost not to show how unnerved she was. "I could not sleep. I thought some tea might help."

He nodded toward the kettle, his gaze never leaving hers. "I already made some. Yer welcome to it."

Relieved to have something to do that allowed her to turn away from him and busy her hands, Charlotte set about pouring her tea, but her attention remained riveted on the man behind her. She heard him set his cup, then the biscuit, down on the counter. Heard his shuffling gait as he crossed the floor, then stopped behind her.

"Why couldn't ye sleep, Charlotte?"

He stood close. Too close. It took all of her strength not to step backward until her back touched his chest. "My . . . my mind is just busy. Wondering how Meredith is faring at Vauxhall. How about you?"

The instant the question left her lips, she longed to snatch it back. What if he couldn't sleep because he'd been thinking about some beautiful young thing he was smitten with? He'd never spoken of anyone, but she knew all about young men his age and the urges that ruled them.

"I couldn't sleep, because, like ye, my mind was busy."

She drew a deep breath, summoned her courage, then turned to face him.

He stood no more than two feet away from her. "Are you worried about Meredith?" she asked. "It *is* after midnight."

"No. If she were alone with that Greybourne bloke who looks at her as if she were a pork chop and he were a hound, I might be. But other folks are there. Actually, it's *you* I'm worried about, Charlotte."

"Me? Whatever for?"

"Ye haven't seemed yourself lately."

Dear God, had she revealed herself? "In what way?"

He frowned. "Can't explain it exactly. Like yer out of sorts. With me." His gaze searched hers. "Have I done somethin' to upset ye?"

"No. I've merely been tired lately."

"I can see that. Ye've circles under yer eyes." Before she realized what he was about, he reached out and brushed the tip of his index finger under her eye. She drew in a sharp breath at the heat his feathery touch shimmered through her. Jerking her head back, away from his hand, she pressed her hips against the counter and leaned as far away from him as possible.

He slowly lowered his hand. There was no mistaking the stricken look in his eyes. "Charlotte . . . I'm sorry. I shouldn't have . . ." He dragged unsteady hands down his face. "But surely ye know I'd never hurt you."

Shame filled her that her reaction would make him think for even an instant that she'd believe he'd hurt her. But how could she tell him that she'd rejected his touch not because she didn't trust him, but because she did not trust herself? Unable to form a word around the lump in her throat, she merely nodded.

None of the tension left his expression or stance. "I'm glad ye know that. And I'd never let anyone else hurt ye. Not ever again."

What was left of her heart simply melted. He looked and sounded so fierce, like a robe-garbed warrior defending his castle. "Thank you, Albert." She'd certainly had no intention of touching him, but somehow, of its own volition—perhaps because she wanted to so very badly—her hand lifted, and she laid her palm against his cheek.

The instant she touched him she realized her grave error. Her gaze riveted on the provocative sight of her hand resting against his face. His skin was warm, and the stubble of his beard lightly abraded her palm. The urge to stroke her fingers over his cheek, to explore the stark panes of his face, overwhelmed her. And she might well have given in to the temptation . . . but then she realized he'd gone completely, utterly still. A muscle jumped spasmodically beneath her fingers, indicating he clenched and unclenched his jaw. His eyes were squeezed shut, as if he were in pain—the sort of pain one suffered when placed in a grossly uncomfortable situation. Like being touched by someone you did not want to touch you.

Embarrassment and humiliation scorched her, and she snatched her hand away as if he'd turned into a pillar of fire. To her further mortification, hot tears pushed at the backs of her eyes, threatening to spill over. She needed to get away from him.

"I . . . I think I heard Hope," she said, grasping at the first excuse that came to mind. "I must go. Good night." She ran from the room, not stopping until she'd reached the safety of her bedchamber.

What an impossible situation. She could not continue living like this much longer. Her only hope was to avoid him completely, but how could that be accomplished while they lived under the same roof? If she remained, it was only a matter of time before she gave herself away. Yet she had nowhere else to go. She ached at the thought of leaving here, the only true home she'd ever known. Of taking Hope away from Meredith and Albert. Of taking herself away from them. What on earth was she going to do?

Just before one A.M., after safely delivering first Meredith, then Catherine to their respective residences, Philip pushed aside the green velvet draperies in his private study. After yanking off his cravat, he removed his glasses, pinched the bridge of his nose, then rubbed his hands down his face. A knock sounded at the door, and he blew out a resigned sigh. He had no desire to rehash the evening, but knew there was no point attempting to put off the conversation. "Come in, Andrew."

Andrew entered the room, closing the door behind him. He crossed the maroon and gold Axminster rug, pausing at the brandy decanters. "You look as if you could use some revivification. Would you like one?"

Philip lifted the snifter he'd set on his desk. "Beat you

to it." Watching Andrew pour himself a fingerful of amber liquor, he mentally counted off the seconds. *Five, four, three, two, one* . . .

As if on cue, Andrew said, "Clearly the evening did not go as you'd hoped."

"On the contrary, I thought the orchestra quite good."

"I was not referring to the music."

"Ah. Well, it's true the food was only adequate, and the portions quite sparse, but as none of us were particularly hungry, it did not bother me."

"Nor was I referring to the food."

"The wine was excellent—"

"Nor the wine. As you damn well know, I meant Miss Chilton-Grizedale." He gently swirled his brandy. "Where did you two disappear to?"

"Were you worried about us?"

"Actually, no. Your sister expressed some concern, but I assured her you merely wished to discuss the finding of your future bride with Miss Chilton-Grizedale in private. I then, with my usual wit and charm, managed to keep Lady Bickley's attention diverted until you returned . . . looking a bit disheveled, I might add."

"It was quite breezy."

"Yes, I'm certain that it was the breeze which rendered Miss Chilton-Grizedale's lips swollen and rosy, and retied your cravat in a different knot than the one you'd sported prior to your walk."

Unease slithered down Philip's spine, along with self-recrimination. Damn it all, he should not have risked kissing her in a public place, regardless of the fact that he'd done so under the cover of darkness, hidden away from prying eyes. The last thing he wanted was to further harm her reputation.

"Did anyone else notice, do you think?" he asked. "Catherine—?"

"No. You both did an admirable job of looking perfectly innocent when you rejoined us. I only noticed the differences because I was looking for them. I'm not trying to pry, Philip. I'm merely trying to help. It is obvious you are out of sorts."

Philip tossed back a swallow of brandy, relishing the burn that eased down his throat. Perhaps Andrew *could* help. Could talk him out of this insane attraction to a woman he barely knew. "This woman you care for . . . how long were you acquainted with her before you knew how you felt about her?"

A humorless sound erupted from Andrew. "I'm guessing you want me to say I knew her for months or years, and that my feelings developed slowly over time, but it was nothing like that. It was more like a lightning bolt struck me. She affected me in ways I'd never before experienced the instant I laid eyes upon her." He stared down into his brandy, his voice taking on a rough, almost angry edge. "Everything about her fascinated me, and each detail I learned about her only served to deepen my feelings from that first initial attraction. I wanted her until I ached, both physically and mentally. She was everything I wanted. . . ." Andrew looked up and his lips quirked with an attempt at humor that did not quite reach his eyes. "You have no idea how many times I imagined the untimely demise of her husband. In some very inventive ways, I might add."

"And if he were to meet with such a fate?"

All vestiges of humor were wiped from his expression. "Nothing would stop me from making her mine. Nothing."

"But what if the lady did not share your feelings?"

"Is that what has you out of sorts? You believe Miss Chilton-Grizedale is not enamored of you? Because if so, you are wrong. She is accomplished at hiding her feelings, but they are there, if you know where to look. And to answer your question, if the lady did not share my feelings, or needed some persuasion, I would court her."

"Court her?"

Andrew looked toward the ceiling, shaking his head. "Bring her flowers. Spout poetry. Compose something called 'Ode to Miss Chilton-Grizedale Upon a MidSummer's Evening.' I know romance is not in your scientific nature, but if you want the woman, you must adjust. But before you do, ask yourself how far you plan to let this flirtation go, and where is it going to leave her—and you—when it's over."

A knot tightened in Philip's stomach. Kissing Meredith had been a gross breach of propriety, but still he'd wanted more. If they'd been in a more private setting, would he have been able to stop himself from taking further liberties with her? God help him, he did not know. She certainly deserved better than to be lured into the shadows of Vauxhall. She deserved to be properly courted by a proper gentleman—

His teeth clenched. Damn it, the thought of another man touching her, kissing her, courting her, surged jealousy through him. Unfortunately he had not planned on his heart and thoughts being engaged by the woman in charge of helping him find his bride. No, he had not planned on Meredith.

Andrew cleared his throat, pulling Philip from his brown study. "If you wish to court her—"

"No. I don't. I cannot. Nothing could come of it."

"Why not?"

Philip raked his hand through his hair. "I'm in no position to court her. I'm supposed to be concentrating on finding a bride. A woman from my own social class." The words sounded hollow and supercilious even to his own ears. "Honor dictates that I do so, to keep my promise to my father."

Andrew raised his brows. "And did you *specifically* promise your father to marry a woman from the upper echelons of your lofty Society?"

"No . . . but it is expected."

"And since when do you always do what is expected of you?"

Philip couldn't help but emit a short laugh. It was time to put this evening's events into their proper perspective. Meredith aroused his curiosity and interest. He'd wanted to kiss her, and he'd satisfied that urge. As she'd pointed out, it was not something they would allow to happen again. He simply needed to keep his hands and his lips to himself. He was a man of ironclad control. He could do anything he set his mind to.

Before Philip could doubt that thought, Andrew said, "Of course the entire subject of marriage will be moot if we cannot break the curse. How many more crates remain in the warehouse to search through?"

"Twelve. How many at the museum?"

"Only four."

Sixteen crates. Would one of them contain the missing piece of the Stone of Tears? If so, he would soon be married to some woman from his own class. If not, he would be forced to face a future alone. Both prospects equally filled him with dread.

Nine

Meredith stood in the shadows of Lord Greybourne's drawing room and observed the festivities. If judged solely on the attendance, the party was a raging success. Out of the two dozen invitations issued, they'd received not even one refusal. The room was filled with a bevy of lovely unmarried ladies, all properly chaperoned, of course, all of them either interested in, or at the very least, curious about, Lord Greybourne.

Her gaze panned around the room until it located the guest of honor, Lord Greybourne himself. When she saw him, her heart lurched in that annoyingly familiar way it had every time she looked at him, only this evening her heart lurched *and* skipped several beats. Resplendent in formal evening attire, with even his cravat properly tied, he took her breath away. His thick chestnut hair gleamed under the light cast by the crystal chandelier, lit with dozens of beeswax candles. He'd clearly tried to tame his hair into submission, but an errant lock fell over his forehead. He stood near the fireplace, engrossed in conversation with Countess Hickam and her daughter Lady Penelope. Lady Penelope was a diamond of the first water, and very sought-after since her coming out last Season. With her shining blond beauty, angelic singing voice, and family fortune behind her, Lady Penelope was a stellar choice for a bride for Lord Greybourne. Indeed, the only reason Meredith had chosen Lady Sarah over her was because of the advantageous landholdings that marriage would have resulted in.

Now Lord Greybourne appeared engrossed in whatever Lady Penelope was saying to him. And Lady Penelope appeared equally engrossed, her perfect complexion highlighted to optimum advantage by the candlelight, her gown displaying an enviable curve of bosom, her perfect blond hair coiffed in flattering curls about her perfect face, her wide, cornflower-blue eyes gazing up at Lord Greybourne with innocent adoration.

Damnation, Meredith wanted to march across the room and just slap all that perfect blue-eyed blondness. She hated the feelings edging through her, and although she longed to lie to herself about what they were, she'd learned long ago that while she could tell falsehoods to other people, there was no point in telling them to herself. And the unvarnished truth was that she was jealous. Spectacularly jealous. Jealous to the point that she could cheerfully imagine packing off every single one of these vapid marriage-minded twits on the next ship to some very faraway locale. Indeed, any one of them would make a perfectly respectable wife for Lord Greybourne. And that made her detest each and every one of them even more. Watching them flutter their eyelashes and fans at him, giggling and flirting, made her want to break things. Namely assorted blondes' arms, legs, and noses.

Drawing a deep breath, she gave herself a severe mental shake. Very well, there was no denying she felt like a cat who'd been dunked in the lake and was now being petted the wrong way. But she could hide her jealousy and frustration, as she hid so many other things. Lord Greybourne was a client. And the sooner she saw to his marriage, the sooner her life could resume some semblance of normalcy.

* * *

The quadrille had just ended when Philip caught sight of Bakari standing in the doorway, his gaze panning the room. When their gazes met, Bakari nodded once. Excusing himself from Lady Penelope, Philip made his way around the perimeter of the room. When he reached Bakari, he asked, "What is it?"

"Your study."

Philip studied him for several seconds, but as always, Bakari's expression remained inscrutable. "Where were you earlier?" Philip asked. "I looked into the foyer several times, but you weren't here."

"Stepped away."

Philip raised his brows, but Bakari offered nothing further, instead turning on his heel and heading back toward the foyer. Mystified, Philip walked down the corridor and entered his private study, closing the door behind him.

Edward stood near the French windows, tossing back a brandy. Philip started toward him. "Edward, how are . . . ?" His voice trailed off and his footsteps faltered as Edward turned to face him. His one eye was swollen shut, his cheek badly bruised, his bottom lip sporting a mean cut. A white bandage encircled the knuckles and palm of his right hand. "Good God, man, what happened to you? Let me fetch Bakari—"

"He's already seen to me. Cleaned me up and bandaged my hand and ribs." Edward winced. "Hurts like a bastard."

"What the devil happened? Who did this to you?"

"I don't know who." He started pacing, with short, jerky steps. "As for how it happened . . . I couldn't sleep. I'm exhausted, but I can't sleep." He paused to look at Philip through haunted eyes. "Every time I close my eyes, I see her."

Pity and guilt stabbed Philip in the gut. "I'm sorry, Edward. I—"

Edward held up his hand. "I know." He took a long swallow of brandy, then continued. "I decided that rather than spend the night in useless pacing, I'd put my time to use by going through a crate of artifacts. I went to the warehouse and set to work."

"The warehouse? How did you get in?"

"The watchman. I trust that is not a problem."

"No, of course not. I'm just surprised." He spread his hands. "I didn't realize watchmen were such trusting creatures."

"Normally it would have surprised me as well, but I was acquainted with the bloke—name of Billy Timson. Seen him at the pub a number of times. He showed me to your crates, and I set to work. I'd been at it for an hour or so when I heard someone come up behind me. I turned around to find a stranger. Holding a knife.

Philip's stomach fell. "Did you recognize him?"

"No." Edward's pacing increased in speed. "He wore a black mask. Covered his entire head, except for his eyes and mouth. 'Who are you?' I asked. He said, 'I want what's in the crate.'" Edward halted and stared at Philip with a bleak expression. "I fought him . . . I tried. I managed to get the knife away from him. Kicked it under a crate. But he was too strong. Must have knocked me out. When I came around, I was alone. He'd clearly searched through the artifacts in the crate I'd been working on, as the area was ransacked." He drew a deep, shuddering breath. "It looked as if several pieces were broken, and some may be missing. I could not tell. I tried to leave, but the doors were secured from the outside—the bastard must have locked me in. The only way for me to escape was to break a window. I tripped and fell in the glass in my haste to get out. I looked around for Billy, but didn't see him. He must have gotten away. Then I ran until I managed to find a hack and get here. I'm sorry, Philip. . . ."

Philip laid a comforting hand on his shoulder. "Don't apologize, please. I'm just thankful you're all right. You are all right, aren't you?"

"According to Bakari, yes. Nothing broken. A cracked rib. Some bruises. Head hurts like the devil." He gently rubbed his bruised jaw. "Bastard had fists like bloody bricks." He appeared about to say something, then stopped.

"What?"

Edward shook his head. "Nothing. It's just . . . his voice. There was something vaguely familiar about it."

"So this could be someone you know? Perhaps someone who sailed with us aboard the *Dream Keeper* who knows the value of the contents of the crates?"

"It's possible, yes. There is something else." Reaching into his waistcoat pocket, he withdrew a small, wrinkled piece of foolscap, then handed it to Philip. "I found this shoved into my pocket."

Philip looked at the offering, and he stilled at the brief message: *The suffering begins now.*

"I don't like this, Philip," Edward said. "The bastard made me suffer, no doubt about that, but I can't help but feel there's something more . . . sinister going on here. And why would he want *me* to suffer? I've no enemies that I know of."

"I think," Philip said slowly, "that this note may not have been meant for you."

"As comforting as it would be to believe that, the note was in *my* pocket, and *I'm* the one who was pummeled to dust. Who else would it have been meant for?"

"Me." Philip quickly told him about finding his journals out of place, and the note on his desk. "I asked every member of the household staff if they'd touched my journals. They all denied it, and I've no cause to doubt them. This note you found and the attack on you makes it clear that this person is serious. The bastard most likely believed it was *me* in the warehouse tonight, examining my crates."

Edward nodded slowly. "Yes, you're probably correct."

A sharp edge of guilt sliced through Philip. Damn it, Edward had been hurt because of him. Had the guard, an innocent bystander, been hurt—or worse—because of him as well? Mary Binsmore's death already lay heavy upon his heart. Would someone else be hurt? If so, who? Father? Catherine? Andrew? Bakari? Meredith? Bloody hell. If someone wanted him to suffer, what more effective way to accomplish that than to harm the people he cared about? *The suffering begins now.*

Moving to his desk, he withdrew the note he'd received and compared the handwriting. "These were written by the same person."

"I had the distinct impression that he was looking for something specific."

"What makes you say that?"

Edward closed his eyes. "It's difficult to say. It all sort of happened in a blur. But he was muttering things as we fought. Things like 'It's mine' and 'Once it's mine, you're finished.'" He opened his eyes. "I'm sorry I can't recall anything else. Based on the size of the lump on my head, I was hit pretty hard."

"I'm sorry, Edward. And grateful your injuries weren't more serious."

"Yes, it could have been much worse. As much as I hate to be the bearer of bad news, Philip, we need to ask ourselves two questions: What if the thing he spoke of is the missing piece of the Stone of Tears? And what if he found it?"

With Edward's disturbing questions still buzzing through his mind, Philip instructed Bakari to arrange for transportation for Edward.

"I'll report the evening's events to the magistrate before returning home," Edward promised.

"I still think I should go with you—" Philip began.

"No. There is nothing to be gained by you leaving your

guests. I'll take care of it and report back to you in the morning."

Philip reluctantly agreed. "All right. I'll plan to arrive at the warehouse directly after breakfast." He rested his hand on Edward's shoulder. "We'll find out who did this."

Edward nodded, then departed. The instant the door closed behind him, Philip turned to Bakari. "How serious are his injuries?"

"Most troubling is lump on head and glass embedded deep in back of hand. He'll hurt, but heal."

Philip's relief did nothing to assuage his concern. "There may be . . . trouble. I want you to take extra precautions."

Bakari merely nodded. Philip's request was one he'd heard numerous times during their adventures together. Bakari was well acquainted with trouble, and Philip had every confidence in the man's ability to circumvent it.

Casting a meaningful glance toward the drawing room, Bakari harrumphed, and Philip nodded. Time to return to his guests. After taking a deep breath to compose himself, he returned to the drawing room. He'd barely set foot in the room when Meredith appeared beside him.

"There you are! Wherever have you been? The waltz is about to begin, and . . ." She frowned. "Is something amiss?"

His gaze settled on her concerned blue eyes, and his insides squeezed tight. No harm would come to her. Or to anyone else. He would see to it. "Just a small matter that required my immediate attention."

She studied his face, and he forced his concerns aside—for now—and willed his expression to go blank. Still, some of his turmoil must have shown, for she asked, "Not Mr. Stanton, I hope? Lady Bickley reported he's feeling under the weather—"

"No, Andrew is safely ensconced in his bedchamber

with one of Bakari's restorative toddies, which will render him cured by morning, I'm certain." He glanced around the room, noting the speculative gazes resting upon him. "Was I missed?"

"Yes. Everyone's been asking for you."

He turned and looked directly at her. "I meant by you."

Color rushed into her cheeks, charming him, making his fingers itch to reach out and brush over that beguiling blush. "Well, of course. I didn't know where you'd hidden yourself. Lady Bickley and I were about to form a search party. There's a roomful of women waiting to receive your invitation to waltz."

"Excellent. May I have the honor of this dance?"

"Certainly not. I am not here to dance. I am here to—"

"Make certain all these young women believe I'm some sort of fascinating explorer, and to drop hints in gossipmongers' ears that reports of my inability to . . . perform are grossly false."

She cocked a brow. "You make it sound as if that is a bad thing."

"Heavens, no. What man wouldn't want a bevy of beauties to think him fascinating?"

"Exactly."

"And no man wants to be thought of as unable to . . . perform."

"Precisely."

"Between those two recommendations and the fact that I've all my hair and teeth, not to mention my lack of a paunch, I'm certain I've already made great strides with the good ladies in my drawing room."

"Indeed."

"Therefore, I insist you dance with me." Before she could refuse, he leaned a bit closer and confided, "You would be doing me a great service. I'm afraid I'm not a proficient waltzer. If I were able to work out my deficiencies with you, rather than trodding upon the toes of any potential future brides and thus alienating them . . ." He raised his brows in a meaningful fashion.

She pursed her lips. "Perhaps you are right—"

"Of course I am. Come. The music is starting." Tucking her hand into the crook of his elbow, he led her to the dance floor.

"It's a very simple dance," she whispered. "All you need to do is count. One-two-three. One-two-three. And alternate your feet."

The quartet struck up a tune. Philip held her one hand raised at the exact proper height, settled his other hand in the precisely proper position on her back, then swept her around the floor. She looked up at him, her beautiful eyes vividly blue, a delicate rose staining her pale skin. Her sweet, delicious scent wafted up to him, and he drew a deep breath to capture the elusive fragrance.

Pie. This evening she smelled like blackberry pie. His favorite dessert. Her turquoise gown accentuated her extraordinary eyes, and while the garment was undeniably modest, it still offered a teasing glimpse of cleavage. His gaze settled on her full, moist lips, and he swallowed a groan.

Bloody hell, so much for keeping things in their proper perspective and his suddenly nonexistent ironclad control. Dancing with her definitely fell into the category of "very poor idea." Yes, he'd wanted to hold her in his arms, but he had not considered what sweet torture it would be. It required all his concentration to hold her at the proper distance and not yank her against him and bury his face against her tempting skin. To taste her lips. Her lips . . . God. He gritted his teeth, and counted furiously to himself, one-two-three. One-two-three.

After their third trip around the floor, her eyes narrowed suspiciously. "I believe you told me a Banbury tale, my lord. You're a very fine waltzer."

He lost count, faltered, then trod upon her toes. She gasped.

"Dreadfully sorry, my dear. You were saying?"

She glared at him. "Lord Greybourne. That little display was very much like the sort of tricks young boys play, a topic I am well versed in. If you think to fool me with such carryings-on, you are destined for disappointment."

"I would never step on your toes on purpose, Meredith." Her eyes widened slightly at his use of her Christian name. "However, I must confess I did recently learn the basics of the waltz."

"How recently?"

"This afternoon. I commandeered Catherine and forced her to teach me so I wouldn't disgrace myself this evening."

"She made no mention of this to me."

"I asked her not to. I wanted to surprise you."

"I . . . see. Well, she did an admirable job. You've quite got the hang of it. So well, in fact, that you need not waste any more time dancing with me. Lady Penelope is standing by the punch bowl. I suggest you partner her first." She steered him toward the punch bowl with a purposeful gleam in her eye, and he, just as purposefully, swung her in the opposite direction.

"I believe you are leading, Meredith. That is the gentleman's prerogative, if I'm not mistaken."

"I'm trying to get us to the punch bowl," she said in a hissing whisper.

"I'm not thirsty."

"Tongues will wag if you don't stop dancing with me."

"Tongues are already wagging about me, so I cannot see that it matters. Indeed, further speculation would no doubt only add to my ever-growing mystique."

"You are impossible! A quick turn around the floor is one thing, and I appreciate it, as it lends to my credibility that you clearly still have confidence in me and my matchmaking abilities. However, the reality of the situation is that you are a viscount, and I am the hired help, and this dance is quickly approaching the time past what is proper."

Annoyance skittered through him. "You are my *guest*."

"If you insist upon looking at it like that, fine. Then you will recall that you also have more than two dozen other guests to whom you must now pay attention." She lowered her gaze for several seconds, then looked back up at him with an expression that nearly stilled his heart. "Please."

That single, softly spoken plea, combined with the knowing, imploring look in her eyes, told him that more lay behind her request than simply duty to his other guests. Did she find being this close to him as distracting and unnerving as he found her nearness? Was she suffering the same discomfort and longings as he?

Bloody hell, he certainly hoped so. He hated to suffer alone.

But neither could he ignore her request. There were duties he needed to perform for the duration of this party. But this party would eventually end . . .

With a resigned nod, he steered them toward the punch bowl.

"You must tell us, Lord Greybourne, what you think about"—Lady Emily's voice dropped to a whisper—"*you know what*."

Philip stared at her, certain he'd misunderstood. "I beg your pardon?"

"Oh, yes, do tell us," urged Lady Henrietta, with a flirtatious giggle. "Everyone is afraid to talk about *you know what*, but we understand that *you* harbor no such fear."

Philip looked at their expectant faces and inwardly shook his head in stunned disbelief that two such innocent-looking creatures were asking him to discuss *sex*. "I'm afraid it's not proper for me to do so." He swallowed a laugh at how prim he sounded. Wouldn't Meredith be proud of him?

"We promise we won't tell," vowed Lady Emily.

"Not a word. Ever," seconded Lady Henrietta.

Understanding suddenly dawned. "You want my opinion as an *antiquarian*?"

The young ladies exchanged a baffled look, then said in unison, "Yes."

Well, it probably wasn't strictly proper, but at least these two showed some interest in his study of ancient cultures. Clearing his throat, he began, "The male phallus was frequently depicted in hieroglyphs as a symbol for male virility."

Lady Emily's eyes widened to saucers. Lady Henrietta's mouth dropped open.

Warming to his subject, he continued, "The erect penis, especially, was often used in ancient drawings. While in Egypt I discovered some particularly fine examples—"

"Is everything all right?" asked Meredith, joining the group.

Before he could reply, Lady Emily said in a strained voice, "I need to sit down for a moment."

"I do, as well," whispered Lady Henrietta. "Please excuse us." Arm in arm, the two young women beat a hasty retreat.

"Good heavens, what did you say to them?" Meredith whispered.

"Damned if I know. They asked for my opinion regarding ancient sexual customs—"

"What?"

"I was as surprised as you, believe me, but they insisted. Wanted my opinion as an antiquarian."

"They actually asked for your opinion about . . ."—she cast a furtive glance around, then lowered her voice—"about *that*? What exactly did they say?"

"They asked what I thought about *you know what*. I'd

barely begun my explanation, which was purely scientific in nature, I assure you, when you arrived."

Her eyes widened and all the color leached from her face. "Dear God. They must have been referring to Lord Pickerill's upcoming surprise birthday party."

He said the only word that came to mind. "Huh?"

"Lord Pickerill's party. Lady Pickerill has been planning it for months and it's the latest *on dit*—besides you. In the hopes of keeping the plans secret from Lord Pickerill, the soiree is being referred to by everyone as *you know what*."

Annoyance skittered through him. "Well, that is not what *you know what* means. *You know what* refers to sexual matters. At least it did when I left England ten years ago. Who in God's name is making these bloody rules?"

Her eyes all but spewed smoke. "The more pertinent question is, what would possess you to discuss such a topic with proper young ladies?"

"You told me to mingle. So I mingled. And you're *still* not happy. Has anyone ever told you that you're very difficult to please?"

"I prefer to call it simply expecting decorous behavior—"

"I'm certain you do."

"—which unfortunately seems beyond you a good portion of the time."

"Well, since I seem to have committed such an undecorous *faux pas*, we can only be grateful that you happened along when you did. Otherwise I no doubt would have shown them the sketches I'd drawn of the hieroglyphs I was discussing."

"Yes, we can only be grateful." She drew a breath. "All right, remain calm—"

"*I* am perfectly calm. You, however, may require a dose of laudanum."

She shot him a glare clearly intended to incinerate him where he stood. "There *must* be some way to cast a positive light upon this. If not, dear God, I can see the headline in *The Times*: *Cursed, Impotent Viscount Caught Showing Indecent Sketches to Ladies of the Ton.*"

He glared right back at her. "The sketches depict ancient glyphs and are not indecent, nor did I even show them to the young ladies. And for the last damn time, I am *not* impotent."

Although she clearly recognized his anger, she didn't step back. Rather, she lifted her chin another notch. "Fine. But what we need to concentrate on now is fixing this situation before Lady Emily's and Lady Henrietta's mouths run amok and ruin everything. Our best recourse is for you to squelch any rumors before they start, and the best way to do that is with flattery. *Lots* of flattery. Talk your way around the room, commenting on how both young ladies are so very intelligent and their conversation so stimulating. Applaud their curious natures." She raised her brows. "Do you think you can do that?"

"I suppose, although I fear it will prove a strain to think of *lots* of flattering things to say about those two nincom—"

"Lord Greybourne. You will recall that the purpose of this evening is to find you a suitable bride—not to scare off every eligible young woman in the room. Now go undo the damage that you've done. And *please* behave yourself."

Before he could reply, she glided away, regal as royalty, leaving him gnashing his teeth. He watched her leave the room, her gown swaying against her feminine curves. Damn annoying, dictatorial, autocratic, infuriating woman. A slow smile tugged at his lips. He couldn't wait until this damn party was over so he could tell her exactly what he thought of her.

With the last of the guests finally gone and his home restored to rights thanks to the army of servants Catherine had engaged and brought from her own home, Philip breathed a sigh of relief. He escorted Catherine down the cobbled walkway to the waiting carriage, followed by Bakari.

"The party was a success," Catherine said. "Speculation and curiosity about you is rampant."

"And I gather that is preferable to rumor and innuendo?"

She laughed. "Most assuredly. Um, Miss Chilton-Grizedale apprised me of the"—she coughed delicately into her hand—"*you know what* situation with Lady Emily and Lady Henrietta."

"Ah. Well, fear not. Through gobs of insincere flattery I was able to divert a disaster."

Amusement glittered in her eyes. "According to the rumors I heard, several of the young ladies are 'cautiously smitten' with you."

"How excruciatingly complimentary."

His desert-dry tone elicited a smile from her. "Considering how dire the circumstances were only days ago, we've made good progress. Did any of the young ladies capture your interest?"

"You could perhaps categorize me as cautiously smitten with one of them."

"Indeed?" Her voice was ripe with interest. "With whom?"

He chucked her lightly under her chin, a childhood gesture he'd never outgrown. "If I told you now, Imp, we'd have nothing to talk about when I visit you tomorrow."

She stuck out her tongue at him, a childhood gesture *she'd* never outgrown. "That's beastly, Philip! I shall expire from curiosity before tomorrow."

"Yes, well, you know what a beast I've always been."

"Actually, *I* was the beastly one. But I'm glad someone has gained your attention. Father will be very pleased.

He's been much improved in the past few weeks, anticipating your homecoming and wedding."

"I'm glad."

"Have you resolved your differences?"

"Not yet."

"Don't wait too long, Philip. Even though he's experiencing a number of 'good' days, he slips a bit further
away every day. I'd hate for you to have any regrets, of
things left unsaid, when he passes away."

Sadness, guilt, and remorse reared their heads, glower-
ing at him, but he bludgeoned them back. "Don't worry,
Imp. I'll make things right." Then, resting his hands on
her shoulders, he said, "I've something to tell you. Someone broke into the warehouse this evening and ransacked
several of my crates."

Instant concern reflected in her eyes. "Was anything
stolen?"

"I'm not yet certain. I don't want to alarm you, but it's
possible this may be more than a simple robbery attempt.
It might be more personally directed—at me. Promise me
you'll be extra careful and not go anywhere alone. Bakari
will see you home."

Her eyes widened, but she nodded. "All right. I promise. But what about you?"

"I'll be careful as well." When she expectantly lifted
her brows to an imperious height, he added, "I promise."

He handed her into the carriage, offering a wave and a
reminder to expect him to visit her tomorrow. He then
strode quickly back up the walk to face the only guest
who remained. Just as he closed the door behind him,
Meredith entered the foyer and their eyes met. His heart
performed a crazy roll and he had to clamp his jaws together to keep from laughing aloud at himself and his
strong reaction to the mere sight of this woman.

"I'll escort you home after Bakari returns with the carriage," he said, crossing the marble-tiled floor. "May I offer you a drink while we wait? Perhaps a sherry?"

"Thank you. This time together will also afford us the opportunity to compare notes on the evening."

"Er, yes, compare notes. That is exactly what I wish to do."

"So you've reached some conclusions regarding the young ladies, then?"

"Indeed I have. Come. Let us retire to my study."

Philip led the way down the corridor, then closed the door behind them. Leaning back against the oak panels, he watched her cross the room, his eyes drawn to the generous curve of her hips hinted at beneath her gown as she walked. His gaze wandered upward, resting on the vulnerable nape of her neck showing where her lustrous hair was upswept into a Grecian knot. Turquoise ribbons, the same shade as her gown, twined through her curls. God help him, she looked as delectable from the back as she did from the front. What had he called himself? Cautiously smitten? Not bloody likely. There was nothing in the least bit cautious about the feelings this woman inspired.

He expected her to sit on the settee, but instead she appeared to sink out of sight. Concerned she'd fallen, he quickly crossed the room to discover her kneeling on the hearth, tickling her fingers over Prince's belly, much to the squirming puppy's delight.

"Is this where you hid yourself all evening, you little devil?" she crooned. "I'd wondered where you were."

Prince jumped up and planted several enthusiastic kisses on her chin, for which he was rewarded with a cuddle and a delightful sound that could only be described as a giggle. Prince then squirmed free and promptly flopped himself once again onto his back, paws dangling in the air, shamelessly presenting her with his belly to rub, which she did.

Laughing, she looked up at Philip. "I place him firmly

in the category of 'Sweetest Dog Imaginable.' "

Philip looked at Prince, and he swore the puppy winked at him. Sweetest dog? He'd more likely place the cunning devil in the category of "Smartest Dog in the World." His gaze riveted on her fingers tickling over the Prince's belly. Or "Luckiest Dog in the World."

A vivid image flashed in Philip's mind, of him and Meredith, naked, lying on the hearth rug, her hands skimming over his abdomen. He instantly swelled against his breeches, and he had to press his lips together to keep from groaning out loud. Blinking to dispel the erotic image, he crossed to the crystal decanters, hoping she wouldn't notice the slight limp in his gait. He poured himself a brandy, which he tossed back in a single, bracing gulp. After refilling his drink, he prepared a sherry for her, then, feeling much more in control, and thankfully able to walk properly once again, he rejoined her. During his brief absence she'd seated herself on one corner of the settee. Prince lay sprawled beside her, his head resting on her lap, gazing up at her with adoring puppy eyes. As the settee was only long enough for two people—or one person and a dog—Philip opted to stand. Leaning his shoulders against the mantel, he shot a glare at Prince who blithely ignored him. By God, it was a sad day when a man was actually jealous of his dog.

She lifted her cordial glass and smiled. "A toast, Lord Greybourne, to the success we achieved this evening. In spite of that near-disastrous misstep, I have a feeling tonight will result in everything we wanted."

With his gaze steady on hers, Philip reached out and touched the rim of his glass to hers. The ring of crystal echoed in the quiet room. "To getting everything we want."

She inclined her head, then took a delicate sip. "Delicious," she murmured. After setting her glass on the round mahogany end table, she opened her reticule and withdrew a piece of foolscap and a sheet of vellum. While unfolding them, she said, "I jotted down some notes during the cleanup process, which I referenced to the notes I took the other evening regarding your preferences."

"Very efficient. So you meant, quite literally, for us to compare notes. I'm afraid I failed to take any. But never fear. This"—he tapped his forehead—"is like a sealed dungeon, filled with all my impressions of the evening."

"Excellent." She looked down and consulted her two pages of notes. "There are a number of young ladies I feel are suitable; however, one in particular stands out. She is—"

"Oh, let's not begin with your first choice," Philip broke in. "Where's the fun in that? I suggest you begin at the bottom of your list, then work your way up to the grand finale. Makes the anticipation so much greater, you know."

"Very well. We'll begin with Lady Harriet Osborn. I believe she is an excellent candidate."

"No, I'm afraid she won't do at all."

"Whyever not? She is an accomplished dancer, and possesses a lovely singing voice."

"She doesn't like dogs. When I mentioned Prince, she wrinkled her nose in a way that indicated the beast would be immediately banished to the country estate."

Prince raised his head at that and issued a low growl, impressing Philip. By God, he very well might be the Smartest Dog in the World.

"See there? Prince wants nothing to do with a woman who would cast him from his home, and I'm afraid I have to agree with him. Who is next on your list?"

"Lady Amelia Wentworth. She is—"

"Completely unacceptable."

"Oh? Is she not fond of dogs?"

"I've no idea. But it doesn't matter. She is an abysmal

dancer." He lifted one booted foot and waggled it about. "My poor abused toes may never recover."

"I cannot see how her dancing ability enters into this, especially since I distinctly recall you saying that you yourself were not fond of dancing."

"Exactly. Your list of my preferences should read that my future bride be an accomplished dancer so as to instruct *me*."

"Surely Lady Amelia can improve her dancing with lessons."

"Impossible. She possesses absolutely no sense of rhythm whatsoever. Next?"

She glanced down at her list. "Lady Alexandra Rigby."

"No."

There was no mistaking the flare of impatience in her eyes. "Because . . . ?"

"I'm not the least bit attracted to her. In fact, I find her most off-putting."

Confusion replaced the impatience. "But why? She is extremely beautiful *and* an accomplished dancer."

"It goes back many years. Her family visited mine at Ravensly Manor the summer I was eleven. Lady Alexandra was two. One afternoon I came upon her in the gardens and caught her eating . . ." He cleared his throat. "For lack of a more delicate way to say it"—he dropped his voice to a whisper—"*rabbit droppings*."

Although she tried to disguise it as a cough, there was no mistaking the horrified laugh that emitted from Meredith's lips. "She was only *two* years old, Lord Greybourne. Surely many children that age do such things."

"*I* never did any such thing. Did you?"

"Well, no, but—"

He raised his hand, cutting off her words. "It is a most unfortunate image of Lady Alexandra I have never been able to erase from my mind. I'm afraid I must insist you file her under the category of 'Lips that have touched rabbit poo shall never touch mine.'" He waved his hand in rolling motion. "Who is next?"

"Lady Elizabeth Watson."

"Impossible."

"Really? Did she also make unfortunate food choices as a toddler?"

"I haven't a clue. However, I know she makes them as an adult. She smelled like Brussels sprouts."

"Don't tell me, let me guess. You've a particular dislike for Brussels sprouts."

"Yes. And cabbage, too, which is why you must cross Lady Berthilde Atkins off your list as well."

"Because she smells like—"

"Cabbage. I'm afraid so." He heaved a dramatic sigh. "Quite unfortunate really, as she had potential."

"I'm certain Lady Berthilde could be persuaded to adjust her eating habits."

"I couldn't dream of asking her to give up—for a *lifetime*—a food item she is obviously so very fond of. Next?"

She eyed him with clear suspicion. "Do you possess any other strong food aversions?"

He offered her a wide smile. "None that I can think of."

"All right." She consulted her list, then looked up at him. "Lady Lydia Tudwell."

He winced. "Won't do. She smells strongly of—"

"I thought there were no other food aversions—"

"—brandy, which is not a food. She quite reeked of the stuff. Clearly she . . ." He mimed tossing back several drinks in quick succession. "On the sly. Completely unacceptable. Next?"

"Lady Agatha Gateshold."

"No."

She huffed out a clearly exasperated breath. "We are

establishing a pattern here, my lord, that is not lost upon me. However, according to your list of preferences, Lady Agatha is a perfect candidate."

"I agree. Except for one thing. She carries a tendre for Lord Sassafrass."

"*Sassafrass?* I've never heard of him."

He shrugged. "Some foreign title. Italian, I believe. On the mother's side."

Doubt was written all over her face. "Lady Agatha made no mention of this attachment to me."

"Really? I'm certain she meant to. She sang his praises to me during our conversation. 'Lord Sassafrass this, Lord Sassafrass that.' It was obvious she was letting me know, in a rather unsubtle way, that she was not interested in me. I've certainly no wish to marry a woman who is in love with another man. Next?"

"Well, Lady Emily and Lady Henrietta—"

"Impossible. They both nearly swooned at the mere *mention* of sexual matters—"

"As any gently bred young woman would."

"Clearly you do not understand as much about the workings of the *ton* as you believe. No, neither Lady Emily nor Lady Henrietta will do. I'm certain their delicate constitutions could not withstand the actual act of lovemaking, and I *am* expected to produce an heir— hardly a feat I can accomplish by myself."

Color rushed into her face, and she stared at him for several seconds. He arranged his features into the picture of innocence. Clearing her throat, she said, "I distinctly recall you saying that you were not necessarily particular about the bride, so long as she was not overly off-putting. Yet now you seem to be most *extremely* particular."

"Hmmm. Yes, I suppose it must seem that way. Who is next?"

"Based on our lack of success thus far, I think I shall

simply move to the top of the list and hopefully save us both some time."

"And who sits upon the top of your list?"

"Lady Penelope Hickam."

"Ah, yes, Lady Penelope."

"Lady Penelope possesses *each and every* trait you yourself said you found admirable in a woman." Looking down, she consulted her list. "She enjoys music, plays the pianoforte, and sings like an angel. She appeared interested in your field of antiquarian studies, voiced no strong objection to dusty relics, and proved a proficient conversationalist on a variety of topics. Romantic drivel holds no appeal to her, and she is an expert at handling servants and running a household. In addition, she is fond of animals, an accomplished dancer, speaks French fluently, and adores embroidering." Looking up from her list, she favored him with a triumphant gleam in her eye. *Find something wrong with* her, that gleam clearly challenged.

"Hmmm. I believe you left one thing out."

Frowning, she once again looked at her list. Then, with a laugh, she looked up. "Only the 'classic, willowy beauty.' I did not mention it, as I felt it unnecessary. Lady Penelope is unquestionably beautiful."

"I think she's rather . . . pale."

Her eyes widened with obvious disbelief. "She's *blonde*."

"Ah, and therein lies the problem. I prefer dark hair."

With an exclamation of clear exasperation and impatience, she gently extricated herself from beneath Prince's sleeping form, then jumped to her feet, clutching her lists. Marching to the mantel, she planted her fists on her hips, then stuck out her jaw at an unmistakably stubborn angle. "What is this nonsense? You most certainly do not prefer dark hair."

He puckered his face into an expression of bewilderment. "Are you certain? Because I'm quite positive I do. And surely that is something I would know."

"You are making sport of me, Lord Greybourne, and I do not like it." She shook her list under his nose. "It is written right here. I wrote it myself the other evening. You said you liked"—she looked at the list, then pointed to the words—"classically beautiful blondes."

"Actually, it was *Andrew* who said that."

"You said nothing to indicate he was mistaken."

"He wasn't mistaken. I'd be hard-pressed to name any man who would not admire—however briefly—a classically beautiful blonde. However, *I* prefer dark hair."

He heard a tapping sound and realized it was her shoe hitting the stone hearth in a staccato click of clear annoyance. "You made no mention of this the other evening."

"I confess my preference is of a rather recent nature."

The tapping increased. "Indeed? How recent? Since I paraded a roomful of 'classically beautiful blondes' through your drawing room?"

"No. Before that."

"When?"

His gaze shifted to her hair. Reaching out, he captured one of the shiny tendrils framing her face, rubbing the glossy strands between his thumb and index finger. The tapping abruptly stopped, and she drew in a sharp breath.

"Do you really want to know, Meredith? Because I can tell you, almost to the exact moment, when my preference changed."

Everything inside Meredith went perfectly still. His words, the soft, husky voice in which they were spoken, the heat simmering in his gaze, effectively shut her up, halting her breath. Dear God, there was no mistaking his meaning or the desire all but emanating from him in waves. Her heart sputtered back to life with a slow, hard pound so loud it echoed in her ears. So loud he surely must hear it.

"Actually, there was one woman at the party who captured my interest, and, I would very much like for you to arrange another meeting between us."

She swallowed once. Hard. She had to stop this. Now. "Lord Greybourne, I—"

"Philip. Please call me Philip. Would you like me to tell you about this woman?" Before she could reply—which would have taken a while, considering she could not seem to locate her voice—he said, his fingers still playing with her hair, "Her hair is dark, like a desert night. Its glossy color is like the rich, black soil deposited along the banks of the Nile each year after the spring floods. Her hair is, in fact, identical to yours."

Desperate to add some levity, to dispel the foglike tension, she attempted a smile. "Are you saying my hair reminds you of *dirt*?"

Instead of answering, he eased pins from her hair until her tresses spilled over his hands. *Stop him!* her inner voice commanded, but her lips refused to vocalize the command. All vestiges of mirth disappeared, leaving her floundering in a sea of awareness and aching longing that threatened to drown her. He sifted his long fingers through her curls, and she had to bite down on her lip to keep from purring.

"Dirt? No. Your hair . . . her hair . . . is vibrant. Silky. Glossy. Lovely."

He slowly traced his fingertips over her face. Every nerve ending tingled, and her eyes slid closed at the sheer pleasure of his touch. "This woman who has captured my interest . . . she is not a classic beauty. Her features are too stark and angular."

The feathery caress of his fingertip tickled over her lips, and her eyes flew open. His gaze was fixed on her lips with a compelling intensity that sizzled heat straight to her core. "Her mouth is too wide and mobile, her lips too rosy and plump. Yet it is the sort of mouth that inspires sensual fantasies, and distracts me from all the other things I should be thinking about."

Breathless, heart thumping, she listened, as if in a trance, while his fingers continued their exploration of her face. "Her nose is a shade too wide, and her jaw far too stubborn. Yet she attracts me like no classic beauty ever has. Her smile is enchanting, and illuminates her entire face. She has a tiny dimple, just there"——he skimmed the pad of his thumb over the corner of her mouth—"that winks when she grins. Her skin is like velvet cream stained with peach that deepens and pales in the most fascinating way depending on her mood. And her eyes . . . her eyes are extraordinary. The same vivid aqua as the Aegean, just as deep, just as fathomless. They are expressive, yet they hide things as well, which only serves to intrigue and bewitch me further. Her features are, in fact, identical to yours."

He stepped closer to her, drawing her into his arms. It seemed the most natural thing in the world to slip her arms around his waist. He pulled her closer, until their bodies touched from chest to knee. His hardness pressed against her, flooding her with heat that settled between her thighs. Her nipples hardened, and she knew her cheeks flamed bright, knew her eyes and expression and flushed face gave away everything she was feeling. Still, she could not look away from him. From his eyes, the want and need in them magnified all the more by his spectacles. From the muscle jerking in his cheek, a testament to his fight for control—the same fight waging in her, and a battle she very much feared she was on the brink of losing.

He leaned down and kissed the side of her neck. Her eyes slid closed. A long, breathy sigh escaped her, and she tilted her head to allow him better access.

"Her scent," he whispered, his warm breath caressing her neck, "drives me mad. She smells like fresh-baked goods . . . warm and enticing, tempting and delicious. How is it that a woman can smell so sweet? Every time I'm near her I want to just take a bite." His teeth scraped gently against her skin, eliciting a shiver of delight. "Her scent is, in fact, identical to yours.

"And her form," he continued, before she could catch her breath, "puts that of any so-called classic beauty to shame." His hands slowly roamed her back, from her shoulders to her buttocks, pressing her closer to him while he continued to trail drugging kisses along her neck, his words breathing heat against her skin. "She fits against me as if the gods fashioned her for me alone. I danced with two dozen women this evening, but she was the only one who felt right in my arms. She felt, in fact, exactly as you feel now."

He lifted his head, and she instantly mourned the loss of his lips against her. "Meredith. Look at me."

With an effort, she dragged her heavy eyelids open. He was looking at her as if he wanted to devour her. As if she were the most beautiful, desirable thing he'd ever seen. Surely that should have alarmed her. Brought back her missing common sense. But instead it enthralled her. Excited her. And filled her with the reckless sort of abandon she'd strived to pummel into submission for as long as she could remember.

Keeping one arm wrapped around her, he combed the fingers of his other hand through her hair. "Those golden-haired society diamonds you paraded in front of me this evening all pale in comparison to you. I have never, in my entire life, been so painfully attracted to a woman as I am to you. I cannot stop thinking about you. God knows I've tried. After our kiss last night, after I'd tasted you, I thought it would be enough, that I could forget you. But I cannot. That kiss only made me crave more. . . ."

He lowered his head until his lips hovered just above hers. "Is it only me who feels this way, Meredith? Or did our kiss make you want more as well?" His warm, brandy-scented breath touched her, intoxicating her as if she'd actually partaken of the potent liquor. Her heart and mind waged a brief battle, but there was no contest. Raising up on her toes, she spoke a single word against his lips. "More."

All the pent-up longing and need Philip had held in check erupted like a volcano. He captured her lips in a wild, desperate kiss, all fire and raw need. His tongue caressed the silky heaven of her mouth, while his arms tightened around her. His inner voice tried in vain to inject reason, warning him that he was exhibiting an appalling lack of finesse. But any small chance reason might have had of exerting itself was instantly banished by her heated response.

Lost in a mindless, heated fog, his hands skimmed down her back to cup her rounded buttocks, then raced upward to tangle in the fragrant silk of her hair. One hand then smoothed downward again, tracing her delicate collarbone, absorbing the frantic pulse throbbing at the base of her throat. Then lower, until he cupped the fullness of her breast. Her breath caught, a tiny sound of feminine arousal that tensed every muscle in his body. Her nipple beaded against his palm, and his fingers circled the aroused peak through the thin muslin of her gown.

She squirmed against him, and his erection jerked in response, eliciting an animal groan from him. He cursed the clothing that barred her soft skin from him. He was desperate to touch her. Desperate to have her hands on him. So desperate that in the infinitesimal part of his brain that was still functioning, he recognized that if he didn't stop this now, he would be unable to stop at all.

Breaking off their kiss, he rested his forehead against hers. Eyes squeezed shut and pulling in ragged, shuddering breaths, he tried to calm his racing heart, but it was damn difficult while her soft body remained flush against his. While her breast still filled his palm. While she still clung to him in a way that indicated her knees were less than steady—much like his own.

After several seconds, he straightened and opened his

eyes. And saw nothing but fog. Damn spectacles. Fabulous invention for many pursuits, but kissing was most definitely not one of them. Reluctantly releasing her breast, he lifted his hand to remove the steamed-over lenses, only to feel her small, soft hand halt his halfway to his face.

"May I?" she asked softly.

He wasn't certain what she was asking permission to do, but he wasn't about to deny her anything. "Of course."

She gently removed his glasses, then set them carefully on the mantel. He blinked, feeling very much like an owl. Bloody hell, he no doubt looked like one, too. Since a piece of vellum could not have fit between them, he saw her face clearly. He knew if he took one step backward, she would turn blurry.

After studying his face with unabashed curiosity, the remnants of unmistakable arousal still lingering in her eyes, she said softly, "I'd wondered what you looked like without your spectacles." She tilted her head from side to side, as if viewing a museum piece

When the silence stretched between them, he finally asked, "Well?"

Her lips twitched. "Are you casting about for compliments again?"

"I wouldn't presume to hope for one. I'm merely curious."

"You look far less studious. Rather boyish, in fact." She reached up and brushed a lock of hair from his forehead, an intimate gesture that stilled him. "Or perhaps that is just because your hair is disarranged."

"As is yours. In a very charming way."

Meredith looked into his brown eyes, at the passion still simmering in their depths, and felt an answering stir in her body. Her common sense coughed back to life, bringing with it all the reasons that she should not be doing this. Drawing a deep breath, she stepped back, out of the circle of his arms.

"Lord Greybourne—"

"Philip. Surely after what we just shared you can call me by my given name."

Warmth crept up her neck. He looked so incredibly tempting, his hair tousled from her explorations, his cravat askew, his eyes dark with unmistakable desire.

Two steps. It would require only two steps forward for her to be once again wrapped in his strong arms, to feel his warm, hard body against her, to again experience the magic and wonder of his kiss. And the urge to take those two steps was so overwhelming it frightened her. This interlude was something she never should have begun. But since she had and couldn't change it, it was certainly time that she ended it.

Lifting her chin, she adopted her most businesslike brisk air. "Philip, about what happened here this evening, it was . . ." *Incredible. Intense. Heart-stopping. Frightening.*

And impossible.

She cleared her throat. "It was the result of a lapse of judgment on my part."

"I beg to differ. It was the result of this powerful attraction between us." He reached out to touch her, and she quickly sidestepped him, moving to put the settee between them. This was difficult enough to say. If he touched her, she feared she'd lose her resolve altogether. He made no further move to touch her; rather, he plucked his spectacles from the mantel and slid them on.

Pressing her hands together, she straightened her back and looked him directly in the eye. "Obviously I cannot deny I find you attractive."

"Just as I cannot deny I find you attractive." He shifted a bit. "Painfully so."

Heat crept up her neck as she recalled the delicious sensation of his hardness pressed against her. "Be that as it may, last night, at Vauxhall, you said, and I agreed, that allowing this to happen again would be a mistake of gargantuan proportions."

"When I said that, I was merely stating what I thought would be *your* view of the situation. It was not my view, nor did I agree."

"Semantics. The fact remains that we cannot act upon this attraction again."

"Why?"

"*Why?* Surely you can see this is impossible. There are dozens of reasons why."

"Then please, share these dozens of reasons with me, for I cannot think of one." He leaned his shoulders against the mantel, folded his arms across his chest, and crossed his booted ankles. "You have my full attention."

"You're making sport of me again."

"On the contrary, I am very serious. We've admitted we are attracted to each other. Even after our kiss last evening, I still thought I could ignore what's between us, but clearly I am mistaken. *I* would very much like to see where this attraction leads. You clearly have objections, whereas I have none."

"But that is the entire point! This attraction cannot lead anywhere."

"Again, I must ask. Why?"

"Are you being deliberately obtuse? Where precisely do you think it could lead? You are bound by your promise to *marry*. I am supposed to be finding you a suitable *bride*. We can hope that in a matter of mere days you will have a *wife*. Please, let us be honest with each other. There is absolutely no room for me in your life. The only two possible outcomes for this attraction are utterly impossible—I cannot marry you, and I won't be your mistress."

Silence, thick and heavy, descended between them, broken only by the ticking of the mantel clock. Nearly a minute passed before he spoke. "Just out of curiosity, assuming I am able to break the curse and marry at all, would marrying me prove such a dreadful hardship?"

The quiet note of underlying hurt and confusion in his question tugged at her heart in a completely unacceptable way. A lump clogged her throat, forcing her to swallow twice before she could trust herself to speak. "Whoever you choose will be a very fortunate woman. I've no doubt you will be a wonderful husband and . . . father. And that woman will, of course, be of impeccable breeding and from a station similar to yours. I am, obviously, not that woman. And even if I were, as I've told you before, I've no desire to ever marry."

"A statement I find most curious. Why do you harbor this aversion to the one thing most women aggressively strive for?"

If you only knew . . . "I am very satisfied with my life exactly as it is. I enjoy my work and the measure of independence it affords me. In addition, Albert, Charlotte, and Hope depend on me, and the feeling is mutual. I would never do anything to disrupt the close-knit family we've built. As for the other option—"

"Becoming my mistress?"

"Yes. I refuse to endanger my reputation, as it would harm not only me, but my family as well. I fought too long and hard to earn my respectability to risk it."

His gaze turned questioning, and she instantly realized she'd said too much. To forestall any questions, she rushed on. "I've learned that it is futile to look back, to wallow in regrets. We can only move forward and hope to learn from our mistakes."

"An admirable philosophy, yet I hear the voice of experience there, Meredith. What sort of mistakes have you made?"

"We all make mistakes," she said, forcing her tone to remain light. "My most recent one occurred only moments ago in this very room."

He stared at her with an unreadable expression for several heartbeats, then blew out a long breath. "Well. One of the things I liked about you right from the start was your ability to state things in a clear, concise manner." He inclined his head in salute. "You've quite outdone yourself this time."

Guilt, for the hurt in his voice, and profound regret that things could not be different, collided in her. Drawing a deep breath, she said, "I'll always treasure what we shared, Philip. I'm not sorry it happened. We simply cannot allow it to happen again."

Yet even as the words passed her lips, her inner voice yelled, *Liar!* For she was sorry. Deeply sorry. For herself and the torment the memory of his kiss, his touch, would bring to her. And deeply sorry because those few precious moments in his arms had opened the floodgates to the feminine yearnings she'd so carefully guarded for all these years, making her ache with needs and desires she knew would haunt her long into the lonely nights ahead.

She'd told him she didn't wallow in regrets, but she knew that tonight, once she was tucked under the covers, she would allow herself one night to wallow, to grieve for her past that would forever keep her from having a man like Philip.

Not trusting himself to be alone with her, Philip arranged for Bakari to accompany Meredith home. Before she left, he explained what had occurred at the warehouse, and cautioned her to be careful. After watching his carriage disappear down the darkened street, he sat on the settee, next to the still-sleeping Prince. Propping his elbows on his knees, Philip lowered his head into his hands.

Bloody hell, what a night.

Pushing aside his conflicted thoughts regarding Meredith for the moment, he turned his attention to the matter he'd forced aside for the bulk of the evening—Edward's disturbing revelations. Who had attacked him? Had he stolen anything? If so, what? And why? A knot formed in his stomach. Surely it couldn't be the one item Philip sought. *The suffering begins now. . . .* Bloody hell, what did that mean? He didn't know, but he was determined to find out who was behind this. He'd arrive early at the warehouse and assess the damage. He hoped Andrew would feel well enough to accompany him.

Pulling off his spectacles, he rubbed the heels of his palms against his forehead as thoughts of the other part of the evening bombarded him. The party. Granted, most of the young women had been pleasant, and all were undeniably beautiful. Unfortunately, not one had kindled the least spark of interest in him.

Except Meredith.

What had she meant about fighting too hard and long for her reputation? Had it been compromised at some point? Something in her voice when she'd spoken of mistakes led him to wonder exactly how serious some of her past mistakes might have been.

But did any past mistakes really matter? No. Meredith Chilton-Grizedale was without a doubt the woman he wanted. There were some things you could fight, and others you simply could wage no defense against. There was no doubt which category Meredith fell into.

Now he just needed to decide what the bloody hell he was going to do about it.

Ten

Philip was just finishing his predawn breakfast when Bakari appeared in the dining room doorway. "Your father," he said.

The earl entered the room. His cheeks were pale, and dark circles shadowed his eyes, but he otherwise appeared surprisingly fit, walking with a spry step. He was, as always, perfectly turned out in a Devonshire brown coat, fawn breeches, blinding white shirt, and intricately tied cravat. Philip idly wondered if Father's valet ever slept.

"Good morning, Philip." He nodded at the footman. "Coffee, if you please."

"Father. How are you feeling today?"

"Quite well, thank you. Better, in fact, than I've felt in weeks."

"Glad to hear it." Philip glanced pointedly at the mantel clock. "Although perhaps you should be resting? It's rather early for a visit."

"I wanted to catch you before you took yourself off for the day. I knew you'd be awake—you've always been an early riser, and obviously I haven't dragged you from your bed." His sharp gaze raked over Philip's appearance. "Or have I? You're looking a bit disheveled, although that is hardly surprising."

"I didn't sleep well." He nearly laughed at the understatement. He hadn't slept at all. The question of what he should do about Meredith had kept him tossing and turn-ing, weighing his options, examining the facts, until he'd finally drawn his conclusion—the only possible solution.

"Mind filled with images of all those lovely beauties, eh, Philip?"

"Something like that, yes."

"That's why I'm here—to discuss last night's festivi-ties." Father cocked a single brow. "Well, did the party have the desired result? Did you meet a woman willing to take you on?"

No doubt Philip should have been offended by the brusquely worded question, but instead his lips twitched with amusement. "I'm not quite sure."

"Meaning what, precisely?"

"Meaning I met a woman *I'd* like to take on—"

"Excellent."

"—but the lady has expressed some reservations."

"Bah. What woman wouldn't want to marry the heir to an earldom?

"For starters, one who isn't eager to risk expiring two days after the nuptials."

His father waved his hand in a dismissive gesture. "Who is the chit?"

"I'd prefer not to say just as yet. Suffice it to say I've made my choice. Now I just need to convince the lady—which is exactly what I plan to do." Indeed, in order to keep his agreement with his father, he'd been fully pre-pared to marry a woman he didn't even know. Well, he *knew* he desired Meredith. And he believed they'd be well suited. Surely he could convince her of that. The bigger problem would be finding a way to protect her and con-vincing her to take him on if he was not able—because of the curse—to marry her.

The footman set the coffee at Father's elbow, and the earl absently stirred the richly fragrant brew with his spoon. "You haven't much time to court her, Philip. I met with Doctor Gibbens yesterday. He says I've two, perhaps three months left. I want to see you settled, maybe even know there's an heir on the way."

A wave of sadness, regret, and loss washed over Philip. For all the things he and his father hadn't shared. Would never share. He made a mental vow that he'd never allow the walls that separated him and Father to be erected between him and his children. "I am doing, and will continue to do, everything in my power to honor our agreement, Father. But you also need to accept the possibility that I may be unable to honor it."

"I'm not a man who likes to contemplate failure, Philip."

"Neither am I. Most especially now that I've found the woman I want."

"Toward that end, I suggest you quit dawdling over breakfast and get yourself to the warehouse to continue your search."

"I plan to do just that, but first I need to tell you something." He quickly related the events that took place at the warehouse last night, concluding with a request that his father be extra careful and alert. "It's clear to me that something more than simply the curse is going on, but I don't know what, or who is behind it. But rest assured I'll find out." Swallowing his last sip of coffee, Philip rose. "Now, if you'll excuse me, Father, I wish to ready myself to depart for the warehouse."

Father's jaw tightened with grim determination as he, too, rose. "I'll come with you. The more of us searching, the quicker we can get through the crates."

"It is dirty, exhausting work—"

"I shall not overtire myself. I'm having a 'good' day today, and I'll not spend it lying about in bed. I want to help you."

"All right." It was useless to argue once Father made up

his mind. He'd simply make certain his father did nothing more strenuous than marking the ledger books.

"You sound surprised that I would offer my assistance, Philip. I'm concerned for your welfare and do not like the ominous sound of the note Edward found. And as for this curse, well . . . although I remain unconvinced of its authenticity, in spite of what you might believe, I would want you to have nothing less than the woman you want . . . son."

Philip's throat tightened at his father's gruff-voiced statement. His father hadn't called him son since Mother's death. Not once, either in conversation or during their correspondence. The fact that he had now clearly indicated Father was extending an olive branch, a peacemaking gesture Philip grasped, as it gave him hope that perhaps they could, upon Philip's marriage, put the past behind them.

"Thank you. I welcome the company." As they exited the dining room, Philip said, "Since Andrew has not yet arisen, I can only assume he is still not feeling well. I hope he will feel better later on and join us as well."

"Stanton is ill, you say? Too bad. Must have come upon him quite suddenly. He looked quite fit when I saw him last evening."

"Last *evening*? What time?"

"Must have been close to eleven, as I was in my carriage, coming home from my club. He was walking along Oxford."

"And what were *you* doing out at eleven last evening, Father? Surely the doctor does not recommend such late-night excursions."

Red suffused his father's pale cheeks. "I felt quite fit last evening and stopped by my club. The doctor encourages such outings if I'm up to it. Raises my spirits and all that."

"I see. But as for Andrew, you must be mistaken. He took to his bed shortly before seven."

"I was certain it was he. . . . Obviously I was mistaken. But your friend Stanton has a double here in London."

" 'Tis said that everyone has one somewhere," Philip said. He chuckled. "Although heaven help us if there are actually two Andrew Stantons running about."

Philip turned in a slow circle, his boots scraping against the rough wooden warehouse floor, as he surveyed the area surrounding two of his crates. Signs of a struggle were obvious in the scuff marks in the wood and the scattered pieces of broken artifacts. Crouching down, Philip picked up a jagged piece of glossy red pottery. Samian, second century A.D. He'd purchased the vase from an artifact dealer in Rome known for acquiring exquisite pieces, sometimes through dubious means. The loss of something so beautiful, which had survived for hundreds of years, offering a priceless glimpse into the past that could never be replaced, cramped his stomach with sick anger. And even more sickening was the realization that Edward could easily have ended up as broken as the pottery. With painstaking care, he could endeavor to reconstruct the vase. The same could not be said if that bastard had killed Edward.

"Has much been lost?" Father asked.

"Difficult to tell. I'd guess several pieces. I will know more after I compare the remaining contents to the ledger." He dragged his hands down his face. "It could have been much worse."

Father's hand swept in an arc, encompassing the debris. "Can they be salvaged?"

"I'll try, although they will, of course, never be the same." He retrieved the leather pouch he'd set down near one of the crates. Opening the drawstring, he pulled out a piece of cotton sheeting. "I need to gather the pieces on this sheet, leaving space between them, then roll up the cloth to protect the fragments. The chair in the office is quite comfortable."

"I did not come here to sit."

"I know, but I'm afraid this task requires crawling about on the hands and knees."

One of Father's brows shot upward. "I'm not the creaking relic you clearly think me. My hands and knees are in perfectly good condition."

In spite of the serious circumstances, a smile pulled at Philip. "As an expert on creaking relics, I can confirm that you are not one. I was thinking of your fashionable attire. If you kneel on this floor, an act of Parliament won't get those breeches clean."

"Pshaw." He slowly lowered himself into a kneeling position, moving so gingerly, his face twisted into such a grimace, Philip had to clench his teeth to keep from laughing.

"There," Father said, his voice tinged with pride when he'd accomplished the task.

"Excellent. Just move carefully so as not to crush any fragments."

While they worked, gently setting broken pieces of various colors on the sheet, Philip answered his father's myriad questions regarding the rugs, furniture, silks, and other goods he'd brought from abroad for their joint importing business venture. More than an hour of surprisingly companionable conversation had passed when Father said, "Look what I found under this crate. It looks much too new to be one of your artifacts. Indeed, it looks very much like the one I carry."

Philip turned. A knife dangled between Father's fingers, its shiny, lethal blade reflecting the morning sunlight streaming through the windows. Philip reached out, and his father carefully passed him the handle.

"This is most likely the assailant's knife. Edward said the bastard lost it during their scuffle." Philip examined the piece but could not discern any distinguishing marks. It was simply a common boot knife. Most men he knew, himself included, carried one just like it—Andrew, Edward, Bakari, and, as he'd just learned, his father.

Slipping the knife into his own boot, Philip said, "I'll hand this over to the magistrate." He resumed the painstaking task of gathering the pottery fragments. They were nearly finished when the creak of the warehouse door announced someone's arrival. "Lord Greybourne, are you here?"

His body instantly tightened at the sound of Meredith's smoky, feminine voice, and he swallowed the humorless sound that rose in his throat. What defense could he ever wage, what prayer of restraint could he hope to achieve, against a woman who affected him so with merely her _voice_?

"I'm here," he said, wincing at the strained, husky note in his own voice. Turning to his father, he said, "Miss Chilton-Grizedale." The sound of a heavier, scraping tread reached his ears. "Accompanied by her butler, Albert Goddard." _Who loves her._

Both Philip and his father rose, and he pressed his lips together to keep from grinning at the dirt staining the knees of Father's formerly pristine breeches. He'd never seen his father looking so untidy. Yet in spite of his ruined attire, satisfaction for a job accomplished gleamed in Father's eyes. Seconds later Meredith and Goddard appeared around the corner. His gaze locked with Meredith's, and for the barest instant a knowing, intimate look flared in her eyes. Then, as if a curtain shrouded her expression, her eyes filled with a cool indifference that set his teeth on edge.

Philip's gaze flicked to Goddard, who stood next to Meredith like a knight errant guarding his lady, glaring at

Philip. If Philip weren't grateful to the young man for protecting Meredith, he'd most likely be highly annoyed at the visual daggers being thrown in his direction. He quickly introduced Father and Goddard. His father then made Meredith a formal bow.

"You are to be congratulated, Miss Chilton-Grizedale," Father said. "Last evening's party produced the desired results."

"I'm not certain I know what you mean, my lord."

"The goal was to find a suitable bride for my son. He told me this morning that one particular young lady made quite an impression on him. I've every confidence the wedding will take place on the twenty-second as we'd hoped."

Twin crimson flags rose on Meredith's cheeks. Her gaze flew to Philip's. Myriad expressions flashed in her eyes, so rapidly he couldn't read them. Confusion? Concern? Dismay?

"I'm happy to hear it, my lord," she said, her voice tight. She averted her gaze, panning over the fragments spread out on the sheets. "Oh, dear." Once again she looked at Philip, this time her eyes filled with distress. "These were broken last night?"

"I'm afraid so."

"I'm so sorry. It hurts *me* to see this—I cannot even fathom how heartbreaking it is for you. You must be sick over the loss."

Her sympathetic commiseration washed over him like a warm, soothing rain, overwhelming him with the desire to draw her into his arms. Not, of course, that he would have forgotten himself in such a way, but even if he had, he was certain the scowling Goddard would have happily reminded him—with his fists.

"How can we help?" she asked.

He explained the procedure, adding, "I think we've collected most of the broken pieces. Once we're finished, we can start on the opened crates to see if anything is missing." Guessing that Goddard might find it painful to crawl about on his bad leg, but suspecting the young man would rather die than admit as much, Philip said to him, "I haven't as yet had the opportunity to look around the rest of the warehouse to see if anything else might have been disturbed. Care to join me?"

A muscle jerked in Goddard's jaw, and Philip could almost read his thoughts. He was damning his physical limitations that had prompted Philip's offer, knowing exactly why Philip had made the suggestion, and resenting the hell out of it. Finally Goddard nodded.

Philip slowly led the way through the labyrinth of crates, deliberately moving away from the area where Meredith and his father worked. When he was assured they were far enough away not to be overheard, he turned to face Goddard.

"You have something to say to me." It was a statement rather than a question.

A dull flush crept over the young man's face. Reaching out one hand to balance himself, he drew himself up to his full height and glared at Philip. "I don't like the way ye look at her."

Philip didn't pretend to misunderstand. Damn it, he knew how he looked at her. And in all fairness, he couldn't blame Goddard. Philip would feel precisely the same way about any other man who looked at Meredith with the desire he knew he himself was unable to hide. And he also couldn't stop the sympathy coursing through him. He had no wish to stomp upon Goddard's emotions. While he hadn't suffered from a physical affliction as serious as Goddard's, he'd been physically awkward, clumsy, and pudgy until he reached his majority. He recalled the pain all too well.

Yet he knew that while Meredith's feelings for Goddard ran deep, she was not in love with him. She wasn't the sort of woman who would kiss him as she had if her heart belonged to another man. What exactly was the nature of their relationship?

Keeping his gaze steady on Goddard, Philip said quietly, "And I can tell by the way *you* look at her that you love her."

"Damned right I do, and that gives me certain rights. Like warnin' off fancy blokes what look at her like she's some tasty morsel to sample, then spit aside when the flavor's gone."

"That is not my intention."

"Is that so?" Goddard stuck out his jaw at a belligerent angle. "What exactly are yer intentions, then?"

"That is personal, between Meredith and me. But, knowing how you feel about her, I want to assure you that I . . . care for her. And would do nothing to hurt her."

"Ye already have, you and yer bloody curse. Her reputation is *everything* to her. Ye've already damaged her business. And the way ye look at her makes it obvious ye think to ruin her as well." Goddard's lips curled back in a sneer. "Ye high-and-mighty lords think that any piece that catches yer fancy is fair game for yer attentions. But Miss Merrie's too smart to fall victim to that. She's run her whole life from it."

"What does that mean? Run her whole life from what?"

Something flashed in Goddard's eyes, something that clearly indicated he'd said too much, and he pressed his lips together. When it became clear Goddard wasn't going to elaborate, Philip asked, "And how do you know that *your* feelings won't get the better of you, won't lead you to do something that could compromise her?"

A muscle jerked in Goddard's jaw. His gaze raked over Philip, as if trying to decide how to answer. Finally he said, "I love her, but not in the way ye're implyin'. She ain't old enough to be my mum, but that's what she's been to me, and that's how I love her. She took care of me all those years, and now that I'm old enough, it's my turn to look after her. I'd do anythin' for her." Goddard's eyes narrowed to slits. "*Anythin'*."

There was no mistaking the young man's meaning. Clearly if Meredith said, *Chop off Lord Greybourne's head,* Goddard would sharpen his axe. One could only hope she wouldn't make such a request. There was no denying his relief that Goddard wasn't in love with Meredith. Yet his words only led to more questions.

"What do you mean, she's been a mum to you?"

Again he hesitated, as if debating whether to answer or not. Finally he said, "Had no mum or dad, least not as I can remember. Only person I had was Taggert, the chimney sweep. I was one of his climbin' boys." Goddard's eyes and voice went flat. "He had others besides me. Kept us all together in a small, filthy room. One day, while cleanin' out a chimney, I fell." His gaze flicked down to his leg. "I remember fallin', but I must have hit my head hard, 'cause I don't remember nothin' else till I woke up and found meself starin' into an angel's blue eyes. Thought I'd died and somehow made it to heaven. Soon found out that the angel was Miss Merrie, a stranger to me. She'd picked me up out of the gutter where Taggert had dumped me. I weren't no use to him anymore."

"Good God," Philip muttered, a sensation akin to nausea rolling through him at such unspeakable cruelty. "How old were you?"

He shrugged. "Not sure. 'Bout eight. At least that's wot Miss Merrie figured. Didn't know when my birthday was, so Miss Merrie named that day my birthday. She's given me a fine party every year since, with cake and biscuits and presents."

"What ever happened to this Taggert?"

A combination of hatred and fear burned in his eyes. "I don't know. I can only hope the bastard's dead."

"So Meredith brought you home to live with her family?"

"She took me in to live with *her*. She were like a mum to me. Fed me, clothed me, taught me to read and cipher numbers. It were just Miss Merrie and me till five years ago when Charlotte and Hope came along."

"She lived *alone* when she found you? She couldn't have been more than fifteen, sixteen. How—?"

"Forget that. Don't matter none." Goddard's voice resembled a low growl, and his hands fisted at his sides. "Wot's important is you knowin' wot kind of lady she is. Kind. Respectable. I owe her my life, and by God, I won't let you or anyone else do her harm in any way."

A fissure of shame snaked down Philip's spine. The bumps he'd viewed as hardships in his privileged life faded to insignificance when compared to the horrors this young man had suffered.

His gaze steady on Goddard's, Philip said, "I would never harm her. And even before you told me your story, I knew she was kind and respectable."

"And what of this lust ye feel for her?"

"I won't deny I feel it, but it is only one portion of the emotions she inspires. You're assuming that this is only one-sided. What if she has feelings for me as well?"

Uncertainty flickered in Goddard's eyes. "I hadn't considered that," he conceded with obvious reluctance. "If she decided you made her happy . . . well, I want her happy."

Philip nodded. He felt a strong need to say something, but damned if he knew exactly what. His gaze involuntarily slipped down to Goddard's damaged leg. He instantly sensed the young man's tension.

"I don't be wantin' yer damn pity."

He looked up and met Goddard's glare. "That's not what I was thinking at all, although I cannot help but feel sorry for what you suffered as a child. No one, most especially a child, should be treated in such an inhumane manner. Indeed, rather than pity, you have my deepest admiration. Not many people would have been strong or brave enough to overcome such adversity. Thank you for telling me something so personal and painful, Goddard. Your loyalty and bravery toward Meredith are commendable."

Goddard blinked in clear surprise, then his tense features relaxed a bit. "I thank God every day she found me. I'm a lucky man."

Philip extended his hand. "I think you're *both* lucky."

The two men shared a measuring look. Then, after a nod, Goddard gripped his hand in a firm clasp. "Thank ye. Have to admit, ye're not exactly what I expected. Ye don't seem too bad, for a titled bloke, that is."

"Thank you. Now let's see if we *all* can't get lucky and find the missing piece of stone."

They walked back to where they'd left Meredith and the earl, this time walking along the outer wall, near the windows. They'd just turned the final corner when Philip halted so suddenly, Goddard bumped into his back. An arc of broken glass littered the wooden floor, sunlight pouring in from the broken window glinting off the jagged shards.

Goddard stepped around him and surveyed the situation. "Miss Merrie told me 'bout last night's break-in. This window's probably how the bloke what hurt yer friend got in."

A frown pulled down Philip's brows. "Perhaps . . . but from what Edward described, I thought the robber had subdued the guard, then simply walked in." Hell, had someone *else* broken in? After Edward's altercation? The sound of the heavy wooden door opening interrupted his thoughts. Brisk footfalls, obviously a man's, thudded on the floor. Seconds later, Mr. Danpry, the warehouse manager, rounded the corner. Philip had met the large-boned man the day the *Dream Keeper* had docked and his crates had been delivered.

Danpry stopped short at the sight of Goddard and Philip. "Lord Greybourne. I just heard about what happened here last night." His gaze skimmed over the broken glass, and his jaw hardened. "I'm confident they'll catch the fiend, my lord. The magistrate wants him, and the warehouse owner has personally hired a Runner."

"Excellent. I've looked around. It appears that nothing other than two of my crates were disturbed."

"You might have been the only one robbed, my lord, but this ain't just a simple burglary."

"Of course not. My friend and quite possibly your guard, were injured."

"The guard, Billy Timson, was more than injured, Lord Greybourne. He was found an hour ago. Floatin' in the Thames. This is now a murder."

They paired off, Meredith and Albert taking one crate, Philip and his father the other, a fact which relieved Meredith greatly. It was difficult enough being in the same room with Philip; standing shoulder to shoulder with him, their hands brushing as they removed the delicate artifacts, would prove pure torture.

For more than two hours, conversation consisted solely of naming items as they were removed from their respective crates and settled on the blankets covering the floor, during which time the air had grown unbearably warm.

Slipping her handkerchief from her sleeve, she dabbed at the moisture beading on her neck. Although she'd had no intention of looking at him, her errant gaze wandered toward Philip. He was lifting a small statue from the crate, his back toward her. Dusty streaks marred his white linen shirt, which also bore a T-shaped darkened stain that ran across his wide shoulders and bisected the center of his back where the material rested against his damp skin.

Her gaze traveled downward, over his hips and buttocks, continuing down the backs of his long, muscular
legs, all of which his snug breeches accentuated in a way
that did absolutely nothing to cool her.

At that moment he turned around, and her gaze
snapped upward, mortified to be caught staring. But his
attention was riveted on the palm-sized statue he held.
Just as her attention was riveted by the sight of him.

His hair was damp, the burnished streaks darkened by
the result of his toils. His glasses had slid down his nose,
and she had to plant her feet to keep from giving in to the
temptation to walk over and adjust the spectacles for him.
But even as the thought entered her mind, he pushed them
up himself.

Her gaze again wandered downward. Along with his
jacket, he'd discarded his cravat and loosened his shirt
around his neck, allowing her a pulse-quickening glimpse
of his tanned throat and a bit of his chest. She caught a
flash of shiny metal. The chain that held his gold coin. A
coin she knew lay nestled against his vibrantly warm skin.

Thanks to his labors, the front of his shirt also bore a
T-shaped stain, the material clinging to his chest and abdomen in a way that fired her imagination and curiosity.
His sinewy forearms drew her avid gaze next, and she
vividly recalled the feel of those strong arms holding her,
urging her closer. To his hands . . . strong, sun-browned
hands that now gently cradled a piece of ancient history.
Magic hands, with callus-tipped fingers that belied his
status as a titled gentleman, that had sifted through her
hair. Touched her lips. Caressed her breasts.

Down, down trailed her gaze, over his flat stomach,
then lower, to linger over the material stretched snugly
over the part of him that fascinated her in a way she desperately did not want to be fascinated.

Tearing her gaze away from *that,* she continued track-
ing lower, over his muscled thighs, down to his dusty,

scuffed black leather boots. He was dirty, disheveled, sweaty. She shouldn't find him the least bit appealing. And in truth she didn't. In truth, she found him *devastatingly* appealing. *Dangerously* appealing. Instead of being put off by his disordered appearance, she wanted nothing more than to strip him of his dirty clothing, then offer to bathe him.

Heat that had nothing to do with the oppressive warehouse air whooshed through her at the disturbing, unwanted erotic image of her running slick, soapy hands over a naked, aroused Philip. Giving herself a mental shake, she raised her gaze. And met his intense stare.

Behind his lenses his eyes burned with compelling awareness, the flames smoldering in those dark brown depths, leaving no doubt that he knew she'd looked at him in a way that no one would ever call proper. While he could not divine her exact thoughts, he clearly recognized the gist of them.

"Feeling overheated, Miss Chilton-Grizedale?" he asked in a silky voice.

Yes, damn you, and it's entirely your fault. "I think we are all suffering from the furnacelike temperature in here."

His gaze skimmed over her, and she inwardly grimaced. Surely she must resemble a bedraggled, limp dust rag. When their eyes met again, his expression was no less compelling, but now tempered with concern.

"Please forgive me. I was so wrapped up in my work, I failed to realize how uncomfortable you must be. As much as I appreciate your help, these are no conditions for a lady. I would be happy to escort you home."

"Nonsense. While I appreciate your concern, I am not a hothouse flower in need of pampering. I insist upon helping with the search. Time is of the essence, and I've a vested interest in you locating the missing piece of stone."

"Vested interest meaning that without the missing

stone, you will not be able to marry me off, preferably to one of those hothouse flowers whom I met last evening."

"I prefer to call them properly bred young ladies—"

"I'm certain you do."

"—and yes, marrying you off is the plan. We both stand to lose a great deal if you cannot break the curse."

Something she could not decipher flashed in his eyes. "No argument here on that point."

"I'm glad we understand each other."

"Beggin' yer pardon, Miss Merrie, Lord Greybourne," Albert broke in, making Meredith want to kiss him with gratitude for the interruption, "but I've just checked off the last item in the crate. Nothin's missing."

There was no mistaking Philip's relief, a sentiment Meredith wholeheartedly shared. "Excellent news," he said.

"Perhaps not," came the earl's grim voice. "I've just finished with our crate, Philip, and there's an item unaccounted for." He tapped his finger on the ledger. "According to your records, a 'gypsum vessel' should have been packed in this crate."

Philip gently set down the marble statue he still held, then looked at the spot where his father pointed. An odd expression passed over his face, then his complexion visibly paled. He dragged his hands down his face. "Damn. I should have noticed . . . should have made the connection."

"Noticed what?" Meredith asked, unable to keep the alarm from her voice.

"I recall seeing this entry when I examined the ledgers, but when I noted 'vessel' it didn't seem of any special significance, as I read it to be 'vessel' as in 'boat.' Not surprising, as you'll note that there are a predominance of nautical items in that particular crate. I assumed a boat carved from gypsum. But I should have considered that vessel might just as easily have meant 'box' of some sort.

And I certainly should have made the gypsum connection."

"What do you mean?" the earl asked. "What is gypsum?"

"It's a common mineral, been used for centuries to carve into vases, boxes, and such. It's also called alabaster . . . which is what the box I found containing the Stone of Tears was carved from." He exhaled a long breath. "It would seem that there was an alabaster box in this crate. And now it's gone."

Eleven

Only nine crates remained.

By six o'clock that evening, they'd completed searching through three more crates—without success. Discouraged, Philip called the work to a halt. His muscles ached, his damp shirt clung to him like an uncomfortable second skin he longed to shed, and hunger he couldn't ignore much longer grumbled in his stomach. Indeed, the work effort would have ended hours earlier if Meredith hadn't had the foresight to bring a basket filled with biscuits, scones, cheese, jam, and jars of cider.

He had no intention of quitting for the day, but some food and a change of clothing were in order. Besides, he couldn't expect anything more from his father, Meredith, or Goddard today. They'd all worked the entire day without a single word of complaint. He'd made his father take several breaks, but the earl appeared to thrive with the work, and was reluctant to quit each time Philip insisted he rest.

In addition to eating and changing his clothes, Philip also wanted to catch up with Andrew, who either was still not feeling well, or had gone to the museum. There was much they needed to discuss.

His father, followed by Goddard, headed down the long walkway toward the exit. Before Meredith fell in behind them, Philip asked, "May I have a word with you, Meredith?"

Goddard halted, looking over his shoulder at Meredith with a questioning gaze.

"It's all right, Albert," she said with a tired smile. "I'll be along in a moment."

With a nod, Goddard continued down the walkway.

When he was certain he couldn't be overheard, Philip walked toward her, halting when only two feet separated them. Streaks of dust marred her creamy cheeks and grayed her lustrous dark hair, to say nothing of the havoc her labors had wrought upon her brown gown. She looked tired, rumpled, and dirty. Yet even as guilt slapped him for causing her untidy state, he couldn't deny that even tired, rumpled, and dirty, he found her more appealing than any perfectly turned-out female he'd ever seen. His fingers all but itched with the desire to grab hold of her and rumple her further.

"I want to thank you for your tireless help today— yours and Goddard's—and for thinking to bring a hamper of food and drink. I'm afraid I tend to forget such mundane matters as hunger and thirst when I'm embroiled in something. Your forethought falls in the category of 'sheer genius.'"

She favored him with a tentative smile. "Thank you, but the truth is it falls more into the category of 'self-preservation.' I deduced we'd be here for most of the afternoon, and further suspected that no one would think of food or drink until we were all faint from hunger. I knew if *I* were the first person to suggest we abandon our work to seek out sustenance, I would be branded a—"

"Hothouse flower?"

"Precisely. And clearly my plan worked beautifully, for rather than categorizing me as a 'limp, weak, female,' you believe I'm a genius."

"Well, your offering was much appreciated, and absolutely delicious. One of the finest meals I've had in ages."

"That's only because you were so hungry. I'd wager that even if I'd served you sawdust patties you would have gobbled them up with nary a complaint."

"Hmmm. You may be right. But be that as it may, you quite saved the day, and in return for your generosity in providing me with such a wonderful meal, I would like to return the favor. Will you dine with me tomorrow evening?"

Wariness filled her gaze. "Dine with you?"

"Yes." His lips quirked upward. "I'm certain you don't mean to look and sound so horrified. I promise you won't be served sawdust patties."

He could see that she meant to refuse him. Before she could do so, he added, "This would be a perfect opportunity for me to get better acquainted with some of the ladies from last night's party."

She blinked twice, then a look of unmistakable relief, which he found most discouraging, passed over her features, instantly followed by what could have been a flash of disappointment, which he found most *en*couraging. "Oh! You mean to invite other people to join us?"

"I shall write the invitations myself. I think eight is a nice number for a dinner party—you, me, and six other young ladies. I'll look over last night's guest list and make my choices. May I count on you to come?"

"Yes. I'd be delighted."

"Excellent. I'll send Bakari 'round in my carriage to pick you up. Shall we say eight o'clock?"

"That will be fine." She looked at him for several seconds, then said quietly, "Philip . . . I'm glad that you're taking steps to further your acquaintance with these young ladies. Any one of them will make you an admirable, respectable wife."

"I'm counting on it, Meredith. We both want me to choose an admirable, respectable wife, and rest assured, I plan to see that we both get exactly what we want."

When Philip arrived home, Bakari informed him that Andrew had spent the day at the museum and was still not home. Philip ordered a hot bath, and while he waited for the tub to be filled, he retired to his private study with Bakari and took the edge off his appetite with several slices of freshly baked bread and a wedge of cheese.

After bringing Bakari up to date on the day's proceedings, he said, "I have a bad feeling, Bakari, this missing gypsum vessel might be the very thing we're searching for. And you know how my bad feelings have a disturbing propensity for proving correct."

Bakari shuddered. "The sandstorm in Thebes, the storm off Cyprus, the grave robbers in Cairo—don't remind Bakari."

"I find it extremely odd that it was the only thing missing, and you know I'm not one to put faith in coincidence. I didn't dwell on my concern, as I did not want to alarm the others. And I refuse to give up hope. There are still nine crates at the warehouse, and the *Sea Raven* with her cargo of the remaining artifacts will, I hope, arrive in the next several days. Perhaps this gypsum vessel was indeed a boat." He raked his hands through his hair. "Damn it all, I should have made the connection. I can only pray that this doesn't prove to be the most costly error of my life."

"Bakari pray, too," the small man said in a grave tone Philip recognized all too well. It was Bakari's "I'll pray for all I'm worth, but it probably won't do much good" voice. Bloody hell.

After finishing off his last bite of bread, Philip said, "There's something else I need to discuss with you. I'd like you to arrange a small, intimate dinner party for tomorrow evening. Mediterranean-style."

Bakari's black eyes glittered. "Intimate?"

"Yes." Philip outlined what he wanted, knowing Bakari would commit his instructions to memory and carry them out to the letter. When he finished his instructions, he rose. "My bath must be close to ready by now. By the time I'm finished, Andrew should be home. The dinner hour draws near, and it isn't like him to miss a meal."

Sure enough, when, freshly bathed and clothed, Philip entered the dining room forty-five minutes later, Andrew was seated at the cherrywood table, enjoying a bowl of what appeared to be a hearty soup. Nodding at the hovering footman to bring him the same, Philip slid into the chair across from Andrew, whose clothing and hair bore evidence of dust and grime.

"Glad to see you're feeling better."

"Not nearly as glad as I am." His gaze flicked over Philip's clean clothes and still damp hair. "I envy you your bath. I requested one, but I had to eat first. I think I quite horrified your staff by reporting to the dining room looking like something that's been dragged across a dusty floor. Thank God Bakari is here to act as a buffer, else I think I'd have been tossed outside."

After the footman set a steaming bowl in front of Philip, Philip dismissed him. He and Andrew ate in concentrated silence for several seconds before Philip spoke. "As you didn't pounce the moment I walked in with the good news that you'd found the missing stone, I assume today's search at the museum was unsuccessful?"

"Unfortunately, yes. Only three crates remain. Edward assisted me, at least as well as he could with his injured hand. He told me what happened last night. Nasty business. He's lucky he lived to tell the tale. Said he thought some artifacts were broken during the scuffle."

"Sadly, five were. However, it could have been much worse."

Andrew shot him a questioning look. "Was anything stolen?"

Philip filled him in on the day's events, reporting the guard's death and the missing gypsum vessel. "Damn it Andrew, I should have made the connection."

"I looked those ledgers over, as did Edward and Bakari. None of us picked up on it, Philip. Stop blaming yourself."

Philip nodded absently. "Clearly the same person is responsible for the robbery and the threatening notes. I need to discover his identity before anyone else is hurt. Toward that end, I'm planning to hire a Bow Street Runner to investigate. I think the person responsible is most likely someone who sailed on board the *Dream Keeper* with us. Someone who is familiar with the artifacts and the curse."

Andrew studied him for several seconds, then said, "Why not let me conduct the investigation? Edward can handle the remaining crates at the museum. I'm already acquainted with everyone from the *Dream Keeper,* and you know I'm capable of ferreting out information."

"Yes, you proved that when you recovered the stolen Aphrodite statue in Athens, and you're certainly capable of defending yourself should the need arise. You're certain you want to do this?"

"Yes. I want this bastard stopped as much as you do. I'll begin tomorrow morning."

"Excellent. Thank you." Relieved, and confident that Andrew would hunt down the truth, Philip said, "I also had an interesting conversation with Meredith's friend and butler, Albert Goddard, today." He briefly outlined the story Albert had related about how he'd come to live with Meredith.

"Goddard's fortunate to have survived such a horrid

childhood," Andrew said grimly. "Clearly there's more to your Miss Chilton-Grizedale than meets the eye."

"Yes, the lady is something of an enigma. And you know how I enjoy a puzzle."

"Is that what you intend to do? Enjoy her?"

"Actually, I've decided to take your advice."

"As well you should, since I am, ahem, rarely wrong. Er, which piece of wisdom, exactly, have you chosen to follow?"

He eyed Andrew over the rim of his wineglass. "I'm going to court her. Before I met Meredith, I was fully prepared to marry a woman I didn't know to honor my agreement with my father. Now that I must choose someone else to be my wife, I'd prefer to marry someone I . . . like. Someone I desire."

"A wise decision. I couldn't imagine marrying someone I didn't know. Of course, it would be undeniably better if you more than . . . liked Miss Chilton-Grizedale."

"I barely know her."

"From where I stand, you know all you need to. But liking and desiring her are certainly a good start. Since the sweeping romantic gesture is not your forte, I'd be happy to offer a few suggestions."

Philip narrowed his eyes. "Contrary to what you believe, I have made several such gestures before." *Several?* his inner voice snickered. *Fine. None.* But he'd certainly thought about it, had meant to make such a gesture. He'd just never met a woman who'd inspired him to do so. Until now. "And toward that end, I've invited Meredith to join me here for dinner tomorrow evening."

"A dinner party? I'd love to come."

"Pity. You're not invited."

"Ah. So it is *that* sort of party. Not to worry, I'll toddle off and make myself scarce. Believe I'll go back to Gentleman Jackson's Boxing Emporium. Quite enjoyed it last evening, and I'd like another crack at it." A lazy smile lifted one corner of Andrew's mouth. "Great way to work out the frustrations—pounding the piss out of someone in the ring. You know how I love a good fight."

"Last evening?" Philip's gaze dipped to Andrew's hand, and for the first time noticed the swollen, bruised knuckles. "I thought you'd taken to your bed."

"I had. I fell asleep after drinking Bakari's concoction, and awoke feeling much improved. Decided to head out and see something of the city. I recalled you mentioning Gentleman Jackson's during one conversation or another, and I decided to pay the establishment a visit."

"My father thought he saw you out and about, but I assured him it wasn't you. My relief knows no bounds that there aren't two of you running amok in London." A frown pulled his brows. "I wonder why Bakari didn't mention you'd gone out."

"I slipped down the servants' stairs so as not to disturb the party."

"You were welcome to join us."

"Very kind of you, I'm sure; however, I was afraid if I attended, all the ladies who were there for your perusal might be swept away by my fascinating American charm." He coughed modestly into his hand. "Didn't want to steal your thunder."

"Believe me, you were welcome to the lot of them. Save one."

"Hmm, yes. Miss Chilton-Grizedale. You may have fancied a young lady before, but I'm sure you realize there's a difference this time."

Philip nodded slowly. "Yes. This time it matters."

"Courting her will prove a challenge, especially since all her energies are focused on finding you a bride."

A slow smile pulled at Philip's lips, and he lifted his wineglass in salute. "Ah, but she needn't bother, as I've already chosen one. Besides, you know how I love a challenge." He glanced at the mantel clock. "And speaking of challenges, are you up for some crate-searching at the warehouse tonight?"

"Of course."

"Excellent. And while we're in the East End, on our way home, let's stop in a pub."

"Sounds intriguing. Are we looking for something—besides trouble?"

"Information."

"About . . . ?"

"A chimney sweep named Taggert."

The following morning, her eyes gritty from lack of sleep, Meredith sat in the gig, staring straight ahead while Albert handled the reins. He appeared lost in thought, for which she was grateful, as her own preoccupation rendered her silent.

Philip. Damnation, she had to stop thinking about him. But how? Last night he'd occupied every corner of her mind—which was bad enough, but it was the *way* he'd occupied her mind that was so unsettling.

She kept imagining stripping off his clothes, then running her hands over his warm flesh, exploring every muscle and plane. Then Philip returning the favor, slipping her gown from her body, his mouth and hands touching her everywhere, then making love to her with slow, languorous, exquisite care.

The images had danced in her head all night, invading her dreams when she'd managed to doze off. She'd lain in her bed, alone, heart pounding, her body tense with longing and frustration, the flesh between her thighs aching and moist. In the past, whenever such yearnings had gripped her—to experience the passion of a man's kiss, the feel of his hands on her skin, the sensation of him inside her body—her fantasy lover had been merely a nameless, faceless figment of her imagination. And therefore dismissable.

Philip was no figment of her imagination.

He was a flesh-and-blood man who appealed to her on every level. She liked him. Liked his easy smile and teasing demeanor. The intelligence so evident in his warm brown eyes. His passion for his antiquarian studies. Admired the part of him that had rescued a helpless puppy, and the kindness with which he'd treated Hope. His acceptance and thoughtful understanding of Albert's affliction. It had not escaped her notice that Philip had assigned Albert tasks that accommodated his disability. Botheration, she even found his stubbornness and flouting of propriety—which was, thank goodness, growing less frequent—no longer overly off-putting. In the short time she'd known him, he'd engaged her sense of humor, her curiosity, her mind, and God help her, her body. If she were looking for a man for herself, she would certainly not need to look any further . . .

Reality came back with a jarring thump. She was *not* looking for a man for herself. And even if she were, Philip, engaging though he was, was an impossible choice. Why could she not seem to remember that? Thank goodness, after their talk the night of the soiree, he clearly realized that *she* was not that woman, as proved by this evening's dinner party. He'd abandoned his pursuit of her, gone over the list of young ladies, and found six that interested him. Excellent.

A sensation that felt uncomfortably like a cramp gripped her stomach. Excellent? She was nothing but a bald-faced liar. She wasn't glad at all. She was miserable and jealous and wanted to hiss at any woman who touched him. The thought of him making love to one of those perfect, young, nubile, blond beauties made her want to scream.

A wave of resentment washed over her, drowning her in its wake. Resentment that she could not allow herself to hope for a relationship with a man like Philip. That she could not tell him the truth as to why. Resentment that decisions that had been made years ago, that she'd had no hand in making, still ruled her life and would until she drew her last breath. Resentment that she could never be more to him than a mistress. While such an arrangement would satisfy her physically, it would destroy her emotionally, forcing her to give up the respectability she'd fought so hard for, not to mention the pain she'd suffer when their affair ended, as it inevitably would. She knew all too well how such arrangements worked. And the fate that faced a discarded mistress. She couldn't allow that to happen to her. Not after she'd run so far to avoid it. Never again.

Surely after tonight's dinner party Philip would make his choice for a bride. As soon as the curse problem was solved, as it certainly would soon be—she refused to believe otherwise—the wedding could take place. All that could happen within a matter of days. Only a matter of days, and then she'd never have to see Philip again. And that was very good. Her heart tried to refute that statement, but her mind flattened her heart's attempt like an insect. And as for tonight's dinner party, she'd simply concentrate on her role as matchmaker by ensuring that the conversation remained lively, but she'd otherwise remain in the background.

Drawing a deep breath, she straightened her spine, grateful that she'd managed to realign things into their proper perspective. Especially since they'd almost arrived at the warehouse. "I appreciate you escorting me to the warehouse and helping search through the crates, Albert."

"Wouldn't have it any other way, Miss Merrie. 'Specially since it seems like somethin' evil's afoot, wot with the robbery and all. Lord Greybourne asked that I be extra careful watchin' over ye."

They arrived at the warehouse minutes later. Meredith walked into the vast building, marching through the dust motes dancing in the warm air, fully intent upon concentrating on the search and ignoring Philip. Her good intentions took a serious jolt when she turned the final corner and found herself staring directly at him.

It appeared he'd been at work for some time, for a film of dust covered his mussed, sun-streaked brown hair, and his glasses had slid halfway down his nose. He'd discarded his jacket and cravat, and rolled his shirtsleeves up to his elbows. He looked nothing short of delicious. Dear God, this was going to be an excruciatingly long day.

Over the course of the morning, Meredith immersed herself in cataloging the artifacts, her tension at being in such proximity to Philip tempered by her wonder and delight at the pieces of the past she held in her hands.

About an hour into their work, a gentleman arrived who was introduced to her and Albert as Mr. Edward Binsmore. Meredith recognized the name as that of the gentleman whose wife had died, allegedly as a result of the curse. He appeared tired and drawn, his dark eyes bleak pools of misery, and his palpable sadness kindled her sympathy. Clearly his wife's death had affected him deeply.

After the introductions, Mr. Binsmore looked around, then frowned. "I thought Andrew would be here."

"He's conducting some inquiries to discover who is responsible for the robbery," Philip said.

"Oh? Has he made any progress?"

"He only started this morning. I'll let you know if he discovers anything."

"Good. Speaking of discovering things . . . I finished cataloging the remaining crates at the museum before coming here." Mr. Binsmore shook his head. "There was no sign of the missing piece of stone."

Philip's jaw tightened. "There's still hope it may be amongst the remaining crates here. And if not, there's still

the items on the *Sea Raven,* which is due to dock soon."
He dragged his hand down his face. He looked so worried,
Meredith had to fight the urge to go to him, to touch the
crinkle between his brows, to enfold him in a commiserat-
ing hug.

Work resumed, with Meredith and Albert working on
one crate, Philip and Mr. Binsmore on yet another. She
could easily identify many of the pieces, as a large per-
centage of them were recognizable items such as vases,
bowls, and goblets. Although it slowed down the process,
she couldn't help but cradle each precious piece in her
hands for several seconds, closing her eyes, trying to imagine to whom it had belonged, and what that person's life in
an ancient civilization, in a distant land, had been like.

She froze as her senses suddenly recognized his presence directly behind her.

"I do the same thing," Philip said softly, walking
around so that he faced her. He offered her a lopsided
smile that she found far too endearing. "I touch these
things and my mind wanders as I try to envision who
owned them and what their lives were like."

Heart thumping, she returned his smile. "I'd just decided the spoon and ladle had belonged to an Egyptian
princess who spent her days dressed in fine silks while her
every whim was pampered to."

"Interesting . . . and intriguing. A silk-clad princess
whose every whim is pampered to. Tell me, does that reflect your own desires?"

Heat sluiced through her at the mere mention of desires, especially when the object of hers was looking at
her with compelling, dark brown eyes. "I think a small
part of every woman secretly dreams of that. Indeed, I'm
certain most men also dream of having their every whim
pampered to, also."

He offered her a broad wink. "Especially by a silk-clad
princess."

A genuine laugh escaped her. Then, noticing that Mr. Binsmore was regarding them with a curious expression, she sobered and pointed to an item resting on the corner of the sheet. "I set that aside," she said, "because I was not certain what it was."

Crouching down, he picked up a metal instrument shaped very much like a question mark. "This is a strigil. It was used by ancient Greeks and Romans for scraping moisture off their skin after bathing."

Their eyes met, and something seemed to pass between them. A secret, silent, private message that made it seem as if they were the only two people in the room. She instantly recalled her vivid fantasy of yesterday, of removing his dusty clothing and bathing him, her soap-slick hands gliding over his naked, aroused body. Heat crept up her neck, made all the worse because she knew he saw the flush staining her cheeks.

"The Romans were famous for their warm-water baths, and frequent bathing in the healing waters was an important part of their culture. Therefore, the strigil was a very common bathing utensil. When a person was done bathing, she would run the strigil over her skin like this." He gently pulled her arm until it was outstretched, rested the curved part of the strigil against her gown, just above her elbow, then slowly scraped the instrument toward her wrist.

"Of course," he said softly, "you wouldn't be wearing any clothing, having just come from the bath." Still holding her hand, he continued, "The strigil was also used to remove oil from the skin. Oil was massaged onto women's bodies; then, after an hour or so, the strigil removed the excess oil, leaving behind soft, fragrant skin." As he said *soft, fragrant skin,* his thumb gently caressed the back of her hand.

Looking into his eyes, a myriad of images rolled through her mind. Of him, and her, in ancient Roman times, naked in the bath. Of him massaging oil over her body. Touching. Kissing. Philip laying her down on the warm tiles . . .

"Are you imagining them using the strigil?" he murmured in a low voice clearly meant only for her ears. "Picturing them in the bath? Rubbing oil on each other?"

She had to swallow twice to locate her voice. "Them?" Good heavens, had that throaty sound come from her?

"The people in your imagination. Ancient Romans . . . or perhaps not?"

There was no mistaking the speculation in his eyes, and she quickly pulled her hand from his and averted her gaze lest he read her true thoughts.

Adopting her most brisk tone, she said, "Thank you for the edifying lesson, Lord Greybourne. I shall check the strigil off on the ledger." With that, she pointedly applied her attention to the ledger with the zeal a master chef would bestow upon a prized recipe. Risking a quick peek at him from beneath her lashes, she watched him lean down to replace the strigil on the sheet, then walk over to discuss something with Mr. Binsmore.

She breathed out a sigh of relief. Good. He now stood way over there. She could forget all about him and concentrate on her work.

Except she could still hear the low-pitched timbre of his deep voice as he spoke to Mr. Binsmore. Could still feel the warm imprint of his hand where it had held hers. Still feel the lingering tingle where his thumb had caressed her skin. She squeezed her eyes shut and prayed for this morning and afternoon to end. A humorless sound lodged in her throat. Morning and afternoon to end? Why, yes. So then she could look forward to spending the entire *evening* in his company as well.

By God, she'd been right. This was going to be a *very* long day.

* * *

Late that afternoon, Philip called a halt to the work. Everyone was dusty, and tired, and sadly their efforts had not yielded any sign of the missing piece of the Stone of Tears. Forcing aside his discouragement, he wiped his hands on a rag, then approached Goddard.

"A moment of your time?" he said, inclining his head toward the office.

Surprise flashed in Goddard's eyes, but he nodded. Once the two men entered the office, Philip closed the door. He watched Goddard limp to the center of the room, then turn to face him with a questioning expression. "Well?" the young man asked.

"I've learned something I think you might find interesting."

Goddard's eyes turned wary, and Philip wondered what secrets he was hiding. "Why do ye think *I'd* find it interestin'?"

"Because it concerns a chimney sweep named Taggert."

What appeared to be relief flashed in Goddard's eyes. Interesting. But the emotion was almost instantly replaced with bitterness, followed by a flicker of fear.

"Taggert?" Goddard's voice resembled a growl. "Only thing of interest I'd want to know about him is that the bastard is dead."

"He is. Died last year, in debtor's prison, where he'd spent the final two years of his life."

All the color seemed to drain from Goddard's face. "How do ye know this?"

"I asked some questions of the right people."

"The right people? Only way you and Taggert would have any people in common would have been if he'd stolen from yer fancy friends."

"It wasn't my fancy friends I questioned. I found several acquaintances of Taggert's at a pub near the docks."

Goddard's eyes narrowed. "Why were ye askin' about Taggert?"

"Because I thought you'd want to know. Because if I were you, I'd have wanted, needed to know. I wouldn't want him always in the back of my mind, wondering if he might someday find me. Or if I might see him on the street. And be tempted to wrap my hands around his neck and kill him on the spot. I didn't want him to have that power over you. He's dead, Goddard. He can't hurt you or any other child ever again."

Confusion flickered across his face. "How did you know—?"

"Because it's exactly how I would have felt."

Goddard's hands clenched at his sides, and his throat worked. A sheen of moisture glittered in his eyes, and he squeezed them shut. "I wanted to know," he whispered. "But I was terrified to try to find out. Terrified that it might somehow get back to him that someone were askin' about him, and he'd put it together. Might do somethin' to hurt Miss Merrie. Or Charlotte or Hope. He were an evil, heartless bastard, and I couldn't risk that he might touch our lives in any way. But it ate at me, always there in the back of my mind. Was he waitin' 'round the next corner? Would he recognize me? I wondered . . . God help me, I wondered."

"You don't have to wonder any longer. You're free, Goddard."

The young man opened his eyes. He made no move to wipe the tears dampening his face, and Philip pretended not to see them. "I'm not certain wot to say to ye . . . except that ye have my thanks."

"You're welcome." With a nod, Philip turned to leave, but Goddard's voice stopped him.

"Why would ye do this? Risk yer safety goin' to such dangerous places for me—someone ye barely know?"

Philip studied him for several seconds, debating how truthful to be, then sighed. Nothing less than the full truth would do. "Because the story you told me about how Taggert treated you affected me deeply. Not only due to the horrors you suffered, but it made the slights and humiliations I endured as a lad, which until that moment had seemed important, pale into insignificance."

Goddard raised his brows. "Who'd slight a rich bloke like you?"

"Other rich blokes. But there's one other reason, Goddard."

"What's that?"

"You're important to her. And she's important to me."

By the time Meredith handed over her bonnet and cashmere shawl to Bakari that evening, she had her emotions well in control. She would make certain to maintain her distance from her host, keep the conversation rolling, and concentrate on the other female guests. Then escape as soon as possible.

She followed Bakari down the corridor, surprised when they walked past the doors leading to both the dining and drawing rooms. He halted at the very last door. "What room is this?" she asked, mystified.

"Private study." His black-eyed gaze searched hers for several seconds with an inscrutable expression. "Hope you like."

Before she could question him further, Bakari knocked on the oak-paneled door. A muffled voice answered from within, and Bakari opened the door.

"Miss Chilton-Grizedale," he said solemnly, indicating she should enter.

With her best impersonal smile firmly in place, Meredith crossed the threshold. And froze.

Private study? This room in no way resembled a study. Indeed, she felt as if she stood inside an opulent tent. Yards of jewel-toned silks and satins covered the walls, draping from a central point in the ceiling, pooling in luxurious puddles upon the floor. She reached out and touched a hand to the fall of burgundy silk covering the wall nearest the door. Except for Madame Renée's Emporium, Meredith had never seen such an abundance of beautiful material.

Her gaze slowly panned the room. A gorgeous rug, woven with an intricate design she did not recognize, covered the floor. A cozy fire burned in the grate, casting the room with intriguing shadows. A half dozen low-slung tables were scattered about the room, the flickering glow of dozens of candles of varying heights reflecting off their dark, polished surfaces. A low, rectangular table nestled before the fire. Covered silver platters rested upon the table, as did an array of both stoneware and sparkling crystal goblets. Massive tasseled pillows in deep sapphire, emerald, topaz, and ruby flanked the table, and were strewn invitingly all about the room, urging one to recline upon their soft, plump, decadent depths.

Only two other pieces of furniture decorated the room: an ornate changing screen in the far corner, and a beautiful chaise lounge in the opposite corner. Her heart tripped over itself when she spied Philip standing in the shadows next to the chaise lounge.

"Good evening, Meredith." His deep voice sent a tingle down her spine, and although she meant to return his greeting, she could not seem to dredge up her voice. And just when she might have done so, he thwarted her attempt by moving toward her with his graceful, sleek gait that instantly reminded her of a predatory jungle cat.

Her eyes widened at his attire. Instead of a proper linen shirt and cravat, a loose-fitting shirt that appeared made from silk covered his broad upper body, leaving his tanned throat bare. His shirt was tucked into . . . She swallowed.

Instead of proper breeches, he wore loose-fitting, midnight-blue trousers that appeared to be held onto his body with nothing more than a drawstring at the waist. Soft brown leather boots encased his feet. With his perennially mussed hair, he looked dark and dangerous in a way that raced blood through her veins. Only his spectacles reminded her that this wildly attractive man was a scholarly antiquarian—or they would have, if the lenses hadn't magnified the compelling heat emanating from his gaze.

He stopped when less than three feet separated them. His gaze never wavering from hers, he offered her a formal bow, then took her hand and pressed a warm, lingering kiss to her fingers. The touch of his mouth against her skin sizzled heat and awareness through her like a lightning bolt, which, although unsettling, at least served to rouse her from the stupor into which she'd fallen.

Cheeks burning, she snatched her hand away, then backed up. Unfortunately, she'd retreated only two steps when her shoulders hit the closed door. Even worse, he erased her two backward steps with a single long-legged stride that brought him close enough to touch. Close enough to breathe in his clean, masculine scent. A feeling akin to panic—peppered with a dose of indignation—skittered through her.

"What on earth are you doing?" she said in a hissing whisper, wiping her hand on her gown in a vain attempt to erase the lingering tingle of his kiss. "And why is your study decorated in such a . . . a decadent fashion? And what on earth are you wearing? Good heavens, what will your guests think?" She cast a quick glance around the room. "And where exactly *are* your guests?"

"So many questions. As for what am I doing—do you mean when I kissed your hand or right now?" Before she could answer, he continued, "I kissed your hand in greeting, and right now, I am simply admiring how lovely you look. The room has been transformed to resemble a tent, similar to one belonging to a wealthy Egyptian trader I met during my travels. As for my attire, it is what I grew accustomed to wearing while abroad, and I can attest it is infinitely more comfortable than English clothing. As for what my guests will think, I anxiously await your opinion."

"It is scandalous. All of it. An absolute disaster looms upon the horizon." She swept her hand in an arc, her fingers inadvertently brushing his arm as she encompassed the entire room. She pulled her hand away as if she'd touched fire. "Have any guests other than me seen this?"

"No."

"Thank goodness. Now you must go and immediately don some proper clothing before the other guests arrive."

"All the guests have arrived."

Her relief vanished like a snuffed-out candle. "Dear God. If any of those proper young women get wind of these seductive dinner arrangements . . ." She briefly squeezed her eyes shut, unable to bring that scenario to fruition. "Where are they? I'll keep them entertained while you dress and—"

He cut off her rush of words by resting a single fingertip against her lips. "Meredith. All the guests, the *only* guests, are here, in this room."

Twelve

It took several seconds for his meaning to penetrate through Meredith's racing thoughts and budding panic. Then the full import of his words dawned. Damnation, what sort of game was he playing?

Raising her chin, she folded her arms across her chest and tapped her foot against the thick carpet. "No one else is coming?"

"No."

"No one accepted your invitation?"

"No."

Her toe-tapping ceased, her annoyance tempered by confusion and sympathy. "Good gracious, what is wrong with these young women? From all accounts the guests enjoyed themselves at your soiree. Perhaps the *you know what* problem was not solved as successfully as we'd thought?"

"I couldn't say."

Sudden suspicion narrowed her eyes. "Did you indicate your, er, dinner theme to them?"

"I did not."

Perplexed, she pursed her lips. "Then I cannot imagine why they *all* refused. Perhaps one, or even two of them, but all six?"

"Actually, there's a very logical explanation."

"Indeed? And what is that?"

"They never received invitations."

She simply stared. "You said you would write the invitations yourself."

"And so I did."

"Then how do you know they did not receive them?"

"I never sent them."

"Never sent them! I—"

He stepped closer to her, effectively silencing her outraged reply with his disturbing nearness. She surreptitiously pressed her back more firmly against the door, but to little good. He settled one hand against the jamb, near her head, then leaned closer. So close she could see the subtle amber flecks in his eyes. So close she could feel the heat of his body surrounding her. She drew in what she'd meant as a slow, calming breath, but it did nothing but fill her head with his delightful scent.

"Do you want to know why I never sent the invitations, Meredith?" His warm breath brushed over her face, tingling all her nerve endings into instant awareness. The urge to touch him was so overpowering, she was forced to grip the sides of her gown to keep her hands to herself. When she didn't reply, he whispered, "I didn't send the invitations because I didn't want anyone else to come. I only wanted you here. I did this for you. Only you."

She swallowed, hard, and looked heavenward for strength. Dear God, where had her anger disappeared to? Why was she not appalled? Where was the outrage at his temerity for tricking her? She cast about in her mind, desperately trying to find some inkling of umbrage, a whiff of annoyance, a thimbleful of irritation, and failed. Utterly. Instead, the myriad emotions battering her were a disturbing combination she did not want to feel: Flattered and excited by the obvious thought and effort he'd gone to on her behalf. Curious and filled with anticipation to experience an evening with him in such lush, exotic surroundings.

And worst of all, relieved that his affections were not otherwise engaged. *I did this for you. Only you.*

A tremor shook her, a shudder she recognized as cold, stark fear. Fear, because she wanted, so very badly, to stay. Because she doubted her ability to resist him. And because she wanted, so very badly, *not* to resist him.

"Philip, I cannot stay."

"Please don't say that. I know this was presumptuous of me, but I wanted to share with you the flavors of the cultures I have known. I thought you would enjoy the food and atmosphere of a distant land."

"I would, but—"

"Then stay. If not for me, then as a courtesy to Bakari, who went to a great deal of trouble to prepare the room and the meal. You have to eat." He leaned closer, until his lips almost touched her ear. "Please."

That single whispered word brushed against her ear, crumbling her already unsteady resolve. Her mind shouted a dozen warnings, reminding her that any relationship other than that of matchmaker and client was impossible with this man, that she needed to strongly discourage his obvious interest in her, admonishing her that this evening could result in consequences disastrous to both their reputations, but her heart refused to listen. To leave after such effort had been expended would be inexcusably rude, her heart rationalized. He'd shown kindness not only to her, but to Albert as well. She could not repay that kindness with ungraciousness. Besides, Bakari and no doubt numerous other servants remained in the house, so it wasn't as if they were truly *alone*.

And really, while she found Philip undeniably attractive, it was ridiculous to imagine that she would not be able to control herself—should the need to even arise. Her inner voice made a noise that sounded suspiciously like an incredulous, *Ha!* She managed, with a great deal of effort, to ignore it.

He leaned back and looked at her. His dark brown gaze met hers—serious, and compelling. Yet it was the unmistakable flash of worry that pulled at her heart. Clearly he was afraid she would turn down his invitation. The fact that this strong, masculine, brave man would fear such a thing tugged at something deep and feminine inside her.

Offering him a smile that felt more wobbly than the confident, coolly impersonal effect she strove for, she said, "In view of the considerable effort made on my behalf, it would be churlish of me not to taste the food."

Unmistakable relief relaxed his features, and he smiled. Clasping her hand, he led her toward the table. Warmth from where his palm pressed against hers seeped into her, and she involuntarily squeezed his fingers. He squeezed back, his smile growing broader. Indeed, his eyes practically glowed with such excitement, she could not help but chuckle.

"What is funny?"

"You. Your expression reminds me of the time when Albert, at age eleven, surprised me with a poem he'd composed in my honor. Even though I was the recipient of the gift, he was more excited than me—"

Her words cut off in dismay as she realized what she'd just inadvertently revealed—that she'd known Albert when he was a child. Except for Charlotte, she'd never told anyone how Albert had come to live with her. It was no one's concern, and she had no desire to entertain questions on the subject, especially as they might lead to other topics she refused to discuss. Perhaps Philip had not noticed her slip of the tongue. Did her disconcertment show?

Clearly it did, for he gave her a searching look, then said, "It's all right, Meredith. I know about Albert's childhood as a chimney boy. And how you rescued him. How he's lived with you ever since."

A chill snaked down her spine. Dear God, how had he

learned that? And if he knew about Albert, could he also know about *her* past as well? Her mind instantly conjured an image of Philip, with his inquisitive nature, unearthing information about her as he might dig up artifacts on an antiquarian expedition. Part of her deemed such a concern a stretch, but fear of someone finding out about her past was a worry that constantly lurked in the back of her mind, like a demon waiting to spring from the recesses of hell and pounce.

Forcing a calm into her voice she was far from feeling, she asked, "How did you happen upon that information?"

He appeared surprised by her question. "Albert told me."

"He *did*?" She shook her head, relieved that he obviously hadn't been making inquiries and didn't know about her past, yet utterly stunned. Albert *never* spoke of the horrors of his childhood. "When? And why would he tell you something so . . . personal?"

"We spoke the other day at the warehouse. As for his reasons, he was motivated by his deep caring for you. He wanted me to understand exactly what sort of woman you are: Kind. Generous. Giving. Not the sort of woman to be trifled with."

"I . . . I see." Dear Albert. He'd shared something deeply painful to himself with a man who was all but a stranger to him, shared something that could easily make him the object of ridicule or pity. All in the name of protecting her. "I hope you won't judge him harshly. He cannot help his unfortunate childhood." *None of us can.*

"Is that what you think of me, Meredith? That I'm the sort of person who would look with disfavor on a young man because he was brutalized as child?"

The unmistakable hurt in his eyes and voice shamed her. If nothing else, Philip had proven himself to be a decent and kind man. A man of integrity. "No, I don't think you would. But I'm sure you will agree that many people would not be so generous. And I am very protective of Albert."

He squeezed her hand. "He is a fine young man, Meredith. I admire his loyalty and bravery. His inner strength. And while I appreciated him pointing out your finer qualities to me, there was no need. I already knew."

His soft words, the compelling look in his eyes threw her emotions into chaos. Before she could recover, he smiled. "So what is this gift that eleven-year-old Albert gave you that somehow reminded you of me?"

She swallowed to find her voice. "When I first met Albert, he did not know how to read or write. After I taught him, his first effort was a poem he'd composed in my honor. He wore the same sort of unbridled, joyous expression as you when I told you I'd remain for dinner. And as I was then, I'm flattered."

"I'd wager that you still remember the words to that poem."

"Oh, yes. I still have it, tucked safely away with my most treasured possessions." In her mind's eye she could see each word, written with such painstaking care. "Would you like to hear it?" The instant she asked, she wondered what had prompted her unprecedented offer. She'd never shared Albert's poem with anyone. Not even Charlotte.

"I'd be honored."

Too late to renege on her offer now. Drawing a breath, she said, "It read: 'About Miss Merrie. Her cheeks are like cranberry, her eyes like blueberry. Her smile glows like a luminary. She gave me sanctuary. No more am I solitary.'"

Silence stretched between them for several seconds, a blessing, as a lump had formed in Meredith's throat. Those simple words, penned in her honor by a broken, damaged boy, still wrenched her. And humbled her.

"A beautiful testimonial," he murmured. "And very astute for an eleven-year-old. He managed to capture your very essence, your vividness, your nature, in only a few words. I can see that that poem is very important to you." He reached out and gently trailed his fingertips over her cheekbone. "Thank you for sharing it with me."

Heat suffused her cheeks. "You're welcome."

"Come. Let me introduce you to the delights of Mediterranean and Mideastern fare. Bakari is an excellent chef." He led her toward the low table in front of the fireplace, then lowered himself to sit upon a plush maroon pillow, his long legs folded crosswise in front of him. Patting the pillow next to him in an inviting fashion, he looked up with a teasing grin. "I'm going to develop a dreadful crick in my neck if you remain standing."

Meredith looked down at that pillow and doubts assailed her. If merely *standing* next to this man was problematic, *reclining* next to him certainly fell into the category of "most unwise." She shifted her gaze to Philip, whose expression reflected amusement.

"You have my word I shall not bite you, Meredith."

Suddenly feeling ridiculous for her hesitation, she gingerly lowered herself to the silk-covered emerald pillow.

"It might seem awkward at first," he said, stuffing several more pillows behind her, "but after you've eaten like this, trust me, the formality of the dining room will lose all its appeal."

Rising to his knees in a fluid motion, he turned his attention to the array of wares on the table, and she took the opportunity to shift about, arrange her skirts, and fold her legs in the same fashion as he had. Once she'd properly situated herself, she had to admit that this was far more comfortable than a hard wooden chair.

"May I offer you a drink?" he asked, extending a stemmed crystal goblet filled with a deep claret liquid.

"Thank you."

With his gaze steady on hers, he touched the rim of his glass to hers, and the gentle chime of fine crystal rang in the air. "To a memorable evening."

Afraid to trust her voice, she merely nodded, then sipped her drink. "Delicious," she said, savoring the lingering lightly sweet, crisp flavor upon her tongue. "I've never tasted anything like it. It is like wine . . . but not. What is it?"

"In truth, I'm not exactly certain. It is a secret recipe of Bakari's, one he fiercely guards. I once tried to watch while he made it, but he discovered me. And punished me."

She raised her brows. "Punished you? How?"

"He refused to make the drink for a month. Never made that mistake again. I don't know how he makes it. I simply enjoy it when he does."

Setting his goblet aside, he lifted the cover off a small tureen. A delicious, savory scent unlike anything she'd ever smelled before wafted toward her on a puff of fragrant steam. Her stomach rumbled with hunger. Leaning forward, she watched him ladle out creamy soup into delicate porcelain bowls. "What is that?"

"Avgolemono. It's a Greek egg-lemon soup."

Her first spoonful had her eyes sliding closed in delight as the flavor slid over her palate. "Incredible." By the time she'd finished her soup, Meredith's trepidation and awkwardness had disappeared as she eagerly awaited the next course. He handed her a plate of delicate steamed fish, flavored with hints of aromatic spices she did not recognize, accompanied by steamed asparagus. After each bite, her eyes again drifted shut, and pleasure-filled *mmmmm*'s escaped her.

"You are clearly a woman of great passion, Meredith."

Her eyes popped open, and she found him studying her over the rim of his wineglass with a half-amused, half-heated expression.

"Why do you say that?"

"Because only someone with a passionate nature could enjoy food with such abandon."

Embarrassment scorched her. Good heavens, in these unfamiliar surroundings, she'd completely forgotten herself.

"Don't be embarrassed," he said, his words and the fact that he'd so clearly read her reaction only serving to burn her cheeks further. "Your enthusiasm is a great compliment not only to Bakari, but to me as well. I am flattered that you feel comfortable enough with me to lower your guard."

Comfortable? She nearly laughed. There was nothing comfortable about the heat and tremors, excitement and pulse-racing this man inspired. Yet, even as that thought entered her mind, she could not deny that in a completely different, difficult-to-define way, she did indeed feel comfortable with him. She enjoyed his company. The sound of his voice. His laugh and quick wit. She could not help but feel that if their situations were different, they might perhaps be . . . friends.

Friends? With the heir to an earldom? Dear God, she was a candidate for Bedlam.

"You've a most interesting expression," he said. "Would you care to share your thoughts?"

She briefly considered not doing so, but then decided perhaps she should, if for no other reason than to remind him of their divergent stations. "I was thinking how very different we are."

"Indeed? That is interesting, as I was just thinking how much alike we are."

"I cannot imagine how you arrived at the conclusion that two people who hail from such different social upbringings are alike."

"Perhaps our upbringings are not as opposite as you imagine. Why don't you tell me about yours?"

Panic fluttered in her stomach, and her gaze flew to his. Nothing in his expression or tone indicated anything other than mild interest . . . or did it? *Relax. It is not unusual he would ask. He is merely making conversation.* Forcing a light laugh, she said, "You grew up in splendor, as an esteemed member of Society. The heir to an earldom. I'm afraid that is quite difficult to top."

He shrugged. "Perhaps. But wealth and social standing do not guarantee happiness." Something in his voice indicated he spoke from experience, and although it pulled at her curiosity, caution kept her from pursuing this conversation that was leading toward questions she couldn't answer truthfully. And for the first time in years, the thought of lying did not sit right with her.

Looking down, she noticed that a small section of the flounced hem of her gown rested upon his knee, the pale yellow muslin a splash of color against his dark trousers. The sight of her gown touching those fascinating, loose-fitting trousers was inexplicably intimate. Arousing. And stirred her in a way that arrowed heat straight to her core.

"What were you like, Meredith?"

She snapped her gaze back to his. He was looking at her through eyes that appeared far too watchful and full of speculation. "I beg your pardon?"

"As a child. What were you like? What did you enjoy doing? What was your family like?" One corner of his mouth lifted in a sheepish gesture, yet the expression did not quite reach those watchful eyes. "I find myself insatiably curious."

Images she'd fought years to erase flashed through her mind, and she batted them away. She hated lying to this man. Yet, she had no choice.

Forcing aside the guilt, she uttered the same falsehood she'd told more times than she cared to admit. "My childhood was normal and happy," she said, the fantasy she'd woven tripping off her tongue. "We were not wealthy, but comfortably off. Over the years, we lived in several places, resettling as my father's livelihood as a tutor demanded. After my father died, my mother secured a position as a governess with a prominent family in Newcastle. I lived there with Mother until her death, at which time I came to London, and established myself as a matchmaker. I'd already had a number of successes which helped toward that end."

"You have no brothers or sisters?"

"Sadly, no." Anxious to swing the conversation away from herself, she offered him a smile. "Unlike you. You are most fortunate to have Lady Bickley. I always wanted a sister."

"I am indeed blessed. My childhood would have been unbearably bleak without Catherine."

Clearly her surprise showed, for he added, "Just because I was surrounded by material comforts does not mean I was happy, Meredith."

Confusion and undeniable curiosity assailed her, along with sympathy, for there was no mistaking the pain in his eyes. What could have made him unhappy? She'd spent countless hours longing for what he'd had—a normal family, a respectable life, a decent home. Why had it not been enough for him?

"I . . . I'm sorry you were not happy, Philip."

"And you're very surprised that I was not. You're wondering how I could grow up in surroundings like this"—his gestured to encompass the opulent room—"yet be sad."

"I cannot deny I find it difficult to fathom."

Setting aside his plate and wineglass, he leaned forward, propping his forearms on his knees. "Have you ever been lonely, Meredith? So lonely that you just . . . ached with it? Felt alone, even though you were surrounded by people?"

Memories, feelings she'd buried long ago rushed to the

surface. Dear God, she'd spent most of her life feeling exactly that way. Unwilling to respond, yet unable to tear her gaze from the distress simmering in his eyes, she simply looked at him, praying he wouldn't see the answer in her own eyes.

"As a child," he said softly, "I always felt as if I were standing outside, looking through the window with my nose pressed to the glass. I was clumsy and awkward, shy and pudgy, forced to wear thick spectacles—all traits made even more glaring when I was in the company of my contemporaries, whom I viewed as everything I was not. I saw little of my father, as he spent much of his time traveling to his estates. My mother was very beautiful, but she suffered from fragile health. After her death, when I was twelve, my relationship with my father grew increasingly strained. . . ." His voice trailed off, and his eyes took on a faraway expression filled with anguish.

Without thinking, she reached out and squeezed his hand. As if coming out of a trance, he looked down at her hand resting upon his. Then he raised his gaze, and her breath stalled at the utter, bleak despair in his eyes. "It was my fault," he said in a voice devoid of emotion, in stunning contrast to the torment burning in his gaze. "I'd promised Father I'd stay with her, keep her occupied until he returned from an appointment with his solicitor. She was feeling better, as she sometimes did, and as always, when she had strength, she wanted to be outdoors. Father told me not to let her go out until he returned. I gave my word. . . ."

He swallowed, then continued. "I gave my word, but then I . . . fell asleep." He shook his head, a bitter sound escaping his throat. "Fell asleep while she read to me. She left the house to walk in the park. Got caught in the rain, and caught a chill. She died three days later."

"Oh, Philip . . ." Sympathy crushed her heart as she

imagined a young boy, blaming himself, and his father, doing the same. "You were a child—"

"Who did not keep his word." He looked up from their joined hands and met her gaze. "If I'd kept my word, she wouldn't have gone outdoors."

"She was a grown woman who was the victim of an unwise decision—a choice *she* made."

"A choice she would not have made if I'd kept my word." His eyes seemed to burn into hers. "When my father learned that I'd failed, that she'd left the house, he told me that a man is only as good as his word. That a man who does not honor his word is nothing. I've never failed to keep my word ever since that day. I've failed in other ways, but not in that way. Nor do I intend to, ever again."

And suddenly she understood his single-minded determination to solve the curse so he could marry before his father succumbed to his illness. It wasn't simply a matter that he'd struck an agreement with his father—Philip had given *his word* to do so.

"Mother's death drove a deep wedge between Father and me. He blamed himself and he blamed me. I blamed myself, and we couldn't seem to breach the ever-widening chasm separating us. Catherine tried to help, reminding us that even before that fateful day, Mother's illness had advanced beyond hope. Father and I both knew that, but we were both with her when she died, we both saw her suffering and struggling for each breath. She hadn't had many more months to live, but she died sooner than she had to."

He blew out a long breath. "With Father spending most of his time seeing to his estates, I spent mine with an array of disinterested private tutors. The situation grew worse when I was sent away to Eton, where I learned that boys, no matter how supposedly well-bred, can inflict great pain, not only with their fists, but with cruel words as well. The fact that I was a failure at school in every way—except academically—did not help the situation with my father. Seeing Catherine during my school holidays was the lone ray of sunshine during those dark years. Her, and the comfort I found in my studies, when I lost myself in the wonders of the past, in the lives of people I did not know."

He paused for several seconds, then he appeared to shake off the remnants of the past and his gaze focused back on hers. "With both my father and I needing to escape the tension festering between us, he offered me the chance to further my studies abroad, and I grabbed the opportunity. We struck our bargain—that I would return to England and marry in exchange for his financial backing. As much as I desperately wanted to go, I was terrified to leave my home. I was painfully shy, still awkward and clumsy."

The ghost of a smile touched his lips. "But once I departed England, no one knew me, or had knowledge of my past failures, and I reveled in the freedom this afforded me. The strenuous physical activity my travels required, along with the fresh air, all strengthened me, and for the first time in my life, I felt as if I belonged. I met Bakari, then Andrew, who is not only a keen pugilist, but an accomplished fencer. He taught me the finer nuances of pugilism and swordplay, and I taught him how to read ancient scripts. He was no more anxious to discuss his past than I was, and we became fast friends. Indeed, except for Catherine, Bakari and Andrew were the first real friends I'd ever had."

His words faded, and silence surrounded them. She wanted to say something, but what could she say to a man who had just bared his soul to her? A man she'd fed nothing but a pack of lies to? *Don't be naïve—honesty only works if you have nothing to hide.*

Feelings bombarded her so quickly, and with such force, she couldn't separate them, couldn't bring one into sharp focus before it was shoved aside by another. Sympathy. Guilt. Compassion. Commiseration.

Deep, abiding affection.

The need to touch him, comfort him, overwhelmed her, and it took all her strength not to draw him into her arms. Instead, she merely squeezed his hand. "I'm sorry, Philip," the inadequate words and gesture in no way expressing the depth of her jumbled feelings.

"Thank you." A bit of the tension left his features. "Over the years, I corresponded regularly with Father. Our letters were stilted at first, but after a while some of the tension dissipated, as clearly we both found it easier to communicate through letters than face-to-face. But all the tension returned three years ago when he wrote, demanding my return to England, as he'd arranged a marriage for me. I refused. Partly because I was not yet ready to come home, but also because I'd become quite stubborn in my own right and I did not take kindly to such an autocratic order. As you can guess, our relationship suffered anew because of it. We still corresponded, but it was strained. And then I received his letter telling me he was dying. That, of course, made me realize it was time to come home. I'd hoped that my return to England and my marriage would heal the rift between us. But then I stumbled upon the Stone of Tears."

Another wave of sympathy washed over her. "Yes. An extremely unfortunate bit of luck."

"In some ways, yes, with Mary Binsmore's death being the most tragic. But the curse has not brought only bad luck."

Her brows shot upward. "How can you say that? The curse lost you Lady Sarah."

Lifting her hand to his lips, he pressed a kiss to her fingertips, shooting a tingle up her arm. "Yes. But the curse led me to you."

Thirteen

Meredith's heart stuttered to a halt, then slammed against her rib cage. *The curse led me to you. . . .*

Before she could think of an appropriate reply—no doubt because there wasn't one—he smiled. "Forgive me, please. I did not mean to inject our evening with ghosts from the past. There are still several more courses to enjoy, and Bakari will treat me to his most fearsome scowl if I do not serve his masterpieces in a timely manner."

Clearly he wished to change the subject, and she was more than willing to comply. Surely the simple routine, the ordinary nature of sharing the remainder of their meal would dispel the air of intimacy that had closed in on them during their conversation. Although how she would ever erase the unsettling feelings his story had wrought upon her, she did not know.

The next two courses consisted of thinly sliced duck, then a savory lamb stew, after which she felt warm and sated and relaxed. Surrounded by the fluffy pillows, it was as if she were encased in a velvety cocoon.

"I cannot decide which dish was more delicious," she said, watching him lift the lid off yet another platter. "Bakari is a gifted chef. If I were you, I'd station him in the kitchen rather than the foyer."

He laughed. "Wait until you taste this." He held a small china bowl containing what appeared to be a combination of custard and thin layers of cake, decorated with a drizzle of chopped nuts and a golden syrup. Obviously a dessert, but one unfamiliar to her. Scooping up a spoonful of the concoction, he held the spoon to her lips. The delicate scents of honey and cinnamon teased her, urging her to eat the offering, but she hesitated, her earlier tension rushing back at the intimacy of his gesture. It was one thing to share a meal with him. It was quite another for him to feed her.

"Try it, Meredith," he said softly. "I promise you'll enjoy it."

She parted her lips, and he fed her the morsel, then slowly slipped the spoon from between her lips. A heady combination of tastes and textures delighted her mouth— silky-smooth custard, spongy cake, crunchy nuts, sweet honey, the tang of cinnamon. Her gaze locked to his, she slowly chewed, then swallowed, trying to ignore the sudden racing of her heart. The heated awareness of him that she'd managed to push aside roared back to life, inching tingling warmth up her spine.

To her dismay—and utter fascination—he leaned back, reclining onto his side on the pile of pillows, his upper body propped up on his left elbow and forearm. Her gaze involuntarily wandered down his length, taking in his tanned throat, the enticing expanse of his broad chest, his long, outstretched muscular legs.

"Do you like it?" he asked in a husky voice.

She jerked her gaze back to his and found him studying her with deep concentration. Like it? *More than anything I've ever seen before.* She glanced down at the china bowl cradled in his left hand and fire raced into her cheeks. Heavens, he'd meant the dessert.

"It's, um, delicious." When he dipped the spoon into the bowl again, she asked, "Are you going to have some?"

"I'd love some." Sitting up, he handed her the bowl and

spoon, then scooted around to face her, moving closer until their knees bumped.

A tingle shot up her leg, and she stared at the bowl and spoon she now held. His meaning was unmistakable. Everything cautious in her warned her to set the food back on the table and leave. Everything feminine and curious in her wanted to know what it was like to feed a man. *This* man.

Heart beating hard, she scooped up a bit of the creamy dessert and brought the spoon to his lips. Fascinated, she fed him the bite, withdrawing the spoon slowly from his mouth as he'd done to her. She watched him chew. Dear God, the man had a beautiful mouth. She instantly recalled the thrilling sensation of that firm, sensual mouth brushing against her lips and skin.

Reaching out, he brushed a single fingertip against her lower lip. "A drop of custard," he murmured. He then brought his finger to his own mouth and licked off the creamy dollop.

She felt as if he'd tossed her into the fire. Before she could think of what to say or do, he gently took the bowl and spoon from her, setting them back on the table. He then picked up an oval ceramic platter filled with an assortment of cut fruits, olives, and shelled nuts.

Setting the platter next to him, he picked up a small piece of fruit. "This is a fig, very popular with the Greeks since ancient times. Taste." He reached out with the offering, but when she held out her hand, he shook his head and brought the fruit closer to her lips. "It is customary for a guest to eat a handheld offering from the host—if the guest enjoyed the meal. It symbolizes a harmonious end to the dinner."

"I see." She tried to tell herself that she would eat from his fingers solely so as not to flout ancient custom and offend him, but it was such a blatant lie she banished the excuse as quickly as it formed. Ancient custom had nothing to do with it as she leaned forward and ate the bit of fig from his fingers. Somewhere in the back of her mind it registered that the fruit was sweet and luscious, but all she could concentrate on was the sensation of his fingers touching her lips.

"The guest may return the favor to the host, if she wishes," he said, "to indicate that she found the company pleasing."

Dear God, she found him so much more than merely pleasing. Tempting. Tantalizing. Exciting. Unable to refuse, she reached out and picked up a small section of peeled orange, which she then held out. His gaze steady on hers, he lightly grasped her wrist and pulled her hand closer to his mouth. He drew the sweet citrus and her two fingers between his lips. She gasped as the warmth of his mouth surrounded her fingertips, his tongue brushing over them. Her own lips involuntarily parted in response, and her breath caught. He withdrew her fingers, then dropped a kiss on them.

He chewed, swallowed, then said, "Delicious." He then picked up a plump, dark olive, the pit clearly removed. "After the sweet fruit, the host offers something salty—to show that he holds his guest in the highest regard."

As if in a trance, Meredith watched him bring the olive to her mouth, her heart skipping a beat when he slowly ran the offering around the perimeter of her parted lips before allowing her to eat it. The salty tang slid over her tongue, a sharp contrast to the sweet fig.

"The guest may offer the same to the host. If she wishes," he said, his brown gaze searching hers.

Just as she couldn't deny she found his company pleasing, nor could she deny she held him in the highest regard. Of course, to do something that admitted that—openly, and to him—was more than a bit frightening. And most certainly unwise.

Yet she could not stop herself from picking up an olive

and offering it to him. His eyes darkened behind his lenses, and a tremor shook her hand. Again he lightly clasped her wrist and drew her hand closer to him, gently sucking the olive and her fingers into the heat of his mouth.

The desire she'd attempted to bludgeon back gushed through her, bubbling in her veins, quickening her pulse. She wanted his mouth on hers. So badly her lips tingled.

"And last," he said, "to finish the meal, is this." From the center of the platter he picked up an object about the size of an orange, but it was a deep purplish red in color.

"What is that?"

"A pomegranate."

She looked at it with interest. "I've never seen one, although I've heard of it."

"It is called the Fruit of Paradise, and throughout history it has been cited in the myths and legends of many different cultures and civilizations, as well as in art and literature."

"Actually, I first heard mention of one in *Romeo and Juliet,*" she said. "A lark's song tells Romeo that morning has come and he must leave his love. But Juliet tells him, 'Nightly she sings on yon pomegranate tree; believe me, love, it was the nightingale.'"

"Yes, I recall that passage. She assured him it was the nightingale rather than the lark . . . because she did not want him to leave. You enjoy Shakespeare?"

Speak. Talk. Say something, anything *to dispel this unbearable tension.* "Yes. And *Romeo and Juliet* is my favorite. I've always loved losing myself in a book, shutting out everything else and being immersed in a story that transported me to another time and place. . . ." Her voice trailed off as an image of herself at age twelve flashed in her mind. Someone had left a book at the house, and she'd found it. *Romeo and Juliet.* She'd immediately added it to her precious hoard of reading material. That night, as she had so many other nights, she'd hidden in the cupboard under the stairs and read by candlelight, this time whisked back in time to Verona and the heartbreaking love that would never be. The beautiful words drown out the noises she did not want to hear, allowing her to escape, for a few hours, all that from which she so desperately longed to escape.

"Meredith . . . are you all right?"

His softly spoken question yanked her back to the present. She blinked to dispel the lingering cobwebs of the past. "Yes, I'm fine."

"You looked very sad."

She forced a smile. "*Romeo and Juliet* is a sad story." Not wishing to dwell on stories of impossible love, she asked, "How do you eat a pomegranate? Like an apple?"

"No. You cut it open and eat the seeds." Still holding the fruit, he handed her a small china bowl filled with tiny, red, pearllike seeds. "The inside is filled with such an abundance of these seeds, the pomegranate has long been a symbol of fertility, bounty, and eternal life. Ancient Egyptians were buried with pomegranates in the hope of rebirth." Reaching into the bowl, he withdrew one seed. It looked like a miniature red teardrop resting on his fingertip. He brought it to her lips. "There's a tiny seed within this kernel that is edible. Taste."

After a brief hesitation, she accepted the offering, her lips brushing against his fingertip like a kiss. His eyes darkened, and he dragged his finger over her bottom lip as he moved his hand away. Lips tingling, Meredith gently bit down on the seed. A tiny burst of flavorful juice touched her tongue, and her eyes widened.

"Deceptive, is it not?" he asked with a smile.

"Indeed. I didn't expect something so small to contain so much flavor. It's tart and sweet at the same time."

He held out another seed for her on his fingertip. "Do you like it, Meredith?"

Her name, said in that husky, deep voice, touched her like a caress. The question in itself was simple enough, but by the heat simmering in his gaze, there was no mistaking that he was asking if she liked more than the taste of the fruit. He wanted to know if she liked being with him like this, being fed by him, feeding him. Touching her fingers to his lips, tasting his fingers against her mouth. As much as she wished it otherwise, there was only one answer—to all those questions.

But should she admit it? She could pretend to misunderstand the deeper meaning behind his question. She *should* pretend. Yet the air of intimacy surrounding them, the opulent décor, the delicious food and wine, the personal, vulnerable details of his life he'd shared with her, the desire all but emanating from him, all served to cast a hypnotic spell upon her that blurred the lines of what she should and should not do . . . of what was wise and unwise. Yes, she should pretend. But she could not.

"Yes, Philip. I like it."

His eyes darkened further at her whispered reply.

Without a word, he took the china bowl from her, setting it and the pomegranate back on the platter. He then rose.

Before she could shove aside her disappointment and search for the relief she should have felt at this obvious signal that their meal was over, he stepped around her, then lowered himself to sit on her pillow, directly behind her.

"Straighten out your legs, Meredith." His soft request brushed by her ear, shooting a shiver of pleasure down her spine.

She did as he bade, then sat ramrod-stiff, afraid to further move lest she encourage—or discourage—him. Behind her, he adjusted his position, shifting closer, and stretching out his long legs on either side of hers. The inner part of his legs touched the outer part of hers, from her hips downward, while his chest brushed her back. A shiver raced down her spine, raising goose bumps on her flesh, inexplicable, as she was not in the least bit cold. Indeed, she'd never felt *less* chilled in her entire life. She felt surrounded by him, the heat of his body enveloping her as if he'd wrapped her in a warm, velvety quilt.

"After the meal," he said, the words tickling over the back of her neck, "relaxation is essential." He began rubbing her shoulders with a gentle yet firm kneading motion that shot delight through her. "You're very tense, Meredith. Relax."

Relax? With him touching her? Yet even as she thought it impossible to do so, she suddenly found she could not maintain her stiff posture against the muscle-weakening magic his strong hands wrought upon her.

"Much better," he said. "This is how a silk-clad princess was pampered . . . fed upon pillows, then stroked until her body released all its tension." His fingers slowly worked their way up her neck, then started to gently slip the pins from her hair. She lifted her head, her mind trying to summon a protest, but her lips refused to voice the words. Released from the confines of the pins, her hair fell about her shoulders and down her back.

"Seeing you like this, surrounded by silks and satins, your hair falling down, you could be Queen Nefertiti herself." The words whispered against her nape, his lips and warm breath caressing the vulnerable skin there. A desire-filled shudder vibrated down her spine.

"Do you know what 'Nefertiti' means, Meredith?"

Incapable of speech, she shook her head.

"It means 'the beautiful woman has come.' Ancient Egyptians celebrated such feminine charms in lyrics they composed to the objects of their affections. I translated several such lyrics I discovered during my travels. One was particularly lovely. Would you like to hear it?"

Again, she merely nodded. She felt him lean closer, his chest pressing against her back. Her eyes slid closed, absorbing the sensation. Soaking in the pleasure. With his lips hovering a hairbreadth from her ear, he whispered:

She looks like the rising morning star,
At the start of a happy year,
Shining bright, fair of skin,
Lovely the look of her eyes,
Sweet the speech of her lips . . .
With graceful step she treads the ground,
Captures my heart by her movements,
She causes all men's necks
To turn about to see her;
Joy has he whom she embraces,
He is like the first of men.

His arms came about her waist, drawing her back against his chest, his warm lips nuzzling the side of her neck. "Meredith." He breathed her name so softly. Kissed her neck so gently. Desire and passion coursed through her veins, awakening needs and longings she'd fought so hard to suppress. Arousing her unbearably, yet confusing her. How was he able to make her feel this way by barely touching her? Everything she'd ever witnessed, seen, and heard had led her to believe that what occurred in the dark between men and women involved rough, groping hands and coarse language. She knew she could resist that.

But this soft caressing, this aching tenderness, shattered her defenses, rendering her unable to resist the seductive lure his gentle voice and hands promised. With a low moan of surrender, she leaned back against him and tilted her head to give his wandering lips easier access to her throat.

He pushed aside the hair from her neck and traced his tongue over her sensitive skin. A shudder ran through her, and she squirmed in a helpless effort to relieve the sweet, heavy ache between her legs. Her movements brushed her buttocks against his hard arousal, and he sucked in a sharp breath. *Just one more touch . . . just one more kiss . . . then I'll stop him. . . .*

Philip heard her moan, felt the gentle vibration against his lips. His control was vanishing at an alarming rate, but even as he recognized that fact, he seemed unable to rein in his desires. He'd arranged this evening to court her, not to seduce her. But now that she was this close, ensnaring all his senses, need ripped through him. *Just one more touch . . . just one more kiss. Then I'll stop.*

He slipped off her lace fichu, exposing more of her creamy, fragrant skin to his hands and lips. He kissed the gentle slope of her shoulder while his hands glided down her throat, then lower, to cup her full breasts through her soft gown.

"Philip." His name whispered past her parted lips in a smoky sigh of need, igniting him as if she'd set a match to dry kindling. And the battle Philip had been waging against the demands of his body was lost.

With a growl, he shifted her in his embrace enough so that their lips could meet—in a kiss he'd meant to be gentle, but instantly turned hot and demanding. He slipped one hand into her bodice, palming her bare breast. While his tongue explored the sweet-tart silkiness of her mouth, his fingers explored the lush softness of her breast, the pebble-hard arousal of her nipple. He drank in her soft gasp, and all semblance of time and place faded away, replaced by an aching, white-hot need. More. He wanted, needed, more.

With a groan that bordered on pain, he broke off their kiss, taking grim satisfaction in her similar groan of protest. He impatiently yanked off his fogged-up spectacles and tossed them onto the table, then shifted her again, until she reclined across his lap. Breathing hard, he looked down at her, lying in his arms. He reached out and touched a single fingertip to the delicate hollow at the base of her throat, absorbing the frantic beat of her pulse. "Do you have any idea how lovely you are? How exquisite you feel in my arms? How profoundly you affect me?"

He caught her hand and pressed her palm against his chest at the spot where his heartbeat pounded as if he'd run across the desert. "That is what you do to me, Meredith. Every time I see you. Think of you. Touch you." Unfastening several buttons on his shirt, he slipped her hand into the opening, then moved her palm across his chest. He squeezed his eyes shut against the acute pleasure of her skin against his. "Touch me."

After a tiny hesitation, she splayed her fingers, then slowly dragged her hand over his skin, her fingertips brushing his nipples. A need-filled shudder shook him. Fighting the overwhelming urge to simply devour her, he lowered his mouth to hers and ran his tongue over her plump bottom lip. She returned the favor, and their kiss melded into a long, sensual, deep mating of lips and tongues.

He shifted their position again, easing her back until she lay fully reclined on the fluffy pillows, angling himself on his side next to her. Leaving the temptation of her delicious mouth, he trailed kisses across her jaw, down her throat, then brushed his tongue over the swells of her breasts. With an unsteady hand he eased down her bodice, exposing plump, pale breasts topped with aroused, coral-hued nipples.

He licked slow circles around her nipple, laving the bud before drawing it into his mouth. A long, sultry *ooohhhh* escaped her, and she tunneled her fingers through his hair, arching up, an offering he took immediate advantage of. Yet it still wasn't enough.

Need pulsing through him, coherent thought lost in a fog of want, his hand skimmed down her rib cage, over her abdomen, then along the length of her thigh and calf. Capturing the soft muslin of her gown between his fingers, he slowly dragged the material upward. Slipping his hand beneath her gown, he stroked his palm up her leg.

With her skin like silk beneath his fingers, her breasts beneath his mouth, her breathy sighs of pleasure echoing in his head, any control he may have believed he still possessed evaporated like a puddle under the desert sun. When he encountered the tie-on drawers, he quickly dispatched with the barrier.

Want her. Need her. The words pounded through him, a mantra fueling the fire raging in his veins. *Need to touch her. Now.*

At the first brush of his fingertip against her feminine flesh, they both stilled. She drew in a sharp breath, and he lifted his head. Lying there, hair in wild disarray, eyes closed, dark lashes resting on cheeks flushed with arousal, lips parted and swollen, breasts bare, nipples damp and erect from his mouth and tongue, she completely undid him. Bathed in the flickering, golden firelight, she looked like a wild temptress, an enchanting siren he could not resist.

She opened her eyes and their gazes collided. "Spread your legs, Meredith."

Without a word, she obeyed, and he glided his fingertip over feminine flesh that was slick, moist, and plump . . . for him. Her eyes slid closed. "Oh, my. . . ." The words whispered past her lips, and she spread her legs wider.

Watching her face, studying the myriad expressions flitting over her features, he aroused her with a slow, circular motion. Her hips began to slowly undulate in response, each movement brushing her hip against his erection, until he felt as if he were about to explode. His fingers quickened their pace, and her breathing turned choppy, her movements jerkier as she sought release. Leaning over her, he kissed her deeply, his tongue slipping into the warmth of her mouth at the same time he eased first one, then another finger into the heat of her body.

She stilled for several heartbeats, and he absorbed the taste of her in his mouth, the feel of her tight, wet heat surrounding his fingers, imagining her wrapped around his erection. Sweat broke out on his forehead, and with a moan, he deepened their kiss, his tongue imitating the act his body ached to share with hers, his fingers stroking inside her in unison. Her hands clutched at his shoulders, digging into his flesh. She tightened around his fingers and arched her back. Breaking off their kiss, he watched her, pressing his hand tightly against her, drinking in the feel of her spasming around his fingers, lost in the erotic sight of her in the throes of orgasm.

A long sigh escaped her, and her grip on his shoulders loosened. He slipped his fingers from her and drew a deep, shuddering breath. The musky scent of her arousal filled his head, and he squeezed his eyes shut and gritted his teeth against the clawing need to free himself and simply bury himself in her silky wet heat.

The sensual fog enveloping Meredith slowly lifted, leaving her steeped in a loose-limbed, sated state she'd never before experienced, one her imagination had never even conceived. Forcing her eyelids open, she stilled at the sight of him. On his side, his upper body propped upon his elbow and forearm, he was perfectly still except for the muscle ticking in his clenched jaw. His gaze was fastened upon her face, his eyes burning with intensity. He took her limp hand from his shoulder and pressed a hard kiss into her palm, then pressed it against his chest. His heartbeat thundered beneath her fingers.

Her gaze roamed over him. His hair was badly rumpled from her fingers, his shirt badly wrinkled and hanging open, and God help her, she wanted nothing more than to remove that shirt altogether to explore the play of muscles her fingers had danced over. Her gaze drifted downward, settling on his arousal that tented his loose trousers in the most spellbinding way. She ached to touch him, to strip away the barriers of his clothing and look at him, to feel him inside her body and share the most intimate of touches with him. And clearly he ached to do the same. Yet he had not. And the truth smacked her like an open-handed slap—she would not have stopped him from making love to her. Indeed, if she'd been capable of speech at the time, she might well have *asked* him to make love to her.

That reality cut through the lingering sensual cobwebs still obscuring her wits, bombarding her with a plethora of self-recriminations. Dear God, what had she been thinking? In the blinking of an eye, she'd surrendered her respectability, and had very nearly turned herself into the very sort of woman she'd sworn she'd never become.

Snatching her hand from his chest, she struggled to sit up. Hellfires burned in her cheeks as she yanked her bodice over her naked breasts, then jerked down her skirts. An image of herself, legs splayed, back arched, wantonly offering him her body, flashed through her mind. The upbringing she'd fought so hard against, that she thought she'd beaten, had defeated her the instant it was put to the test. She supposed she should be thankful for his restraint, because clearly she did not possess any.

Leave. She had to leave. Immediately. Before she said or did anything else to humiliate herself. Because even now, with the cold reality of her actions staring her in the face, she still wanted nothing more than to fall back into his arms and let the magic begin all over again. His intoxicating, gentle touch stripped away her control, leaving her vulnerable in a way that terrified her.

Hot tears pushed behind her eyes, and she pressed her lips together to contain the sob rising in her throat. She frantically tried to tame her wild hair by twisting it into a knot while she looked about in panic for her hairpins.

Spotting several, she grabbed them, and began jabbing them into her hair.

"Meredith. Stop." He reached out and grasped her wrists, halting her efforts to repair herself. She tried to pull away, but he wouldn't let her. She drew in a deep breath, fighting off the panic threatening to overwhelm her.

Gathering what scraps of her dignity remained, she forced herself to meet his gaze. "Please let me go. I want to leave."

"I can see that. But I cannot let you leave . . . not like this. We need to talk."

"There's nothing to say . . . except I'm sorry."

"What the devil for?"

"For my . . . behavior." Dear God, it was nearly impossible to look him in the eye.

His eyes filled with concern, and, releasing one of her hands, he gently brushed a tangled curl from her cheek. "My God, Meredith, you've nothing to apologize for. You were . . . extraordinary. If anyone should beg pardon, it should be me, but God help me, I cannot apologize for something that was so beautiful. The only thing I am sorry for is that you so obviously feel regrets over what we shared."

"How can I not? It was a mistake."

His eyes darkened. "It was nothing of the sort. It was incredible. And inevitable, given the attraction between us. Although it was perhaps precipitous." He brushed his fingers over her cheek. "Although I desperately, and obviously, want to make love to you, it was not my intention to seduce you this evening."

She pointedly looked about the room. "Indeed? Then why did you go to all this trouble?"

"To court you. Properly."

"There is *nothing* proper about any of this, Philip." And she knew it. Had known it from the moment she'd walked into this room. Yet she'd stayed. She had no one to blame for the outcome of the evening but herself. Damnation. It would have been so nice to assign the blame somewhere, anywhere else. On him—but he'd taken nothing she had freely given. On the wine—but she'd only had one glass.

"I assure you my intentions were honorable. Yet once you were in my arms, I'm afraid I forgot everything else." He cupped her cheek in his palm. "You intoxicate me, Meredith. Everything about you captivates me. Yes, I want to make love to you, but I want much more than that."

Everything in Meredith stilled, and she stared at him with dawning dread. His words, his serious, hopeful expression, his declaration that he'd arranged this evening to properly court her and that his intentions were honorable . . . she actually felt the blood drain from her head.

Dear God, did he intend to ask her to be his wife?

Fourteen

Meredith jumped to her feet, trying to hide her mounting alarm. Abandoning the idea of fixing her hair, she scanned the room for her reticule, every fiber of her being intent on escaping. Before he gave voice to an impossible proposal.

Philip rose and grasped her shoulders. "Meredith, I—"

She rested her fingers against his lips, cutting off his words. Trying to keep her voice calm, she said, "Don't say anything else."

Hurt and confusion flashed in his eyes. "Why not?"

Because I know a simple "no" will not satisfy you, that you'd want more of an explanation. And I cannot think of a lie in my current state of confusion that would satisfy you. And I cannot tell you the truth. And because it's now obvious where talking to you leads—to me lying on my back. "Because I . . . I am not ready to hear anything more. I need time to think, and I cannot do that in your presence. You're far too . . . distracting."

A measure of the tension left his face. "You affect me in exactly that same way. Which is why—"

"No!" Full-fledged panic rose in her, doubled by the unmistakable hurt and confusion in his gaze. "Please, Philip. *Please* do not say anything else. Not now."

His unwavering gaze completely unnerved her. "You know what I want to ask you, Meredith."

She didn't dare pretend she didn't, lest he indeed ask her. "Yes. But not here. Not now. I . . . I need to think."

He studied her for several seconds. "Very well. But we will discuss this, Meredith."

She nodded. "But not now." *Not until I've had a chance to gather my thoughts and shore up my defenses against you.*

"I'll return for you here once I've seen to the carriage." He quit the room, closing the door quietly behind him. The instant she was alone, Meredith buried her face in her hands.

Dear God, what had she done?

•

Albert pushed aside the heavy blue velvet drapes and stared out the drawing room window. Without even a glimmer of moonlight, nothing save blackness and his own somber reflection greeted his stare. He listened to the mantel clock chime, announcing it was midnight. Surely Miss Merrie would return home soon from the fancy dinner party. Would Lord Greybourne choose one of the fine ladies he'd invited to be his wife? Or would he follow his heart?

An image of Charlotte rose in his mind's eye. Squeezing his eyes shut, he rested his forehead on the cool glass and blew out a long breath. She'd gone upstairs hours ago to put Hope to bed and had not returned. Obviously she'd retired as well.

Instantly the image in his mind shifted, and he imagined Charlotte, lying in bed, her blond hair fanned out across the pillow, firelight flickering across her golden skin. His body tightened, and he gritted his teeth, trying to banish the sensual image, but to no avail. Reaching out her arms, she said, "Albert . . ." A groan of misery-filled longing he could not suppress escaped him.

"Albert . . . are you all right?"

His eyes popped open, and he jerked upright. Reflected in the window, he saw her standing in the doorway.

Heat rushed into his face. Biting back a curse, he tried to will away his obvious arousal, but it was hopeless. And damn it, he'd left his jacket and waistcoat in his bedchamber. There was nothing to shield his condition from her.

"I'm fine." The words came out in a strained, hoarse voice.

He watched her reflection, watched her hesitate, praying for all he was worth that she'd turn and leave him. Instead she frowned, then walked slowly toward him.

"You don't sound fine. I heard you groan . . . did you hurt yourself?"

"No." The word felt ripped from his throat. His heart pounded harder with every step she took. She didn't stop until she stood next to him. Her delicate, flowery scent wafted over him, and he clenched his jaw and fisted his hands at his side. Although she'd retired hours ago, she still wore her gray day gown. Thank God. If she'd shown up in her night rail . . .

Bloody hell, don't think of her wearin' a night rail. He felt her staring at his profile and resolutely fixed his gaze out the window, but that didn't help, as he could clearly see her reflected in the glass. Her lovely profile. Her full lips. Her soft hair. Her feminine curves. God help him. Perhaps if he ignored her she would leave. Before she saw the effect she had upon him.

"I came down to make a cup of tea. Would you care for one?"

"No." The word came out much harsher than he'd intended, and he saw her flinch, saw the look of hurt, surprised confusion pass over her features at his biting tone. Damn it all, he was making a muck of things. He had to get away from her. Now. Intent upon escaping as quickly as possible, he turned swiftly. Too swiftly. As he did so often, he tripped over his own bloody feet, and would have fallen flat on his face had she not grabbed hold of his upper arms to steady him.

He straightened and found himself standing less than a foot away from her, her hands grasping his upper arms. The heat of humiliation at his clumsiness instantly changed into heat of an entirely different sort, radiating need and want through him from where her hands touched him. Somewhere in the back of his mind a small voice screamed at him to move away from her. But instead he looked into her eyes.

Beautiful gray eyes that stared up at him with an expression he couldn't name, but that halted his breath just the same. By God, the feel of her hands, even through his shirt, burned fire through him. She was so close. She smelled so delicious. He loved her so deeply. And God help him, he wanted her so badly. . . .

He'd meant to step away. Surely he had. But the longing and desire he'd fought against for so long overwhelmed him, and he stepped forward. Cupped her pale face with one unsteady hand. Wrapped his other arm around her waist to draw her flush against him. Heart slamming against his ribs, limbs shaking, he leaned in and touched his lips to hers, kissing her with all the pent-up love in his soul. For several euphoric seconds. Until he realized he was the only one participating. Abruptly ending the kiss, he straightened. And froze.

She stood wooden in his embrace, face devoid of color, eyes wide and filled with shock. Nothing *but* shock. No warmth, no desire, no tenderness.

He released her as if she'd burned him, and took two hasty steps backward. And finally another expression filled her eyes.

Pity.

Jesus. Anything but that. Anger. Hatred. Disgust. But not *pity*. For the virginal cripple who'd made a complete ass out of himself. And destroyed years of friendship with a single, thoughtless act. How could he have been so incredibly stupid?

"I . . . I'm sorry, Charlotte. Please, forgive me."

She said nothing, just stood rigidly, hands clenched at her sides, staring at him with that same stunned, pity-filled expression that jabbed a knife straight through his heart. Turning, he strode from the room as swiftly as his lame leg allowed, not stopping until he reached the privacy of his bedchamber. Sitting on the edge of his bed, he propped his elbows on his shaking knees, then lowered his head into his hands.

God Almighty, never, never had anything hurt like this. Not Taggert's fists, not his leg, nothing. And just when he thought he couldn't be more mortified, hot tears pushed at the backs of his eyes and a shudder shook him. Bloody hell, he hadn't been reduced to tears since he was a lad. But these weren't tears of pain. They were tears of loss.

Another shudder racked him, and a litany of self-directed obscenities whispered past his lips. He'd ruined everything. That one-sided kiss, her utter rejection, and his utter humiliation would always stand between them. Christ, how could he ever look her in the eye again? He'd betrayed her trust. She no doubt thought him nothing more than a randy bastard, the same sort who'd misused her for years.

Raising his head, he dragged his hands down his face. He had two choices. He could try to find some way to accomplish the impossible—to find the words to make amends to her, then pray they could go on as if tonight had never happened. Or he could leave Miss Merrie's house.

His heart shattered as it recognized that there was really only one choice.

Charlotte stared at the empty doorway where Albert had disappeared, and slowly emerged from the stupor that had afflicted her since the instant he'd stumbled into her arms. Raising a shaking hand, she pressed her fingers to her lips.

Lips that only moments before he'd touched with his own.

Heat swamped her, awakening her senses that his unexpected kiss had frozen with shock. Her eyes slid closed, and she allowed herself to relive those few seconds. Never had a man kissed her like that. With sweet, heart-stopping gentleness. With all her experience, she hadn't known a kiss could be so . . . beautiful. Hadn't known it could rob her of breath. Of movement. Render her wide-eyed, stunned, and speechless.

Yet she should have known that Albert would kiss like that. Everything about him was good and kind, tender and sweet. And heaven help her, she wanted all that goodness and kindness for herself. She wanted Albert for herself. And after the way he'd held her against him, after she'd seen the blatant desire burning in his eyes, there was no denying he'd wanted her.

Pity had suffused her that someone as fine as Albert would waste his desires on someone like her. Which brought to mind the most nagging of questions. *Why* would he want someone like her? Had he been drinking? No, there'd been no hint of spirits about him. Perhaps it hadn't been *her* he'd desired—maybe she'd just happened upon him when he'd been thinking about some other woman, a woman he desired. Yes, most likely she'd simply found Albert at a randy moment. She well knew that men had plenty of those. A man got hard, and any woman would do.

Yet the instant the thought entered her mind, her heart rejected it. No. Albert wasn't just any man. He was honorable. He'd kissed her because he'd wanted *her*. And it wasn't just his body that told her that. It was the look in his eyes.

But that still did not answer *why*. Why would a decent young man desire a used-up, former whore? *'Cause he's lookin' fer a little tumble, you nodcock. You haven't*

*wanted a man to touch you fer the past five years. Now
you do. Why not give 'im what he wants? You'll both get
yer itches scratched.*

No! She clapped her hands over her ears to drown out
the guttural voice from her past. That voice she'd worked
so hard, with Meredith's help, to bury. She wasn't that
woman anymore. She'd made a decent life for herself and
for her daughter. And Albert wasn't the sort of man who'd
expect a tumble from her. No, Albert was the sort of man
who only would have kissed her if he . . .

Cared for her. As she cared for him.

Everything inside her stilled. Dear God, was it possible?
She hadn't allowed herself to hope for such a miracle. She
squeezed her eyes tight, recalling how unresponsive she'd
stood in his arms, and his stricken expression. He would
naturally assume her wooden reaction stemmed from being repulsed by him.

She had to know if he cared for her. Had to. Now. If he
didn't, well, she'd take that blow as she'd taken so many
others. If he did . . . She pressed her hands over the spot
where her heart beat frantically. Either way, her life was
about to change.

Drawing a deep, resolute breath, she walked swiftly
from the room and headed toward the stairs. When she
reached Albert's closed bedchamber door, she paused.
She heard his distinctive shuffle as he moved about. Summoning all her courage, she knocked.

Nearly a minute passed before he opened the door.
Their eyes met, and her insides squeezed at his bleak ex-
pression. Stepping across the threshold, she said, "Albert,
I . . ."

Her voice trailed off at the sight of his worn leather portmanteau setting on his neatly made bed. Her gaze panned
around the chamber, and her heart sank to her toes. Even in
the dim glow of a single candle, she could see that all signs

of his personal belongings were gone. His hairbrush. His shaving equipment. Hope's childish drawings that he'd proudly framed and hung upon his wall as if they'd been painted by Gainsborough himself. His open wardrobe gave testimony to the fact that it was empty.

A deafening silence engulfed them. Charlotte licked her dry lips, and managed to find her voice. "What are you doing?"

A muscle jerked in his cheek. "I'm leaving, Charlotte."

Three little words. How was it possible for three little words to wreak such havoc? To hurt so badly? "Why?"

Pain flashed in his eyes, then his expression went blank. Shifting his gaze down to the open portmanteau, he said, "I just . . . need to leave."

A flicker of hope sparked in her chest at his abject misery. Surely he wouldn't be so utterly forlorn if he didn't care deeply? *'Tis now or never, Charlotte.*

Summoning every ounce of bravery she possessed, she asked, "Are you leaving because of me, Albert?"

His head jerked up, and he stared at her through tortured eyes. When he did not reply, she said softly, "Are you leaving because of what just happened between us?"

Color rushed into his face. "I'm sorry, Charlotte. I—"

"It's not an apology I seek, Albert, but an explanation. *Why* did you kiss me?"

"I lost my head. I don't know what I was thinkin'."

"Were you thinking about me . . . or was someone else in your mind?"

"Someone else? What do you mean?"

She pressed her hands to her midriff. "Was *I* the person who inspired that kiss, or was I merely a substitute for another woman?"

A myriad of emotions paraded across his face: confusion, comprehension, then an unmistakable dash of anger. "I'd never use ye in such a way, Charlotte."

Her knees nearly buckled with relief, and the flame of hope burned brighter. "That kiss—"

"Was a terrible mistake."

"Why do you say that?"

He stared at her as if she'd gone mad. Then a short, humorless sound escaped him. "Yer horrified reaction made it very clear. Not that I blame ye, of course. I had no right to touch you."

Her heart squeezed. "I wasn't horrified, Albert. I was surprised. Shocked, actually. I couldn't imagine why you would kiss me at all, but most especially like *that*."

"Like *that*? Ye mean like a piteously green lad." He all but spit out the words.

"No. I mean like a man kisses a woman he cares for deeply. A woman he . . . loves."

Albert prayed for the floor to split open and swallow him. Never, in his entire life, had he been more mortified. Bloody hell, with his clumsy kiss, he'd given away the show.

"Is that how you kissed me, Albert?"

His shoulders slumped at her soft-spoken question. He wanted to deny it, to spare himself from being the further object of her pity, but how could he hope to convincingly lie about something so obvious? Besides, he wouldn't have to see her pity for long. He'd be gone from here within a matter of hours. "Yes, Charlotte, that is how I kissed you."

"Because you love me?" Her voice was barely a whisper.

He jerked his head in a nod. "Yes. Tonight my feelin's . . . they got the better of me. And since I can't promise that they never would again, I have to leave here. For both our sakes."

"Oh . . . my. Albert, that kiss was the most wondrous I've ever received. I didn't even know a kiss *could* be wondrous until tonight."

Confusion filled him. "Wondrous? Are ye sayin' you *liked* it?"

"Yes, Albert, that is what I'm saying. But you so surprised me, I did not have the presence of mind to react as I should have. I wouldn't be so surprised if you were to try it again . . . now."

He could only stare, certain he'd misheard her. "Are ye sayin' you want me to kiss you?"

"More than anything."

She couldn't have struck him more dumb with a brick to his head. Half of him wanted to simply grab her and take advantage of this obvious leave-taking of her wits, but the other half demanded caution. And the assurance that his hearing had not suddenly become afflicted.

"Why would ye want me to kiss you?" he asked carefully, studying her, terrified by the seed of hope struggling to bloom in his heart.

Her eyes filled with such unmistakable tenderness, his breath cut off. "I want you to kiss me because I love you."

Sweet God, he'd lost his mind. Daft, that's what he was. Hearing things. Bedlam was the next stop for him.

Clearly he must have looked as dazed as he felt, because her eyes filled with concern. "Albert, did you hear me?"

"I'm not certain. Doesn't seem possible that I heard what I think I heard. Could ye . . . say it again?"

A smile trembled on her lips. Then she cleared her throat and said in a slow, distinct, and quite loud voice, "I want you to kiss me because I love you."

Sweet God, he *hadn't* lost his mind! Reaching out, he framed her face between his unsteady hands. She stepped closer to him and lifted her face, sliding her arms around his waist.

"Charlotte . . ." He brushed his mouth softly across hers, almost afraid to touch her, fearful that he'd suddenly awake and discover this was nothing but a dream, a figment of his imagination. But there was nothing imaginary about the way her lips parted beneath his, or the feel of her arms tightening around him.

Forcing himself to end their kiss before the increasingly urgent demands of his body overrode his judgment, he lifted his head. And looked at the most incredible, beautiful sight he'd ever seen. Charlotte. In his arms. Her lips moist and reddened—from his kiss. Her skin flushed with arousal—from his touch. Her eyes filled with tenderness and love—for him.

He blinked twice, still certain that she would disappear, but she remained in his embrace. God knows he didn't want to say or do anything to disrupt this magical moment, but he had to ask. "Are ye certain, Charlotte? Certain ye want to take on a man like me?" He looked pointedly down at his leg, then raised his gaze to hers. "I'm damaged goods."

"So am I. I can't change my past, Albert."

"Any more than I can change mine." He touched her soft cheek, marveling that he could do so. "I'm only interested in yer present and yer future."

"I'm five years older than you."

"I don't care." Taking her hand, he raised it to his lips and kissed the backs of her fingers. "I can't believe ye're right here, that I'm touchin' you, that you love me. But by God, I'm not goin' to let this slip away. Charlotte, will you marry me?"

Her eyes widened; then, to his alarm and dismay, a big tear dribbled down her cheek. "Bloody hell! I didn't mean to make ye cry." He brushed away the drop with his fingers, but another tear, then another, followed.

"I'm not crying," she whispered.

"Well, then ye've sprung a leak, 'cause there's water coming out of yer eyeballs."

A noise that sounded like a sob and laugh combined rushed from her. She flung her arms around his neck and buried her face against his chest. Feeling utterly helpless, he patted her back, smoothed her hair, and lightly kissed her temple. "Charlotte, please, I can't stand to see ye cry. Why are ye so upset?"

She raised her head at that. Framing his face between her palms, she said, "I'm not upset. I'm overcome. Stunned. It hadn't occurred to me that you'd want to *marry* me."

"What did ye think I'd want?" Yet the instant he asked the question, he read the answer in her eyes. "I wouldn't dream of dishonorin' ye, Charlotte."

"I'm not the sort of woman a man marries."

"The hell ye're not. I want you to be my wife. I want Hope to be my daughter. I guess the only question is, do you want me to be yer husband and Hope's pa?"

"If you want us—"

"It's what I've always wanted."

She drew in a visibly shaky breath. "Then yes. Yes, I will marry you."

It was as if the sun broke out from behind a balloon of dark clouds. Clasping her tightly against him, he kissed her long and deep, until he had to break away to keep his sanity. He rested his forehead against hers for half a minute, catching his breath. "There's somethin' ye should know. I've . . . I've never been with a woman."

"I wish I could tell you that I've never been with a man. But I can honestly say that I've never *made love* with a man before."

He lifted his head and smiled. "Is it true? Are ye really goin' to be my wife?"

She smiled in return. "Yes. Are you truly going to be my husband?"

"Yes. And the sooner, the better. I, um, hope you won't be wantin' a long engagement."

"Albert, it's not necessary for us to wait until we're married to—"

He silenced her with a kiss. "Yes. It is. Ye deserve all

the respect due a proper lady, and I'll not besmirch yer honor by taking ye before we're wed. I never thought I'd have ye, Charlotte. Now that ye're mine, I can wait."

The love and gratitude shining in her eyes nearly brought him to his knees. "I cannot wait to tell Hope and Meredith our happy news," she said. "Won't she be surprised to learn that while she was attending a dinner party to find Lord Greybourne a perfect match, we found a perfect match of our own?"

"A mighty successful evenin' as far as I'm concerned," he said, returning her smile. "I only hope Miss Merrie's was as successful."

Fifteen

The following morning, Philip left his bedchamber and started down the stairs toward the dining room, intending to eat quickly, then depart for the warehouse. He hoped Andrew would be present to update him on his progress with his investigations. Bakari stood in the foyer, and Philip noted that his face bore subtle signs of a sleepless night.

"Bad night?" he asked, studying Bakari's face.

Something flashed in Bakari's obsidian eyes, but vanished so quickly Philip decided he'd imagined it. "Sleep hard to find."

"Yes, I know exactly what you mean," Philip murmured. Actually, sleep had been impossible to find. "I want to thank you again for all your hard work in planning and executing last night's dinner." He laid his hand on Bakari's shoulder, a gesture of thanks and friendship, but the smaller man winced.

Philip immediately removed his hand. "Sorry. Didn't mean to hurt you."

"Sore from hanging material in study."

"Oh, well, yes, I imagine you would be, which is why I wanted to again express my appreciation. I meant to say so last night when I returned from escorting Miss Chilton-Grizedale home, but you weren't about." He offered Bakari a smile. "Was odd not having you awaiting my re-

turn, but with all the extra work you did, I deduced you'd
retired due to exhaustion."

Again, something flashed in Bakari's eyes. Then he inclined his head. "As you say, extra work exhausting. Did
she like?"

"Yes. It was a most enjoyable evening." Until he'd allowed his passions to overwhelm him and thus scare her
like a mouse cornered by a cobra. Until they'd shared a
silent, uncomfortable journey back to her home.

Bakari's sharp gaze studied him. "You marry her?"

"I hope so."

"What she say when you ask?"

"I didn't ask her. But I plan to. The next time I see her."

"Next time might be too late."

Philip considered asking him to explain his cryptic
comment, but he knew from the stubborn set of Bakari's
lips that his friend would say nothing further. Besides,
Bakari, in his reticent way, had merely voiced the concern
that Philip hadn't been able to erase from his mind. He'd
honored Meredith's request to postpone asking her to be
his wife, but he'd begun to fear that her time spent thinking would be used for coming up with excuses *not* to
marry him, instead of reasons why they were well suited.

He suspected he knew why she'd balked at him asking
her. The information he'd inadvertently discovered about
her past while questioning one of the tavern keeps about
Taggert would certainly give her pause. Perhaps he should
have told her that he knew. But he wanted to give her the
chance to tell him. To trust him with the truth. He'd tried
to draw her out about her past last evening, but she'd sidestepped his efforts. Perhaps now that he'd told her of his
own painful past, she'd be more willing to confide in him.

Bakari handed him a note. "This just arrived."

Philip took the folded vellum, broke the wax seal, then
scanned the brief missive. "The *Sea Raven* has been spot-
ted off the coast. It is expected to dock this evening. Start-

ing tomorrow, the search for the missing piece of the Stone of Tears can be expanded to the artifacts aboard the *Sea Raven*." He tucked the vellum into his waistcoat pocket. "Is Andrew about?"

"Dining room."

Nodding his thanks, Philip proceeded down the corridor. He entered the dining room and halted at the sight of Andrew, whose normally amiable countenance bore a bruised jaw and swollen lip.

"Does that hurt as much as it appears to?" he asked.

Andrew winced. "Makes eating rather unpleasant, but my ribs hurt enough so that I barely notice."

"Is this a result of your investigations?"

"I'm not certain. I'll tell you once you're seated across from me. It requires too much effort to talk across the room."

Frowning, Philip crossed to the sideboard, where he helped himself to some eggs and thinly sliced ham, then settled himself across from his friend. "I'm listening."

"First tell me how your evening with Miss Chilton-Grizedale fared." Andrew made a great show of examining Philip's face. "Doesn't look as if she bruised you."

"Well, she didn't cosh me." At least not physically.

"A good sign, that. Is that as good as the news gets?"

"I'm afraid so. After a bit of a bumpy start, things were going along quite well—until she realized I planned to propose. Then she all but panicked. Asked me to please not ask her then, to give her time to think first."

Andrew raised his brows. "A curious reaction, don't you think?"

Not anxious to pursue that line of conversation, Philip gave a noncommittal shrug. "She is cautious. And with this bloody curse over my head, not to mention my alleged inability to . . . perform—which is still being alluded to in *The Times*—I'm not precisely the most eligible man about. Unlike you."

An inexorably sad expression passed over Andrew's features, and guilt tweaked Philip that his attempt at levity had clearly caused his friend distress. "Yet I would gladly relinquish my bachelor status if I could have the woman I love," Andrew said softly.

Love. It was a topic that, along with many others, had plagued Philip through the long, sleepless night. And Andrew was just the man to help him. "You say you love this woman," he said. "How do you know?"

Andrew studied him through serious eyes. "You know because your heart pounds at the sight of her, at the sound of her voice. Your thoughts become jumbled when she's close to you. No matter where you are, what you're doing, she's in your mind. Whether you're together or apart, you're completely *aware* of her. You know because you'd do anything to have her. Anything to be with her. And when you contemplate your life without her, the years just stretch before you like a dark, empty void."

Philip leaned back in his chair, absorbing Andrew's words with a dawning sense of amazement. By God, he felt all those things, and so many more, for Meredith. This didn't simply fall into the category of "she appealed to him" or "they were well suited" or "he enjoyed her company." No, this was—

"Bloody hell. I'm *in love*."

Andrew laughed. "Well, of course you are. Surely that cannot surprise you."

Philip stared at him. "You knew? Before me?"

"God, yes. Your love for her is so obvious, I don't know how you can see, for all the little arrow-bearing cupids circling about your head, obscuring your vision. It's been obvious from the first time I saw you and Miss Chilton-Grizedale together."

Damn. When had he become so transparent? And when had Andrew become so bloody perceptive? "I see. And

Meredith . . . does she have these little vision-obscuring, arrow-bearing cupids flitting about her head as well?"

Andrew stroked his chin, wincing when he touched his bruised jaw. "Miss Chilton-Grizedale is not an easy woman to read. She is clearly attracted to you, and it is my guess that she cares for you deeply. Whether or not she will allow herself to act upon her feelings is difficult to predict. However, if she is like most people, given the correct enticements, she can be persuaded." A muscle ticked in Andrew's jaw. "I envy you, Philip. You're free to pursue the woman you love."

"I'm free to *pursue* her, but to what end? Unless I rid myself of this curse, I am not free to marry her." His words settled upon him like a dark shroud of gloom. If he didn't find a way to get rid of the curse, Meredith would be lost to him. Bad enough that he'd break his word to Father—that would cost him his honor and integrity. Now he stood to lose his heart as well.

"Regarding the curse—I've some good news about the *Sea Raven*," Philip said. Withdrawing the note from his waistcoat pocket, he handed it to Andrew, who scanned the few lines. "I'm planning to go to the docks this evening to supervise the unloading and transporting of the crates. We can start searching through them tomorrow."

Andrew nodded his agreement, then passed back the note. Tucking the missive away again, Philip said, "Now, tell me about your interesting evening."

"I spent the day and evening near the docks, interviewing crew members from the *Dream Keeper.* Unfortunately, I didn't discover anything helpful. On my way home I stopped at Gentleman Jackson's, hoping to relieve some of my frustrations brought on by my unsuccessful inquiries."

"Knowing firsthand your pugilistic abilities, I find it incredible that your face bears such a colorful array of bruises."

"Actually, I pounded the piss out of several dandies at the esteemed boxing emporium, suffering nary a scratch myself. It was afterwards that I received these mementos of the evening."

Philip looked at him over the rim of his coffee cup. "Afterwards?"

"Yes. Moments after I departed Gentleman Jackson's, I was attacked. Bastard jumped me from behind." Reaching up, he touched the back of his head and winced. "Didn't manage to knock me out, but hit me hard enough to get me down. He was introducing his boot to my ribs when several gentlemen happened upon us. The bastard ran off, luckily before he inflicted any serious damage."

Unease slithered down Philip's spine. "Did you see him?"

"No. The gentlemen who ran him off helped me back into Gentleman Jackson's, where my injuries were tended to. Then I hired a hack and returned here."

"Damn it, Andrew, why didn't you tell me last night?"

"Bakari wasn't in the foyer when I returned, so I deduced he had retired. On the chance that you were still, ah, occupied with your guest, I chose not to seek you out. There was nothing you could have done."

"I don't like this, Andrew. First Edward was attacked, now you, only hours after you questioned crew members." The words of the second note echoed through his mind. *The suffering begins now.* "This is no coincidence. In fact—"

His words were cut off by Bakari's appearance in the doorway. "Mr. Binsmore," Bakari said. He withdrew, and Edward entered the room.

"Good morning, Philip, Andrew," Edward said, heading toward the nearest chair.

Philip instantly noted his friend's gingerly walk. "Are you all right, Edward?"

"Yes, of course. Why do you ask?"

"You're limping."

"Am I? Well, I'm afraid I'm still sore from the attack at the warehouse the other evening."

"Ah. Well, although I'm sorry you're still hurting, I'm relieved you've suffered no further injuries since then."

"Further injuries?" He lowered himself into the chair next to Andrew and winced. "What do you mean?"

"Andrew was accosted last night."

Edward's eyes widened and he turned toward Andrew. "Egad, your face is bruised! Are you all right?"

"Yes. Just sore."

"Were you robbed?" Edward asked.

Andrew shook his head. "Perhaps that was his intent, but he was frightened off before he had the chance."

Philip's hands fisted with anger. "Bakari should have a look at your injuries. Both of you."

"He's already seen to mine," Andrew said. "First thing this morning. Has my ribs trussed up like a goose on its way to the oven."

"And I'm fine," Edward added quickly. "Except for some stiffness in my back, the only thing still troubling me is this." He raised his bandaged hand. "I unwrapped it yesterday and discovered several bits of glass still embedded in the back of my hand. I removed them, then put on a clean dressing. It's feeling better already."

Philip nodded. "All right. Tell me, Andrew, did your attacker leave any sort of note with you, as he did with Edward?"

"No."

Edward's brows shot upward. "You think the same person is responsible?"

"I'm afraid I do."

Bakari again appeared in the doorway, his lips set in a grim line that trickled unease down Philip's spine. "Your study," Bakari said to Philip. "Come quickly."

Philip, Andrew, and Edward exchanged a quick look,

then all three hurried down the corridor after Bakari. Philip entered the room first. All remnants of last night's dinner had vanished—the opulent fabrics, the plush pillows, leaving nothing behind save his memories. His gaze swiveled toward his desk, and his blood ran cold.

Striding quickly across the room, he halted alongside his mahogany desk. Sticking up from the center was the silver hilt of a knife whose blade was embedded in the polished wood and thrust through a folded piece of vellum.

"What the devil . . . ?" Edward murmured as he, Andrew, and Bakari joined him.

"When did you find this?" Philip asked Bakari in a sharp voice as his eyes scanned the room for anything else out of place.

"Just now."

"You didn't see this when you cleaned the room this morning?"

"Cleaned room last night. Started after you leave with lady."

"What time did you finish?"

"Three."

"And then you retired?"

Bakari nodded.

"That means this was left sometime between three A.M. and now." Curling his fingers around the hilt of the knife, Philip pulled the blade free, then held the glinting blade up to the sunlight filtering in through the window. "It's identical to the knife found in the warehouse after the robbery."

"Yes," agreed Edward. "Which means that there's nothing remarkable about it. It's the same sort of knife most men carry."

Philip picked up the vellum and unfolded it. *Those you hold dear are suffering. As will you.*

His blood ran cold.

"What does it say?" Andrew asked.

His mind racing, Philip passed him the note. "It is the same handwriting as the other two notes."

"Do you recognize it?" Andrew asked.

"No."

"Which means it is someone you don't know," said Edward.

"Perhaps," Philip said. "Or it could be someone I know, who is disguising his handwriting so I do not recognize it." *Those you hold dear are suffering.* "First Edward, now Andrew . . . bloody hell, who does he plan to hurt next?" The instant the question left his lips, Philip froze. "Bloody hell, *plan* to hurt? Has this bastard already harmed someone else I love? I need to check on my father, Catherine, and Meredith immediately."

The front door brass knocker sounded. They all exchanged a quick glance, then filed out of the room, Philip in the lead. Striding quickly to the foyer, Philip yanked open the door. Catherine stood on the porch. One look at her pale face tightened his gut with alarm.

The instant she stepped across the threshold, he grasped her by the shoulders. "Are you all right, Catherine?"

"Yes." But her bottom lip trembled and a sheen filled her eyes, giving the lie to her claim.

"But something has happened," Philip said, his insides cramping with dread.

"I'm afraid so. Did Father send you a note this morning?"

"No." He shot a questioning look toward Bakari for confirmation, and his friend shook his head.

"He no doubt thought you'd already have departed for the warehouse. But I stopped here on my way to Father's house, hoping you'd still be home. Father was attacked on his way home from his club last night."

Philip's hands tightened on her shoulders, and he

fought to control the dread and rage curling through him.
You bastard. "How serious are his injuries?"

"His arm was broken. The doctor reset the bone, but it's
very painful. He also has an egg-sized lump on the back of
his head. According to the note he sent me this morning,
he'd just departed White's when he was accosted from behind. Father recalled a sharp pain in the back of his head,
then nothing else until he awoke, on a sofa in White's, being tended to by the doctor. A gentleman leaving the club
found Father lying in the street." Her chin quivered and
she blinked rapidly. "With his frail health, we're lucky he
survived at all."

Philip's gaze sought out Andrew's, whose lips were
pressed into a flat line. Edward and Bakari looked equally
grim.

"I'm afraid there's more," Catherine said, regaining his
attention. "Last night, an intruder entered my bedchamber."

Everything in Philip froze, and for several seconds he
couldn't speak as full-blown fury raced through him. Before he could find his voice, she continued, "I was awakened by a noise on my balcony. At first I thought it was the
wind, but then I saw a black-garbed figure entering my
chamber through the French doors."

"What did you do?" Philip asked, biting back his outrage that whoever wanted to hurt him was doing so in this
way. *If you want me, come after me, you cowardly bastard.*

"I jumped up, grabbed the fire poker, and swung it at
him for all I was worth. As it was very dark, I'm not quite
sure what part of him I hit, but I believe it was his upper
arm. I raised the poker to swing again, and he ran. Vaulted
over the balcony to the garden and disappeared into the
mews." She rested her palm against Philip's cheek. "Stop
looking so worried. He didn't hurt me. Truly."

Despite the tension cramping his stomach, a ghost of a
smile whispered across Philip's lips. "Coshed him with

the fire poker, did you? Good girl, Imp. You always were a spitfire."

A shaky laugh sounded from her throat. "At that moment, perhaps, but seconds later I was shaking, and, I'm embarrassed to admit, quite weepy. I kept thinking, what if I had not awakened when I did?"

A shudder ran through her, and Philip gathered her into his arms, pressing a kiss to her forehead. "You've always been the bravest girl I know. And even the bravest warriors sometimes cry after the battle is over."

"You're certain you weren't hurt, Lady Bickley?" Andrew asked, his voice tight.

Catherine turned toward Andrew. "Yes. I—" Moving from Philip's embrace, she stepped toward Andrew, her eyes filling with surprise and concern. "Good heavens, Mr. Stanton. It seems I should be asking that question of you."

"Andrew was also attacked last evening," Philip said. He quickly told her about the threatening notes. Just as he finished, the brass knocker again sounded. Bakari answered the door, then handed Philip a note. Breaking the seal, Philip scanned the few lines, and relief flooded him.

"It's from Meredith, advising she plans to call upon me this morning"—he pulled out his pocket watch and consulted the time—"an hour from now. She writes that Goddard will drive her, so she is obviously safe and not alone, thank God." Turning toward Andrew, Edward, and Bakari, he said, "I'm going to escort Catherine to our father's townhouse to see her safely settled and to check on him. You three go to the warehouse and continue to search through the remaining crates, which will serve the dual purpose of protecting them. I'll meet you there—after I've spoken to Meredith. When we've finished with the last crates, we'll go to the dock to await the *Sea Raven*'s arrival."

"The *Sea Raven*?" Edward asked.

"Yes. I received word this morning that she is scheduled to dock this evening."

As they all quickly donned their coats, Philip said, "Andrew, you and the others use my carriage."

"And what will you use?" Andrew asked.

"I'll ride in Catherine's carriage to Father's, then hire a hack." Grabbing his walking stick from the porcelain stand in the foyer, he stepped outside. "Be careful, and I'll see you soon," he said to his friends, then escorted Catherine to her waiting coach.

As their father's townhouse was well within walking distance, the ride took only a few minutes, during which time Philip tightly clasped Catherine's hand and inwardly thanked God that she had not been hurt. Or worse.

When they arrived at their father's townhouse, Catherine was immediately escorted to the master bedchamber, while Philip took a moment to speak to Father's butler. "Instruct the staff that no one other than myself is to enter this house, Evans. No one. For any reason. Nor do I want Lady Bickley or Father to leave for any reason."

Evans's thin face paled. "You think there's danger about, my lord?"

"No, Evans. I *know* there's danger about." He quickly told him about the other attacks, and the intruder entering Catherine's bedchamber.

Evans drew himself up to his full height. "Rest assured, my lord, that I'll not allow any further harm to come to your father or sister."

"I know, Evans. And now I'd like to see Father." When Evans made to escort him, Philip said, "I know the way. Better for you to talk to the staff, then keep your post at the door."

"Of course, my lord."

Philip climbed the stairs, then turned down the corridor

toward the master bedchamber. He knocked on the door, and was bade to enter by a muffled voice. Entering the room, he closed the door, then crossed the royal blue Axminster rug to the bed. Catherine sat in a wing chair next to the far side of the bed, clasping Father's hand.

Philip's insides tensed as he took in the white bandage encircling Father's head, and his arm supported by a splint and heavily bandaged as well. Pain radiated from his pale, pinched face and was clearly reflected in his eyes, but he managed a wan smile.

"Good to see you, son."

Philip grasped his hand, and fought to push back the guilt and anger stabbing him. "Good to see you as well, Father. How are you feeling?"

"A bit worse for the wear, I'm afraid, but Doctor Gibbens assures me I'll make a full recovery." He pursed his lips. "Damn impertinent man. Told me it was fortunate I possessed such a hard head. When I asked him if he recalled to whom he was speaking, he had the temerity to *wink* at me and say, ''Tis fortunate you possess such a hard head, *my lord*.' Can you credit such impudence? Clearly he thinks that simply because we've known each other since we were lads he can take such verbal liberties. Well, I let him know that as soon as I am not laid so low I intend to give him a dressing-down *and* a thrashing at the chess table."

A lump swelled Philip's throat. Although in pain, clearly Father was attempting a bit of levity for his and Catherine's sake, a fact which made Philip feel worse rather than better. Forcing a smile and what he hoped passed for a light tone, he said, "I'll wager Dr. Gibbens said he would look forward to that."

"As a matter of fact, those were his exact words."

"Ah, yes, mind-reading. One of the talents I developed abroad. Did I not mention that?"

"No," Father said. "And I would like to point out that I am not hardheaded."

"Of course not," Philip and Catherine said simultaneously.

Father winced with obvious discomfort and all remnants of Philip's levity vanished. Clasping his father's hand between both of his own, he briefly explained about the other attacks, concluding with, "I believe there is a connection between these attacks and my search for the missing piece of the Stone of Tears. Someone is attempting to make me suffer by hurting those close to me. Unfortunately, he has succeeded. Until now." He looked steadily into his father's eyes. "I will find out who is responsible and I will stop him. I give you my word, Father."

A long look passed between them. Then Father nodded and squeezed his hand. "You're a fine man, son. I have every faith that you will keep your word."

A breath he hadn't even realized he held whooshed past Philip's lips—a breath that carried away a bit of the millstone weight that had hung about his heart since his mother's death. Neither he nor Father were great communicators, a fact that had compounded the stilted awkwardness and distance between them over the years. But with those simple words his father had just uttered, he felt as if a bridge had been constructed. And he had every intention of crossing its span. He hoped his news would provide the first step.

"Father, regarding my marriage . . . I want you to know I am more determined than ever to solve the curse because I've met the woman I wish to marry—and the thought of not having her as my wife is unthinkable."

Catherine clasped her hands over her heart, a sound of surprised delight coming from her. "Oh, Philip, I'm so happy you found someone you care for."

Before he could tell Catherine that he more than merely *cared for* his future wife, Father said, "Excellent news.

Clearly last night's dinner party was a success. Knew that Miss Chilton-Grizedale would come up with the goods. Highly intelligent chit, even though the first arrangement she planned sank like a stone. So, who is the young lady you've chosen? Must tell you, the betting book at White's is leaning heavily in favor of Lady Penelope."

"Actually, it is Miss Chilton-Grizedale."

"What about her?"

"*She* is the young lady I've chosen."

"She is the lady you've chosen to select a suitable bride for you, yes?"

"No. She is the lady I've chosen to *be* my suitable bride."

A deafening silence permeated the room. Then Catherine rose from her chair. Without a word, she moved around the bed until she stood in front of him. "I have one question," she said softly, her concern-filled eyes searching his. "Do you love her?"

"Completely."

Some of the tension drained from her gaze. "Does she love you?"

"That is *two* questions, Catherine."

"Indulge me." Reaching out, she rested her hand against his face. "I want only your happiness, Philip." Lowering her voice to a whisper, she added, "I would not want you to make the same mistake I did and marry someone who does not care for you."

A spurt of anger toward Bickley rushed through Philip, and he renewed his vow to have a long talk with his brother-in-law as soon as his own affairs were settled. "Not to worry, Imp," he whispered in her ear. "She cares for me. She makes me happy. And I'll make her happy. And we'll both make you an aunt many times over."

She favored him with a dazzling smile—a smile that could have been snuffed out if that bastard had gotten his hands on her last night. "Then it would seem that congratulations are in order. I wish you and Miss Chilton-Grizedale much happiness, Philip."

He chucked her under the chin. "Thank you."

From the bed, Father cleared his throat. "I must say, Philip, that your announcement caught me quite off guard." He looked at Catherine. "Will you excuse us for a moment?"

"I'll be in the drawing room." After giving Philip's upper arms a bracing squeeze, she quit the room, closing the door behind her with a quiet click.

"I'm afraid I do not have time right now for a lengthy discussion, Father. Indeed, there is nothing to discuss, as my mind is made up. I am going to marry Meredith."

A red flush crept up Father's face, made all the more pronounced by the stark white bandage. "How can you consider such a thing, Philip? You gave me your word—"

"To marry. And I shall. As soon as the curse is broken."

His father's lips thinned into a flat line of disapproval, erasing the fragile unity they'd achieved just moments ago. "She is not of our class, Philip. Good God, the woman is in *trade*. What do you know of her family? Where does she come from? Who are her parents?" Before Philip could utter a word, Father plowed on, "I may not know her parents' names, but I know who they are. They are *nobody*. People of no consequence."

"It matters not. She may not be a peer's daughter, but she is perfectly respectable. In addition, she is kind, generous, interesting—as you yourself said—intelligent, and she makes me happy."

"I'm certain she's delightful. So take the chit as a mistress. And marry properly."

Philip clenched his hand to keep his temper in check. "By 'properly' you mean to someone who will bring money, prestige, and perhaps holdings to the marriage."

Father looked relieved. "Precisely."

"I'm afraid I'm not willing to sacrifice my happiness to further fatten the already rotund family coffers, Father."

Silence stretched between them for several seconds. "Your years abroad changed you, Philip. I never thought you would dishonor your heritage this way."

"I find no dishonor in marrying for love rather than fortune. Now, I don't want to appear abrupt, but I must leave, and I consider this subject closed. I'm sorry you were hurt, and very relieved you are all right."

"Believe me, this subject is not at all closed."

"It is entirely and permanently closed. I am getting married, and I'm afraid, Father, that you do not get to cast a vote on my choice for a wife. Although I very much would like your blessing, I intend to have her, with or without it. I shall visit you again as soon as I am able."

He quickly departed the room, then hurried down the stairs, where he said a quick good-bye to Catherine, and reiterated to Evans his instructions regarding not allowing anyone entry into the house. He then hastily donned his coat and accepted his walking stick from Evans. It was only a few minutes' walk back to his own townhouse, where he would await Meredith.

God help that bastard if he thought to venture anywhere near Meredith. *If you do, you bastard, I suggest you enjoy these next few hours. Because they will be your last.*

Sitting on a stone bench situated along her favorite shady path in Hyde Park, Meredith breathed in the cool morning breeze, which lifted the gentle scent of flowers and earth and encouraged birds to twitter. Her gaze fell upon Charlotte, Albert, and Hope, who examined a group of butterflies fluttering near a group of colorful blooms a short distance away.

Tears pooled in Meredith's eyes at the sight of her friends. Tears of joy, because Charlotte and Albert clearly loved each other deeply, and they were obviously so happy together. And, if she were completely honest with herself, tears of envy, because she wanted that sort of love for herself, and it could never be.

When they'd told her this morning that they planned to marry, she'd been momentarily stunned into silence. Charlotte and Albert? Why, she'd never considered such a thing. Yet, turning the idea over in her mind, she saw how well suited they were. They had much in common, knew and accepted each other's pasts, and Albert couldn't love Hope more than if she were his own child. She recalled looks given when the other was not aware and the odd tension she'd occasionally felt between Albert and Charlotte—tension she'd shrugged off as one of them being tired or preoccupied. She had not, even once, considered that they might be preoccupied with *each other.* Good Lord, what sort of matchmaker was she, failing to see love when it resided directly under her nose?

A humorless laugh escaped her and she blinked back her tears. Obviously she wasn't a very good matchmaker at all, for a good matchmaker would not be so foolish as to fall in love with the man for whom she was supposed to find a suitable bride.

During the sleepless night, she'd taken a hard, cold, bald-faced look at the facts and had not allowed herself the luxury of hiding behind platitudes and rationalizations or looking the other way.

The disturbing fact was that she had—very unwisely—fallen in love. Bad enough that she should do so, but the fact that she'd fallen in love with a viscount—the heir to an earldom—well, that fell in the category of "unequivocally stupid."

Philip needed a wife, and after last night, it was clear he planned to overlook their glaring class differences and propose. Her heart lurched, sick with loss and regret. She would have given anything, *anything,* to be able to accept.

But as she painfully knew, much more than glaring class differences kept her from being a suitable bride for Philip. And although she dreaded doing so, it was time to tell him that even if he broke the curse, she could never be his wife.

She rose, and together with Albert, Charlotte and Hope, they walked back to the gig, which they'd left near the Park Lane entrance, almost directly across from Philip's townhouse. All she had to do was walk across the street and tell him.

"Are ye certain ye don't want us to wait?" Albert asked as he helped Hope up onto the gig's seat.

"No, thank you," Meredith said, with what she hoped passed for a cheerful smile. "I'm not certain how long my discussion with Lord Greybourne will last."

"But how will you get home, Aunt Merrie?" Hope asked.

"I'll ask Lord Greybourne to arrange transportation for me."

When Albert appeared about to voice an objection, she added quickly, "Lord Greybourne no doubt plans to go to the warehouse to continue searching through the remaining crates, and I may accompany him." She bit back her guilt at that falsehood. After her conversation with Philip, she wouldn't be seeing him again.

When they were all settled in the gig, Albert took up the reins. "We'll see you later," Charlotte said, her eyes glowing with happiness.

A lump swelled in Meredith's throat, and, not trusting her voice, she simply smiled and nodded.

"'Bye, Aunt Merrie," Hope said, waving.

"Good-bye, Poppet," she managed, then blew the child a kiss.

The gig moved down Park Lane, and Meredith watched it, waving, until the conveyance vanished from her sight. Then she stood for another minute, oblivious to the pedestrians moving in front of and behind her, staring across the road at Philip's townhouse, gathering her courage, trying desperately to ignore the little voice that cruelly reminded her that everything she wanted was inside that house. And that she would never have it. And because she never would, it was time to sever all ties with Philip.

Drawing a resolute breath, her gaze riveted on her destination, she stepped into the street. She'd taken half a dozen steps when she heard a familiar voice yell a frantic, "Meredith!"

Surprise halted her steps. Looking about, she saw Philip running toward her, his face a mask of panic. "Meredith, watch out!"

Suddenly aware of the sound of pounding hooves, she looked over her shoulder. A carriage, drawn by four black horses, their legs flashing at full gallop, was bearing down on her. Her mind screamed at her to run, but terror froze her for several seconds. Seconds, she realized in a flash, that would cost her her life.

Sixteen

Philip ran as he'd never run before, his
every muscle straining to reach her in time. He saw the
terror flash in her eyes, saw her freeze for those few vital
seconds before she moved. Too late . . . too late.

He leapt toward her, grabbing her around the waist,
knocking her off her feet and propelling them both forward. They landed near the edge of the road with a bone-
jarring, skidding impact, just as the carriage thundered by
them, spewing dirt and grit, shuddering vibrations
through him as the wheels passed them with only inches
to spare.

Heart pounding, breath scorching his lungs, he pushed
himself off her. He'd tried to twist sideways to protect her
from the impact, but they'd gone down hard. Shaking with
fear, he gently rolled her onto her back.

His stomach dropped at the dirty scrape marring her
cheek, and the trickle of blood seeping from a cut on her
temple. Her chin was smeared with dirt and already showing signs of bruising. Her gown was torn in several places,
and covered with road dust, as was her hair. She stared up
at him, her normally crystal-clear eyes glazed and unfo-
cused, but at least she was conscious.

"My God. Meredith." He gently touched shaking fingers to her uninjured cheek. The rational part of his
mind shouted out a litany of things he should be doing—

checking her for broken bones, moving her from the side of the road—but every other part of his mind was immobilized with stark fear. And fury. Turning his head, he noted the carriage had nearly disappeared from view. He briefly squeezed his eyes shut. Jesus. One more second. Just one more second and she'd have been killed under those churning hooves, those speeding wheels. "Please say something," he implored.

She blinked, and some of the cobwebs left her eyes. "Philip."

He had to swallow to locate his voice. "I'm right here, darling."

"Are you all right, sir?" a gentleman asked, running over to them.

"I'm fine. I'm not yet certain about her." Philip didn't look up, but he was aware that several people had gathered around, all of them murmuring about how it wasn't safe to cross the road these days, how the speeding carriage had seemed to appear from nowhere, and what a splendid rescue he'd made.

"Meredith, I want you to remain still while I check to see if you've broken any bones." He examined her arms and legs, then gently pressed on her ribs. "Nothing appears broken," he said, his voice hoarse with relief. Scooping her up into his arms, he rose, trying to push down his alarm at her silence. If she were completely herself, his Meredith would surely scold him for scandalously hauling her about like a sack of potatoes, especially in public. And God knows he'd have given anything to hear such a reprimand, to know she was truly all right.

"She's going to be fine," he said to the half dozen people who had gathered. A collective sigh of relief went up, but Philip didn't waste any more time. He strode quickly across Park Lane, then up the steps to his house, where he banged on the door with his boot. A young footman named James opened the door, his face set in a fierce scowl.

"Now, see here—" He cut off his irate words as Philip marched across the threshold.

"Miss Chilton-Grizedale is hurt. I need warm water and bandages. Lots of them." He headed down the corridor to his private study, cradling his precious cargo close to his chest. "Also, there's a bowl of Bakari's ointment in the kitchen. Cook will know where. Bring that as well. Then I want a bath made in my bedchamber."

"Shall I send for the doctor, my lord?"

"Not yet. There are no broken bones, and I've some experience in treating injuries. I'll let you know if the doctor is needed."

After opening the door to Philip's private study, James hurried off to do as he'd been ordered. Philip strode to the sofa in front of the fire and gently laid Meredith on the cushions. Kneeling beside her, he gently pushed a tangled skein of dusty midnight hair from her scratched cheek. "Move your arms and legs about a bit," he instructed. "Does anything hurt?"

A moment later she shook her head. "Nothing hurts, although I'm a bit sore all over." She looked up at him, her wide, serious gaze searching his face. Reaching up, she brushed her fingertips across his chin.

"You've a terrible scrape," she whispered.

Damn it, words felt beyond him. Never in his life had he felt this undone. This frightened. "I'm fine." His voice sounded like he'd swallowed a mouthful of rusty nails.

"And your spectacles. They're all bent and . . . askew."

"I have another pair."

"I owe you my thanks." He heard her swallow. "You saved my life."

"Barely. The sight of that carriage speeding toward you

will haunt me for the next decade. At least." Lifting her hand, he pressed a fervent kiss against her fingers. "I was walking home from my father's townhouse when I saw you standing on the opposite side of the street. You stepped into the road . . ." A shudder ran through him. "In your note, you wrote that Goddard would be with you. Why were you standing alone outside the park?"

"I hadn't been alone. I'd just seen Albert, Charlotte, and Hope off. I was on my way to call upon you. To talk to you."

A long look passed between them. Her expression gave him little hope that he would like what she had to say. Well, he had a few things to say to her as well. And as soon as he bandaged her up, she was damn well going to listen. But first he needed to warn her. He quickly told her about last night's attacks on Catherine, his father, and Andrew.

"Meredith, you almost being run down was *not* an accident. Whoever did this knows your importance to me, tried to harm you *because* of your importance to me."

Before she could reply, a knock sounded on the door. Without looking away from her, Philip said, "Come in."

James entered, bearing a tray laden with two pitchers of water, an assortment of linen bandages, and a blue ceramic bowl covered with a handkerchief. "The bath you ordered will be ready directly. Do you need any assistance, my lord?" he asked, setting the tray on the floor next to Philip.

"No, thank you."

The young man quit the room. Philip removed his filthy, torn jacket, rolled up his sleeves, and made a quick adjustment to his bent spectacles. Then he dampened several strips of snowy linen and began gently cleansing the dirt from her face.

"A bath will be good for you," she said, wincing when he touched the cut at her temple. "You're very dirty."

"Thank you. I'm a fool for such flattery, you know. However, the bath is for you."

Her eyes widened. "Me? I cannot bathe in your home!"

If he'd been capable of it, he would have smiled. His decorous Meredith was back. "You most certainly can. A warm soak will help relieve the soreness in your muscles."

Her lips flattened into a prim expression. "My muscles are not sore."

"Perhaps not now, but they will be. We hit the ground with a most resounding thump. Besides, you calling me dirty is rather like a dog calling a cat hairy."

"Oh, dear. You mean I'm—"

"Filthy. I'm afraid so."

She tried to sit up, but he gently pushed her back on the cushions. "Do not distress yourself. I need to examine and clean the scrapes on your face. After you've bathed, I'll bandage you. While you're bathing, I'll arrange for your gown to be cleaned and repaired." When she seemed about to protest, he rested his fingers upon her lips. "No arguments. Let me take care of you."

Meredith looked into his brown eyes, so earnest, so serious, so filled with concern and guilt, she couldn't refuse his request. Besides, she still felt rather shaky. And her cheek stung like the devil himself had set fire to her skin.

Let me take care of you. She could not recall anyone, ever, having uttered those words to her. It was an odd notion, giving herself over to someone else's care, *his* care, but certainly not an unpleasant notion. And one that allowed her to postpone for a few more precious minutes the words that would forever deprive her of him.

With a nod, she relaxed back into the cushions, torn between her desire to shut her eyes and simply absorb the feel of him touching her, and keeping her eyes wide open, to watch him, memorize his features, for this would be her last opportunity to do so.

Opting to keep her eyes open, she watched him carefully clean, then examine, her cuts and scrapes. He
worked carefully and methodically, his eyes intent, his
hands steady. A lock of dusty, disheveled hair fell over his
forehead, and her fingers itched to brush the strands back.
But he wasn't hers to touch.

Her gaze lowered to the scrape on his chin, and her
stomach dropped. Dear God, he'd risked his life to save
her. With that same heroic spirit he'd exhibited the first
day she'd seen him outside Madame Renée's shop. Had
that only been a matter of days ago? Impossible. She felt
as if she'd known this man her entire life. And had yearned
for him all that time. She longed to dampen a strip of linen
and press it to his hurt chin. But he wasn't hers to heal.

Her gaze then focused on his mouth. That beautiful,
sensual mouth that had kissed her with both tender perfection and white-hot passion. A flood of memories of that
beautiful mouth touching hers swamped her, remem-
brances she would never be able to erase from her mind.
Her lips tingled with the overwhelming desire to kiss him.
But he wasn't hers to kiss.

He touched a piece of dampened linen to her bottom
lip, yanking her from her reverie. Her gaze flew to his, and
she saw his attention was riveted on her lips as he dabbed.
A muscle ticked in his jaw, and she realized that he was
suffering from her nearness just as she was suffering from
his. The knowledge should have appalled her, but instead
a completely inappropriate wave of feminine satisfaction
raced through her. A minute later he turned to place the
used linen back on the tray. He took a moment to cleanse
his own face, then dab some sort of ointment from the ceramic bowl onto his scraped chin. When he returned his
attention to her, their gazes locked, and her breath caught
at the intense, compelling look in his eyes. He went perfectly still and she heard him swallow.

"I'm finished," he said in a husky voice. "Neither the

scrape on your cheek nor the cut near your temple are serious, thank God, nor is the bump on your chin." He held up the small blue ceramic bowl. "This is one of Bakari's concoctions. It will aid in the healing process. I don't know how he makes it, but it works wonders." Still kneeling next to the sofa, he gently dabbed on the cream, which stung a bit at first, but then seemed to evaporate the burning sensation from her scraped skin. When he finished, he set the bowl aside, then asked, "How do you feel?"

"Much better, thank you." She smiled to show him she was telling the truth. "But what about you? That scrape on your chin—"

"I'm fine. I'm—" He blew out a long breath and raked his hands through his hair. "No, I'm not fine. I'm sick inside that you're hurt, that you were very nearly killed. Furious that someone is trying to hurt me by hurting everyone I care about. Frightened that he might somehow inflict more damage before I can stop him." Taking her hands, he pressed her palms against his chest. Through the soft material, she felt his heart beating, hard and fast.

"You were almost lost to me today, Meredith. Before I ever had a chance to tell you all the things I want to tell you. It brought home the sobering fact that we never know what the future holds. Every minute is a gift, and should not be squandered, for it might well be your last. I therefore refuse to waste so much as another second." His brown gaze locked with hers, and he pressed her palms more firmly against his chest. "I love you, Meredith. With all my heart. Will you do me the honor of becoming my wife?"

Seventeen

Meredith had known since last night that he intended to ask her to marry him, and she was prepared to answer him. But she had not anticipated a declaration of love. *I love you, Meredith.* Those words, spoken in that deep, serious voice, left her reeling.

Hot tears pushed behind her eyes and she bit down on the inside of her cheeks in an effort to gain control. She wanted to scream, to rail at the fates and circumstances that would rob her of her chance of happiness with this man . . . this man she loved. Who, incredibly, loved her in return.

But he doesn't truly love you, Meredith, her inner voice interjected. *How could he? He doesn't really know you. The real you. The lying, cheating, stealing you. The you that your respectable, matchmaker persona hides. You tell him the truth, and his love will disappear.*

And, she realized with a sinking heart, she would have to do just that—tell him the truth—all of it, thus extinguishing the tiny flame of hope that she might be able to convince him of their incompatibility without revealing her past. But she knew him well enough to realize that as long as he harbored the belief that he loved her, she would never convince him that a marriage between them was impossible. And if his heart wasn't free of her, he would not pursue another woman. So she'd have to prove to him that he didn't love her after all. Give him back his heart. So he could give it to someone else.

Feeling far too vulnerable in her reclined position, she said, "I'd like to sit up, please." He helped her, his hands warm and firm on her shoulders. Once she was upright, he poured her a tumbler of water, from which she gratefully sipped. Then she looked down at her forest-green gown and grimaced at the dirt marring the material, a fitting symbol of the mess her life had recently become.

She turned toward Philip, who now sat next to her, his eyes serious. And hopeful. Gathering her courage, she met his gaze and forced herself to speak the words her heart wanted so desperately not to say. "Philip, I cannot marry you."

"May I ask why not?"

How she longed to snap out, *No, you may not.* But she owed him the truth. Unable to sit still under his regard any longer, she slipped her hands from his, then rose. Drawing a bracing breath, she lifted her chin. "I'm afraid I have not been entirely honest with you, Philip. There are things about me, about my past, that you do not know. Things that prevent me from considering marriage."

"Such as?"

She began to pace in front of him. Her muscles protested, but she simply could not remain still. "We are not just simply from different social backgrounds, Philip," she began. "I'm afraid that my past is the sort that, if the circumstances were to come to light, would cast shame and scandal upon your family's name and render us both outcasts. I . . . I left my home at an early age. It was an unhappy place from which I could not wait to escape. I made my way to London, but unfortunately I did not realize the hardships I would face on my own. My meager funds quickly ran out, as did my choices. My options narrowed down to dying of starvation or doing what I had to in order to survive. I chose to survive. In order to do so, I had precisely two choices. I could prostitute myself, which I adamantly refused to do." She paused in front of him and pressed her hands to her jittery midsection. "That left stealing. And that is what I did."

She quickly resumed her pacing, not wanting to see the inevitable disgust enter his eyes. "I stole anything I could. Money. Jewelry. Food. At first I wasn't very good at it, and the only thing that saved me from capture on numerous occasions was my ability to run fast. But I learned quickly. I had no choice. There were times I was so hungry, I risked my life for a slice of bread." Images she'd spent years forgetting rushed to the front of her mind. Huddled in dark, frightening alleyways. Running for her life.

Shaking off the memories, she continued, "I became an amazingly adept pickpocket. I moved about to different places to avoid capture, saving every farthing I could, because I wanted to leave the sordid life I was leading as soon as possible. I was determined to become respectable. To lead a decent, honest life. As far from the one I'd run away from as possible. When I'd stolen enough money, I purchased some decent clothing, then set about finding employment. I was fortunate enough to meet Mrs. Barcastle. She was a wealthy widow in need of a traveling companion."

Pausing in her pacing, she turned and faced him squarely. "Traveling with Mrs. Barcastle over the course of the next year, I pickpocketed my way through Brighton and Bath, Bristol and Cardiff, and every place in between."

Something that looked like compassion, but surely could not have been, flickered in his eyes. "You are fortunate you were not caught."

"I was very good. And quite invisible. In the social circles in which we traveled, no one glanced at me—the plain, hired companion. I was like a white spot on a white wall."

Drawing another bracing breath, she continued, "Under Mrs. Barcastle's kind tutelage, I practiced to improve my speech and manners. By the time we returned to London, I had enough money to abandon my larcenous ways and begin establishing my new, respectable identity. As I possessed a flair for matching compatible personalities, I decided to try my hand at matchmaking. I was successful almost immediately, with Mrs. Barcastle herself being my first client. She recommended my services to her friends, and little by little my reputation grew. I eventually purchased the house where I now live, and have managed to maintain a comfortable existence. The marriage I arranged between you and Lady Sarah was the culmination of fifteen years of hard work, and a lifetime of dreams."

Standing before him, she gripped her hands together at her waist and forced herself not to avert her gaze. "After much soul-searching, I have come to terms with my past. But I'm not naive enough to believe that anyone else would or could do the same. Especially the members of Society. Now that you know the truth, I'm sure you can understand why I cannot consider accepting your proposal. For a certainty, you never would have issued a proposal if you'd been in possession of the full truth." A little voice reminded her that he *still* was not in possession of the full truth, but surely she could be spared telling him the rest. . . .

Without breaking eye contact, he rose and stood before her. He made no move to touch her, a fact which did not surprise her, but hurt just the same. Clenc g her hands, she braced herself for the recriminations she knew were coming.

The most deafening silence she'd ever heard stretched

between them, until she thought she would scream. Finally he said quietly, "Thank you for telling me, Meredith. I can only imagine how difficult it was for you to do so."

Dear God, he had no idea how difficult it had been. To say the words that would cost her him. And free his heart. "You're welcome."

"You're wrong about one thing, however."

"What is that?"

"That I never would have issued a proposal if I'd been in possession of the full truth." Reaching out, he lightly grasped her shoulders. Looking directly into her eyes, he said, "I knew, Meredith."

Her heart seemed to stall, then stumble over itself. Surely she'd misheard him. "I beg your pardon?"

"I knew. About your past as a pickpocket."

She could only stare at him in stunned amazement, grateful for his grasp upon her shoulders, as her knees suddenly felt decidedly wobbly. Her mind raced. The only people who knew were Charlotte and Albert, and they would never reveal such details about her to anyone. "How . . . ?" It was the only word she could manage.

"Quite by accident, I assure you. The night I made inquiries regarding Taggert, I spoke to a tavern keep named Ramsey who'd been acquainted with Taggert. Ramsey told me quite a bit about the vile bastard, including a story of how he once witnessed, through the tavern window, Taggert dump a chimney boy on the side of the road like a sack of garbage. Ramsey left the tavern and started toward the boy, but before he reached him, a young woman, scarcely more than a girl, ran to the boy. She knelt next to him, then scooped him up in her arms."

"Dear God," she whispered. "A man came up to me. He asked if the boy was all right. I said, 'He's hurt. I must bring him home.' He asked if the boy was my brother. I lied and said yes. I was afraid if I said I didn't even know him that someone would take him away from me. Toss him into the street again and leave him there. Or give him back to that horrible man who'd thrown him away like yesterday's trash."

"Ramsey told me that the girl who carried off the boy seemed familiar. It took him a few minutes to place her, as she'd grown up, and cleaned up, since he'd seen her last, but there was no mistaking those vivid, aqua eyes. She was the same street urchin who used to steal food from his tavern and pick the pockets of his clientele." One corner of his mouth lifted. "You were quite the bane of his existence for a number of months."

Meredith began to shake all over, battered by incredulity and confusion. "You've known. Since that night you asked about Taggert."

"Yes."

"You knew when you invited me to your home for dinner."

"Yes."

"When you arranged that elaborate meal and decorations."

"Yes."

"And you said nothing about it."

"No."

"But why?" She felt the strong need to sit down, and locked her knees to stiffen the watery sensation suddenly plaguing them.

"Because I was hoping you'd tell me yourself." Releasing her shoulders, he framed her face between his palms. "I am humbled by your trust in me. And the feelings you must have for me, to tell me something so deeply private."

Dear God, this was not going at all the way it was supposed to! Stepping away from him, she said, "I did not tell you out of any deep feelings, Philip. I told you because you would not accept a simple no for an answer. Because you needed to understand how stupendously mismatched we are."

"You mean how stupendously mismatched *you* think we are. Because of things you did *to survive* when you were little more than a child. Well, I disagree with your assessment. Actually, my disagreement falls into the category of 'strenuously disagree.' I've seen the lengths people can be driven to by poverty and fear and hunger. I do not think any less of you for surviving. Indeed, I greatly admire that you overcame such tragedy to become the intelligent, kind, decent woman you are. It has been my experience that adversity either breaks people or strengthens them. And those that it strengthens are often blessed with a special sort of compassion for others who face the same sort of adversity. You have that compassion, Meredith. That strength of spirit. And they are just a few of the many things I love about you. Now, I shall ask you again. Will you do me the honor of becoming my wife?"

Dear God, he meant what he said. But he still did not know the entire truth. "There's more, Philip. It . . . it has to do with the reason I left home. Do you recall me telling you that my father was a tutor and my mother a governess?"

"Yes, of course."

"That was but another lie." She licked her dust-dry lips. "There's no easy way to tell you, so I shall simply say it. I have no idea who my father is. Neither did my mother. He was just one of many men she entertained at the brothel where she worked. At the brothel where I grew up. The brothel I ran away from when I turned thirteen because it was time for me to start earning my keep and I refused to do so. The brothel that my mother refused to leave because she thought being a whore was the only thing she was good at. The brothel where she died of syphilis." Tears wetted her cheeks, but she could not stop the flow of words now that she'd started. It was as if she'd lanced a wound and all the poison was flowing out.

"I went back once. After I was settled in London. I tried

to convince her to come live with me, but she refused. It was the most awful visit." She shut her eyes briefly, vividly recalling her mother's haggard appearance. And the house . . . God, she hated that place. Hated the crude, raucous noises, the smells of stale liquor and smoke and bodies. "I never saw her again. The last correspondence I had from her arrived six months later. She'd written me a letter and asked one of the girls from the brothel to deliver it to me. That girl was Charlotte."

"Your friend, Mrs. Carlyle." It was impossible to gauge his reaction from his neutral tone and expression.

"Yes. The story of her being a widow was but yet another fabrication. Charlotte, who was pregnant, was accosted on her way to my home and arrived beaten and bruised. Albert and I nursed her back to health, and she has lived with us ever since. When she gave birth to her daughter, we all agreed that the perfect name for the child was Hope." She drew in a long, deep breath, then slowly exhaled.

"The reason my matchmaking enterprise is so important to me is because of my upbringing. I used to hide in the cupboard under the stairs thinking, if only Mama had married, how different both our lives would have been. And the same for all the other girls in the brothel—if only they'd found kind, decent men to marry, their lives would have been so different. . . ."

Shaking off the remnants of the past, she said softly, "So now you see why any further association, let alone a marriage, between us is impossible. I told you on more than one occasion I've never intended to marry. I would find it impossible to keep up the pretense and lies regarding my past with a husband—someone I'd have to live with on a daily basis. Nor would I expect any man to accept not only my past, but the pasts of the people closest to me, for I would never abandon Albert, Charlotte, and Hope. The fact that this tavern keep Ramsey recognized

me all those years ago—what if he were to see me again?
The whole ugly truth could come out. It is a fear, and a
possibility that lives inside me every day. A woman with a
past like mine could cost you everything, Philip. Your social standing, your future, *everything*."

They stood in silence, looking at each other, the six-
foot expanse of rug between them seeming like an ocean,
his expression impossible to decipher. She'd told him.
Everything. All that was left was to say good-bye. A simple word, yet she could not seem to push it past her lips.

Finally, after what seemed an eternity, he spoke.
"You've presented everything in your usual clear, concise
manner, but there are still three questions I'd like to ask
you—if you have no objections."

"Of course."

"My first question is, except for details regarding your
background, have you ever lied to me?"

"No." A humorless sound escaped her. "But with regard
to my background, I've accumulated an impressive number of offenses. What is the second question?"

"Do you love me?"

The question stilled everything inside her. *Do you love
me?* How could she deny it? Yet how could she admit it?
And to what end? Telling him how she felt about him
would only make their parting more painful. "I cannot see
how that matters, Philip."

"It matters a great deal to me." Eyes steady on hers, he
stepped toward her, not stopping until less than two feet
remained between them. Her heart pounded so hard, she
could feel her blood drumming through her veins. Reaching out, he clasped her hands, then raised them to his lips.
"It is a simple question, Meredith." His words warmed his
breath against her chilled fingers.

"There is nothing simple about it."

"On the contrary, it requires nothing more than a simple yes-or-no response. Do you love me?"

She wanted to lie. Damnation, she'd uttered so many untruths over the years, surely telling one more should not cause such anguish. But she couldn't push the falsehood past her lips. Lowering her chin, she stared at their clasped hands and whispered, "Yes."

He squeezed her hands, then pressed her palms against his chest. Through his shirt, his heartbeat thumped against her hands, strong and steady. Wrapping one arm around her waist, he touched his fingers beneath her chin and raised her face until she had no choice but to look into his eyes. Eyes whose expression in no way reflected the disgust she'd anticipated. Indeed, his gaze was warm with tenderness. And unmistakable love.

"My third question is, will you marry me?"

Her breath left her lungs in a whoosh. She tried to step back, but his arm tightened, holding her in place. "Have you not been listening?" she asked, her voice rising to an incredulous level. "I am a *bastard*. I grew up in a *brothel*. My mother was a *prostitute*. I spent years as a *thief*."

"You told me you'd made peace with your past. Yet you cannot seem to let it go."

"I *have* made peace with my past. But just because *I* can accept it doesn't mean anyone else would. The things I've done, my background, are unacceptable. Society, your own family, would never accept me. You know they wouldn't."

"You cannot help nor be blamed for the circumstances surrounding your birth, Meredith. Nor are you responsible for your mother's actions. What you see as insurmountable obstacles, I view as reasons to admire your strength and determination to overcome such daunting odds. As for Society rejecting you, yes, I'm certain most of them would if they were to learn the things you confided in me today. However, I don't care a jot about Society. I suffered at the expense of their petty cruelties until I left England. I owe them nothing—most especially the woman I love. As for my family, Catherine has already given our union her blessing. She married a man from our social class—a baron with a pedigree and fortune—but they do not love each other, and she is miserably unhappy. She does not want the same misfortune to befall me."

He moved one step closer, leaving only a hairbreadth between them. "When I returned to England, I was fully prepared to marry a woman I barely knew in order to keep my word to my father. I am no longer willing to do that. The thought of marrying anyone but you is completely impossible. Other people may not accept you, Meredith. But *I* do. Exactly as you are. And isn't that really all that matters?"

Meredith started to tremble. Thank God his arm supported her, or she surely would have wilted to the floor. He'd listened to all her objections, then had swept them aside as if he wielded a broom.

"What if you are unable to break the curse, Philip?"

"Then I would humbly request that you be the wife of my heart, Meredith. I would not shame you, or our feelings for each other, by asking you to live openly in England as my mistress—especially now that I fully understand all the reasons for your aversion to such an arrangement. If I cannot rid myself of the curse, then we could leave England, travel abroad, anywhere you wished, and represent ourselves as husband and wife. If the curse prevents me from pledging my life to you in a church, it still cannot prevent me from pledging it to you."

He tucked a stray curl behind her ear. "Whether it is because of the decade I spent away from Society, or simply my nature, there are very few people whose opinion truly carries any weight with me. Your past, our arrangement— whatever we decide it is to be—is private, between you and me. What anyone else thinks does not matter."

Dear God, he made it all seem so reasonable, and possible. Still, one small matter remained. . . .

She shifted out of his arms, and put several feet between them. "Um, Philip, I'm afraid I have a confession to make. Several minutes ago, I pilfered your watch from your waistcoat pocket." She slipped her hand into the deep pocket of her gown to retrieve the piece. "I did it to demonstrate how completely unacceptable I would be as a candidate for your wife, and had every intention of returning it to you. . . ." Her voice trailed off and a frown pulled down her brows as her fingers swept through her pocket. Her *empty* pocket.

"Is this what you're looking for?"

Her gaze riveted on him slowly extracting his watch from his waistcoat pocket. "H-how . . . ?"

He casually snapped open the gold cover, consulted the time, then returned the piece to his pocket with equal nonchalance. Then a slow, devastating smile curved his lips upward. "I picked up several skills while abroad. The ability to pinch items from someone's pocket, for instance. Bakari instructed me on the finer points, strictly for survival reasons, you understand. Came in quite handy on more than one occasion."

She actually felt her jaw drop open. "You *stole* things?"

"I prefer to call it retrieving my own personal items that were stolen from me first. Many places I visited were rampant with thieves and pickpockets. Since I strongly objected to being relieved of my property, I merely beat them at their own game."

Meredith shook her head in amazed disbelief. "Incredible. You're very good. I didn't feel a thing."

"Thank you. Heartwarming to know I haven't lost my touch. However, as long as we're exchanging confessions, I must tell you that I did, on one occasion, use my talents to confiscate something that did not belong to me. While in Syria, Bakari, Andrew, and I, through a rather circuitous series of events, were imprisoned in a dungeon. I pinched the key from the guard's pocket, and we escaped."

Her eyes goggled. "Imprisoned in a dungeon? Did you accidentally lock yourselves in?"

"Not exactly. It is a very involved tale, one I will happily share with you—but not right now. Right now we have much more important things to discuss." Erasing the distance between them with a single long stride, he drew her into his arms. "Do you have any other last-minute confessions to make?"

Dazed, she shook her head.

"Excellent. Neither do I. Therefore, all that is left is for you to answer my question. Will you marry me?"

He was looking at her with an expression that robbed her of breath. Love, tenderness, admiration, and heated longing all emanated from his gaze. Everything she'd always wanted but had been convinced could never be hers now stood before her. All the feelings and yearnings she'd ever hidden in her heart burst free, flooding her with a happiness she hadn't dared hope possible.

Staring at him in wonder, scarcely able to believe this wasn't a dream, she reached up and framed his face between her hands. "I love you, Philip. With all my heart. Yes, I will marry you. And I will strive every day to be a good and proper wife to you."

She felt the tension drain from his body. Lowering his head, he pressed his forehead to hers. "Thank God. I thought you were going to say no."

"You were very persuasive."

"Because I love you so very much." He gently touched his lips to hers, a kiss filled with love and promise, and one that quickly flared into a passionate mating of lips and tongues. Heat raced through her, and, wrapping her arms around his neck, she raised up on her toes, pressing herself against him.

Philip tightened his arms around her, and tried his damnedest to curb his ardor, but he was lost. Lost in the soft, supple feel of her. The delicious, sweet taste of her.

Lost in the knowledge that she loved him. That she would be his wife. That she was his to love and touch and kiss. To laugh with and love with.

Her fingers wreaked havoc with his hair while his hands ran restlessly down her back, urging her closer, then skimming lower to cup her buttocks. His erection strained against his tight breeches, and a guttural groan vibrated in his throat. Summoning his last ounce of will, he broke off their kiss. He blinked behind his fogged-up lenses, then impatiently pulled off his spectacles and tossed them onto the end table.

He looked down into Meredith's glazed eyes, and a groan of pure masculine need pushed past his lips. With her lips damp and parted, her eyelids at half mast, and her color high, she looked well kissed and thoroughly aroused. And he knew if he kissed her again, he'd give in to the need clawing at him. "Meredith, if we don't stop now, I'm afraid I won't be able to stop at all."

She looked at him with an expression that stilled him. "I don't recall asking you to stop."

Eighteen

Her words shot fire through his veins and robbed him of speech. *I don't recall asking you to stop. . . .*

"You said I was almost lost to you today," she said, her eyes serious and intent upon his. "Well, I almost lost you as well. You said that we never know what the future holds, that every minute is a gift, and should not be squandered. I don't want to waste so much as another second, Philip."

Without hesitation, he bent his knees and scooped her up. Holding her tightly against his chest, he moved swiftly toward the door. "Have I mentioned how much I love the way you not only listen to me, but can repeat my own brilliant words back to me, almost verbatim?"

A smile curved her lips. "No, I don't believe you've mentioned that."

"Very remiss of me. Of course, there are so many things I love about you, it will take me an enormous amount of time to tell you all of them. Years. Decades. Especially as I am continually discovering new things."

Leaving the study, he strode down the corridor, forcing himself not to break into an undignified gallop. As they entered the foyer, James asked anxiously, "Is Miss Chilton-Grizedale all right, my lord?"

Philip halted and beamed at the young man. "Actually,

James, Miss Chilton-Grizedale is extraordinary. And what's more, she shall not remain Miss Chilton-Grizedale much longer. She is soon to be Viscountess Greybourne. As she just accepted my proposal only minutes ago, you may be the first to congratulate us."

"I . . . I'm honored, my lord," James stammered, clearly dumfounded at being the first to hear such a momentous announcement. "Best wishes to both of you."

"Thank you." Without further ado, Philip climbed the stairs, two at a time, then headed swiftly down the corridor toward his bedchamber.

Crimson stained her cheeks. "Good heavens, whatever must that young man think, with you carrying me upstairs like this?"

"He thinks you are going to make good use of the bath set up in my chamber, which you are. And he thinks I am the luckiest man in the world, which I am."

"Your announcement of our betrothal quite shocked him. One normally shares such news with one's family before telling the servants. And certainly not while carrying one's betrothed. And most certainly not while carrying one's betrothed toward the bedchamber where a bath has been prepared." She heaved an exaggerated sigh. "Whatever am I going to do about your stunning lack of propriety?"

"Hmmm. I can think of half a dozen things without even setting my mind to it. And do you really believe that was shock in his eyes? Odd, I thought it was envy. Still, how fortunate am I that my future bride is well versed in such etiquette-related details, the likes of which I've clearly forgotten over the years." Arriving in his bedchamber, he crossed to the oversized brass tub set before the fire and gently lowered her to her feet. He then returned to the door to close and lock it. The click reverberated through the quiet room.

Rejoining her, he lifted her hands to press a kiss against

each of her palms. The delicious scent of freshly buttered scones teased his senses, mingling with the heated steam rising from the bath.

He slipped the pins from her hair, allowing the fasteners to fall silently onto the Axminster rug. Midnight tresses spilled over his hands and down her back. Gently sifting his fingers through the strands, he loosened the tangles and the dust, until only smooth, shiny curls fell over his fingers.

Slowly. He had to go slowly with her. But bloody hell, he wasn't certain he would be able to, especially if she continued to look at him with eyes that reflected love and trust and desire, shadowed with just a shade of trepidation.

"Nervous?" he asked.

A short breath pushed from her lungs. "Yes."

"I imagine you witnessed a great deal more than a child should. And I would guess that most of it was of a crude nature."

She swallowed audibly. "True."

He tucked a silky stray curl behind her ear. "You know I would never hurt you."

"Of course."

"We will be beautiful together, Meredith."

"I know, Philip. I'm not afraid."

"I'm glad." One corner of his mouth lifted. "If it makes you feel any better, I'm nervous as well."

There was no mistaking her surprise. "Surely not for the same reason I am?"

Heat crept up his neck. "No. At least not exactly, as I am not a virgin. But nothing in my experience has prepared me for *this*. For making love to a woman I *love*. To a woman I desire so much I can barely think properly. To a woman I want, more than anything, to please. That, coupled with the fact that it has been many months since I was last with anyone . . . well, suffice it to say that I am nervous as well."

He felt some of the tension ease from her body. "In that case," she said, a smile trembling on her lips, "I shall do my utmost to be gentle with you."

He smiled in return. "My darling Meredith, you have no idea how much I anticipate you doing so."

Without taking his gaze off her, he unbuttoned her bodice, then slowly slipped her gown from her shoulders, revealing her delicate clavicle, and porcelain skin stained with a faint blush. "The first time I kissed you, at Vauxhall, my only regret was that it was so dark. I wanted to see you. Your skin. Your body. Your eyes. Your reactions. And now I have you in the light. . . ." He eased her gown downward, over her arms, past her hips, then let it go to spill into a forest-green puddle at her feet.

Meredith drew in a quick breath and all the tension she'd only just pushed aside roared back at standing before him wearing only her undergarments. Taking her hand, he helped her step from the center of her fallen gown. He then picked up the garment and draped it over the back of a leather chair. Returning to her, he dropped to one knee. "Hold on to my shoulders."

She did as he bade, and he gently lifted one foot, then the other, sliding off her shoes. He smoothed his hands up her calves, then the backs of her thighs, shooting shivers of delight up her spine. When his fingers skimmed near the edges of her garters, he looked up at her.

"The first time we met, after you'd swooned in St. Paul's—"

"I prefer to call it an uncharacteristic moment of light-headedness."

"I'm certain you do. After you swooned, I told you I would not dream of touching your garters without your express permission."

"Actually, you said you *probably* would not dream of touching them without my express permission. I thought you were incorrigible."

"I am."

"I also recall assuring you that you would never receive such permission."

"You did. May I touch your garters, Meredith?"

"Yes," she whispered. "Please do."

He untied the ribbons and slipped off her stockings, leaving her to curl her bare toes into the fire-warmed rug.

Then he rose, and her breath stalled when he edged his fingers beneath the straps of her chemise and slowly drew the garment down her body, letting it fall at her feet.

His gaze tracked slowly downward, touching her everywhere like a heated caress, leaving a trail of fire in its wake. Her nipples hardened into aching points, and her breathing turned shallow.

Reaching out, he took her hands, entwining their fingers. "Meredith . . ." Her name passed his lips in a rough whisper. "You're beautiful. So beautiful." Lifting her hands to his lips, he pressed a fervent kiss against the sensitive inside of her wrist. Tingles raced up her arm, shooting liquid heat through her, which settled low in her belly. Surely she should feel some embarrassment at standing naked before him, yet all she felt was breathless exhilaration. Heady anticipation. And an overwhelming impatience to remove his clothing so she could see him as well, feel him against her, skin to skin.

Disentangling one of her hands from his, she reached out and skimmed her fingers down the front of his shirt. "One of us is wearing far too many garments."

His eyes darkened with a combination of heat and amusement. Releasing her hand, he pulled his shirt from his breeches, then settled his arms at his sides. "I am at your disposal, madam."

Intrigued at the thought of undressing him, she applied herself to the row of buttons down the front of his shirt. When she finished the last one, she slowly parted the material, slipping the fine lawn over his shoulders and down his arms. Her avid gaze took in his wide shoulders, broad chest, and muscled arms. Golden, tanned skin, sprinkled with dark brown hair that narrowed into a fascinating ribbon that bisected his ridged abdomen, before disappearing into the waistband of his breeches.

Encouraged by the desire so evident in his eyes, she placed her hands on his chest, then splayed her fingers, absorbing the warmth of his skin, delighting in the sensation of his hair tickling against her palm, his heartbeat thudding beneath her fingertips. She inhaled deeply, filling her head with the delightful, woodsy-clean scent that belonged to him alone. Captivated, she experimentally glided her hands across the expanse of firm muscles, and was rewarded with a masculine groan. Emboldened by that response, she smoothed her hands over him again, marveling at the firm, smooth texture of his skin, his hard muscles contracting beneath her palms. But when she feathered her fingertips down, over his abdomen, he sucked in a breath and grasped her wrists.

"If you continue to do that, I won't last very long, and I am not yet finished taking care of you. There is still your bath to see to. Let me help you into the tub. The warm water will relax you, and relieve any soreness from our fall."

"But what about you? You fell as well."

"Which is why I intend to join you in the bath."

His words, coupled by the sensual glitter in his eyes, fired a tingling flame through her. Pulling her gaze from his, she turned to look at the shiny brass tub, noticing for the first time its size. It was wider and considerably longer than any tub she'd ever seen, and did indeed appear large enough to fit two people—provided they sat *very* close to each other. "I've never seen a tub such as this."

"I had it made in Italy. As I enjoy the healing and relaxation properties of a soak in warm water, and do not care to fold myself up like a paper fan, I required something considerably larger than a hip bath. I'm certain you'll enjoy it."

Holding his hand for balance, she climbed upon the small wooden stool, stepped over the edge of the tub, then lowered herself into the heated water.

He dropped a quick kiss on her lips. "Close your eyes and relax. I shall return in a moment."

"Where are you going?"

His gaze slid down her body. "To fetch my strigil."

Admiring his broad back, she watched him walk toward a door she assumed led to his dressing room, and recalled their conversation in the warehouse about the strigil . . . how it was used by ancient Greeks and Romans for scraping moisture off their skin after bathing. And the wealth of sensual images that conversation had inspired. Of him, and her, naked in the bath—never daring to hope that such fantasies could become reality. Was it only an hour ago she'd told herself that he wasn't hers to touch? Hers to kiss? Yet now he was all that, and so much more. He was hers to love. And marry. And care for. *And bathe with* . . .

The curls of steam rising from the water had nothing to do with the heat coursing through her. The door he'd disappeared through opened, and he walked toward her, wearing a dark blue silk robe, the sash loosely knotted about his waist. She noted his bare feet, and her heart sped up at the realization that the robe was all he wore. In one hand he carried a folded towel, in the other hand he carried a strigil, identical to the one she'd cataloged at the warehouse, except this one was made of highly polished brass and looked considerably newer.

After setting down the towel and strigil next to the towel whoever had prepared the bath had already left, he crouched down alongside the tub. Dipping his hand into the water, he trailed his fingers along her thigh. "How does the water feel?"

"Nice. Warm." Summoning her courage, she added, "Lonely."

Heat flickered in his eyes, and without a word, he rose, untied the sash securing his robe, then shrugged the garment from his body. Her gaze wandered slowly downward, from his shoulders and chest, following that captivating silky line of hair down his abdomen to his . . .

Oh, my.

Lower, that silky ribbon spread to cradle his fully erect manhood. Fascination and trepidation collided in her, and her gaze flew up to meet his. His ardor was obvious, but judging by the banked fire in his eyes, it was also clear that he was holding himself in tight control.

He stepped to the edge of the tub. "Move forward a bit," he said softly.

Entranced, she did as he bade her, watching over her shoulder as he stepped over the edge, then lowered himself to sit behind her.

The water rose, coming within inches of sloshing over onto the carpet. He slipped his long legs on either side of her, then, grasping her shoulders, eased her backward until her entire back reclined against his chest, warm water lapping at her shoulders. He fitted his arms beneath hers, wrapping them lightly around her waist.

Sensations bombarded her from every direction. The incredible feel of his naked body surrounding hers, their skin slippery and sleek from the water. The gentle tickle of his chest hair against her shoulders. His heartbeat thumping against her back. His arousal nestled snugly against the base of her spine. Her temple resting against his smoothly shaven cheek. The sight of his strong, golden brown arms and legs enveloping her, her skin so pale in comparison. One of his large hands cupping the underside of her breast beneath the water, her nipple erect, as if begging for his touch. She drew in a deep breath and her eyes slid closed as his unique scent rose on the steam, surrounding her in a heated, sensual cocoon from which she never wished to emerge.

Yet just when she thought it impossible to be steeped in further sensations, his hands began to move beneath the water. Her eyelids fluttered open and she watched his hands glide slowly upward, over her breasts. His palms skimmed over her taut nipples, but he did not linger, instead continuing his upward journey to her shoulders, where his fingers lightly massaged. A low moan of pleasure purred in her throat.

After his hands wrought their limb-weakening magic upon her shoulders for several moments, he whispered against her cheek, "Raise your arms and wrap them around my neck."

Languid from his ministrations, she did as he bade, linking her upraised hands together at his nape. With his lips bestowing lingering kisses along her temple, his hands slowly smoothed down the undersides of her arms, slipped under the water to continue over her breasts. Each of his fingers teased over her nipples, quickening her breath. Before she could recover, he continued downward, over her rib cage and abdomen, then along her inner thighs. When he reached her knees, he reversed direction and slowly stroked his way back up her body to her elbows.

"Do you like that?" His question tickled by her ear.

"Yes." Her response came out in a long sigh of pleasure.

He repeated the long, drugging stroke, kindling an inferno in her that quickly threatened to consume her from the inside out. With each passing of his hands over her body, she experienced an insistent, heavy pull between her thighs. Moans she could not suppress accompanied her every exhale. How was it possible that his touch both soothed and aroused her unbearably at the same time?

Each time his fingers brushed over her nipples, she lifted her breasts, craving more of his touch. When his palms meandered along her thighs, she spread her legs wider, increasingly desperate for him to put out this relentless fire he'd ignited. Turning her head, she pressed her lips against his throat, squirming against him when he lingered over her breasts and teased her aching nipples between his fingers.

Philip sucked in a sharp breath as she moved against him, the curve of her buttocks rubbing against his erection. He gritted his teeth against the pleasure, fighting to remain in control, but the feel of her all but vibrating beneath his hands, the sight of her taut nipples seeking his touch, her straining to splay her legs wider, offering him the sensual wonders hidden by the triangle of dark curls at the apex of her thighs, the erotic scent of feminine arousal rising from her skin, her increasingly uninhibited response, all conspired to rob him of his command over himself.

"Philip . . ."

His name, whispered against his neck in a smoky, need-filled moan, stripped him of another layer of restraint. Shifting slightly to have better access to her lips, his mouth came down on hers in a hot, demanding, open-mouthed kiss. While one hand continued to play over her breasts, his other hand wandered downward, his fingers cruising over her belly and those entrancing curls, then slid lower, between her thighs, to glide over her sleek, swollen flesh. She gasped against his mouth, and he deepened their kiss, his tongue rubbing against hers in a blatant imitation of the act his body desperately ached to share with her.

He slowly caressed her folds, then eased a finger inside her. A long groan vibrated in her throat. Unlocking her hands at the back of his neck, she ran her palms down his thighs. She broke off their kiss, and whispered against his throat, "Touch you . . . want to touch you."

Slipping his finger from her velvety heat, he grasped her waist and helped her turn over. Rising to her knees between his spread legs, she settled her backside on her heels. A groan escaped him at the sight of her, azure eyes glittering, dark hair mussed, the lower part wet and clinging to her shoulders, color high, lips swollen and reddened from their kisses, full breasts topped with coral-tipped, aroused nipples, water streaming down her body. Before he could regain the wits just looking at her had robbed, she said, "Put your hands behind your head."

Their eyes met, and his heart thudded at her unmistakable meaning. She meant to stroke him just as he'd stroked her. Lifting his arms, he locked his fingers at his nape. And prayed for strength.

Starting at his elbows, she slowly dragged her hands down his arms and over his chest, igniting a trail of flame under his skin. Watching her touching him, her eyes bright with avid curiosity, wonder, and desire, he knew he'd never seen a more arousing sight. Her hands skimmed over his hips, then down his thighs to his knees, where she changed direction and started her upward stroke.

"Do you like that, Philip?"

"God, yes."

By gritting his teeth and clenching his fingers until they turned numb, he endured another slow pass of her hands along his body. On her third downward journey, her fingertips brushed over the head of his erection. He sucked in a sharp breath, then groaned.

Clearly encouraged by his response, she touched him again, this time trailing her fingers down the length of his rigid flesh. Leaning his head back, he closed his eyes, engulfed in raw sensations as her hands caressed and stroked him. When she wrapped her fingers around his shaft and gently squeezed him, a growl of need ripped from him, and he could no longer deny the demands of his body. He needed her, wanted her. *Now*.

Lifting his head, he reached for her, commanding in a raw voice, "Straddle me."

Without hesitation, she rested her hands on his shoulders, then shifted her legs to the outside of his thighs. Grasping her hips, he settled her over the tip of his erection and gently urged her downward until her maidenhead impeded their progress. Their gazes locked, he simultaneously surged up and pressed her down, and buried himself deep within her silky heat.

Her eyes widened and his heart clenched. "Did I hurt you?"

She shook her head slowly, and he forced himself to remain perfectly still, to give her a chance to become accustomed to the feel of him, while he absorbed the exquisite sensation of her tight, velvety heat wrapped around him. Nearly a minute passed before she experimentally moved against him, dragging a groan from him.

Releasing her hips, he skimmed his hands up to her breasts, determined to allow her to set the pace. Watching every nuance of her wonder-filled arousal, he filled his hands with her breasts, while she slowly rocked against him. The effort to hold off his rapidly approaching orgasm beaded sweat on his forehead. Her tempo increased, and the last shreds of his control evaporated, leaving him lost, mindless with need. Gripping her hips, he thrust upward, hard and fast. Her eyes slid closed, and her fingers dug into his shoulders. The instant he felt her tighten around him, he let himself go, his own release pounding through him.

When his tremors finally subsided, he opened his eyes. Her eyes were still closed, and her head hung limply forward, as if too heavy for her neck to bear. Heart still thudding against his ribs, he said the one word he could manage.

"Meredith."

She slowly lifted her head. Her eyelids fluttered open, and their gazes locked. A long, silent look passed between them. He wanted to say something, but damn it, words were beyond him. And even if they weren't, what words could possibly describe what they'd just shared?

"I had no idea . . ." she finally said quietly. "Thank you. For showing me how beautiful that act can be."

The area around his heart went hollow, then filled with such love for her, he ached with it. "Then I must thank you as well, because I never knew it could be that beautiful."

She said nothing for several heartbeats, then a smile pulled up one corner of her lips, and a hint of mischief flickered in her eyes. "Do you think it's possible that it could get even more beautiful?"

Smiling, he fisted his hand in her hair and dragged her mouth down to his. "A very intriguing hypothesis, one which I believe requires immediate experimentation," he said, punctuating each word with a nipping kiss. "But as the water is growing cool, I suggest we remand to the comfort of my bed to conduct our research."

They shared one final lush kiss, after which he helped her to rise. Then he stood and helped her step over the edge of the tub, onto the wooden stool, and down to the carpet. Following her out, he snatched up the strigil. He skimmed the instrument down each of her arms and legs, removing the water from her skin, then wrapped her in a thick towel, warmed from its spot near the fire. He was about to apply the strigil to his own arm when she asked, "May I?"

He set the instrument in her outstretched hand, then enjoyed her gentle ministrations. When she finished, he shrugged into his robe, then led her to stand in front of the fire, where he used the other warmed towel to dry her hair. When he finished, he stood in front of her, sifting his fingers through the long, dark, still slightly damp strands. She smiled up at him, a smile so filled with love and happiness, she dazzled him. "Would you mind terribly if I told you again that I love you?" she asked.

He frowned and pretended to give the question great thought. "Well, I suppose if you feel that you *must* . . ."

"Oh, I must." Rising up on her toes, she looped her arms around his neck. "I love you, Philip."

Pulling her tighter against him, he said, "I love you, too."

Something flickered in her eyes, prompting him to ask, "What is it?"

"I was just thinking, do you think perhaps we might have . . . made a baby?"

The question stilled him. An image of her, large with their child, flashed in his mind. "I don't know. But I *do* know the thought of you bearing our child . . ." His voice trailed off and he lowered his head to touch his forehead to hers. "The mere thought leaves me speechless with joy."

She leaned back in the circle of his arms, her eyes dancing. "I can picture our son now. Strong and intelligent, with your kind eyes behind his spectacles, and your thick, dark hair."

"And I can picture our daughter now," he countered with a grin, "with your vivid coloring, determination, and generous spirit." Taking her hand, he led her toward the bed. "What sort of wedding would you like? Something grand in St. Paul's?"

"Actually, I'd prefer something simple. Perhaps here, in your home."

"Then that is precisely what we shall have. I will arrange for a special license as soon as—"

His words cut off as she stumbled. Her hand slipped

from his, and before he could catch her, she fell forward, landing on her knees, and breaking her fall with her palms. He dropped to his knees beside her and wrapped an arm around her shoulder, helping her to sit back on her heels.

"Are you all right?"

"Y-yes. I must have tripped on something."

He glanced around, but no stray objects littered the floor, nor were there any bumps in the carpet. He was about to ask her if she felt able to stand when she groaned and pressed her fingers to her forehead.

"What's wrong?" he asked, alarmed by her sudden pallor.

She squeezed her eyes shut and drew in a sharp breath. "My head. It hurts. Severely."

He stared at her, a kernel of uneasiness knotting his stomach. A fall . . . then a headache . . . The words from the Stone of Tears reverberated through his mind.

For true love's very breath
Is destined for death.
Grace will fall, a stumble she'll take,
Then suffer the pain of hell's headache.
If ye have the gift of wedded bliss,
She will die before you kiss.
Or two days after the vows are said,
Your bride, so cursed, shall be found dead.
Once your intended has been lo
Nothing can save her from

Bloody hell, what were the missing words to the curse? Could it be 'Once your intended has been *loved*?' His uneasiness turned into dawning, stunned horror. She'd fallen. And now was suffering a terrible headache. By proposing to Meredith, telling her he loved her, then making love to her, had he brought the wrath of the curse upon

`her? If not, then the fall and the headache immediately
following were odd coincidences—and by God, he didn't
believe in coincidence. Especially when his gut tightened
in this foreboding way.

She groaned again and everything inside him froze. No,
this was no odd coincidence. Stark fear iced his veins at
the horrible realization that he'd done exactly that—
brought the wrath of the curse upon her—and had thereby
sealed her fate.

Unless he found a way to break the curse—

She would die in two days.

Nineteen

Philip knelt beside Meredith, who pressed her hands against her forehead and moaned. He struggled to draw a breath and silence the agonized *Noooooo!* ricocheting through his brain. Her falling, the headache, the curse . . . this could not be happening. Not when they'd just found each other. Not when their future, only seconds ago, had bloomed so bright upon the horizon.

Bludgeoning back the talons of fear clawing at him, he hoisted her into his arms and carried her to his bed, where he yanked back the burgundy counterpane, then settled her gently upon the mattress. Her complexion was waxy pale, her features bunched into a pain-filled grimace.

"I've never had a headache such as this," she whispered. "It feels as if the inside of my head is on fire and about to explode.

Suffer the pain of hell's headache. Philip tucked the covers around her, then sat next to her for a moment, holding her hand, and praying to every heavenly force he'd ever heard of to intervene. To save her. To help him find the missing piece of stone. *Please, please, don't take her away from me.*

Leaning over, he brushed his lips against her brow. "I'm going to leave you for a moment to prepare a draught that will relieve the pain."

He crossed to his wardrobe and pulled out a worn leather satchel. Digging through the contents, he extracted a small bottle of one of Bakari's mysterious cures. Philip didn't know exactly what was in the bottle, but he knew from experience that it was effective in relieving headaches. He quickly added several drops to a tumbler of fresh water, then returned to her.

"Drink this," he said, helping her to sit up. After she swallowed the contents, he settled her back on the pillow.

She opened her eyes, and a wobbly half smile pulled up one corner of her lips. "I'm sorry, Philip. I didn't mean to cast such a pall on our research."

"Meredith, I'm afraid this is not an ordinary headache you're suffering."

"What do you mean?"

"The series of events this morning. We professed love for each other. I proposed, you accepted. We made love. Then you fell down, and now you have a headache."

Understanding, along with confusion, dawned in her eyes. "The curse. But we're not married."

"The last two lines read, *Once your intended has been lo* and *Nothing can save her from.* I believe the 'lo' must be from 'loved.' You are my intended. I told you I love you. I made love to you. I'm afraid that by doing so, I unleashed the curse upon you."

Her eyes widened with a combination of fright and disbelief. "Which means that in two days I'm going to . . . *die?*"

His stomach cramped into a painful knot at the question, and he pressed her cold hands between his. "It means that I only have two days to find the missing piece of stone and discover how to break the curse."

"And if you cannot?"

They stared at each other for a long moment in silence, both knowing the frightening answer, one he simply could not verbalize. "I will not fail in this, Meredith. Your life depends upon my success, and nothing is more precious to me than your life."

Her bottom lip quivered, but a flicker of determination fired in her eyes. "Well, it's rather precious to me as well, especially now that my future includes you, and I've no intention of taking this lying down. What can I do to help?"

"You can remain here, in this bed."

"I'll do no such thing! You cannot expect me to just lie about when—"

"Meredith." He cupped her pale face between his hands. "I need you to stay here—*for now*," he emphasized, to forestall the argument he knew was about to burst from her, "so that I know you are safe. Andrew, Bakari, and Edward will help me search through the remaining crates at the warehouse and those on the *Sea Raven*."

"Philip, I can assist with the search. You'll need as many hands as possible. And as for me being safe, I'd feel safer with you than anywhere else."

He blew out a long breath and dragged his hands down his face. She did have a point—he'd know she was safe if she was within his sight. And God knows he didn't want to spend one precious minute away from her. "Do you feel well enough?"

"Yes. My head still hurts, but not as badly."

Reaching out, he brushed his fingertips over her pale cheek, acutely feeling the need to say what he was feeling, but not certain how. "I'm so sorry, Meredith. I didn't know—"

"Of course you didn't." She laid her hand over his and turned her face to press a kiss into his palm. "We'll fix this, Philip. Together. You'll see."

A lump of emotion clogged his throat. Instead of turning on him in anger for bringing the curse's wrath upon her, or succumbing to panic and fear, she'd turned to him with love. And determination. In spite of his own panic and fear, he could give her nothing less. "Together," he repeated. "I won't allow any harm to come to you, Meredith. I give you my word."

She smiled. "That is all I need."

His heart turned over at the trust and confidence in her eyes. He could only pray it wasn't misplaced. "All right. Let's get dressed. There's no time to waste."

The hack was still approximately a half mile from the warehouse when Philip inhaled and frowned. "I smell smoke."

Meredith nodded. "Yes, I do, too."

They exchanged a look, and Philip could tell that she felt the same sense of foreboding that crept through him. But several minutes later his fears were put to rest when they arrived at the warehouse. Whatever was burning, it wasn't the warehouse.

As there was no sign of his carriage, he said to the hackney, "Wait for us here." He assisted Meredith from the vehicle, then they quickly entered the warehouse and made their way through the labyrinth of rows to Philip's cache of crates. The area was empty, but a note was affixed to the outside of one of the crates. Philip scanned the brief missive:

We finished going through the crates here. Nothing regarding the missing piece of stone was found. Have proceeded to docks to await Sea Raven's *arrival.*

The fact that these crates had failed to yield the missing piece of stone felt like a noose tightening around his neck. And he had less than forty-eight hours to solve the puzzle before he stepped off the scaffold. Taking Meredith's hand, he led her toward the exit. When they opened the door, the stench of acrid smoke, stronger than before, filled his nostrils. The hackney jerked his thumb toward a dark plume of smoke rising in the air.

"Looks to be comin' from the docks, it does," the man said, his voice grave.

Again, that tingle of foreboding slithered down Philip's spine. "Take us there, posthaste," he instructed, handing Meredith into the interior.

He clasped her hand tightly as the hack moved swiftly along the narrow streets. "How is the headache?"

"Better."

"But it still hurts?"

She regarded him through serious eyes. "Yes."

She was clearly trying to put on a brave front, but shadows of fear lurked in her eyes. He desperately wanted to comfort her, but he didn't know what to say. Only a fortnight ago, he hadn't even known this woman existed. Now she held his heart in her hands. And he held her future, her life, in his. Her very life depended on his ability to solve the curse.

Unable to keep from touching her, he moved from the seat opposite to sit beside her. Then he wrapped his arms around her and hauled her onto his lap. She looped her arms around his neck and rested her head against his shoulder. Squeezing his eyes shut, he held her tightly against him, absorbing the feel of her in his arms, her warm breath touching his neck, her soft hair against his jaw. *I will not lose her. I cannot lose her.*

A deafening boom rent the air, and the vehicle jerked to a halt. Meredith sat upright, her eyes round. "What was that?"

Philip's stomach dropped. "It sounded like gunpowder exploding." Setting Meredith on the seat, he jumped from the carriage. Thick plumes of black smoke billowed in the distance behind the building directly in front of them. The horse whinnied loudly, and Philip heard the driver trying to soothe the animal.

"Won't be able to take ye any farther, sir," the driver said. "Me horse got spooked by that noise, and she's caught wind of the fire wot's burning. 'Fraid she won't budge."

"We'll walk the rest of the way," Meredith said from directly behind him.

Unease prickling along his nerve endings, Philip jerked his head in a nod. Reaching into his pocket, he tossed several coins up to the driver. Then, tightly clasping hands, they quickly skirted around the building.

The instant they turned the corner, Philip skidded to a halt. Flames and smoke engulfed a burning ship. The vessel drifted in the middle of the river, obviously untied from the dock so as not to allow the fire to spread to the wharf and beyond. Men ran frantically about on the dock, hoisting buckets of water to put out small fires erupting from burning embers landing on the surrounding docks.

Meredith clutched his arm. "How awful."

"Yes." But Philip suspected she hadn't yet realized just how awful. For the ship that was ablaze was the *Sea Raven*.

Squinting through the puffs of black smoke, he saw a familiar figure. "Come. I see Andrew."

Keeping close together, they made their way across the cobblestones. When they reached the dock, Philip touched Andrew on the shoulder. His friend turned, nodded a greeting to Meredith, then looked at him with a grim expression.

"How did this happen?" Philip asked.

"I don't know. After we finished cataloging the last crate at the warehouse, we came here. The ship was just being secured. There were people everywhere, and

Bakari, Edward, and I became separated. The ship some-how caught fire, then there was an explosion."

"Gunpowder," Philip murmured. "There were a dozen barrels on board."

"Yes. I cannot fathom that the cargo traveled safely all the way from Egypt without mishap, only to be destroyed upon its arrival."

"Was anyone injured?"

"Some minor burns, one crewman suffered a broken leg. But no fatalities, thank God. If the gunpowder had exploded sooner, before the crew was able to disembark, it would have been a different story." Their eyes met. "Unfortunately, none of the cargo was saved. All the artifacts on board are lost."

"Where are Edward and Bakari now?"

"I don't know." He made a vague, sweeping gesture with his hand. "Around somewhere, I'm sure."

Philip felt a pressure on his arm. Turning, he met Meredith's distressed-filled gaze. "Artifacts?" she whispered. "Dear God, was that ship the *Sea Raven*?"

"I'm afraid so." His insides clenched at the fear and resignation that filled her eyes.

"So that's it, then," she said, her voice utterly devoid of expression. "There's no hope of finding the missing piece of stone. Which means that in less than forty-eight hours I'm going to die."

"What's that you say, Miss Chilton-Grizedale?" Andrew asked in a perplexed voice. "What is she talking about, Philip?"

Before Philip could reply, Edward and Bakari joined them. Like Andrew, both men's clothing bore black, sooty streaks. "Horrible tragedy," Edward murmured, shaking his head. "Thank God no one was killed." He turned to Andrew. "Where did you disappear to? I haven't seen you since the moment we arrived at the docks."

Andrew raised his brows. "I could say the same about you."

"Many people, much confusion," Bakari said. He then pointed toward the water. "Look."

They all turned toward the ship, and for the next few minutes watched in silence as the burning *Sea Raven* slowly slipped beneath the surface, until it disappeared completely from sight.

"All that work, all those artifacts . . ." Edward shook his head, then clapped a sympathetic hand on Philip's shoulder. "A terrible loss for you, Philip."

"None of that matters. All that matters is finding a way to break the curse. Before it's too late." His gaze shifted between his three friends. "Meredith has been affected by the curse."

"What do you mean?" asked Andrew, his voice sharp.

"I mean that the wrath of this bloody curse has befallen her."

"But how?" Edward asked. "You did not marry her."

"No, but I *asked* her to marry me. And moments after I did so, she fell down, then developed a painful headache."

Andrew, Edward, and Bakari's gazes all shifted to Meredith, their expressions ranging from pity to dread. Not one of them suggested that perhaps her fall and the onset of the headache were merely coincidence.

"What can we do to help?" Andrew asked quietly.

"I want you to escort Meredith back to my townhouse. See that she's comfortable, and watch over her." Philip gave Andrew a meaningful stare, and his friend nodded, knowing that 'watch over her' meant not to leave her side. He turned to Meredith. "Do you wish to stop at your own residence first?"

She shook her head. "Not now. I don't want to alarm Charlotte and Albert. Of course, I shall need to see them . . . soon."

He clasped her hands. "You will be able to see them every day, for years to come." He turned to Bakari. "I'd like you to go to my father's townhouse and keep an eye on him and Catherine. And Edward, if you wouldn't mind, I'd appreciate it if you'd take care of making inquiries regarding the fire, and speak to the necessary authorities."

"What are you going to do?" Meredith asked.

"I'm going to stop at the warehouse to look over the ledgers one last time. Perhaps something will inspire an idea. Then I'll join you at my townhouse."

With a nod and a promise to contact him later, Edward departed. Philip and Meredith followed Andrew and Bakari toward the waiting Greybourne carriage, several blocks away. After Andrew and Bakari rounded a corner, affording them a modicum of privacy, Philip stopped and pulled Meredith against him. Before she could utter a sound, he covered her mouth with his, in a hard, demanding kiss, filled with all the fear and desperation threatening to overwhelm him. She kissed him back with equal desperation, her fear palpable. Gentling the kiss, he cupped her face between his hands, then drew back to look at her.

A tiny smile lifted one corner of her mouth. "Waiting to kiss me until your friends rounded the corner . . . how utterly respectable of you. Although I must point out that kissing me outdoors is highly scandalous."

"Over the course of the next half dozen decades, I fully intend to do more than kiss you outdoors. I'm going to make love to you beneath the stars in a moonlit English garden. In the warmth of the Adriatic Sea. And countless places in between. Show you, and tell you, every day, how very much I love you."

She blinked rapidly to dispel the sheen of moisture he detected in her eyes. "I shall greatly look forward to that."

Allowing himself only one more quick taste of her, he

clasped her hand, then rounded the corner, where the Greybourne carriage stood at the opposite end of the building. Waving off the footman, he opened the door himself, then handed Meredith in, helping her get settled on the seat opposite Andrew and Bakari.

"I'll be along shortly," he said, squeezing her hand.

"Are you not riding as far as the warehouse?" she asked.

"No. It's not very far, and the walk will clear my head." He turned to Andrew and Bakari. "Be careful." With that he closed the door, then signaled the driver to depart. He watched the carriage disappear around a corner, then, firmly gripping his walking stick, he turned toward the warehouse.

Since childhood, walking had always been a soothing, comforting balm, enabling him to gather and align his thoughts in a logical, methodical way. And God knows he'd never needed that more than right now. Moving through the narrow streets, he culled through the myriad thoughts buzzing through his mind and focused on one at a time.

There was no doubt in his mind that the destruction of the *Sea Raven* was deliberate. Whoever had set the ship ablaze not only meant him irreparable harm, but the sheer audacity of the act proved that his enemy was growing increasingly desperate.

Who was doing this? Who was so intent upon seeing him suffer? And why? Unfortunately, Andrew's inquiries had not resulted in an answer.

Rounding the final corner, he arrived at the warehouse. He walked along the rows of stacked crates, heading directly toward the office. He opened the desk drawer where his ledgers were stored, and froze. Lying on top of the ledger was a single, unfolded sheet of foolscap.

I have the stone you seek. You will suffer.

Twenty

Philip stared at the note, which was written in the same hand as the others, and fury and hope collided in him. Fury that this bastard was toying with him like this, but hope . . . God, so much hope that he was telling the truth. *I have the stone you seek.* That could only refer to the missing piece of the Stone of Tears. It existed. He'd wager his last farthing that it had been in the alabaster box stolen the night of the break-in—and this deranged bastard had taken it, which proved that the curse was indeed at the crux of all the attacks. *You won't have the stone for long*, he silently vowed. *I'm going to find you* and *my stone. And then make you the sorriest bastard in England.*

The person responsible for this was no stranger. His were the only crates tampered with. It had to be someone who knew him. Knew where his belongings were stored. Knew the value of that piece of stone. Knew who his family and friends were . . . who was important to him. Of course, that could be anyone who'd sailed home with him. Everyone onboard the *Dream Keeper* knew Andrew, Edward, and Bakari were like brothers to him. Had heard him speak of his father and Catherine, and the fact that the crates in the ship's hold were bound for the museum and the warehouse.

The door creaked on its hinges. "Hallo," an adolescent

male voice called out. "Is there a bloke named Grey-bourne about?"

"I'm Greybourne," Philip called, hurrying toward the door. A boy about twelve years of age, garbed in dirty, torn clothing, stood in the open doorway.

"I've a note for ye." His eyes narrowed. "But it'll cost ye. Bloke what told me to deliver it said ye'd give me a ha'pence."

Philip withdrew a coin from his pocket and flipped it in the air. The boy caught it neatly, his eyes widening at the tuppence resting in his palm. He handed over the note, then dashed away, no doubt worried that Philip would try to wrest the coin back from him. Breaking the wax seal, Philip skimmed the few lines.

> *Spoke to magistrate who believes a crew member careless with a cheroot caused the blaze. No witnesses able to say what happened, but he'll make further inquiries. Have taken a room for the night at the Denby Arms to be close by should you need me. Edward.*

Philip stared absently at the note. He did not agree that the fire was caused by a careless crew member. Nor did he believe anyone aboard the *Sea Raven* was responsible. Whoever set the blaze was the same person responsible for everything else—and that person had not just arrived today on the *Sea Raven*.

Folding the note and slipping it into his pocket, he continued his pacing, his mind churning out possibilities, and tossing them away just as quickly. To the best of his knowledge, he'd made no enemies onboard the ship during his sail home. He couldn't deny he'd made a number of enemies during his travels. Had one of them followed him to England?

An image of that carriage barreling toward Meredith

flashed in his mind, and his footsteps slowed. This person clearly knew that Meredith was important to him—a fact which was a very recent development. And not known by many people. In fact, the only people who knew were those closest to him—

He halted, his mind racing as an awful possibility occurred to him. No, it couldn't be . . . couldn't possibly. But the more he reflected upon the events of the past days, he realized it could be. The puzzle pieces clicked, one by one, into place in his mind, leaving the sickening truth staring him in the face. The attacks, the broken glass, the odd absences, the conversations . . . yes, it all fit. He dragged his hands down his face. Damn it to hell and back, what a blind, trusting fool he'd been! His blood ran cold. And what danger had he unwittingly placed Meredith in by not realizing the truth sooner?

He quickly assessed his possible courses of actions, then with a decisive nod, he hurried back to the office, where he dashed off three brief notes and sealed them. Racing to the door, he ran outside. As he'd hoped, he spied the boy who had delivered Edward's note earlier. The lad leaned negligently against the wooden exterior of the adjacent building, talking with another boy roughly the same age. No doubt the lad had hung about hoping Philip might have a note of his own to send—or he'd hoped that he and his friend might pick Philip's pocket when he departed from the warehouse.

"You there," Philip called to the boys. "I've a job for you."

The boys exchanged glances, then sauntered over, all cunning bravado. "Wot kind o' job?" asked the boy familiar to him.

"I've some letters I want delivered."

"Do ye, now?" the other, taller boy drawled. "And just wot's in it fer us?"

He withdrew two coins from his waistcoat pocket. "A

bob for each of you now. When you return from your deliveries, I'll give you an additional quid."

"A quid fer each o' us?" the taller boy asked, his eyes narrowed with clear suspicion.

"Yes."

"And that's all ye want fer such a grand sum? Just to deliver some letters?"

"That's all I want. What are your names?"

The boys exchanged a quick glance, then moved closer. "I'm Will," said the taller boy. He jerked his head toward the smaller lad. "This here's Robbie."

"Well, Robbie and Will, this is what I need for you to do." Philip gave Will two letters and Robbie one, then carefully recited the direction to which he wanted each delivered. "Any questions?"

"Where's our blunt?" Robbie asked.

Philip handed each of them a bob. They exchanged another look, then turned to leave. Philip mentally counted to five, then called out, "Boys?"

They turned in unison. "I want to stress that we've made a deal and I expect you to live up to your end. You have my word I'll live up to mine. I therefore wouldn't suggest you entertain any thoughts of running off with your bobs and destroying my letters. Because I shall find out if you do. And I can assure you it will be the last time you attempt such a double-cross." He casually withdrew his pocket watch from his waistcoat pocket and consulted the time, hiding his smile at the boys' dumfounded, goggling expressions. "Do you understand?"

Both boys alternated their stunned gazes between Philip and the watch. "I . . . understand," said Will.

"Me, too," said Robbie, nodding so vigorously Philip feared the lad would rattle his brains.

"Then be off with you. There's no time to waste."

The boys ran off as if the hounds of hell pursued them, and Philip reentered the warehouse, satisfied that they would both deliver his letters with the utmost speed and return for their extra money. He gave his watch a fond glance before tucking it back in his waistcoat pocket. Second time today someone had tried to relieve him of his watch. His thoughts turned to Meredith. Someone he'd never have believed capable of such treachery was trying to steal something much more valuable from him than his watch.

Profound hurt pierced him at the breach of trust, but he firmly pushed it aside. *If you wanted to hurt me, you should have come after me and left those I care about alone. But you won't succeed in hurting anyone again. I know who you are, you lying bastard.* A grim smile curved his lips, and he ran his hands slowly down his walking stick.

All I have to do now is wait for you to come to me.

Meredith sat on the settee in Philip's drawing room, sipping a cup of tea she prayed would relieve the nauseating pounding in her temples. Prince's head lay propped on her thigh, and she sifted her fingers over the puppy's soft, golden fur while she watched Mr. Stanton pace in front of the fireplace. Ever since he'd read the note that had been delivered a quarter hour earlier, he'd worn a fierce scowl and had moved ceaselessly back and forth across the hearth, clearly pondering a disturbing problem.

Curiosity tugged at her, but as he hadn't said whom the note was from, she hesitated to question him. Surely he would have told her if the missive was from Philip.

Clearing her throat, she said, "I hope Philip isn't overly fond of that carpet."

He paused, a perplexed frown bunching his brows. "Which carpet?"

"The one you're pacing into a threadbare state."

Looking down at the thick Axminster beneath his

boots, he shot her a sheepish grimace. "Oh. That carpet."

"You're worried about Philip," she said.

He looked as if he wanted to deny it, but then he jerked his head in a nod. "He's been gone longer than I was expecting."

"I'm guessing you want to go to the warehouse."

"Yes."

"But you haven't because you promised Philip you'd look after me."

A tired smile creased his face. "Philip did not mention you were clairvoyant, Miss Chilton-Grizedale."

"It requires no special intuition to see how concerned you are. I think you should go."

"I promised him I wouldn't leave you."

"So bring me with you. I'm worried about him, too."

He studied her for several seconds, an unfathomable expression in his dark eyes. Then a slow smile turned up the corners of his lips. "Yes. I'll bring you with me. That might work out perfectly."

At the Denby Arms, Edward opened his door in answer to a discreet knock. A footman held out a silver salver bearing a wax-sealed note.

"This just arrived for you, sir." The footman sniffed. "Delivered by a most raggedly dressed lad, you should know."

Frowning, Edward took the letter, closed the door, then broke the seal.

Approaching the foyer in her father's townhouse, Catherine noted Bakari intently reading from a piece of foolscap.

"I heard the knocker," she said as she stepped into the foyer.

She clearly startled Bakari, who hastily shoved his letter into a fold of his loose-fitting trousers. Raising her brows, she said, "I was hoping Philip had arrived."

"He has not."

"Who came to the door?"

"Delivery boy."

When he did not elaborate, Catherine prompted, "And what did he deliver?"

"Letter. For me."

Obviously the contents of the letter had upset Bakari, as he was clearly agitated. Before she could question him, however, he murmured, "Please excuse me," then he hurried down the corridor leading to the kitchens.

Seated in the carriage, the words of Greybourne's note seared through his brain, infuriating him anew. *I've figured out how to break the curse without the missing piece of stone. Meet me at the warehouse.*

Break the curse? *I'll not let you, Greybourne. Oh, no. You have not yet begun to suffer. But you will, you bastard. You will. I'm on my way.*

Twenty-one

When Will and Robbie returned to the warehouse, both reporting the successful delivery of his letters, Philip breathed a sigh of relief. He paid them their quids, along with an extra pound each for proving so trustworthy. Their eyes nearly popped from their sockets at such a windfall. Pity tugged at Philip's heart for the two dirty-faced lads. He'd seen so many like them, both here in London and abroad. Children, who through no fault of their own were forced to live on the cruel streets, fighting each day for survival. Children who viewed the world with flat-eyed expressions that hid hunger, fear, hopelessness, and despair. It was exactly what Meredith had faced, and he marveled anew at the strength, character, and determination it had taken for her not only to successfully rise above such circumstances, but to help Albert and Charlotte do so as well.

Before sending the lads on their way, he said, "If you boys are interested in work—*honest* work—you come see me." He rattled off his direction.

"That's where I delivered one of yer letters," said Will. His eyes widened. "Were that fancy place yer house?"

"Yes." He fixed them both with a penetrating stare. "There's work available, but know that I will not tolerate being lied to or stolen from. Not once. The decision is yours." He made a shooing motion with his hands. "Now go buy yourselves something to eat."

The boys studied him for several seconds, then dashed off. Philip watched them disappear from view, hoping that they would take him up on his offer. God knows he couldn't hope to save all the children of London, but perhaps he could help Will and Robbie to help themselves. He'd given them the opportunity. The rest was up to them.

Alone again, Philip paced in front of the office, forcing himself to take deep, calming breaths. His gaze swept the area, noting the careful placement of his walking stick, hidden by the shadows of the crate it leaned upon. Everything was ready for him to confront his enemy.

His enemy. A humorless laugh pushed past his tight throat. *And all this time I'd thought you were my friend. . . .*

His pacing halted when he heard the door open. A familiar voice called out, "Are you here, Philip?"

"Yes. By the office."

Rapid footfalls sounded against the wood floor. When his guest rounded the corner and faced him, Philip stilled from the impact of staring into the dark eyes of this man he'd for so long believed to be his friend. Emotions pelted him from all sides, and he frowned. Damn it, he hadn't anticipated that under his anger he'd experience this deep sense of loss. And sadness that it had come to this. Bludgeoning back his unwanted feelings, he said, "Glad you could come. There's something we need to discuss."

"So I gathered from your note. You've found a way to break the curse without the missing piece of stone? How extraordinary. You must tell me how."

"And so I shall. But first, tell me, how are your injuries?"

Philip watched him roll his shoulders and flex his hand. "Improving."

With a lightning-quick moye, Philip reached out and

grabbed Edward's upper arm and squeezed. A sharp cry of pain erupted from Edward's lips and he jerked himself free of Philip's grasp, backing up several paces.

"It's a miracle that Catherine didn't break your arm when she hit you with the fire iron last evening," Philip said coldly. "She's quite a strong woman."

They stared at each other in silence for several seconds, then a frigid calm settled over Edward's features, a frightening contrast to the hatred blazing in his eyes. "So you know." He shrugged. "It was inevitable that you would discover the truth sooner or later. If you hadn't done so on your own, I would have revealed myself to you . . . eventually. After I'd had the pleasure of watching you suffer the loss of those you love. But satisfy my curiosity. How did you figure it out?"

"Several things regarding your story about the night of the break-in here at the warehouse bothered me, but I couldn't figure out what they were." Philip's gaze dropped to Edward's wrapped hand. "The morning after the robbery, I noticed broken glass scattered all about the floor, which would only make sense if someone had broken the window to *gain* entry. Yet you claimed that you broke the glass to *escape* the warehouse, in which case the glass would have broken in the other direction and have been scattered *outside*. The guard didn't let you in. *You* broke the glass to enter the warehouse, which resulted in your injury."

His gaze dropped to Edward's wrapped hand. "Both you and Bakari mentioned that you had glass embedded in the *back* of your hand. If you'd tripped, as you'd claimed, the glass would have embedded itself in your palms. But if you'd used your fist to shatter the glass to break into the warehouse, then it would have cut the back of your hand. My mistake was in blindly accepting your version of the events of that evening when they were all lies."

Philip pinned him with a narrow gaze. "*You* killed the guard. You being beaten was a result of trying to escape him after he discovered your presence in here. You were the one who robbed me. And the minute it occurred to me to doubt your word, the pieces clicked into place."

Edward inclined his head. "It is as you say. How very clever you are. Unfortunately for you, not clever enough to live to tell your tale to anyone else."

In spite of his anger, Philip couldn't squelch the pity tugging at him. He hated what Edward had done, yet losing his beloved wife had obviously driven him to this madness. "I want you to know, Edward, that I am deeply sorry for what happened to Mary. I never meant for anyone else to see the Stone of Tears. I kept it hidden in my cabin onboard the ship—"

"Did you think I didn't know you were hiding something?" Edward said, the words spitting out like a cobra's venom. "Something of great value that you did not want to share? I was determined to find it. During the storm I was finally given my opportunity to search your cabin. Very clever hiding spot, in your boot, but not clever enough."

Philip's heart skipped a beat. He *had* hidden the stone before he'd rushed from his cabin. In the confusion of the storm, the mast breaking, the details had become a blur. A layer of the guilt he carried peeled away, along with his pity. Narrowing his eyes, he said, "*You* brought this curse down upon yourself and Mary by your own greed. I wasn't trying to keep some treasure from you—I was trying to keep anyone else from translating that infernal stone. I'd hidden it. You went looking for it. Invaded my cabin, my privacy, and look what it got you."

"You dare to shift the blame for Mary's death to me? You're the one who found the stone. If it weren't for you, she'd be alive."

"As she would be if you hadn't allowed your greed to get the better of you."

"Stop! Damn you, the fault is yours. And you're going to pay for it." His gaze darted about the area. "Not that it matters, as you will be dead in less than a minute, but I assume that either Andrew or Bakari—perhaps both of them—are on their way here as well?"

"No. This is between you and me."

"Pity. Their arrival here would have saved me the trouble of going to them, but it matters not. Their hours are numbered." With a quick movement, he withdrew a pistol from his jacket and pointed it at the center of Philip's chest. "Unfortunately, you will not still be alive to see them die, but *you* will die knowing that those you hold dear will soon follow you."

Philip shook his head. "I won't allow you to hurt anyone else."

A sharp bark of laughter erupted from Edward. "Indeed? You cannot stop me. You *will not* stop me."

Philip didn't move so much as an eyelash as he studied his foe. He needed time, had to keep Edward talking. "I'm sorry about Mary, Edward—"

"*Sorry?*" he repeated in an awful voice. His eyes narrowed into hate-filled slits. "That doesn't bring her back, now, does it? Nothing will. Not your pity, nor your useless financial gestures. Do you think that *money* can take her place? Assuage your responsibility? Could money replace the woman *you* love, Philip?"

The mere thought turned his stomach. "If there was a woman I loved . . . no."

"Don't lie to me. 'Tis obvious how you feel about Miss Chilton-Grizedale. Of course, I won't have to actually kill her. You've taken care of that for me, by professing your love and asking her to marry you. Who knew that that would activate the curse?" A high-pitched laugh escaped him. "How bloody perfect!"

"You're not going to hurt anyone," Philip repeated in a frigid voice.

Edward's expression turned to one of amusement as he looked pointedly between the pistol and Philip. "I'm afraid I must disagree."

"Meredith isn't going to die because I am going to break the curse."

"So you indicated. How do you intend to do that without the missing piece of stone?"

Philip smiled. "You're going to give me the missing piece of stone."

"Again, you are mistaken."

"You have the missing piece. You wrote as much in your last note. You stole it the night you robbed me. It was in the alabaster box."

Madness glittered in Edward's eyes. "It was. I read it. I alone hold the answer to breaking the curse, and I will never share it with you. Never."

Knee-weakening relief smacked Philip. Edward's words made it clear that there was indeed a way to break the curse. Now all he had to do was get that missing piece of stone. And survive this encounter. Moving slowly, he maneuvered himself so that his walking stick was directly behind him.

"Show me the stone, Edward."

Edward laughed. "Oh, I intend to. What better way to make you suffer than to show you that which you shall never have? It's rather like leaving a man tied in the desert, just out of reach of an oasis." Slipping his hand into his pocket, he withdrew a stone, half the size of his palm.

Philip's heart pounded. Without a doubt, it was the missing piece of stone.

"You want to know what it says, don't you?" Edward taunted. "Well, you'll never know. You're going to your grave, Greybourne—the same place you sent my Mary. And I want your last thoughts to be of losing everything you love."

"Killing my family won't bring back Mary."

"But it makes you suffer. Of course, killing your family is not as important as killing Miss Chilton-Grizedale." An unpleasant smile curved his lips. "An eye for an eye, Philip."

"You'll never get away with this. You'll hang."

"It matters not. My life is over. You and your curse saw to that."

His gaze locked on Edward's, Philip took a half step forward. "Give me the stone, Edward."

"Don't come any closer, Philip."

Philip moved another half step. "Why not? You're going to kill me anyway." Another step. Then he looked over Edward's shoulder, widened his eyes, and shook his head.

"What—?" The instant Edward swiveled around to see who or what was behind him, Philip reached for his walking stick.

Realizing he'd been duped, Edward whirled back around. Philip swung the walking stick, catching Edward across the chest. Edward's eyes widened in surprise, then narrowed in mad fury, but he quickly recovered, dodging Philip's next swing. With an inhuman roar of rage, Edward rushed forward, smashing into Philip, sending him crashing against the stacked crates. The walking stick fell from his grasp.

"You bastard," Edward heaved, trapping Philip against the wall with the full weight of his large body. Philip struggled to move, but ceased when he felt the pistol jammed directly under his ribs. One twitch of Edward's finger would end his life. He'd heard that insanity drove men to great strength, and Edward was proving that correct. His forearm pressed against Philip's throat, cutting off his air. Black dots began to swim in front of his face. Knowing it was now or never, he heaved himself forward, throwing Edward back several paces. He grabbed Edward's wrists. One hand held the pistol, the other the stone. Eyes riveted on each other, they struggled fiercely.

Sweat coating his skin, muscles screaming against the strain, Philip tried to direct the pistol away from him.

"You think you're going to win this?" Edward ground out, his face only inches from Philip's. "Think again, you bastard. I'll see to it that no matter what happens, you'll not win."

A dull thud, followed by the sound of Edward's boot smashing down, turned Philip's blood to ice.

"The stone is destroyed," Edward whispered. "And so are you. I hope you rot in hell."

The pistol fired.

The carriage had just halted outside the warehouse when the sound of a pistol shot rent the air. Heart pounding with fear and dread, Meredith grabbed Mr. Stanton's arm. "Dear God. That came from inside the warehouse."

"Stay here," he said, opening the carriage door and jumping to the ground.

"I'll do no such thing. Philip is in danger. I can help."

He slipped a knife from his pocket. "Help? How?"

Jumping to the ground, she hefted her rock-laden reticule. "I'm armed." She lifted her chin. "And determined. You're not leaving me here."

He raised his brows. "You any good with that thing?"

"Would you care for a demonstration?"

They stared at each other for several seconds, then he jerked his head in a nod. "You'll do. Don't make a sound, stay behind me, and for God's sake, don't get yourself killed."

Clasping her hand, he led her silently forward. They'd only taken half a dozen steps when she halted and squeezed his hand. Heart pounding, she whispered, "There's someone in the shadows."

No sooner had the words left her mouth than Bakari stepped forward, a long, curved knife held in his fist.

"What are you doing here?" Andrew whispered.

"Same as you. Hope to save his life."

Andrew nodded, then indicated with a jerk of his head that Bakari should bring up the rear. The warehouse door stood ajar, and they slipped in the opening. Moving silently forward, Meredith forced long, slow, deep breaths into her constricted lungs, fighting back her fright. If something had happened to Philip . . .

Keeping close to the shadows cast by the crates, they crept forward. She strained her ears, but heard nothing save the thumping of her own heartbeat pounding in her ears. When they came to the final corner before they'd reach Philip's crates, Mr. Stanton stopped. They listened for several seconds, but heard nothing. Then he cautiously peeked around the corner.

She heard his sharp intake of breath, then his agonized groan. "Philip . . . oh, God . . . bloody hell."

Twenty-two

 Mr. Stanton rushed around the corner. Knees shaking, heart lodged in her throat, Meredith immediately ran after him. Several yards away, obscured by the shadows, a man lay face down in a dark pool that was obviously blood. Another man crouched next to the prone body, his back to Meredith.

"Philip," she whispered, fear icing her blood.

The crouching man stood and turned. Their eyes met, and she skidded to a halt. His hair was wildly mussed, his cravat untied, his spectacles askew, his clothes and face streaked with heaven knew what. And he was absolutely the most wonderful, beautiful sight she'd ever beheld.

"Meredith." Philip opened his arms to her, and with a sob, she ran toward him, not stopping until he'd enveloped her in his strong embrace.

Philip caught her against him and held her tightly against his heart. She was safe. For now. But with Edward dead and the missing piece of stone shattered, how could he hope to save her from the curse?

"Are you all right?" Andrew asked quietly.

No. "Yes."

Andrew's gaze flicked down to the motionless figure. "Is he dead?"

Philip looked down at Edward's body, and an emotion-filled shudder ran through him. Regret at the loss of a man he'd thought was his friend. Sorrow for the madness that had claimed him. Guilt for his unwitting part in contributing to that madness. And stark fury at the harm he'd wreaked—harm that could still cost him Meredith. "Yes."

"What happened?" asked Meredith.

He quickly told them how he'd deduced that Edward was the man they sought, about the note he'd sent to lure Edward to the warehouse, and what had transpired once he'd arrived. He concluded with, "We struggled for the pistol, and it fired. It is only by the grace of God that the lead ball struck him and not me."

He felt a tremor shiver through Meredith. Lifting her head, she looked up at him, her eyes huge. "I've never been so frightened as when I heard that pistol shot."

The area surrounding Philip's heart went hollow. Unless he broke the curse, she had a little more than a day to live—and her most frightening moment had been fearing he'd been hurt. Bloody hell.

She laid her hand against his face. "I know you're hurt by Mr. Binsmore's death. And his betrayal. You feel sorry for him, but at the same time you hate him for what he tried to do to all of us. You're feeling guilty that he's dead, that his wife died."

He looked into her wide, worried eyes, and love hit him like a punch in the heart. She understood. Everything he was feeling. Without him saying a word.

Her gaze searched his. "Philip, it was his own greed that killed them both. It is not your fault. You were a victim. His greed nearly cost you your life. Please don't feel guilty for being alive. Especially when I'm so grateful that you are all right."

He pressed a kiss into her soft hair, then shot Andrew a meaningful look over the top of her head. "I hadn't anticipated you—*and Meredith*—coming here, Andrew."

"I thought you might need someone to watch your back."

"As much as I appreciate that, I needed someone to watch Meredith."

"I never took my eyes off her."

"I meant for you to do so at my townhouse—as you well know. By coming here, either of you might have been hurt. Or worse." His gaze swiveled to Bakari. "Same for you."

Bakari held up his curved blade. "Have big knife. Thought you could use."

A resigned sigh escaped Philip. "Thank you. But we obviously all need to talk about what the phrase 'do not leave the house' means."

Walking over, Andrew clapped Philip on the shoulder. "My friend, if you think you are going to be able to talk this woman out of anything she's set her mind to, you're sadly mistaken. When I tried to, she threatened to cosh me with her reticule, in which she apparently carries an anvil."

"Stones," Meredith clarified. "Although an anvil is an excellent suggestion."

"Speaking of stones . . ." Philip looked down at the broken fragments of stone scattered on the floor, and his stomach clenched. "Andrew, will you please advise the magistrate as to what's happened here?"

"Of course."

"While you're gone, Meredith and I will gather up the broken pieces of stone." He forced a smile at Meredith. "Then all I have to do is piece it back together and do as it says to break the curse."

They shared a long look, and he clearly read the question in her wide eyes: What if he could not do it in time?

And unfortunately, they both knew the answer.

Meredith would die.

During Andrew's absence, Philip and Meredith painstakingly picked up the broken stone fragments, placing them in a leather pouch. Picking up sliver after sliver, Philip's frustration, anger, and fear grew. It would take days to put the pieces back into order—and he had only a matter of hours. How could he hope—

"Philip, look at this."

He turned to Meredith, who knelt on the rough wooden floor several feet away. In between her thumb and index finger, she held a pale spherical object, which, if it hadn't been the size of a quail's egg, he would have guessed was a pearl.

Moving closer to her, he asked, "Where did you find it?"

"Half hidden beneath these two pieces of the broken stone." She held out her other palm. "It looks as if it was secreted inside the stone."

Taking the fragments and the sphere from her, he carefully affixed them together. The two pieces of stone perfectly fitted around half of the sphere.

"It looks like a pearl," Meredith remarked.

"Indeed it does." Carefully placing the stone pieces in the pouch, he examined the sphere, running his fingers over its slightly uneven surface. He held it up to the light, the afternoon sunlight glowing warmly against the gentle patina. He then gently ran it across his teeth. "Unless I am very much mistaken, this is a genuine pearl." He couldn't hide the disbelief in his own voice.

Her eyes widened. "If so, it must be worth an enormous amount of money."

"Yes. And the fact that it was hidden inside the stone means it must have some significance regarding the curse. Come, let us finish gathering the remaining pieces."

A quarter hour later, just as they'd determined that there were no further fragments to be found, Andrew returned with the magistrate. As soon as Philip had answered all the man's questions, he requested that Andrew and Bakari remain to see to the body, then he left with Meredith.

He didn't need to consult his watch to know how much time he had left to piece the stone back together.

Not nearly enough. And he would need every second.

When they reached his townhouse, Philip tried to get Meredith to rest, especially since she'd admitted on the ride home that her head still hurt, but she adamantly refused.

"I'm praying that I'll have a lifetime with you, during which time I promise to rest frequently." Her bottom lip trembled, a marked contrast to the stubborn tilt of her chin. "But if I do not, I will not spend what short time we have left apart. I'm going to help you. And if I cannot help, I am, at the very least, going to remain close to you."

Since he wanted her to remain close, he didn't argue. He led her to his private study, where he opened all the curtains to bring extra light into the room. Before they began piecing together the fragments, Meredith said, "I'd like to write a note to Charlotte and Albert, to let them know about our betrothal and that I'm planning to remain here to help you piece together the stone. I'm not going to tell them I've been affected by the curse unless I have to. If we are unsuccessful by tomorrow afternoon, I would like to send for them, and Hope. I . . . I would need to see them, talk to them, before . . ." Her voice trailed off, and she averted her gaze.

He grasped her hands and squeezed them. "I understand. But when you send for them, it's going to be to invite them to our wedding." He waited for her to look at him, then he leaned forward and gently kissed her, allowing himself only a brief taste.

While she wrote to her friends, he composed a quick note to Catherine and his father assuring them all was well, and one to his solicitor as well. After instructing James to deliver the letters posthaste, he and Meredith set about the painstaking task of trying to arrange the dozens of pieces back together.

After several hours, the light began to wane, and Philip lit not only candles but the fire as well. He could tell that Meredith's head was aching; indeed, his was as well, from staring at the minute bits of the ancient language, trying to fit them together. Andrew and Bakari arrived, and although they wanted to help, Philip refused them.

"I do not want you to be exposed to the curse. If I cannot break the curse, such exposure would prove fatal should either of you decide to marry in the future."

They'd argued, but Philip stood firm. After they'd all eaten a quick meal, Philip insisted that Meredith rest. Bakari mixed her a draught, after which she curled up on the sofa in his study, Prince cuddled in her arms, and soon was asleep.

Philip labored into the night, eyes straining against the poor light, muscles cramping with fatigue. Yet little by little the words came to life, renewing his determination, as did the sight of Meredith sleeping, bathed in the glow from the fire.

As dawn bloomed, he fitted the last pieces together. It was clear that the pearl had indeed been secreted inside the missing piece, but he did not put it back in its place, instead leaving the gem on his desk. Several bits of the stone were missing, but it was mostly legible.

Heart pounding with anticipation, he dashed to his bedchamber, his stiff muscles screaming in protest. He extracted the original piece of the Stone of Tears from its hiding place in his leather satchel at the bottom of his wardrobe. Returning to his study, he set the stone beside the puzzle he'd just completed and read the ancient language:

As my betrothed betrayed me with another,
So shall the same fate befall your lover.
To the ends of the earth

From this day forth,
Ye are the cursed,
Condemned to hell's worst.
For true love's very breath
Is destined for death.
Grace will fall, a stumble she'll take,
Then suffer the pain of hell's headache.
If ye have the gift of wedded bliss,
She will die before you kiss.
Or two days after the vows are said,
Your bride, so cursed, shall be found dead.
Once your intended has been loved in word and deed
Nothing can save her from my curse's greed.
There is but one key
To set the cursed free.
Follow the beauty to a risky feast
As she shows her lover she is not the least
And proves through sheer daring that never shall fail,
Do the same so love, not death, shall prevail.

He rubbed his hands over his face, the stubble of his beard abrading his palms. He knew the words. Now he just needed to figure out what the bloody hell they meant. He glanced at the clock.

He had less than twenty-eight hours left to find out.

Only twelve hours remained.

Striving to fight off the panic threatening to strangle him, Philip raked his hands through his hair. With Meredith's help, he'd spent the entire day going through his journals, searching for a clue as to what the curse meant, but without success. For Andrew's and Bakari's safety, Philip refused to reveal the exact words he'd pieced together, but sent them off to the museum to search through the documents there regarding anything to do with pearls, a feast, or the price of true love. He'd suggested that

Meredith write another note to Charlotte, asking that she, Albert, and Hope come to the townhouse so she could break the news to them and prepare them for the worst, but she'd refused.

"Not yet. To do that makes it seem as if I've given up hope, and I haven't. I have every intention of being your bride."

Forcing his gaze from hers lest she see the fear curling through him, he continued to pore over his journals. He swallowed his mounting dread, which increased with each passing minute. Another minute without an answer. Another minute lost. He refused to look at the clock, but each time the mantel clock struck the quarter hour, his mind registered that he was swiftly running out of time. He pulled another journal toward him, simultaneously praying and cursing. Damn it! The answer had to be somewhere. Had to. *Had* to. Had to find it. Please . . .

"I don't think we've paid enough attention to this," Meredith said. He looked up. The enormous pearl rested in her palm. "Given its size and age, this single gem is no doubt worth thousands of pounds."

Philip adjusted his spectacles, giving her his full attention. "I agree."

"It's the sort of gem that would be worn by someone very important. A queen, perhaps."

"Yes, a queen such as Nefertiti or Cleopatra . . . both of whom were great beauties . . ." A memory tickled the back of his mind, mingling with the final lines of the stone's message.

"What is it?" Meredith asked.

"I'm not certain, but you've sparked an idea." Rising, he walked to the bookcase in the corner, then crouched to run his finger over the leather-bound spines on the bottom shelf. "There's a story I recall reading years ago—" He found the volume he sought and slid it out. "Give me a moment."

Bringing the volume to his desk, he flipped through the pages until he found the entry he sought. As he read the words, his heart began to pound and his hands to shake.

"I think I've found something," he said.

She leaned over his shoulder. "What book is that?"

"It is one of my earliest journals, consisting of notes I took years ago when I had the opportunity to read Pliny the Elder's *Natural History*. When you mentioned the pearl, and a queen wearing it, coupled with the last lines of the stone, it somehow struck me as familiar."

"Who is Pliny the Elder?"

"A Roman administrator from the first century. In *Natural History* he wrote of an event where pearls played a pivotal role at one of the most celebrated banquets in history. Apparently Cleopatra wagered Mark Antony that she could host the most expensive dinner in history, one that could never be equaled."

Understanding flared in her eyes. "A beauty, and a risky feast."

"Yes. According to the story, she intended to convince Rome that Egypt possessed a heritage and wealth so vast that it was beyond conquest. That also fits in with the curse. Antony was her lover, and she was trying to prove she—Egypt—was strong, and 'not the least.' " He could not keep the excitement from his voice as he read more of his notes. "The banquet indeed proved luxurious, but not any more so than Cleopatra had served on other occasions, and therefore Mark Antony thought he had won. But then Cleopatra, who was wearing a pair of large pearl earrings, removed one, crushed it, dropped it in her cup of wine, and drank it down, whereupon the judge of the wager declared that the astonished Antony had lost the bet."

Her eyes widened. "Sheer daring."

"Yes. It all fits into the words of the curse," Philip said, his heart pounding with the certainty that this was the clue they'd sought. Jumping to his feet, he grasped her shoulders. "The last line of the stone. *Do the same so love, not death, shall prevail.* If we do as she did, love, not death shall prevail."

Her eyes widened with comprehension and hope. Her gaze dropped to the pearl nestled in her palm. "Do you suppose this could be the other pearl, from Cleopatra's other earring?"

"I strongly suspect that it is."

She breathed out a long, slow breath. "Dear God. If it was worth that much then, how much do you suppose this pearl is worth now?"

"Not nearly as much as your life, Meredith."

"But you yourself said it must be worth thousands of pounds. If it was Cleopatra's, I'm guessing that is a conservative estimate. To consider destroying something so rare and valuable—"

He silenced her by touching his fingers to her lips. "*You* are more rare and valuable than anything. Come. It's time to end this curse." Taking her hand, he led her to the decanters, where he poured a goblet of red wine.

Feeling as if she were in a daze, Meredith watched him crush the gem into the crystal. Dear God, that gem was priceless, and he'd crushed it without a thought in his bid to save her.

"Philip . . . what if you're wrong?"

For an answer, he drank from the goblet, then handed it to her. "Drink."

She did as he bade, swallowing the remaining liquid. Then they stood in silence, watching each other. A minute passed. Meredith's heart pounded with trepidation as they waited for a sign, a clue that the curse was broken.

Another tension-fraught minute passed. Nothing. Her trepidation escalated to panic. Philip's eyes reflected the same worry and concern she knew she saw in hers. Dear God, drinking the crushed pearl had accomplished nothing save destroying a priceless gem. The hope that had bloomed in her heart slowly extinguished, leaving despair and heartbreak in its wake.

But suddenly she experienced an odd sensation in her head. Her eyes widened.

"What is it?" Philip asked, his anxious gaze searching her face.

"My headache," she whispered. "It's gone."

A noise from the desk caught their attention, and they turned in unison. Meredith grasped Philip's hand, her amazement turning to stunned shock as the Stone of Tears appeared to tremble upon the desktop. Then, as if pushed by an invisible hand, the stone fell from the desk, hitting the parquet floor with a thud, breaking into hundreds of pieces, which then slowly crumbled until nothing save a pile of sand remained.

Her gaze flew to Philip's. "Dear God, did you see that?" she asked, unable to fathom what she'd just witnessed, afraid to hope that that handful of sand meant what she prayed it meant.

"I did. And except for you, it falls into the category of 'the most beautiful thing I've ever seen.'" A slow smile curved his lips and he drew her against him. "My darling Meredith, it means that we have broken the curse—literally and figuratively. We're free."

Relief weakened her knees. "It's truly over?"

"Yes. As for everything else, it's just beginning." He cupped her face in his hands, and his smile faded. "Bloody hell, you have no idea how frantic I was. How sick inside. How utterly terrified."

"No more so than I, I assure you."

"As much as I hate what Edward did, part of me understands the desperation that drove him. If anything had happened to you, it would have driven *me* mad."

Anxious to erase the tension in his eyes, she smiled. "Well, thanks to you, I am fine. Luckily you had one of your moments of brilliance—at a very convenient time."

"That moment of brilliance was inspired by you."

"Quite the well-suited pair, are we not?"

"*I* was not the one who needed convincing of that." He lowered his head and kissed her with long, slow, deep perfection, until her knees turned to porridge and she sagged against him. He left her lips and trailed hot kisses along her jaw and down her throat.

"This is the second time you saved my life, you know," she murmured, tilting her head to give him better access. "Surely that deserves some sort of reward."

"And don't think for one moment that I won't collect."

He straightened, and she smiled at the sight of his fogged-up spectacles. Sliding them off his nose, he asked, "You know how you frequently comment on my lamentable lack of propriety?"

"I prefer to call it giving discreet hints."

"I'm certain you do. However, I suggest you brace yourself, my dear, for the instant I get you into my bedchamber, you are going to see a shocking lack of propriety."

Anticipation tingled down her spine. "Heavens. No doubt I should swoon at such a statement. Luckily I am not prone to the vapors."

Raw emotion blazed from his eyes. "I'm greatly relieved to hear it." After dropping one quick kiss onto her lips, he stalked to his desk, where he scribbled off a quick note.

"To Andrew and Bakari, letting them know the quest has ended," he explained. Striding back to her, he dipped his knees, then swung her up into his arms. Before she could do more than gasp, he exited the room and strode down the corridor into the foyer, where they were greeted by James, who, bless him, didn't turn an eyelash at the sight of Philip carrying her—again.

Philip handed the footman the note and said, "See that it is delivered to Mr. Stanton at the British Museum immediately, James."

"Yes, my lord."

"And then see to it that I am not disturbed."

"Yes, my lord."

With that, Philip took the stairs two at a time, while Meredith clung to his neck, flames firing her skin. "You truly are incorrigible," she whispered.

"So you are fond of telling me." He entered his bedchamber, kicking the door closed with his boot, then locking it. He then strode to the bed and gently laid her upon the counterpane, following her down, covering her with his body. "Are you ready for me to show you exactly how incorrigible?"

Reaching up, she sifted her fingers through his disheveled hair, absorbing the delicious feel of his weight pressing her into the mattress. Smiling up into his beautiful brown eyes, she said, "My darling Philip, that falls into the category of 'absolutely yes.'"

Epilogue

Looking at his reflection in the cheval glass, Philip tugged his dark blue cutaway jacket into place, proudly noting that not one wrinkle marred his wedding attire. Had only four days passed since he and Meredith had broken the curse? Yes, but waiting even that long to make her his wife had felt like an eternity. Thank God he'd procured a special license to end his suffering.

A knock sounded on his bedchamber door, and he called, "Come in." Expecting Bakari, he hoped with the news that Meredith had arrived for the ceremony which was scheduled to begin in twenty minutes, he was surprised to see his father enter the room. As his father approached him, Philip was pleased to note his healthy coloring.

"Bakari was about to come to inform you that your bride has arrived, but I offered to bring the message, as I need to talk to you."

Anticipation filled Philip. *Your bride has arrived.* Which meant that in less than an hour's time she would be his wife. The future stretched before them like a sparkling, jewel-encrusted sea.

"I'm glad you're here, Father, as I would like to talk to you as well." With his marriage only moments away, he was hopeful they could make their peace with each other and enjoy whatever remaining time they had left before

Father's health failed. He indicated the wing chairs flanking the fireplace. "Shall we sit?"

"I prefer to stand."

"All right. I'm glad you're feeling up to it. Indeed, you're looking very well. Except for the sling supporting your arm, you're the picture of health."

A flush crept up Father's neck. "Er, yes. And that is precisely what I'm here to discuss." He cleared his throat. "I am, in fact, exactly that."

"Exactly what?"

"The picture of health."

"How do you know this?"

"Doctor Gibbens told me."

It took several seconds for the meaning of the words to sink in. Then, with an incredulous smile, Philip erased the distance between them and clasped his father on the shoulder. "This is joyous, miraculous news, Father! To what does Doctor Gibbens credit your recovery?"

"There has been no recovery, Philip. I was never ill."

Philip went still, then his hand slowly slid from his father's shoulder, as a jumble of emotions assaulted him. Amazement. Anger. Disappointment. They stood facing each other, as tension thickened the air between them.

"You lied because you thought I would not keep my word to you." He was unable to disguise the bitterness in his voice.

"I lied because I wanted you to keep your word to me while I was still alive," Father countered. "I wanted you home, and after a decade abroad it was time for you to return. I'd wanted you home three years ago, but in spite of having arranged a marriage for you, you refused to obliged me."

"So this time you claimed to be dying."

"Yes."

Philip's jaw tightened at the lack of remorse in his father's eyes and the defiant angle of his chin. "Surely you realize how despicable your actions were, Father. Not only toward me, but toward Catherine as well. Underneath her brave front, she's been extremely distraught over your impending death."

"I made my apologies to Catherine earlier this morning. Gave me quite the dressing-down, but we've made our peace. She neither likes nor condones what I did, but she understands why I did it. I did not believe you would come home otherwise. Indeed, I wasn't certain that even news of my impending death would drag you back to England."

"Your faith in me never fails to astound, Father. Tell me, how did you achieve your sickly look?"

"I severely cut back on my eating."

"And your pasty complexion?"

"A dusting of flour." Before Philip could say anything further, Father continued, "You have every right to be angry, but I hope you will understand that while my actions were dishonorable, my intentions were not. Although my health thankfully remains good, that of many of my peers does not. I wanted us to have the chance to repair our relationship before it was too late, and you were not showing any signs of returning." Father lifted his brows. "If I'd not lied, would you have come home?"

Philip's hands clenched. "Most likely no," he admitted.

"I sensed as much. I hope you'll forgive me for resorting to trickery, but I felt I had no choice. I'm sorry I lied to you. However, I am not sorry you are home. I missed you, Philip. We once had a good relationship. . . ."

Memories of days spent walking the grounds at Ravensly Manor, afternoons spent reading together in the library, evenings spent bent over the chessboard, swept through Philip, leaving sadness and regret in their wake. "Yes." Philip pushed the word past his tight throat. "Before I failed to keep my word. Before I failed Mother. And you."

A muscle jerked in his father's jaw. "I've waited years

to say this, Philip, and now that the moment is upon me, the words are still difficult. . . ." He exhaled a long breath. "I did us both a great disservice that day when your mother was caught in the rain, then fell so ill. Yes, I was upset and distraught, but not at you. At the fates that were robbing me of her. She'd been so fragile for so long, and we'd known for months the end was near. That day, I said things to you in anger. Hurtful things impinging your honor that I did not mean. But things which, once said, erected an ever-growing wall between us I did not know how to scale . . . a wall I hope we can, as adults, somehow climb over. You're a fine man, son. I should have apologized to you years ago. As I did not, I can only pray that it is not too late. I'm sorry."

His father extended his hand. Philip stared at the gesture of sorrow, friendship, and respect, and swallowed to dislodge the lump in his throat. Feeling as if a huge weight had lifted from his shoulders, he reached out and clasped his father's hand in a firm grip. Philip wasn't certain who made the first move, but seconds later they were embracing in a back-thumping hug. When they stepped apart, both pulled linen handkerchiefs from their pockets. Dabbing at his eyes, Father said, "Blast it, Philip, this place is bloody dusty. You simply must hire more servants. Especially now that you're taking a wife." He slipped his handkerchief back into his pocket. "You said there was something you wished to discuss with me?"

"Yes. Actually, I wished to thank you. It was your efforts to secure me a bride that set into motion the series of events that led me to this moment: anticipating taking Meredith as my bride."

Father's brows rose. "I see. Does that mean you forgive me for deceiving you in order to get you home?"

"I suppose it must, for if you hadn't, I would not have returned. And if I hadn't returned, I would not have met

Meredith. So indeed, it would appear that I am grateful for your deceit."

"About Miss Chilton-Grizedale, Philip . . . although she is not of the peerage, I quite like her. And Catherine assures me she will lend her support to your wife and that she has the makings of a fine viscountess."

"She does, Father. On my word of honor, she does."

"Well, that is good enough for me."

Standing next to Andrew, Philip watched Meredith enter the drawing room, and his breath hitched. She wore a pale blue muslin gown, exquisite in its simplicity, the unadorned column highlighting her extraordinary eyes and vibrant coloring. Her midnight hair was gathered into a classic Greek knot, and strands of lustrous pearls, his wedding gift to her, were wound through the shiny tresses. Her gaze locked onto his, and a smile filled with pure love and happiness trembled on her lips.

She walked slowly toward him, her gloved fingers resting lightly on Albert's sleeve. Albert, who beamed with pride at his "Miss Merrie," and who would be marrying Charlotte Carlyle early next month.

Albert delivered Meredith to Philip's side with a solemn nod, to which Philip responded with an equally grave bow of the head. Then he looked down at the woman who owned his heart. "You look beautiful," he whispered.

"Thank you. So do you," she whispered back. "Your father told me about your conversation."

"Quite the trickster, is he not?"

The vicar cleared his throat and frowned at them.

"Yes," Meredith whispered with a smile, blithely ignoring the vicar. "I thanked him profusely."

He smiled in return. "As did I."

"I think the vicar is growing impatient with you two,"

Andrew whispered into the fray. "His face resembles a thundercloud." He nodded toward Meredith. "You look lovely, Miss Chilton-Grizedale."

She beamed at him. "Thank you, Mr. Stanton, as do you. So lovely, in fact, I'm certain that it won't be long before *you* are standing before the vicar. Indeed, I intend to see to it."

Andrew shot Philip a pointed look, to which Philip shrugged. "She *is* the Matchmaker of Mayfair, you know." He returned his attention to Meredith, whose beautiful eyes glowed up at him.

"You look happy," he whispered.

A slow, beautiful smile lit her face. "Happy? I prefer to call it unequivocal, indubitable, flagrant, euphoric joy."

He laughed, earning him a stern glare from the vicar. "Yes, I'm certain you do. And this time, my darling Meredith, I completely agree with you."

Author's Note

Dear Reader,

I hope you enjoyed Philip and Meredith's love story! I had a wonderful time writing about their adventures, especially as the research I conducted for this book led me to some fascinating information regarding ancient civilizations. Of special note is the story of Cleopatra's very clever way of hosting the most expensive feast in history. This is indeed based upon writings found in Pliny the Elder's Natural History, *a comprehensive work detailing his observations of the world around him, and devoted to a variety of subjects such as agriculture, geography, astronomy, botany, zoology, and medicine, as well as history. Gaius Plinius Secundus (known as Pliny the Elder) possessed a passion for directly observing phenomena and taking notes. Unfortunately, his dedication to this method, along with his curiosity, was directly responsible for his death in 79 A.D., when he ventured too close to Mount Vesuvius during its eruption and the destruction of Pompeii.*

Also of special note is the poem Philip recites to

Meredith during their Mediterranean dinner, which is an actual lyric translated from an ancient Egyptian glyph.

I love to hear from readers! You can contact me through my website at www.JacquieD.com, where there's always something fun going on.

Thank you so much for spending time with Philip and Meredith!

Best regards and happy reading,

Jacquie D'Alessandro

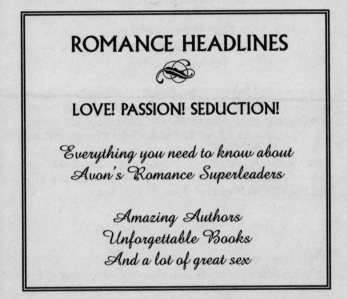

ROMANCE HEADLINES

LOVE! PASSION! SEDUCTION!

*Everything you need to know about
Avon's Romance Superleaders*

*Amazing Authors
Unforgettable Books
And a lot of great sex*

MOTHER OF THE BRIDE KEEPS SANITY
BUT LOSES HEART TO EX-SPOUSE
IN WEDDING GONE AWRY

Once Upon a Wedding
by Kathleen Eagle
September 2003

[Minneapolis, MN] What was Camille thinking? Her determination to make her daughter's wedding a day to remember has gone completely out of control. It's simply too much for one woman to handle! And to make matters somehow worse, Camille's ex-husband, Creed, returns to town, suddenly longing to make up for lost time. Not only does he want to do "the father thing," he's ready, willing, and able to tempt her back into his arms.

"What are you doing here?"

She regretted the words as soon as they came out of her mouth. It was a rude way to greet the man, even though he had no business messing in her kitchen anymore.

He didn't appear to take offense. He went right on putting cream and sugar in her old "Favorite Teacher" mug. But he'd always taken his coffee straight.

"You haven't had your coffee yet this morning, have you? You still buy the best. I still make the best." He handed her coffee with that same old sloe-eyed, sleepy morning smile. "My daughter lives here."

"Is that how you got in?"

He sipped his own coffee. "She says she's getting married. She's not old enough, is she?"

"How old should she be?"

"Older than my little girl." He boosted himself up the few inches that it took to seat himself on the counter. His long legs dangled nearly to the floor. "I always liked Jamie. I thought he was really going to make something of himself. Pick up a couple of instruments, put a band together. He couldn't sing, but he had a good ear."

She let the "make something of himself" jibe sail past her ear.

"How did you get here? I didn't see a strange vehicle in the driveway."

"And you don't see a strange man in your kitchen. You know us both. I'm still driving the same pickup, the one I left here with."

"How old is that thing now?"

"I've lost track. But she had zero miles on her when I got her." He gave his signature wink. "Just like you."

"What a flattering comparison."

"More than you know. That pickup is the only thing I have left that I don't share, but Jordan needed it to haul some stuff." His eyes went soft, as though resting them on her felt good to him. "How've you been?"

"Fine."

"Your mom?"

"Not so fine." She tried to remember what had been going on in her life when she'd last heard from him. "You know she has cancer."

"No, I didn't know. I'm sorry." He wagged his head sadly. "Jordan said she'd moved back, but she didn't say why. How's she doing with it?"

"Jordan, or my mother? Coping, both of them." She took her mothering stance, arms folded. "You haven't given me one straight answer so far. Why are you here, Creed?"

"Jordan called to tell me she was getting married. Actually, she left a message on my new answering machine." He grinned proudly. "I can call from anywhere and check in. So I got this message from her saying she had some news. I was coming into town anyway, so I . . ."

Her undeniable curiosity must have shown, because he was quick to explain. "I've got a gig. Haven't had one here in a long time." His smile seemed apologetic. "Yeah, I'm still at it. And, yeah, I still work construction to pay the bills."

"So why are you here," she repeated with exaggerated patience, "in *this house?*"

"Like I said, Jordan called. Talked to her last night. She called again this morning, wanting to use the pickup. She said you were gone with the van."

"That's right," Camille recalled. "She told me she needed it today."

"Said you'd been gone all night." He shrugged diffidently. " 'Course, we weren't worried."

"I left—"

"I haven't seen the boy yet. What's he like now? Still smart? Still . . ." A trace of the worry he'd disclaimed appeared in his eyes. "I know he's not a boy, and I know I missed my chance to send the bad ones packing and give the good ones fair warning. I left it all to you. He'll treat her right, won't he?"

"I hope so," she said with a sigh. "What am I saying? If he doesn't, she's outta there." Another double take. "*What am I saying?* They'll treat each other right."

"Like partners?"

"They'll make it, Creed."

"They haven't yet?" He gave a nervous laugh. "Just kidding. I don't want to know. I'd have to break his neck, and I don't think that would look too good. A neck brace with a tux." Hunkering down, he propped his elbows on his knees and cradled his coffee between his hands. "She's got her heart set on a fancy wedding, huh?"

"Fancier than ours was, I guess."

"A ten-dollar chapel in Vegas with an Elvis impersonator would be fancier than ours was." His eyes smiled for hers, hauling her into their private memory. "But the wedding night was a different story, wasn't it?"

"It wasn't fancy."

"Neither is heaven."

"Oh?" She raised her brow. "When were *you* last there?"

CURSE MAKES VISCOUNT THE MOST UNMARRIAGEABLE MAN IN ENGLAND

Who Will Take This Man?
by Jacquie D'Alessandro
October 2003

[London, England] Word is out! Philip Whitmore, Viscount Greybourne, is the victim of a curse, making him completely unmarriagable. Despite all attempts by Meredith Chilton-Grizedale, the Matchmaker of Mayfair, to find him a suitable bride, he remains unwed. Then the viscount begins viewing *her* as a potential mate ...

$\mathcal{L}$ord Greybourne stepped in front of her. His brown eyes simmered with anger, although there was no mistaking his concern. Reaching out, he gently grasped her shoulders. "I'm sorry you were subjected to such inexcusable rudeness and crude innuendo. Are you all right?"

Meredith simply stared at him for several seconds. Clearly he believed she was distraught due to the duke's remark which cast aspersions upon Lord Greybourne's ... manliness. Little did Lord Greybourne know that, thanks to her past, very little shocked Meredith. And as for the validity of the duke's claim, she could not fathom that anyone could so much as look at Lord Greybourne and have a doubt regarding his masculinity.

Lowering her hands from her mouth, she swallowed to find her voice. "I'm fine."

"Well, I'm not. I'd have to place myself firmly in the category of 'vastly annoyed.'" His gaze roamed over her face and his hands tightened on her shoulders. "You're not going to faint again, are you?"

"Certainly not." She stepped back, and his hands lowered to his sides. The warm imprint from his palms seeped through her gown, shooting tingles down her arms. "You may place me firmly in the category of 'females who do not succumb to vapors.' "

He cocked a brow. "I happen to know that is not precisely true."

"The episode at St. Paul's was an aberration, I assure you."

While he did not appear entirely convinced, he said, "Glad to hear it."

Clearing her throat, she said, "You came to my defense in a very gentlemanly way. Thank you."

A wry smile lifted one corner of his mouth. "I'm certain you don't mean to sound so surprised."

Indeed, she was surprised—stunned actually—although she had not meant to sound as if she were. But she'd have to reflect upon that later. Right now there were other, bigger issues to contemplate.

Unable to stand still, Meredith paced in front of him. "Unfortunately, with the duke's news, we must now re-categorize our situation from 'bad' to 'utterly disastrous.' Your bride is well and truly lost, thus doing away with our plan for you to marry on the twenty-second, and my reputation as a matchmaker is in tatters. And with your father's ill health, time is short." Her mind raced. "There must be a way to somehow turn this situation around. But how?"

"I'm open to suggestions. Even if we are successful in finding the missing piece of stone, my marrying is out of the question without a bride." He shook his head and a humorless sound escaped him. "Between this curse hanging over me, the unflattering story in the newspaper, and the gossip Lord Hedington alluded to circulating about my ability to . . . perform, it seems that the answer to the question posed in today's issue of *The Times* is yes—the cursed viscount *is* the most unmarriageable man in England."

Unmarriageable. The word echoed through Meredith's mind. Damnation, there must be a way—

She abruptly halted her pacing and swung around to face him. "Unmarriageable," she repeated, her drawn out pronunciation of the word in direct contrast to her runaway thoughts. She stroked her jaw and slowly nodded. "Yes, one might very well christen you The Most Unmarriageable Man in England."

He inclined his head in a mock bow. "A title of dubious honor. And one I'm surprised you sound so . . . enthusiastic about. Perhaps you'd care to share your thoughts?"

"Actually I was thinking you exhibited a moment of brilliance, my lord."

He walked toward her, his gaze never wavering from hers, not stopping until only two feet separated them. Awareness skittered down her spine, and she forced herself to stand her ground when everything inside her urged her to retreat.

"A *moment* of brilliance? In sharp contrast to all my other moments, I suppose. A lovely compliment, although your stunned tone when uttering it took off a bit of the shine. And brilliant though I may be—albeit only for a moment—I'm afraid I'm in the dark as to what I said to inspire you so."

"I think we can agree that Lady Sarah marrying Lord Weycroft places us both in an awkward situation." At his nod, she continued, "Well then, if you are The Most Unmarriageable Man in England, and it seems quite clear you are, the matchmaker who could marry you off would score an incredible coup." She lifted her brows. "If I were successful in such an undertaking, you would gain a wife, and my reputation would be reinstated."

He adjusted his spectacles, clearly pondering her words. "My moment of brilliance clearly remains upon me as I'm following your thought process, and what you've described is a good plan. However, I cannot marry unless I am able to break the curse."

"Which a brilliant man such as yourself will certainly be able to do."

"*If* we are able to locate the missing piece of the Stone of Tears. Assuming we are successful, whom did you have in mind that I would marry?"

Meredith's brow puckered, and she once again commenced pacing. "Hmm. Yes, that is problematic. Yet surely in all of London there must be one unsuperstitious woman willing to be courted by a cursed, gossip-ridden viscount of questionable masculinity who will most likely fill their homes with ancient relics."

"I beg you to cease before all these complimentary words swell my head."

She ignored his dust-dry tone and continued pacing. "Of course, in order to ensure the reinstatement of my reputation, I must match you with just the perfect woman. Not just any woman will do."

"Well, thank goodness for that."

"But who?" She paced, puzzling it over in her mind, then halted and snapped her fingers. "Of course! The perfect woman for The Most Unmarriageable Man in England is The Most Unmarriageable Woman in England!"

"Ah. Yes, she sounds delightful."

Again she ignored him. "I can see the Society pages now—England's Most Unmarriageable Man Weds England's Most Unmarriageable Woman—and praise to Meredith Chilton-Grizedale, the acclaimed Matchmaker of Mayfair, for bringing them together." She pursed her lips and tapped her index finger against her chin. "But who is this Most Unmarriageable Woman?"

He cleared his throat. "Actually, I believe I know."

Meredith halted and turned toward him eagerly. "Excellent. Who?"

"You, Miss Chilton-Grizedale. By the time Society reads tomorrow's edition of *The Times, you* will be the Most Unmarriageable Woman in England."

WOMAN MARRIED FOR JUST
SIX DISASTROUS HOURS STUNS CITY
WITH MURDER CASE INVOLVEMENT

Kill the Competition
by Stephanie Bond
November 2003

[Atlanta, GA] Belinda Hennessey moves to Atlanta to escape all memories of her six-hour marriage. Her new friends are a hoot—they pass time spent in traffic writing an advice book on marriage and men. But the new job is *murder*—literally. When a dead body turns up at the office, Belinda fears for her life. Luckily, she's already acquainted with Officer Wade Alexander . . .

The police cruiser's blue light came on, bathing Belinda's cheeks with condemning heat each time it passed over her face. The officer was male—that she could tell from the span of his shoulders. And he wasn't happy—that she could tell from the way he banged his hand against the steering wheel. Since the cruiser sat at an angle and since her left bumper was imbedded in his right rear fender and since his right signal light still blinked, he apparently had been attempting to change lanes when she'd nailed him.

The officer gestured for her to pull over to the right. When traffic yielded, he pulled away first, eliciting another sickening scrape as their cars disengaged. She followed like a disobedient child, and despite the odd skew of her car and an ominous noise that sounded like *potato potato potato* (probably because she was hungry), managed to pull onto the narrow shoulder behind him. The driver side door of the squad car swung open, and long uniform-clad legs emerged. Belinda swallowed hard.

"Whip up some tears," Libby said.

"What?"

"Hurry, before he gets back here."

"I can't—owww!" She rubbed her fingers over the tender skin on the back of her arm where Libby had pinched the heck out of her. Tears sprang to her eyes, partly from the pain and partly from the awfulness of the situation. She tried to blink away the moisture but wound up overflowing. She was wiping at her eyes when a sharp rap sounded on her window.

"Uh-oh," Carole whispered. "He looks pissed."

An understatement. The officer was scowling, his dark hair hand-ruffled, his shadowed jaw clenched. Belinda zoomed down the window and waited.

"Is everyone okay?" he barked. Bloodshot eyes—maybe gray, maybe blue—blazed from a rocky face.

"Y-yes."

"Then save the tears."

She blinked. "I beg your pardon?"

Libby leaned forward. "My friend is late for an important meeting, Officer."

He eyed Belinda without sympathy. "That makes two of us. I need your driver's license, registration, and proof of insurance, ma'am."

Belinda reached for her purse, which had landed at her feet. "I'm sorry, Officer. I didn't see you."

"Yes, ma'am, these big white cars with sirens really blend."

He glanced at her license, then back at her.

"It's me," she mumbled. The worst driver's license photograph in history—she'd been suffering from the flu, and for some reason, wearing a Mickey Mouse sweatshirt had seemed like a good idea. She was relatively certain that a copy of the humiliating photograph was posted on bulletin boards in DMV break rooms across the state of Ohio.

"I'll be right back."

He circled around to record the numbers on her license plate, then returned to his car, every footfall proclaiming his frustration for inexperienced, un-photogenic female drivers. He used his radio presumably to report her vitals. She'd never been in trouble in her life, but her gut clenched with the absurd notion that some computer glitch might finger her as a lawless fugitive—kidnapper, forger, murderer.

The crunch of gravel signaled the officer's approach. She opened her eyes, but the flat line of his mouth caused the Berry Bonanza with calcium to roil in her stomach.

"Do you live in Cincinnati, Ms. Hennessey?"

"No, I moved here two months ago."

A muscle worked in his jaw as he scribbled on a ticket pad. "I need your address, please."

She recited it as he wrote.

"You were supposed to obtain a Georgia driver's license within thirty days of moving here."

His tone pushed her pulse higher. "I didn't know."

He tore off one, two, three tickets, then thrust them into her hand. "Now you do." He unbuttoned his cuff and began rolling up his sleeve. "I need for you ladies to move to my car, please."

Belinda gaped. "You're hauling us in?"

The officer looked heavenward, then back. "No, ma'am. You have a flat tire and at this time of day, it'll take forever for your road service to get here."

She pressed her lips together, thinking this probably wasn't the best time to say she didn't have a road service. Or a cell phone to *call* a road service.

He nodded toward the cruiser. "You'll be safer in my car than standing on the side of the road."

"I . . . thank you."

He didn't look up. "Yes, ma'am. Will you pop the trunk?"

While the women scrambled out of the car, Belinda released the trunk latch, but the resulting *click* didn't sound right. She opened her door a few inches, then slid out, bracing herself against the traffic wind that threatened to suck her into the path of oncoming cars. The toes of her shoes brushed the uneven edge of the blacktop, and she almost tripped. Her dress clung to her thighs, and her hair whipped her cheeks. The rush of danger was strangely exhilarating, strangely . . . *alluring*.

Then a large hand clamped onto her shoulder, guiding her to the back of the car and comparative safety. "That's a good way to become a statistic," he shouted over the road noise.

She tilted her head to look into reproachful eyes, and pain flickered in the back of her neck. Tomorrow she'd be stiff. "This is very nice of you," she yelled, gesturing as if she were playing charades.

He simply shrugged, as if to say he would've done the same for anyone. Dark stubble stained his jaw, and for the first time she noticed his navy uniform was a bit rumpled. He frowned and jerked a thumb toward the cruiser. "You should join your friends, ma'am."

At best, he probably thought she was an airhead. At worst, a flirt. She pointed. "The trunk release didn't sound right."

He wedged his fingers into the seam that outlined the trunk lid, and gave a tug. "I think it's just stuck." Indeed, on the next tug, the lid sprang open. He twisted to inspect the latch as he worked the mechanism with his fingers. "The latch is bent but fixable." He raised the trunk lid and winced. "I assume the spare tire is underneath all this stuff."

A sheepish flush crawled over her as she surveyed the brimming contents. "I'll empty it."

He checked his watch. "I'll help. Anything personal in here?"

She shook her head in defeat. Nothing that she could think of, and what did it matter anyway?

But her degradation climbed as he removed item after item that, in his hands, seemed mundane to the point of intimate— a ten-pound bag of kitty litter, a twelve-pack of Diet Pepsi, a pair of old running shoes with curled toes, an orange Frisbee, a grungy Cincinnati Reds windbreaker, a *Love Songs of the '90s* CD, two empty Pringles Potato Chips canisters (she'd heard a person could do all kinds of crafty things with them), and two gray plastic crates of reference books she'd been conveying to her cubicle one armload at a time.

Her gaze landed on a tiny blue pillow wedged between the crates, and she cringed. Unwilling to share that particular souvenir of her life, she reached in while he was bent away from her and stuffed it into her shoulder bag.

"I'll get the rest of it," he said.

She nodded and scooted out of the way. "Can I help with—"

"No." He looked up at her, then massaged the bridge of his nose. "No, ma'am. Please."

Glad for the escape, Belinda retreated to the cruiser, picking her way through gravel and mud, steeling herself against the gusts of wind. The girls had crowded into the backseat, so she opened the front passenger door and slid inside, then shut it behind her. The console of the police car was guy-heaven—buttons and lights and gizmos galore. The radio emitted bursts of static. No one said anything for a full thirty seconds.

"How much are the fines?" Carole asked.

She gave up on her hopeless hair and pulled out the three citations signed by—she squinted at the scrawl—Lt. W. Alexander. After adding the numbers in her head, she laid her head back on the headrest. "Two hundred and twenty-five dollars."

"Ooo," they chorused.

Ooo was right.

CLASS REUNION REUNITES "PERFECT" COUPLE
CAN LOVE SURVIVE BAD '80S
COVER BAND MUSIC?

Where Is He Now?
by Jennifer Greene
December 2003

[Michigan] Teen toasts of the town reunite! *Man Most Likely to Succeed* Nick Donneli and *Most Popular* Jeanne Cassiday brace themselves for their class reunion. It's time to discover who still has bad hair, to see who *really* became a doctor ... and to figure out if they can have another chance at love. It's true that sometimes maturity isn't all it's cracked up to be ... but sometimes love really is better the second time around ...

"*B*oots."

The sudden masculine voice shocked her like a gunshot ... but that voice wrapped around her old nickname—the nickname only one man had ever called her—punched her right in the heart and squeezed tight.

It took only a second for her to turn around, but in that second, she saw the round clock with the white face on the far wall. The photographs of old cars—so many they filled one wall like wallpaper. The red leather couch, the red stone counter—furnishings that seemed crazy for a garage, but then, what the Sam Hill did she know about mechanics and garages? She also saw the pearl-choking Martha drop her aggressive stance in a blink when it finally became obvious that Nick Donneli really did know her.

"Mr. Donneli," Martha said swiftly and sincerely, "I'm terribly sorry if I misunderstood this situation. I was trying to protect you from—"

"I know you were, Martha, and you're a wonderful protector. But the lady thinks she's looking for my father instead of me. That's what the source of the confusion is."

"I see." Martha obviously didn't.

Jeanne didn't either. She was pretty sure she'd get what was going on in a second. Or ten. But she needed a minute to breathe, to gulp in some poise, to lock onto some sense somehow.

Only damn. Temporarily her heart still felt sucker punched. Her pulse started galloping and refused to calm down.

He looked just like he always did. More mature, of course. But those dark, sexy eyes were just as wicked, could still make a girl think, *Oh, yes, please take my virginity; please do anything you want, I don't care.* He still had the cocky, defensive, bad-boy chin. The dark hair, with the one shock on his temple that wouldn't stay brushed. The thin mouth and strong jaw, and shoulders so square you'd think they were huge, when he wasn't that huge. He just had so damn much personality that he seemed big.

He was. So handsome. So in-your-face male. So take-on-all-comers wolf.

And double damn, but he'd called her Boots.

She hadn't heard the nickname in all these years. Hadn't and didn't want to. But the fact that he even remembered it completely threw her. For God's sake, she'd been over her head, over her heart, over her life in love with him, and believed he'd felt the same way about her. Then suddenly he'd sent that cold note from Princeton: *Life's changed for me. Everything's different. I'm moving on. I don't want to hurt you, but this relationship isn't going any further. You go on with your life, find someone else. I'm never coming back.*

Those weren't the exact words. She didn't remember the exact words, because it wasn't the words themselves that had devastated her. It was going from one day when she'd believed herself loved, when she'd loved him more than her life, believed she knew him, believed he was The One. Her Prince. The Only Man For her.

To being hurled out of his life after a semester in college because he'd "moved on"—as if that were some kind of explanation. As if real love could die as easily as a mood change.

She'd been stunned. So stunned, she realized now, that it wasn't as simple as being hurt. It rocked her world. And it was from that instant, that time when she'd been knocked flat and crushed, that she'd started down a different road. She'd started making choices she'd never wanted to make. She'd started doing what other people wanted her to do.

It was that letter. His rejection. His dropping her the way he had. That was the catalyst for her losing Jeanne Claire Cassiday. And she'd never found herself since then.

And whatever she'd meant to say, on seeing him again, what came out was "Damn it, Stretch!"

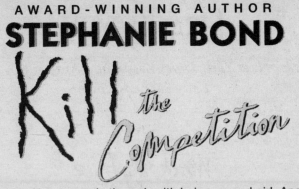

A W A R D - W I N N I N G   A U T H O R

STEPHANIE BOND

Kill the Competition

Belinda Hennessey is through with being a good girl. And her new outlook is paying off. She's found a killer job, spunky gal-pals, and fantasies involving a velvety-voiced traffic reporter. Even a run-in with a drop-dead gorgeous cop bolsters her new bad-girl attitude. Nothing can stop her...until a coworker is murdered, and evidence points to the carpool! With a killer on the loose, her friends at each other's throats, and an abundance of southern (male) comfort, Belinda knows only one thing for certain: success can be murder!

Buy and enjoy KILL THE COMPETITION (available October 28, 2003), then send the coupon below along with your proof of purchase for KILL THE COMPETITION to Avon Books, and we'll send you a check for $2.00.

- -

LISA KLEYPAS

New York Times Bestselling Author of
Lady Sophia's Lover

When is love . . .

Worth Any Price

0-380-81107-3/$7.50 US/$9.99 Can

Marry a nobleman who would control her—never!
So Charlotte runs to the protection of Stony Cross Park.
But it is there she is captured by Nick Gentry, a treacherous
foe reputed to be the most skillful lover in England.

And Don't Miss

WHEN STRANGERS MARRY
0-06-050736-5/$7.50 US/$9.99 Can

LADY SOPHIA'S LOVER
0-380-81106-5/$7.50 US/$9.99 Can

SUDDENLY YOU
0-380-80232-5/$6.99 US/$9.99 Can

WHERE DREAMS BEGIN
0-380-80231-7/$6.99 US/$9.99 Can

SOMEONE TO WATCH OVER ME
0-380-80230-9/$7.50 US/$9.99 Can

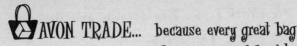